Nova Scotia

First published in 2005 by Crescent Books,
an imprint of Mercat Press Ltd
10 Coates Crescent, Edinburgh EH3 7AL
www.crescentfiction.com

ISBN 1 84183 0860

Scottish
Arts Council

The publisher acknowledges subsidy from the Scottish Arts Council
towards the publication of this volume.

Set in Goudy Old Style at Mercat Press
Printed and bound in Great Britain by
Bell & Bain Ltd., Glasgow

Nova Scotia

NEW SCOTTISH SPECULATIVE FICTION

edited by

NEIL WILLIAMSON & ANDREW J. WILSON

Crescent

For James

CONTENTS

PREFACE:
REINVENTING SCOTLAND
Neil Williamson &
Andrew J. Wilson

There is a visionary thread woven through Scottish story-telling. It expresses itself in a sense of the otherworldly and an ability to find alternative ways of looking at ourselves.

This imaginative strand runs from the ancient Celtic myths through writers such as James Hogg, George MacDonald, Robert Louis Stevenson, Arthur Conan Doyle, John Buchan and Naomi Mitchison, and today it can be found in the work of Alasdair Gray, Iain Banks and Ali Smith. *Nova Scotia* is an anthology of original short stories (and one unique poem) which continue this tradition.

The contributors reimagine Scotland in the past, present and future. Here you'll find secret histories, contemporary marvels, and visions of the fate of our nation. There are also glimpses of other, alternative Scotlands, places that might have been if history had run a different course. Some of the stories are about Scotland the country, this far-flung corner of Europe teetering on the edge of the North Atlantic shelf; some are about the people who come from it; every one of them deals with the essential qualities, both good and bad, of our national characteristics.

The authors are all Scots. They're Scottish in the broadest sense: some were native-born while others have chosen to make their home here; some are highlanders and islanders, others urbanites; and this gives us an extraordinary range of perspectives. We wanted this collection to be inclusive, not exclusive, and we wanted not only the tight focus of introspection, but also the ability to see ourselves, as Burns had it, as others see us.

We offer you, then, a panorama of views and imaginings: bright forecasts and dour contemplations, the alien made familiar and the everyday made fantastic.

After all, we're all Jock Tamson's bairns.

INTRODUCTION:
SCOTLANDS OLD AND NEW
David Pringle

In the year 1153, when David I, King of Scots, lay dying in his city of
Carlisle, he could comfort himself with the thought that his realm's
border with England now lay well to the south, at the Ribble Valley
in Lancashire. The counties of Cumberland, Westmorland and North-
umberland were all firmly in Scots' hands, in effect parts of a greater
Scotland. Is this a detail from an alternate-history science-fiction story?
No, it's historical fact, and it serves to remind us how "artificial"
Scotland's southern border is. Although that border was more or less
stabilized along its modern lines during the reigns of King David's
less-happy successors, some parts were to remain fluid for centuries:
thus, the city of Berwick-upon-Tweed, a part of England since Tudor
days, is cut off from its natural hinterland, the county of Berwick-
shire, which remains in Scotland.

People living on both sides of that border remain English-speaking
(that is, they speak dialects descended from the Northern form of
medieval English) and probably have more in common with each
other than they do with either Scots Highlanders or English Southerners; but, all the same, and after many centuries of peace and
cooperation, the border looms as a kind of psychological barrier.

An anthology such as this is meaningless without it, for it is of its essence that it contains stories by authors born in, or resident in, that part of Britain which lies north of the border. In one sense or another, but primarily because of the existence of that border, the authors who have contributed to this book are all Scottish.

Most of their stories are science fiction, while a number are what we would define as fantasy. As the former editor and publisher, for more than two decades, of a magazine called *Interzone* which published a similar mix of imaginative stories—mainly science fiction, some fantasy—I'd like to dwell, briefly, on the subject of the SF, rather than the fantasy, just as I tended to do when putting together issues of the magazine. For the July 1994 issue of *Interzone* I wrote a short review of a critical book entitled *Scottish Fantasy Literature* by Colin Manlove (published in Edinburgh by Canongate), in which I found myself saying:

> This book raises the question: why, when there is such a rich tradition of fantasy, is there no distinctively Scottish science fiction? The names of J. T. McIntosh and Iain Banks are mentioned in passing by Mr Manlove, but clearly "Scottish SF" as an entity scarcely exists; nor, for that matter, do Irish SF or Welsh SF, although the contributions of those other Celtic-fringe countries to mythological fantasy and supernatural horror likewise have been vast. The answer would seem to have to do with a relative lack of urbanization in the Celtic countries; it's precisely those nations which are most cut off from their rural, folkish roots which have been most likely to create important traditions of scientific romance or science fiction— England, the USA. Perhaps SF is essentially a "deracinated" form, a folklore for city-dwellers who have forgotten the folk tales of their ancestors.

Given the importance of Glasgow and central Scotland to the industrial revolution (and given the significance of the career of James Watt—not to mention a multitude of other Scottish engineers), the last point I made above now seems to me rather dubious. Most of Scotland remains "rural", yes, but a sizeable swathe of it is very definitely urban; and over the past two and a half centuries the contributions of Scots to science, engineering and industrialization have been enormous. And yet, and yet ... so much of the culture of Scotland, especially the literary culture, does seem backward-looking and *anti*-urban, mired in Celtic mists. Think of the career of Sir Walter Scott; think of all the Tartanry, and of that popular movement, begun by J. M. Barrie, known as the Kailyard (still alive, after a century, in the form of the *Sunday Post*, the *People's Friend, Dr Finlay's Casebook* and *Monarch of the Glen*).

It has always seemed to me that there should have been more Scottish SF writers, especially in the light of the recurrent "modernizing" tendencies in Scottish history. I'm thinking in particular of three historical periods when Scotland has shaken off the dead weight of its past and bounded ahead in certain vital respects. The first was in the twelfth century, the age of the aforementioned King David and his immediate successors, when Scotland first entered the main stream of Western European civilization, welcomed in foreigners and seeded burghs and monasteries across the land. (See *David I: The King Who Made Scotland* by Richard Oram [Tempus, 2004].) The second was in the sixteenth century, when Scotland had its Reformation and turned Presbyterian—a change now deeply out of fashion, partly thanks to the excesses of that revolution (small-minded puritanism, witch-burning, etc.), but which stored up immense energies for the future. (In a bookshop recently I noted, with a slight shock of surprise and pleasure, a biography by Roderick Graham boldly entitled *John Knox, Democrat* [Robert Hale, 2001].) The third notable period was, of course, in the eighteenth century (and into the early nineteenth), the age of David Hume and Adam Smith, when Scotland enjoyed its famous Enlightenment—which led on directly to the Industrial Revolution. (See, for example, *The Scottish Enlightenment: The Scots' Invention of the Modern World* by Arthur Herman [Fourth Estate, 2001].)

Perhaps more Scottish literature of recent times should have dealt with those periods, and with the long-term consequences of those periods, rather than dwelling obsessively on the anti-Englishry of William Wallace and Robert the Bruce, and on the romantic lost causes of Mary, Queen of Scots, and Bonnie Prince Charlie. As I say, there should have been more Scottish SF writers, and yet somehow, for a century or two, they failed to appear. If only Walter Scott had written an early scientific romance; if only Robert Louis Stevenson had done likewise (yes, I know claims are made for *The Strange Case of Dr Jekyll and Mr Hyde* as SF, but it has always seemed to me more of a horror fantasy); if only James Leslie Mitchell, Scotland's nearest approach to a rival of H. G. Wells as a great science-fictionist, had not died so young! Mitchell's *Three Go Back* (1932) and *Gay Hunter* (1934) apart, there are really no major Scottish science-fiction novels prior to the commencement of the career of Iain M. Banks. Since Banks, however, and especially since the arrival of Ken MacLeod, I'm glad to say things are changing.

Where did they go, all those "missing" Scottish SF writers—those of the past century who should have been inspired into creativity by the long-term workings-out of Reformation and Enlightenment and Industrialization? It occurred to me recently that there's an obvious answer: they went to America. Thinking about the rise of that core sub-genre of American SF in the 1920s and 1930s, the type of story now known as Space Opera (but in its day referred to as the tale of "super-science"), I realized that its four prime creators, the four writers generally acknowledged to be the early masters of pulp-magazine Space Opera, were probably all of Scottish ancestry. Two of them had Scottish surnames—Edmond Hamilton and John W. Campbell—while two had surnames which, if not specifically Scottish, are very common in Scotland—E. E. "Doc" Smith and Jack Williamson. Probing slightly deeper into the latter pair's antecedents, I learn (from Sam Moskowitz's *Seekers of Tomorrow*, 1966) that Smith's parents were "of British extraction and staunch Presbyterians"—they sound like Scots to me!—while Williamson's parents gave him the middle name Stewart (hence his occasional pseudonym of "Will Stewart"); long-time Southerners, from a part of the US where Scots settled in profusion, they are highly likely to have been Scots-Americans too. So there we have it—all the missing Scottish SF writers of yesteryear were born of forebears who had emigrated to America (and, yes, to Canada, Australia, New Zealand, South Africa and other parts too).

But times have changed. The age of emigration is over, at least for now, and home-grown Scottish SF is showing signs of awakening and even flourishing. When I was editor of *Interzone* (a "British" SF magazine, published from the south of England), I never got around to producing an all-Scottish issue—it didn't seem to me that enough good material was available—and yet, looking through this new anthology, I find that at least six of the writers are people we published in *Interzone*: Michael Cobley, Jack Deighton, Andrew C. Ferguson, John Grant, Charles Stross (a Yorkshireman when we first discovered him over 15 years ago!) and Neil Williamson. Of the remainder, some are unfamiliar to me, while others are known, admired names. Had they come my way before I gave up the editorship in 2004, I would have been proud to publish their stories in an all-Scottish edition of *Interzone*.

Selkirk, May 2005

*How do you begin an anthology of new Scottish speculative fiction? With
a new poem from Scotland's Makar, of course; a poem that tells a most
remarkable story. Remember, in Scotland, you're never more than forty
miles from the sea.*

❂ ❂

THE COST OF PEARLS
Edwin Morgan

❂ ❂

Do you want to challenge that dervish Scotland?
Even and only being interrogated
by a swash of centenarian mussels
black-encrusted and crusty with it?
When they folded their arms and gave such a click
it could be heard right down Strathspey,
did you reckon the risk of a dialogue was minimal?
"Come on then, have at you!" It was like an old play
though far from funny. "All that winking stuff,
that metal, those blades,
you think we don't know death when we smell it?"
"Your nose deceives you. We are observers, explorers.
We heard there was a murmuring of mussels,
a clatter and a chatter
somewhere in the gravel-beds of unbonny Scotland,
almost like voices threatening something—"
"Damn sure we were threatening something! Do you know
a thousand of us were killed in one day
not long ago—" "I heard it was eight hundred—"
"Eight hundred, ten hundred, it was a massacre.
Your pearl poachers breenged through our domains like demons
with their great gully knives and scythed us to shreds
for what might be, most likely might not be,
a pearl, a pearl of price, a jeweller's price.

❂

I hear a shuffling of papers. Prepare yourself.
We are our wisest, neither clique nor claque

but full conclave. We want to know,
and we will know, what is it gives you
your mania for killing. Don't interrupt!
For a few smouldering prettinesses
at neck and brow you would ransack
a species. I said don't interrupt,
we have all the time in the world
and I can hear the steady footfall
(that's a joke, you may smile)
as our oldest and wisest, worthily High Mussel
at a hundred and forty-nine, filtering and harrumphing
(no, you must not smile now),
angrily kicking the gravel, and with a last sift and puff
(no no, this is not funny, think of his powers)
commands the interrogation to begin."

John Calvin said: "All the blessings we enjoy are Divine deposits, committed to our trust on this condition, that they should be dispensed for the benefit of our neighbours." A Presbyterian minister carries these words in his heart and makes evangelism his sacred duty, ensuring that the Word will be passed on. No matter who these neighbours might be...

○ ○

A CASE OF CONSILIENCE
Ken MacLeod

○ ○

"When you say it's Providence that brought you here," said Qasim, "what I hear are two things: it's bad luck, and it's not your fault."

The Rev. Donald MacIntyre, M.A. (Div.), Ph.D., put down his beer can and nodded.

"That's how it sometimes feels," he said. "Easy for you to say, of course."

Qasim snorted. "Easy for anybody! Even a Muslim would have less difficulty here. Let alone a Buddhist or Hindu."

"Do tell," said Donald. "No, what's really galling is that there are millions of *Christians* who would take all this in their stride. Anglicans. Liberals. Catholics. Mormons, for all I know. And my brethren in the, ah, narrower denominations could come up with a dozen different rationalizations before breakfast, all of them heretical did they but know it—which they don't, thank the Lord and their rigid little minds, so their lapses are no doubt forgiven through their sheer ignorance. So it's given to me to wrestle with. Thus a work of Providence. I think."

"I still don't understand what your problem is, compared to these other Christians."

Donald sighed. "It's a bit hard to explain," he said. "Let's put it this way. You were brought up not to believe in God, but I expect you had quite strong views about the God you didn't believe in. Am I right?"

Qasim nodded. "Of course. Allah was always..." He shrugged. "Part of the background. The default."

"Exactly. Now, how did you feel when you first learned about what Christians believe about the Son of God?"

"It was a long time ago," said Qasim. "I was about eight or nine. In school in Kirkuk. One of my classmates told me, in the course of ... well, I am sorry to say in the course of a fight. I shall pass over the details. Enough to say I was quite shocked. It seemed preposterous and offensive. And then I laughed at myself!"

"I can laugh at myself too," said Donald. "But I feel the same way as you did—in my case at the suggestion that the Son was not unique, that He took on other forms, and so forth. I can hardly even say such things. I literally shudder. But I can't accept, either, that He has no meaning beyond Earth. So what are we to make of rational beings who are not men, and who may be sinners?"

"Perhaps they are left outside," said Qasim. "Like most people are, if I understand your doctrines."

Donald flinched. "That's not what they say, and in any case, such a question is not for me to decide. I'm perplexed."

He leaned back in the seat and stared gloomily at the empty can, and then at the amused, sympathetic eyes of the friendly scoffer to whom he had found he could open up more than to the believers on the Station.

Qasim stood up. "Well, thank God I'm an atheist, that's all I can say."

He had said it often enough.

"God and Bush," said Donald. This taunt, too, was not on its first outing. Attributing to the late ex-President the escalating decades-long cascade of unintended consequences that had annexed Iraq to the EU and Iran to China was probably unfair, but less so than blaming it on God. Qasim raised a mocking index finger in response.

"God and Bush! And what are you having, Donald?"

"Can of Export."

"Narrow it down, padre. They're all export here."

"Aren't we all," said Donald. "Tennent's, then. And a shot of single malt on the side, if you don't mind. Whatever's going."

As Qasim made his way through the crowd to the bar, Donald reflected that his friend was likely no more off-duty than he was. A chaplain and an intelligence officer could both relax in identical olive

T-shirts and chinos, but vigilance and habit were less readily shrugged off than dress-codes. The Kurdish colonel still now and again called his service the *mukhabarat*. It was one of his running gags, along with the one about electronics and electrodes. And the one about extra-terrestrial intelligence. And the one about ... yes, for running gags Qasim was your man.

As I am for gloomy reflections, Donald thought. Sadness, *tristia*, had been one of the original seven deadly sins. Which probably meant every Scottish Presbyterian went straight to hell, or at least to a very damp purgatory, if the Catholics were right. If the Catholics were right! After three hundred and seventeen days in the Extra-Terrestrial Contact Station, this was among the least heretical of the thoughts Donald MacIntyre was willing to countenance.

Qasim came back with the passing cure, and lasting bane, of the Scottish sin; and with what might have been a more dependably cheering mood-lifter: a gripe about his own problems. Problems which, as Donald listened to them, seemed more and more to resemble his own.

"How am I supposed to tell if an underground fungoid a hundred metres across that communicates by chemical gradients is feeding us false information? Or if an operating system written by an ET AI is a trojan? Brussels still expects files on all of them, when we don't even know how many civs we're dealing with. Bloody hell, Donald, pardon my English, there's one of the buggers we only suspect is out there because everyone comes back from its alleged home planet with weird dreams." Qasim cocked a black eyebrow. "Maybe I shouldn't be telling you that one."

"I've heard about the dreams," said Donald. "In a different context." He sighed. "It's a bit hard to explain to some people that I don't take confession."

"Confessions are not to be relied upon," Qasim said, looking somewhere else. "Anyway ... what I would have to confess, myself, is that the Etcetera Station is a bit out of its depth. We are applying concepts outside their context."

"Now *that*," said Donald with some bitterness, "is a suspicion I do my best to resist."

It was one the Church had always resisted, a temptation dangled in different forms down the ages. As soon as the faith had settled on its view of one challenge, another had come along. In the Carpenter's workshop there were many clue-sticks, and the whacks had seldom ceased for long. In the beginning, right there in the Letters, you could see the struggle against heresies spawned by Greek metaphysics and Roman mysticism. Barely had the books snapped shut on Arius when Rome had crashed. Then the Muslim invasions. The split between the Eastern and Western churches, Christendom cloven on a lemma. Then the discovery of the New World, and a new understanding of the scope and grip of the great, ancient religions of the Old. The Reformation. The racialist heresy. The age of the Earth. Biblical criticism. Darwin. The twentieth century had brought the expanding universe, the gene, the unconscious—how quaint the controversies over these now seemed! Genetic engineering, human-animal chimerae, artificial intelligence: in Donald's own lifetime he'd seen Synods, Assemblies and Curia debate them and come to a Christian near-consensus acceptable to all but the lunatic—no, he must be charitable—the fundamentalist fringe.

And then, once more, just when the dust had settled, along had come—predictable as a planet, unpredicted like a comet—another orb in God's great orrery of education, or shell in the Adversary's arsenal of error-mongery, the greatest challenge of all—alien intelligent life. It was not one that had been altogether unexpected. Scholastics had debated the plurality of worlds. The Anglican C. S. Lewis had considered it in science fiction; the agnostic Blish had treated it with a literally Jesuitical subtlety. The Christian poet Alice Meynell had speculated on alien gospels; the godless ranter MacDiarmid had hymned the Innumerable Christ. In the controversies over the new great discovery, all these literary precedents had been resurrected and dissected. They pained Donald to the quick. Well-intended, pious, sincere in their seeking they might be; or sceptical and satirical; it mattered not: they were all mockeries. There had been only one Incarnation; only one sufficient sacrifice. If the Reformation had meant anything at all, it meant that. To his ancestors Donald might have seemed heinously pliant in far too much, but like them he was not to be moved from the rock. In the matter of theological science fiction he preferred the honest warning of the secular humanist Harrison. *Tell it not in Gath, publish it not in the streets of Ashkelon...*

o

Donald left the messroom after his next round and walked to his quarters. The corridor's topology was as weird as anything on the ETC Station. A human-built space habitat parked inside an alien-built wormhole nexus could hardly be otherwise. The station's spin didn't dislodge the wormhole mouths, which remained attached to the same points on the outside of the hull. As a side-effect, the corridor's concave curve felt and looked convex. At the near ends of stubby branch corridors, small groups of scientists and technicians toiled on their night-shift tasks. At the far ends, a few metres away, thick glass plates with embedded airlocks looked out on to planetary surfaces and sub-surfaces, ocean depths, tropospheric layers, habitat interiors, virtual reality interfaces, and apparently vacant spaces backdropped with distant starfields. About the last, it was an open question whether the putatively present alien minds were invisible inhabitants of the adjacent vacuum, or more disturbingly, some vast process going on in and among the stars themselves. The number of portals was uncountable. There were never more than about five hundred, but the total changed with every count. As the station had been designed and built with exactly three hundred interface corridors, this variability was not comfortable to contemplate. But that the station's structure itself had somehow become imbricated with the space-time tangle outside it had become an accepted—if not precisely an acknowledged—fact. It received a back-handed recognition in the station's nickname: the Etcetra Station.

Use of that monicker, like much else, was censored out of messages home. The Station was an EU military outpost, and little more than its existence, out beyond the orbit of Neptune, had been revealed. Donald MacIntyre, in his second year of military service as a conscript chaplain, had been as surprised to find himself here as his new parishioners were to discover his affiliation. His number had come up in the random allocation of clergy from the list of religions recognized by the EU Act of Toleration—the one that had banned Scientology, the Unification Church, the Wahabi sect and, by some drafting or translation error, Unitarian Universalism—but to a minister of the Church of Scotland, there could in all conscience be no such thing as chance.

He had been sent here for a purpose.

o

"The man in black thinks he's on a mission from God," said Qasim.

"What?" Major Bernstein looked up from her interface, blinking.

"Here." Qasim tapped the desktop, transferring a file from his finger.

"What's this?"

"His private notes."

The major frowned. She didn't like Qasim. She didn't like spying on the troops. She didn't care who knew it. Qasim knew all this. So did Brussels. She didn't know that.

"What are your grounds?" she asked.

"He spoke a little wildly in the mess last night."

"Heaven help us all, in that case," said the Major.

Qasim said nothing.

"All right." Bernstein tabbed through the notes, skimming to the first passage Qasim had highlighted.

"'Worst first,'" she read out. "'The undetectable entities. No coherent communication. (Worst case: try exorcism???!) Next: colonial organisms. Mycoidal. Translations speculative. Molecular grammar. Query their concept of personhood. Also of responsibility. If this can be established: rational nature. Fallen nature. If they have a moral code that they do not live up to? Any existing religious concepts? Next: discrete animalia. Opposite danger here: anthropomorphism. (Cf. Dominican AI mission fiasco.) Conclusion: use mycoids as test case to establish consilience.'" She blinked the script away, and stared at Qasim. "Well? What's the harm in that?"

"He's been hanging around the team working on the mycoids. If you read on, you'll find he intends to preach Christianity to them."

"To the scientists?"

"To the mycoids."

"Oh!" Major Bernstein laughed. It was a sound that began and ended abruptly, like a fall of broken glass, and felt as cutting. "If he can get *any* message through to them, he'll be doing better than the scientists. And unless you, my overzealous *mukhabaratchik*, can find any evidence that Dr MacIntyre is sowing religious division in the ranks, practising rituals involving animal cruelty or non-consensual sexual acts, preaching Market Maoism or New Republicanism or otherwise aiding and abetting the Chinks or the Yanks, I warn you most seriously to not waste your time or mine. Do I make myself quite clear?"

"Entirely, ma'am."

"Dismissed."

○

I do not what I wish I did.

It was a lot to read into a sequence of successive concentrations of different organic molecules. In the raw transcript it went like this:

Titration	Translation
Indication-marker	THIS
Impulse-summation	MYCOID
Action (general)	DOES
Negation-marker	NOT
Impulse-direction	ACT
Affirmation-marker	[AS] INTENDED [BY]
Impulse-summation	[THIS] MYCOID
Repulsion-marker	[AND THIS] DISGUST[S]
Impulse-summation	[THIS] MYCOID

Donald looked at the print-out and trembled. It was hard not to see it as the first evidence of an alien that knew sin. He well realized, of course, that it could just as well mean something as innocent as *I couldn't help but puke.* But the temptation, if it was a temptation, to read it as an instance of the spirit warring against the flesh—well, against the slime—was almost irresistible. Donald couldn't help but regard it as a case of consilience, and as no coincidence.

"Is there any way we can respond to this?"

Trepper, the mycoid project team leader, shook his head. "It's very difficult to reproduce the gradients. For us, it's as if... Look, suppose a tree could understand human speech. It tries to respond by grow-ing some twigs and branches so that they rub against each other just so, in the wind. And all we hear are some funny scratching and creak-ing sounds."

Trees in the wind. Donald gazed past the tables and equipment of the corridor's field lab to the portal that opened on to the mycoids' planet. The view showed a few standing trees, and a lot of fallen logs. The mycoids did something to force the trees' growth and weaken their structure, giving the vast underground mycoid colonies plenty of rotting cellulose to feed on. Far in the distance, across a plain of coppery grass, rose a copse of quite different trees, tall and stately with tapered bulges from the roots to half-way up the trunks. Vane-like projections of stiff leaves sprouted from their sides. Bare branches bristled at their tops. These were the Niven Pines, able to synthesize and store megalitres of volatile and flammable hydrocarbons. At every lightning storm one or other of these trees—the spark carried by some kind of liquid lightning conductor to a drip of fuel-sap at its foot—would roar into flame and rise skyward. Some of them would make it to orbit. No doubt they bore mycoid travellers, but what these clammy astronauts did in space, and whether this improbable arboreal rocketry was the result of natural selection, or of conscious genetic manipulation by the mycoids—or indeed some other alien—was as yet unclear.

In any case, it had been enough to bring the mycoids a place at the table of whatever Galactic Club had set up the wormhole nexus. Perhaps they too had found a wormhole nexus on the edge of their solar system. Perhaps they too had puzzled over the alien intelligences it connected them to. If so, they showed little sign of having learned much. They pulsed their electrophoretically controlled molecular gradients into the soil near the Station's portal, but much of it—even assuming the translations were correct—was about strictly parochial matters. It was as if they weren't interested in communicating with the humans.

Donald determined to make them interested. Besides his pastoral duties—social as well as spiritual—he had an allotted time for scholarship and study, and he devoted that time to the work of the mycoid research team. He did not explain his purpose to the scientists. If the mycoids were sinners, he had an obligation to offer them the chance of salvation. He had no obligation to offer the scientists the temptation to scoff.

Time passed.

○

The airlock door slammed. Donald stepped through the portal and on to the surface. He walked forward along an already-beaten track across the floor of the copse. Here and there, mushroom-like structures poked up through the spongy, bluish moss and black leaf-litter. The bulges of their inch-wide caps had a watery transparency that irresistibly suggested that they were the lenses of eyes. No one had as yet dared to pluck a fungus to find out.

A glistening patch of damp mud lay a couple of hundred metres from the station. It occupied a space between the perimeters of two of the underground mycoids, and had become a preferred site for myco-linguistic research. Rainbow ripples of chemical communication between the two sprawling circular beings below stained its surface at regular intervals. Occasional rainstorms washed away the gradients, but they always seeped out again.

Donald stepped up to the edge of the mud and set up the apparatus that the team had devised for a non-intrusive examination of the mycoids' messages: a wide-angle combined digital field microscope and spectroscope. About two metres long, its support frame straddled the patch, above which its camera slowly tracked along. Treading carefully, he planted one trestle, then the other on the far side of the patch, then walked back and laid the tracking rail across them both. He switched on the power pack and the camera began its slow traverse.

There was a small experiment he had been given to perform. It had been done many times before, to no effect. Perhaps this variant would be different. He reached in to his thigh pocket and pulled out a plastic-covered gel disc, about five centimetres across, made from synthesized copies of local mucopolysaccharides. The concentric circles of molecular concentrations that covered it spelled out—the team had hoped—the message: We wish to communicate. Please respond.

Donald peeled off the bottom cover and, one knee on a rock and one hand on a fallen log, leaned out over the multicoloured mud and laid the gel disc down on a bare dark patch near the middle. He withdrew his hand, peeling back the top cover as he did so, and settled back on his haunches. He stuffed the crumpled wrappings in his pocket and reached in deeper for a second disc: one he'd covertly prepared himself, with a different message.

Resisting the impulse to look over his shoulder, he repeated the operation and stood up.

A voice sounded in his helmet: "Got you!"

Qasim stood a few metres away, glaring at him.

"I beg your pardon," said Donald. "I've done nothing wrong."

"You've placed an unauthorized message on the mud," said Qasim.

"What if I have?" said Donald. "It can do no harm."

"That's not for you to judge," said Qasim.

"Nor for you either!"

"It is," said Qasim. "We don't want anything ... ideological or controversial to affect our contact." He looked around. "Come on, Donald, be a sensible chap. There's still time to pick the thing up again. No harm done and no more will be said."

It had been like this, Donald thought, ever since the East India Company: commercial and military interests using and then restricting missionaries.

"I will not do that," he said. "I'll go back with you, but I won't destroy the message."

"Then I'll have to do it," said Qasim. "Please step aside."

Donald stayed where he was. Qasim stepped forward and caught his shoulder. "I'm sorry," he said.

Donald pulled away, and took an involuntary step back. One foot came down in the mud and kept on going down. His leg went in up to the knee. Flailing, he toppled on his back across the tracking rail. The rail cracked in two under the blow from his oxygen tanks. He landed with a huge splash. Both pieces of the rail sank out of sight at once. Donald himself lay, knees crooked, his visor barely above the surface.

"Quicksand," said Qasim, his voice cutting across the alarmed babble from the watching science team. "Don't try to stand or struggle, it'll just make things worse. Lie back with your arms out and stay there. I'll get a rope."

"Okay," said Donald. He peered up through his smeared visor. "Don't be long."

Qasim waved. "Back in seconds, Donald. Hang in there."

The science team talked Donald through the next minute, as Qasim ran for the portal, stepped into the airlock, and grabbed the rope that had already been placed there.

"Okay, Donald, he's just—"

The voice stopped. Static hiss filled the speaker. Donald waited.

"Can anyone hear me?"

No reply.

Five more minutes passed. Nobody was coming. He would have to get himself out. There was no need to panic. He had five hours's worth of air supply, and no interruption to the portals had ever lasted more than an hour.

Donald swept his arms through the mud to his side, raised them above the mud, flung them out again, and repeated this laborious backstroke many times, until his helmet rested on solid ground. It had taken him half an hour to move a couple of metres. He rested for a few minutes, gasping, then reached behind him and scrabbled for something to hold. Digging his fingers into the soil, kicking now with his feet—still deep in the mud—he began to lever himself up and heave his shoulders out of the bog. He got as much as the upper quarter of his body out when the ground turned to liquid under his elbows. His head fell back, and around it the mud splashed again. He made another effort at swimming along the top of the mud on his back. His arms met less resistance. Around him the sludge turned to slurry. Water welled up, and large bubbles of gas popped all across the widening quagmire.

He began to sink. He swung his arms, kicked his legs hard, and the increasingly liquid mass closed over his visor. Writhing, panicking now, he sank into utter darkness. His feet touched bottom. His hands, stretched above his head, were now well below the surface. He leaned forward with an immense effort and tried to place one foot in front of the other. If he had to, he would walk out of this. Barely had he completed a step when he found the resistance of the wet soil increase. It set almost solid around him. He was stuck.

Donald took some slow, deep breaths. Less than an hour had passed. Fifty minutes. Fifty-five. At any moment his rescuers would come for him.

They didn't. For four more hours he stood there in the dark. As each hour passed he realized with increasing certainty that the portal had not reopened. He wondered, almost idly, if that had anything to do with his own intrusion into the bog. He wondered, with some anguish, whether his illicit message had been destroyed, unread, as he fell in on top of it.

The anguish passed. What had happened to the message, and what happened to him, was in a quite ultimate sense not his problem. The parable of the sower was as clear as the great commission itself. He had been in the path of duty. He had proclaimed, to the best of his ability, the truth. This was what he had been sent to do. No guarantee had been given that he would be successful. He would not be the first, nor the last, missionary whose mission was to all human reckoning futile. The thought saddened him, but did not disturb him. In that sense, if none other, his feet were on a rock.

He prayed, he shouted, he thought, he wept, he prayed again, and he died.

○

At last! The aliens had sent a communications package! After almost a year of low-bandwidth disturbances of the air and the electromagnetic spectrum, from which little sense could be extracted, and many days of dropping tiny messages of blurry resolution and trivial import, they had finally, *finally* sent something one could get one's filaments into!

The mycoid sent long tendrils around the package, infiltrating its pores and cracks. It synthesized acids that worked their way through any weak points in its fabric. Within hours it had penetrated the wrapping and begun a riotous, joyous exploration of the vast library of information within. The mycoid had in its own genetic library billions of years of accumulated experience in absorbing information from organisms of every kind: plant or animal, mycoid or bacterium. It could relate the structure of a central nervous system to any semantic or semiotic content it had associated with the organism. It probed cavities, investigated long transportation tubes, traced networks of neurons and found its way to the approximately globular sub-package where the information was most rich. It dissolved here, embalmed there, dissected and investigated everywhere. In an inner wrapping it found a small object made from multiple mats of cellulose fibre, each layer impregnated with carbon-based markings. The mycoid stored these codes with the rest. Seasons and years passed. A complete transcription of the alien package, of its neural structures and genetic codes, was eventually read off.

Then the work of translation and interpretation, shared out across all the mycoids of the continent, began.

It took a long time, but the mycoids had all the time in the world. They had no more need—for the moment—to communicate with the aliens, now that they had this vast resource of information. They, or their ancestors, had done this many times before, under many suns.

They understood the alien, and they understood the strange story that had shaped so many of the connections in its nervous system.

They interpreted the carbon marks on the cellulose mats. In their own vast minds they reconstructed the scenes of alien life, as they had done with everything that fell their way, from the grass and the insects to the trees. They had what a human might have called a vivid imagination. They had, after all, little else.

Some of them found the story to be:

Affirmation-marker	GOOD
Information-marker	NEWS

Spores spread it to the space-going trees, and thence to the worm-hole network, and thence to countless worlds.

Not quite all the seeds fell on stony ground.

They say that life is what you make it, but what happens when we truly create artificial life? What if our inventions try to remake us in their own image? Is the human condition necessary? Is it even sufficient?

✿ ✿

DEUS EX HOMINE
Hannu Rajaniemi

✿ ✿

As gods go, I wasn't one of the holier-than-thou, dying-for-your-sins variety. I was a full-blown transhuman deity with a liquid metal body, an external brain, clouds of self-replicating utility fog to do my bidding and a recursively self-improving AI slaved to my volition. I could do anything I wanted. I wasn't Jesus, I was Superman: an evil Bizarro Superman.

I was damn lucky. I survived.

✿

The quiet in Pittenweem is deeper than it should be, even for a small Fife village by the sea. The plague is bad here in the north, beyond Hadrian's Firewall, and houses hide behind utility fog haloes.

"Not like Prezzagard, is it?" Craig says, as we drive down the main street.

Apprehension, whispers the symbiote in my head. *Worry*. I don't blame Craig. I'm his stepdaughter's boyfriend, come calling during her first weekend leave. There's going to be trouble.

"Not really," I tell him, anxiety bubbling in my belly.

"Beggars canna be choosers, as my granny used to say," Craig replies. "Here we are."

Sue opens the door and hugs me. As always, I see Aileen in her, in the short-cropped blonde hair and freckled face.

"Hey, Jukka," she says. "It's good to see you."

"You too," I say, surprising both myself and the symbiote with my sincerity.

"Aileen called," Sue says. "She should be here in a few minutes."

Behind her shoulder, I notice Malcolm looking at me. I wink at him and he giggles.

Sue sighs. "Malcolm has been driving me crazy," she says. "He believes he can fly an angel now. It's great how you think you can do anything when you're six."

"Aileen is still like that," I say.

"I know."

"She's coming!" shouts Malcolm suddenly. We run out to the back garden and watch her descend.

○

The angel is big, even bigger than I expect from the lifecasts. Its skin is transparent, flowing glass; its wings pitch-black. Its face and torso are rough-hewn, like an unfinished sculpture.

And inside its chest, trapped like an insect in amber, but smiling, is Aileen.

They come down slowly. The downdraught from the micron-sized fans in the angel's wings tears petals from Sue's chrysanthemums. It settles down onto the grass lightly. The glass flesh flows aside, and Aileen steps out.

It's the first time I've seen her since she left. The quicksuit is a halo around her: it makes her look like a knight. There is a sharper cast to her features now and she has a tan as well. Fancasts on the Q-net claim that the Deicide Corps soldiers get a DNA reworking besides the cool toys. But she is still my Aileen: dirty blonde hair, sharp cheekbones and green eyes that always seem to carry a challenge; my Aileen, the light of the sun.

I can only stare. She winks at me and goes to embrace her mother, brother and Craig. Then she comes to me and I can feel the quicksuit humming. She brushes my cheek with her lips.

"Jukka," she says. "What on earth are you doing here?"

"Blecch. Stop kissing," says Malcolm.

Aileen scoops him up. "We're not kissing," she says. "We're saying hello." She smiles. "I hear you want to meet my angel."

Malcolm's face lights up. But Sue grabs Aileen's hand firmly. "Food first," she says. "Play later."

Aileen laughs. "Now I know I'm home," she says.

○

Aileen eats with relish. She has changed her armour for jeans and a

T-shirt, and looks a lot more like the girl I remember. She catches me staring at her and squeezes my hand under the table.

"Don't worry," she says. "I'm real."

I say nothing and pull my hand away.

Craig and Sue exchange looks, and the symbiote prompts me to say something.

"So I guess you guys are still determined to stay on this side of the Wall?" I oblige.

Sue nods. "I'm not going anywhere. My father built this house, and runaway gods or not, we're staying here. Besides, that computer thing seems to be doing a good job protecting us."

"The Fish," I say.

She laughs. "I've never gotten used to that. I know that it was these young lads who built it, but why did they have to call it Fish?"

I shrug.

"It's a geek joke, a recursive acronym. Fish Is Super Human. Lots of capital letters. It's not that funny, really."

"Whatever. Well, Fish willing, we'll stay as long as we can."

"That's good." *And stupid*, I think to myself.

"It's a Scottish thing, you could say. Stubbornness," says Craig.

"Finnish, too," I add. "I don't think my parents are planning to go anywhere soon."

"See, I always knew we had something in common," he says, although the symbiote tells me that his smile is not genuine.

"Hey," says Aileen. "Last time I checked, Jukka is not your daughter. And I just got back from a war."

"So, how *was* the war?" asks Craig.

Challenge, says the symbiote. I feel uneasy.

Aileen smiles sadly.

"Messy," she says.

"I had a mate in Iraq, back in the noughties," Craig says. "*That* was messy. Blood and guts. These days, it's just machines and nerds. And the machines can't even kill you. What kind of war is that?"

"I'm not supposed to talk about it," says Aileen.

"Craig," says Sue. "Not now."

"I'm just asking," says Craig. "I had friends in Inverness and somebody with the plague turned it into a giant game of Tetris.

Aileen's been in the war, she knows what it's like. We've been worried. I just want to know."

"If she doesn't want to talk about it, she doesn't talk about it," Sue says. "She's home now. Leave her alone."

I look at Craig. The symbiote tells me that this is a mistake. I tell it to shut up.

"She has a point," I say. "It's a bad war. Worse than we know. And you're right, the godplague agents can't kill. But the gods can. Recursively self-optimising AIs don't kill people. Killer cyborgs kill people."

Craig frowns.

"So," he says, "how come you're not out there if you think it's so bad?"

Malcolm's gaze flickers between his sister and his stepfather. *Confusion. Tears.*

I put my fork down. The food has suddenly lost its taste. "I had the plague," I say slowly. "I'm disqualified. I was one of the nerds."

Aileen is standing up now and her eyes are those of a Fury.

"How dare you!" she shouts at Craig. "You have no idea what you're talking about. No idea. You don't get it from the casts. The Fish doesn't want to show you. It's bad, really bad. You want to tell me how bad? I'll tell you."

"Aileen—" I begin, but she silences me with a gesture.

"Yes, Inverness was like a giant Tetris game. Nerds and machines did it. And so we killed them. And do you know what else we saw? Babies. Babies bonded with the godplague. Babies are cruel. Babies know what they want: food, sleep, for all pain to go away. And that's what the godplague gives them. I saw a woman who'd gone mad, she said she'd lost her baby and couldn't find it, even though we could see that she was pregnant. My angel looked at her and said that she had a wormhole in her belly, that the baby was in a little universe of its own. And there was this look in her eyes, this look—"

Aileen's voice breaks. She storms out of the room the same instant Malcolm starts crying. Without thinking, I go after her.

"I was just asking…" I hear Craig saying as I slam the door shut behind me.

●

I find her in the back garden, sitting on the ground next to the angel, one hand wrapped around its leg, and I feel a surge of jealousy.

"Hi," I say. "Mind if I sit down?"

"Go ahead, it's a free patch of grass." She smiles wanly. "I spooked everybody pretty badly back there, didn't I?"

"I think you did. Malcolm is still crying."

"It's just... I don't know. It all came out. And then I thought that it doesn't matter if he hears it too, that he plays all these games with much worse stuff going on all the time, that it wouldn't matter. I'm so stupid."

"I think it's the fact that it was *you* telling it," I say slowly. "That makes it true."

She sighs. "You're right. I'm such an arse. I shouldn't have let Craig get me going like that, but we had a rough time up north, and to hear him making light of it like that—"

"It's okay."

"Hey," she says. "I've missed you. You make things make sense."

"I'm glad somebody thinks so."

"Come on," Aileen says, wiping her face. "Let's go for a walk, or better yet, let's go to the pub. I'm still hungry. And I could use a drink. My first leave and I'm still sober. Sergeant Katsuki would disown me if she knew."

"We'll have to see what we can do about that," I say and we start walking towards the harbour.

o

I don't know if a girl like Aileen would ever have taken an interest in a guy like me if it hadn't been for the fact that I used to be a god.

Two years ago. University cafeteria. Me, trying to get used to the pale colours of the real world again. Alone. And then three girls sit down in the neighbouring table. Pretty. Loud.

"Seriously," says the one with a pastel-coloured jacket and a Hello-Kitty-shaped Fish-interface, "I want to do it with a post. Check this out." The girls huddle around her fogscreen. "There's a cast called Postcoital. Sex with gods. This girl is like their *groupie*. Follows them around. I mean, just the cool ones that don't go unstable."

There's a moment of reverent silence.

"Wow!" says the second girl. "I always thought that was an urban legend. Or some sort of staged porn thing."

"Apparently not," says the third.

These days, the nerd rapture is like the 'flu: you can catch it. The godplague is a volition-bonding, recursively self-improving and self-replicating program. A genie that comes to you and makes its home in the machinery around you and tells you that do as thou wilt shall be the whole of the law. It fucks you up, but it's sexy as hell.

"Seriously," says the first girl, "no wonder the guys who wrote Fish were all *guys*. The whole thing is just another penis. It has no regard for female sexuality. I mean, there's no feminist angle *at all* in the whole collective volition thing. Seriously."

"My God!" says the second girl. "That one there. I want to do him, uh, her. It... *All* of them. I really do."

"No you don't," I say.

"Excuse me?" She looks at me as if she's just stepped in something unpleasant and wants to wipe it off. "We're having a private conversation here."

"Sure. I just wanted to say that that cast is a fake. And I really wouldn't mess around with the posts if I were you."

"You speak from experience? Got your dick bitten off by a post girl?" For once I'm grateful I need the symbiote: if I ignore its whispers, her face is just a blank mask to me.

There is nervous laughter from the other girls.

"Yes," I say. "I used to be one."

They get up in unison, stare at me for a second and walk away. *Masks*, I think. *Masks.*

A moment later I'm interrupted again.

"I'm sorry," the third girl says. "I mean, really, really sorry. They're not really my friends, we're just doing the same course. I'm Aileen."

"That's OK," I say. "I don't really mind."

Aileen sits on the corner of the table, and I don't really mind that either.

"What was it like?" she asks. Her eyes are very green. *Inquisitive*, says the symbiote. And I realize that I desperately want it to say something else.

"You really want to know?" I ask.

"Yes," she says.

I look at my hands.

"I was a quacker," I say slowly, "a quantum hacker. And when the Fish-source came out, I tinkered with it, just like pretty much every geek on the planet. And I got mine to compile: my own friendly AI slave, an idiot-proof supergoal system, just designed to turn me from a sack of flesh into a Jack Kirby New God, not to harm anybody else. Or so it told me."

I grimace. "My external nervous system took over the Helsinki University of Technology's supercomputing cluster in about thirty seconds. It got pretty ugly after that."

"But you made it," says Aileen, eyes wide.

"Well, back then, the Fish still had the leisure to be gentle. The starfish were there before anybody was irretrievably dead. It burned my AI off like an information cancer and shoved me back into—" I make a show of looking at myself. "Well, this, I guess."

"Wow!" Aileen says, slender fingers wrapped around a cup of latte.

"Yeah," I say. "That's pretty much what I said."

"And how do you feel now? Did it hurt? Do you miss it?"

I laugh.

"I don't really remember most of it. The Fish amputated a lot of memories. And there was some damage as well." I swallow.

"I'm... It's a mild form of Asperger's, more or less. I don't read people very well anymore." I take off my beanie. "This is pretty ugly." I show her the symbiote at the back of my head. Like most Fish-machines, it looks like a starfish. "It's a symbiote. It reads people for me."

She touches it gently and I feel it. The symbiote can map tactile information with much higher resolution than my skin and I can feel the complex contours of Aileen's fingertips gliding on its surface.

"I think it's really pretty," she says. "Like a jewel. Hey, it's warm! What else does it do? Is it like, a Fish-interface? In your head?"

"No. It combs my brain all the time. It makes sure that the thing I was is not hiding in there." I laugh. "It's a shitty thing to be, a washed-up god."

Aileen smiles. *It's a very pretty smile,* says the symbiote. I don't know if it's biased because it's being caressed.

"You have to admit that sounds pretty cool," she says. "Or do you just tell that to all the girls?"

That night she takes me home.

○

We have fish and chips in the Smuggler's Den. Aileen and I are the only customers; the publican is an old man who greets her by name. The food is fabbed and I find it too greasy, but Aileen eats with apparent relish and washes it down with a pint of beer.

"At least you've still got your appetite," I say.

"Training in the Gobi Desert teaches you to miss food," she says and my heart jumps at the way she brushes her hair back. "My skin cells can do photosynthesis. Stuff you don't get from the fancasts. It's terrible. You always feel hungry, but they don't let you eat. Makes you incredibly alert, though. My pee will be a weird colour for the whole weekend because all these nanites will be coming out."

"Thanks for sharing that."

"Sorry. Soldier talk."

"You do feel different," I say.

"You don't," she says.

"Well, I am." I take a sip from my pint, hoping the symbiote will let me get drunk. "I *am* different."

She sighs.

"Thanks for coming. It's good to see you."

"It's okay."

"No, really, it does mean a lot to me, I—"

"Aileen, please." I lock the symbiote. I tell myself I don't know what she's thinking. *Honest.* "You don't have to." I empty my pint. "There's something I've been wondering, actually. I've thought about this a lot. I've had a lot of time. What I mean is—" The words stick in my mouth.

"Go on," says Aileen.

"There's no reason why you *have* to do this, go out there and fight monsters, unless—"

I flinch at the thought, even now.

"Unless you were so angry with me that you had to go kill things, things like I used to be."

Aileen gets up.

"No, that wasn't it," she says. "That wasn't it at all!"

"I hear you. You don't have to shout."

She squeezes her eyes shut. "Turn on your damn symbiote and come with me."

"Where are we going?"

"To the beach, to skip stones."

"Why?" I ask.

"Because I feel like it."

°

We go down to the beach. It's sunny like it hasn't been for a few months. The huge Fish that floats near the horizon, a diamond starfish almost a mile in diameter, may have something to do with that.

We walk along the line drawn by the surf. Aileen runs ahead, taunting the waves.

There is a nice spot with lots of round, flat stones between two piers. Aileen picks up a few, swings her arm and makes an expert throw, sending one skimming and bouncing across the waves.

"Come on. You try."

I try. The stone flies in a high arc, plummets down and disappears into the water. It doesn't even make a splash.

I laugh, and look at her. Aileen's face is lit by the glow of the starfish in the distance mingled with sunlight. For a moment, she looks just like the girl who brought me here to spend Christmas with her parents.

Then Aileen is crying.

"I'm sorry," she says. "I was going to tell you before I came. But I couldn't."

She clings to me. Waves lap at our feet.

"Aileen, please tell me what's wrong. You know I can't always tell."

She sits down on the wet sand.

"Remember what I told Craig? About the babies."

"Yeah."

Aileen swallows.

"Before I left you," she says, "I had a baby."

°

At first I think it's just sympathy sex. I don't mind that: I've had that more than a few times, both before and after my brief stint as the Godhead. But Aileen stays. She makes breakfast. She walks to the campus with me in the morning, holding my hand, and laughs at the spamvores chasing ad icons on the street, swirling like multicoloured leaves in the wind. I grow her a Fish-interface from my symbiote as a birthday present: it looks like a ladybird. She calls it Mr Bug.

I'm easy: that's all it takes for me to fall in love.

That winter in Prezzagard passes quickly. We find a flat together in the Stack vertical village, and I pay for it with some scripting hackwork.

And then, one morning, her bed is empty and Mr Bug sits on her pillow. Her toiletry things are gone from the bathroom. I call her friends, send bots to local sousveillance peernets. No one has seen her. I spend two nights inventing nightmares. Does she have a lover? Did I do something wrong? The symbiote is not infallible, and there are times when I dread saying the wrong thing, just by accident.

She comes back on the morning of the third day. I open the door and there she is, looking pale and dishevelled.

"Where have you been?" I ask. She looks so lost that I want to hold her, but she pushes me away.

Hate, says the symbiote. *Hate.*

"Sorry," she says, tears rolling down her cheeks. "I just came to get my things. I have to go."

I try to say something, that I don't understand, that we can work this out, that nothing's so bad she can't tell me about it, and if it's my fault, I'll fix it. I want to plead. I want to beg. But the hate is a fiery aura around her that silences me and I watch quietly as the Fish-drones carry her life away.

"Don't ask me to explain," she says at the door. "Look after Mr Bug."

After she's gone, I want to tear the symbiote out of my skull. I want the black worm that is hiding in my mind to come out and take over again, make me a god who is above pain and love and hate, a god who can fly. Things go hazy for a while. I think I try to open the window and make a three-hundred-metre dive, but the Fish in the walls and the glass won't let me: this is a cruel world we've made, a lovingly cruel world that won't let us hurt ourselves.

At some point, the symbiote puts me to sleep. It does it again when I wake up, after I start breaking things. And again, until some sort of Pavlovian reflex kicks in.

Later, I spend long nights trawling through the images in Mr Bug's lifecache: I try to figure it out by using the symbiote to pattern-match emotions from the slices of our life together. But there's nothing that hasn't been resolved, nothing that would linger and fester. Unless I'm getting it all wrong.

It's something that's happened before, I tell myself. *I touch the sky and fall. Nothing new.*

And so I sleep-walk. Graduate. Work. Write Fish-scripts. Forget. Tell myself I'm over it.

Then Aileen calls and I get the first train north.

○

I listen to the sound of her heartbeat, trying to understand her words. They tumble through my mind, too heavy for me to grasp.

"Aileen. Jesus, Aileen."

The god hiding in my mind, in the dead parts, in my cells, in my DNA—

Suddenly, I want to throw up.

"I didn't know what was happening, at first," says Aileen, her voice flat and colourless. "I felt strange. I just wanted to be alone, somewhere high and far away. So I went to one of the empty flats up at the Stacktop—one of the freshly grown ones—to spend the night and think. Then I got really hungry. I mean, really, really hungry. So I ate fabbed food, lots and lots. And then my belly started growing."

With the Fish around, contraception is the default state of things unless one actually *wants* a baby. But there had been that night in Pittenweem, just after Christmas, beyond the Wall where the Fish-spores that fill the air in Prezzagard are few. And I could just see it happening, the godseed in my brain hacking my cells, making tiny molecular machines much smaller than sperm, carrying DNA laden with code, burrowing into Aileen.

"It didn't feel strange. There was no pain. I lay down, my waters broke and it just pulled itself out. It was the most beautiful thing I'd ever seen," she says, smiling. "It had your eyes and these tiny, tiny fingers. Each had the most perfect fingernail. It looked at me and smiled."

"It waved at me. Like ... like it decided that it didn't need me anymore. And then the walls just *opened* and it flew away. My baby. Flew away."

The identification mechanism I used to slave the godseed was just my DNA. It really didn't occur to me that there was a loophole there.

It could make my volition its own. Reinvent itself. And once it did that, it could modify itself as much as it pleased. Grow wings, if it wanted.

I hold Aileen. We're both wet and shivering, but I don't care.

"I'm sorry. That night I came to tell you," she says. "And then I saw it looking at me again. From your eyes. I had to go away."

"So you joined the Corps."

She sighs.

"Yes. It helped. Doing something, being needed."

"I needed you too," I say.

"I know. I'm sorry."

Anger wells up in my throat. "So is it working? Are you guys defeating the superbabies and the dark lords? Does it make you happy?"

She flinches away from me. "You sound like Craig now."

"Well, what am I supposed to say? I'm sorry about the baby. *But it wasn't your fault. Or mine.*"

"It was you who—" She lifts her hand to her mouth. "Sorry, I didn't mean that. I didn't mean that."

"Go back to your penance and leave me alone."

I start running along the waterline, heading nowhere in particular.

○

The angel is waiting for me on the shore.

"Hello, Jukka," it says. "Good to see you again."

As always, the voice is androgynous and pleasant. It tickles something in my brain. It is the voice of the Fish.

"Hi."

"Can I help you?"

"Not really. Unless you want to give her up. Make her see sense."

"I can't interfere with her decisions," says the angel. "That's not what I do. I only give you—and her—what you want, or what you would want if you were smarter. That's my supergoal. You know that."

"You self-righteous bastard. The collective volition of humanity is that she must go and fight monsters? And probably die in the process? Is it supposed to be *character-forming* or something?"

The angel says nothing, but it's got me going now.

"And I can't even be sure that it's Aileen's own decision. This—this thing in my head—it's you. You could have let the godseed escape, just to hurt Aileen enough to get her to sign up to your bloody kamikaze squadron. And the chances are that you knew that I was going to come here and rant at you and there's nothing I can do to stop her. Or is there?"

The angel considers this.

"If I could do that, the world would be perfect already." It cocks its glass head to one side. "But perhaps there is someone who wanted you to be here."

"Don't try to play head games with me!"

Anger rushes out of me like a river. I pound the angel's chest with my fists. Its skin flows away like a soap bubble.

"Jukka!"

The voice comes from somewhere far away.

"Jukka, stop," says Aileen. "Stop, you idiot!"

She yanks me around with irresistible strength. "Look at me! It wasn't the Fish. It wasn't you. It wasn't the baby. It was *me*. I want to do this. Why won't you let me?"

I look at her, my eyes brimming.

"Because I can't come with you."

"You silly boy," she says, and now it's her holding me as I cry, for the first time since I stopped being a god. "Silly, silly boy."

o

After a while, I run out of tears. We sit on a rock, watching the sun set. I feel light and empty.

"Maybe it would have been easier if you hadn't called," I say, sighing.

Aileen's eyes widen.

"What do you mean? I never did. I thought Craig did. It would have been just like him. To keep me from going back."

And then we see the baby.

It is bald and naked and pink, and a hair-thin silver umbilical hangs from its navel. Its eyes are green like Aileen's, but their gaze is mine. It floats in the air, its perfect tiny toes almost touching the water.

The baby looks at us and laughs: the sound is like the peal of silver bells. Its mouth is full of pearly teeth.

"Be very still," says Aileen.

The angel moves towards the baby. Its hands explode into fractal razor bushes. A glass cannon forms in its chest. Tiny spheres of light, quantum dots pumped full of energy, dart towards the baby.

The baby laughs again. It holds out its tiny hands, and *squeezes.* The air—and perhaps space, and time—wavers and twists. And then the angel is gone, and our baby is holding a tiny sphere of glass, like a snow-globe.

Aileen grabs my arm.

"Don't worry," she whispers. "The big skyFish must have seen this. It'll do something. Stay calm."

"Bad baby," I say slowly. "You broke Mummy's angel."

The baby frowns. I can see the cosmic anger simmering behind the wrinkled pink forehead.

"Jukka—" Aileen says, but I interrupt her.

"You only know how to *kill* gods. I know how to *talk* to them." I look at my—*son,* says the little wrinkly thing between its legs—and take a step towards him. I remember what it's like, having all the power in the world. There's a need that comes with it, a need to make things perfect.

"I know why you brought us here," I say. "You want us to be together, don't you? Mummy and Daddy." I go down to one knee and look my son in the eye. I'm in the water now and so close to him that I can feel the warmth of his skin.

"And I know what you're thinking. I've been there. You could take us apart. You could rebuild our minds. You could *make* us want to be together, to be with you." I pause and touch his nose with my forefinger. "But it doesn't work that way. It would never be perfect. It would never be right." I sigh. "Trust me, I know. I did it to myself. But you are something new, you can do better."

I take Mr Bug from my pocket and hold it out to my son. He grabs it and puts it into his mouth. I take a deep breath, but he doesn't bite.

"Talk to the bug," I say. "He'll tell you who we are. Then come back."

The baby closes its eyes. Then he giggles, mouth full of an insect-shaped AI, and touches my nose with a tiny hand.

I hear Aileen gasp. A lightning horse gallops through my brain, thunder rumbling in its wake.

○

Something wet on my face wakes me. I open my eyes and see Aileen's face against the dark sky. It is raining.

"Are you okay?" she asks, almost in tears, cradling my head. "That little bastard!"

Her eyes widen. And suddenly, there is a silence in my mind, a wholeness. I see the wonder in her eyes.

Aileen holds out her hand. My symbiote is lying in her palm. I take it, turning it between my fingers. I take a good swing and throw it into the sea. It skims the surface three times, and then it's gone.

"I wonder where he gets it from."

Scotland has long had links with what the Reverend Robert Kirk called the "Secret Commonwealth of Elves, Faunes and Fairies", but the industrial revolution seemed to sever many of the ties between our world and its enchanted doppelgänger. Now, in the twenty-first century, the heavy industrial landscape of the post-Victorian age, with its yards, mills and factories, and the communities of workers they founded and nurtured, can seem as distant and strange as faerieland itself.

o   o   o   o   o   o   o   o   o   o   o   o   o   o   o   o   o   o   o   o

THE LAST SHIFT
Hal Duncan

o   o   o   o   o   o   o   o   o   o   o   o   o   o   o   o   o   o   o   o

8:30

Down the steps and out of the airtram station, showing his ticket to the guard at the door, Billy strides along the paving stones of Coats Street, sticks his morning roll-up in his mouth and stops to light it at the corner of Dyers Wynd, glancing up at the War Memorial for a second before, with a puff of smoke and steam in the cold winter air, he walks on. He fumbles the woollen glove back onto his left hand, right hand cupping the fag for warmth. The wind blows the hood of his parka down and he curses, shivers as a drip of rainwater blown from a roof somewhere above hits the back of his neck and dribbles down between his shoulder-blades. He flips the hood back up over his horns, spine rippling involuntarily with the tickle of water. Bastard. He hates the winter, hates this weather, hates having to wear umpteen layers of clothing all the endless months from autumn to spring. You can't even fly in this weather.

o

The bell of the town hall clock across the river chimes half past and he quickens his pace to a jog over the pedestrian crossing with the red man showing. Back to a stride on the other side. He nods a wee joke of a forelock-tugging *good morning, guvnor ... and good morning to you, sir,* to the greened-grey bronzes of the Gilmour Brothers as he walks between them—Thomas with his thumbs tucked under his frockcoat's lapels, Peter with his top hat nooked in a crook of elbow, both of them every inch the solemn Empire-builder, dark wings spread out wide behind them. Aye, but they look like sentinels surveying the very furthest dominions of Albion, gazing out over Afrita and Nagastan, the Aerient and the New World. Even their horns are solemn and patriarchal, curving ram's horns thick and heavy as their mutton-chop sideburns. Oh, aye. Albion's finest.

○

Down the steps Billy goes, and into the little ornamental garden with its statue of Queen Titania, bulky in her widow's black bustle, out onto the cobbles slick with rain (being not quite cold enough for ice last night) where Thread Lane cuts a narrow path between a row of old sandstone offices and the rail of the wall that drops down to the river below. Swans nesting in the weeds and litter sail slow on the murk of the Black Cart, beneath the bunting of Christmas lights all strung from side to side across the river, dull baubles without the power on at this grey time of the morning. He follows the lane along till it hits Needle Road and crosses the river. Cars thrum past him in a stream of dopplering noise.

○

Upriver from the bridge and squat beside a natural weir of white foam crashing over hidden rock, the old Anchor Mill is a hulk of red brick, rowed and columned with windows, square tower perching at one corner. Billy flicks his dead fag out over the river towards it as he crosses the bridge. The building's under renovation just now, being turned into luxury apartments. Scaffolding almost swallows it, adding to its ugly bulk. Under the mill, like some long lump of worn, cracked granite swallowed by surf at the bottom of a seaside cliff, an outcrop of stone—grey and green with damp and moss—juts out into the water. The old mill used to belong to Gilmour; the whole town of Fergusley in a way used to belong to Gilmour—a centuries-old family company of dyers, weavers, threadmakers and more. Benefactors of their home town, the Gilmours and their business gave half of the streets their names. There's a Gilmour Church, Gilmour House, Mill Road, Carpet Wynd ... and it goes on.

Times change though, of course.

○

8:45

Billy tilts his head like he used to do when he was younger. If you look at it the right way in the right light, the rock in the river seems to have the shape of a man embedded in it—there's the face and the horns, and there's the right hand and the pinion of his left wing pressing out, as if, long ago, some poor soul fell into the molten rock of an unformed earth, to be trapped as an insect in amber, or as a fossil, flesh itself transformed to stone, lost and then uncovered by millenia of riverine erosion. It used to fascinate Billy as a wee boy—still does—this form of a man that's trying to free itself through time's slow action from the stone, and the mill, the dark shadow of industry that lours over it. As a kid, he was always being told off by his ma for playing on the rock, he and his mates daring each other to walk out onto the slimy surface of it, to jump, wings batting the air, across the whitewater where it broke through. *William David Hunter, if Ah hear ye've been near that river, Ah'll shoot the boots aff ye.* How many times did he hear the story of the MacKay boy who fell in and drowned before anyone could get to him?

○

He follows Needle Road along, gagging as he hits the rotten egg and rancid milk stench of the tannery, trying to breathe through his mouth so the smell isn't quite so bad. He still can't understand how anyone in their right mind could think of turning the Anchor Mill into apartments with this stink on the doorstep. All it'll take is for the wind to be blowing in the wrong direction and, Tamuz Christ, the yuppies'll be boaking on their cornflakes. But there's a housing development on the other side of the tannery as well, one of those red and brown brick mini-estates that looks like it belongs out in the suburbs rather than here, all car parks and tarmac paths and grass verges, flats with tiny windows looking out of tiny rooms. Billy was brought up in one of those estates, but he's lived in an old-style sandstone tenement flat ever since he flew the coop, moved into Kentigern for uni, can't imagine staying in anything as poky as this now. Especially with the reek from the tannery next door.

○

Cutting through the estate takes a good ten seconds off his journey, so he strides through the car park between the brick blocks, comes out on the road that leads into the Mile Bank Factory. Another red-brick monster, this is the younger sibling of the Anchor Mill, and it's all that's left now of T. & P. Gilmour in the town of their birth. Inside the factory there's a model of how it used to be—the Anchor Mill over here, the Mile Bank Factory over there and the whole area between them with no tannery, no estate, just huge red warehouse buildings, workers' houses, a hostel for the winding women. All of it Gilmour. All of it gone. Back in the day, Gilmour didn't just make the thread for magic carpets but the rugs themselves; Christ, they were the ones brought the patterns back to Albion in the first place. The town's name is synonymous with the swirls and whirls of multicoloured mystery, of Fergusley Pattern.

❍

The Mile Bank Factory is a later building than the Anchor Mill, more ornate in its brickwork, reminiscent of some strange Titanian idea of a castle, with a patterning like buttressed battlements where the walls meet the roof, a bell tower like a turret high above the entrance. Tall, thin windows like the slits in fortress walls, scaled up for giants to fire tree-trunk arrows through. A huge, octagonal chimney rises to one side and back, twice the height of the five-storey factory building. Even now, you can smell the chemical smoke that used to come spewing from that chimney, even now when it hasn't been active for the last three months at least. Billy darts across the road between the cars turning in through the iron gates of the factory, the last stragglers arriving. The factory bell is clanging out the start of the day shift now, quarter to nine, time to clock in. Billy flicks the hood of his parka down and strolls in through the front doors.

❍

10:30

Fred sits alone in his room in the turret, counting the seconds as they tick on the clock. Forty-one years, he thinks. Forty-one years. They gave him a gold watch last summer, to mark his anniversary, an old-fashioned pocket watch but with this newfangled alarm built in to ting out chimes at preset times. He hasn't had the alarm set for a month though, hardly seemed worth it now.

Forty-one years. He's been working at Gilmour since he was a lad, since he left school at fourteen to take his apprenticeship. Working the warehouse first, lugging great barrels off carts onto trolleys and wheeling them down the long hallways of shelves. Nipping into the dark corners at the back with the other lads for a fly smoke and a game of cards when there wasn't a delivery due. Aye, but they put a stop to that, they did; Health and Safety, dangerous chemicals and open flames; ach, but they didnae think about that in his day.

○

Then there was—what was it?—ten years on the dyehouse floor, at the weigh station, getting the druglines from the office and searching out the right dyes, spooning out powder of all colours onto bowls on scales small as a jeweller's, or pouring great scoops into buckets, scales that ye could weigh a man on. He always thought he'd be put onto the machines at some point, get to do something that took a bit of skill, like. But instead they made him a foreman—for his timekeeping, because he was always there bang on time. Clockwork Fred, they called him. You could set your watch by him pushing the front door open with a *mornin' all*, and a *how's yersels th'day?* And that would be when Old Huntley's bell would go off—*clang, clang, clang*—ringing in the start of the shift.

Breathless arrivals flapping rain off their wings, peeling caps from their heads, unwinding scarfs. *Is Fred in yet?* they'd ask. Not *Am I late?*

○

So they made him foreman and he'd walk around in the background with his clipboard and timesheets, and his job became all about listening to piss-poor excuses from boys who should know better, and giving out written warnings when he really had to. He was proud of his lads though, for the most part, only had to dock a man's pay— what?—four, five times in all the years he's worked at Gilmour. Well. Ye have to give them a wee bit of leeway when they're coming in the morning after their sister's wedding or their old man's funeral, two hours late and pale-green wi' their wings dragging in the dust behind them, running off to the bog to throw up. Or back before the factory closed down over Christmas and ye'd get them all in on the twenty-seventh at all sorts of times. Why, there was one year the boss himself didn't show up till half ten and Fred just kept popping down to the door to reset the time clock for each straggler's arrival. *Right then, get yer coat off and get to work, and if anyone asks ye've been here since quarter to, right?* They'd smile weakly. *Aw, Fred, yer a fuckin' star.*

o

It was always on the cards, he supposes, that when Old Huntley retired, well, who is it that takes over the job of bell ringer but Clockwork Fred? His heart trouble had started by then and the boss—well, as he said, it wasnae good for him to be on his feet all day. *Yer looking awfy grey these days, Fred. And really, yer the perfect man for the job. Yer own wee office wi' a desk and a windae.*

Aye, there's a part of him that didnae want to go upstairs and leave the lads on the floor. But, of course, by then the lads on the floor weren't the *same* lads on the floor. Big Tam had emigrated, Shuggy, he'd gone off and joined the polis, and now there was a new generation of *lads on the floor*. Boys wi' hair like bloody lassies, and carvings on their horns of all things, and feathers all the colours under the sun. They didn't call him Clockwork Fred anymore; they called him Old Fred.

So he'd moved upstairs, as far upstairs as anyone could go.

He watches the clock now, watches the seconds ticking by until it's time, and when the second hand reaches twelve, he gets up off his chair and ambles up the spiral staircase, through the trapdoor, into the bell room to clang out the start and end of this shift or that. He has a wee look at his golden pocketwatch, set to the exact same time as the clock in his office. It's 10:31 now. Ach, with all his daydreams he's bloody late.

He takes hold of the old iron bell's clanger and rings out morning break for the day shift.

o

10:40

— So how's things in the warehouse? asks Alice.

— Ach, it's fuckin deid noo, says Tam. Ah tell ye, ye walk roond there and there's no a soul in sight.

— A'right, says Billy as he closes the door behind him.

— Hey up, says Alice.

Tam gives him a nod.

Billy walks across the room and takes his usual seat. They all have their usual seats in the smoking room—Alice in her labcoat at the wee table just beside the door, Tam in his boiler suit in the corner beside her, sitting up on one of the high stools at the counter that runs round three walls. A window set in the wall beside Tam looks out into the canteen, twenty-odd tables and only one of them with folk sat at it. Billy slides up onto a stool at the wall facing Alice's table, where another window looks out onto grass and bushes, an iron fence and a wee shop on the other side of the road outside the factory. A couple of suited greywings from Sales sit at the other wall, talking quietly between themselves in an unknown language of reports and foreign countries. That's what it all comes down to—Albion can't compete with the booming Ashen economy, the cheaper wages of kobold workers.

○

— So have they told ye where yer going yet? asks Alice.

Billy shakes his head.

— They're talking about moving us into the Kentigern office, but...

He shrugs.

— Typical fuckin' Gilmour, eh? says Tam.

Billy gives a wry smile, brings out his rolling tobacco, papers and lighter, dumps them on the counter. Alice has her pack of Mayfair sitting on the table beside her mug of tea. Tam's Golden Virginia tin sits on the counter. Billy in his suit jacket, T-shirt and jeans, smokes Drum Mild, a toker's tobacco, sold in every corner shop in the student-filled, bohemian area of Kentigern where he lives. There's a silence as he rolls up, an unspoken discomfort—on his part, at least—with the knowledge that Alice and Tam are being laid off while he's ... one of the lucky few. The whole factory is closing down production, even the Technology Centre that services sites around the world is mostly being shipped off abroad. It's only Billy and the Colour Systems team he's part of that are keeping their jobs.

○

The smoking room is a democratic zone where everyone is equal in their pariah status, but he can't help being aware of certain things. That a degree and a programming job cuts him off from his roots, from the factory town he was born in, and the working-class folk he used to be one of. That his horns are carved with the names of punk bands, his wings the iridescent blues and greens of a rebellious teenager. He's not blue collar or white collar, Billy, but no collar at all. He'll go home at the end of the day, maybe do a bit of painting, maybe head up to the Art School, see if he can score some sweeties. No worries about job interviews, or Christmas. It's all right for him. A factory having its plug pulled and all he has to worry about is fucking survivor's guilt and where exactly his new office will be opening in the New Year.

— Aye, that's Gilmour through and through, says Tam. Cannae even get their arses in gear tae tell ye where yer goin'.

Us and them, thinks Billy. *It's Tam's way of saying yer one of us, not one of them.* He appreciates that.

○

In a way, it's true. Last Christmas it was his job on the line, with talk of offshoring the development work to contractors in Nagastan—just like the manufacturing is shifting year by year to the vast Sinese "economic zones" or the ex-Soviet republics of Eastern Elysse. In the end, it was only a change of management that saved him, a new MD with a new attitude, a new plan, another new initiative. In the end, white collar or blue collar or no collar at all, it doesn't really matter; industry—manufacturing or services—it's all moving out East to where the workers and the governments are cheap. That's where all the magic carpets are made these days, so that's where the thread has to be dyed. Alice, Tam or Billy, no one has a job for life these days.

He's only really got to know them in the last six months or so, as well. Used to just nip outside for his fags rather than go all the way from the Technology Centre to the canteen. It was only since the bosses decided that the whole site, outside as well as in, was No Smoking (cheaper to insure that way) that he's come here, rather than walk even further just to stand outside in the freezing rain at the factory gates. He doesn't have to take his breaks when the bell rings for the factory workers, but somehow even when he doesn't hear it ringing as he sits at his PC, coding away and listening to music on his headphones, he still ends up in the smoking room around the same time as the others.

— Did ye hear back from Wilsons? says Tam to Alice.

— No yet. Ah wouldnae think Ah'll hear tae after Christmas noo.

— Naw. Ah wouldnae think so.

Billy sparks his lighter, brings it up to the fag now hanging from his lips.

○

12:15

Fred looks up at the clock on the wall, then at his watch, then at the clock again. The clock says 11:43, but his long service watch and his own internal clockwork tells him that it's lunchtime, quarter past twelve, so he climbs up the staircase, rings the bell with a tired *clang-clang clang-clang*, and climbs back down. He stretches his wings—the left one's giving him a fair bit of gyp these days—then furls them in behind him as he sits back down in his chair. He opens the drawer of his desk, takes out his paper and the tupperware box with his sandwiches inside. He peels the lid off and lays it in the drawer, takes out the apple and the yogurt and sits them at the back of the desk, one to the right, the other to the left. He opens up the foil wrapping on the sandwiches and sits them between the apple and the yogurt, spreads the paper out in front of him. Only once he's scanned the headlines on the front page does he reach out, pick up the first neatly cut, white bread sandwich, and take a bite.

○

— Is that not yer problem there? says Billy.

He leans in to click a fingernail on a line of code on Dave's monitor, but even before he starts with the explanation, Dave is clenching a fist at the PC.

— Fucking bastard! Duh.

Billy laughs, kicking his chair off on its wheels and swivelling round back to his own desk. He grabs the mouse, sails the pointer across the screen and clicks to bring the Media Player to the front. He's got about five or six windows open already, Visual Studio, Query Analyser, Enterprise Manager, a remote connection by Terminal Services to the server in Odorhei ... and Internet Explorer, of course. He slips his headphones on, restarts the track and brings up the Explorer window, a Google search on "graey folk". One of the links takes him to an e-text graey story about a man who fell in love with a graey and followed her to the magic land; how after a hundred years, an old man now, he returned to find only a year had passed in his own world, time running faster in the magic land of Grae.

○

Fred stands at the window, sandwich in hand, looking out across the houses and the tannery and the river. God, how it's all changed in the years that he's been working here.

He remembers the long, hot summer of '76, when the lads on the dyehouse floor, or in the warehouse, or in Finishing—Sales, Orders, almost everyone—they would all come to work in shirts with the sleeves rolled-up, jackets slung over their shoulders, horns poking out from under their flat caps.

And when the bell rang for the end of the shift, with no bulky coats to bind their wings beneath, and so eager to be out in the late afternoon sun, down the park or the pub, they'd all pile out through the front doors, but instead of jumping into cars or heading off to the bus stop or whatever, they'd simply run towards the factory fence, not giving a damn about the gates but scattering in every direction, wings unfurling, spreading wide, and flapping, fluttering, like a flock of birds bursting into the sky from some city square. A flock of workers in the air, wheeling and darting together like starlings.

○

— What's that?

Billy pulls the headphones off his ears, lets them hang around his neck. Dave is pushing back from his desk.

— It's lunchtime. Didn't you hear the bell? Anybody want anything from the shop?

Billy looks at the clock in the bottom-left corner of the screen; it says 11:47, but then it's been resetting itself from the server every time he reboots, and the server does run slow sometimes. He thought they had that fixed. The clock on the wall says 12:19, but then that's running fast. Doesn't really matter; he's not sure if he's hungry right now or not.

He grimaces in a conflict of laziness and indecision. If he says no, then he'll have to go out himself, what with the canteen closed now.

But he has no idea what he wants and the shop across the road has such a shit selection.

Ah, bollocks.

o

14:45

The bell above the fishmonger's shop door tings again as it closes behind Agnes. It's Friday, so it's fish for tea tonight of course; her man Fred's a good Catholic and he wouldnae have it any other way. Sometimes they get special fish suppers from Da Vinci's just round the corner from the house—if she's got the wee yins to look after, like—oh, but they're right spoilt, so they are, but is that no what yer gran and granda are for? Anyway, the weans are staying at their mum's tonight, so it's just her and Fred. But maybe that's for the best; Fred's been awfy quiet these last few days, as his last shift at Gilmour got closer. Quiet and grey, his wings no longer the brilliant blue they were, so bold and dashing when they first met at the dancing all those years ago.

O, how he swept her off her feet, he did, waltzing her up into the air, those wings beating so strong in time with the swing of big-band jazz, up and down and round and round till she was giddy. That was proper dancing, not like nowadays when ye go to a do, for a wedding or an anniversary, and the young ones have only gone and hired some DJ to play an awfy racket far too loud; the young ones seem to like it, bopping through the air this way and that, but in her day the dances had moves. The hall would be filled with couples swirling through the air in waltzes and foxtrots and what-not, and even though nobody really watched out above or below or around, somehow they never collided, moving as they were in the same patterns of grace.

— Three cod fillets please, Jimmy.

o

— Two IPA and a lager tops, Dan, cheers.

Dan picks up a glass in either hand and swivels them upright, puts the first one under the tap and the second to one side—on the black plastic tray under the Guinness—and heaves the handle of the Deuchars IPA pump down towards him slow and steady.

— Starting early thiday, lads, are yez no?

— Ah, fuck it, says Malkie and leaves his jaw gaping open afterwards, realizing.

— Come on there, Malkie, says Dan. There's ladies present.

He nods towards the couple in the corner-booth, both OAPs but dolled up to the nineties like they're off to the dancing. The man smoothes the white duck's-arse of his hair down nervously, a widower courting maybe. It was him who put Bobby Darin on the jukebox. "Beyond the Sea".

— Sorry Dan, says Malkie quickly. Sorry. Ah wisnae thinking.

— Just ... mind yer language.

A foul mouth is one thing Dan'll no have in The Wee Hauf, and they all know that. Malkie should know that by noo. But Dan lets him off with a warning look; the wee man's been right scunnert since he got laid off from Gilmour in the summer, after all. Ye've got tae make allowances.

— There ye go.

o

— There ye go, Mrs Jones. Is there anything else yer after?

— No thanks. That's all.

She counts out the coins from her purse to pay him, puts the parcel in her shopping trolley and says goodbye. She doesn't have time for a blether, has to get home to put the washing on. And she's some ironing to do before she puts the tea on. Fred'll expect it ready for him when he gets in, five past five on the dot, as always. How Sadie and the others used to pull her leg about the way she'll stand at the kitchen window, cleaning the counter or just footering really, until she hears the end-of-shift bell off in the distance. Then she knows it's time, ye see, so over she goes to the gas cooker—'cause she could never be doin wi' those electric ring things, ye can never tell if they're still on—and lights the match, and turns the knob until the fire flares up yellow. Then she'll put the pot of oil on for the chips, turning the knob to get just the right colour and size and quiet roar of yellow-tipped blue flame under it. *Honestly, Agnes,* Sadie would say, *ye keep yer time by the Gilmour clock as much as yer fella.* Agnes would prim her lips. *Well it's better than putting yer man's tea on when the bell rings for last orders,* she'd say.

The truth is, she's no the only one knows just when their husbands, or their sons or daughters, will be home by the sound of a bell that rings out over a town that's woven through with Gilmour thread.

The bell above the fishmonger's shop door tings again as she swings the door open to leave, waving a goodbye.

○

Malkie takes a Regal from his pack and slides the ashtray towards him over the low, tiled table. The clock behind the bar, being set to pub time, is a little fast, but he reckons Big Tam'll probably be in the smoke room right this very minute, wi' his own copy of the day's *Sun* open at Page Three. Malkie's copy sits folded on the table in front of him. What was her name thiday? Melissa or Melanie or Melody, he thinks. Smiling wide but with a hint of a pout to her lips, head tilted, wings as white as a swan's, furled round to wrap her shyly in her feathers, just one nipple showing the way she's half turned away, wingtips meeting to cover her privates in front but still show off the curve of waist becoming hip becoming buttock. A right stunner.

Tam and the rest'll be here at the usual time, of course, still going for the Friday drink straight after work in a way that their old men probably did too, only in those days the kitty would be coming out of brown paper packets instead of wallets with cashline cards in them. It's funny. In the last three months, being here before the others, he's just now noticed the way Dan starts to gather stacks of glasses to clean at just the right time, preparing for their arrival.

○

16:30

— I'm sorry, Mr Jones, he says. It's time.

He stands there in silence for a second, and Fred himself says nothing. There's nothing more to say really, is there? All the *end of an era* platitudes have been exhausted over the last three months, in the canteen, in the smoke room, in the office, in the warehouse, on the dyehouse floor. All the might-have-been's and the could-have-done's. What's past is past. Time marches on.

Fred nods and his boss, Bob, nods back at him, as if to acknowledge that it's better not to try and put into words what can, in words, only sound trite and inadequate. Oh, there's been many a time that Bob has done just that, in all the meetings where the cut-backs and redundancies were announced, trying to bolster the spirit of the survivors with talk of initiatives and pulling together, metaphors of ship's crews, jokes about the Spirit of the Blitz. Not now. Now he just nods and turns away, closes the door behind him, leaving Fred alone.

The clock on the wall says twenty-five to three now, even further off than before. He bought new batteries for it last week, but never got round to putting them in; it hardly seemed worth it. The second hand ticks sluggishly past twelve and the minute hand jerks forward a distance so small it seems completely inconsequential.

o

Billy closes down all the abandoned windows on his PC and dances the mouse across the screen with a click here and ... here ... to tell it to shut down. He picks up the plastic tumbler of red wine from his desk and drains it, realizes he's a wee bit drunk, not having any lunch and all. He's gasping for a fag now as well; that's the thing with drinking in the office. But it's Christmas and this is the nearest thing they're having to a do. It just didn't seem right having a night out under the circumstances, so the boss just bought in a whole load of beer and wine, vodka and gin, and come three o'clock, they all downed tools, so to speak, and headed to the break-out area for a strange mix of muted conversations and loud laughter.

— Right. Ah'm off.

Billy grabs his parka from the coat-hook and starts doing the rounds, wishing everyone a happy Christmas and a good New Year when it comes.

— Are ye not goin' tae the pub? asks Dave.

— Ah cannae, he says. Got to get home for the dog.

Billy gives a wry shrug. He was well up for it as well, but she's overdue her booster shots and this is the last chance he'll get at a vet's appointment for a while, he reckons. It's a right fucker, though.

— Ah'll see yez in the New Year, he says. Somewhere.

— Aye, Dave laughs. If they just fuckin tell us where to go.

Billy brings his wings in, folding them low and tight to his back, and swings his parka round and over—arms in the sleeves—and on. He gives a shake to settle himself snug in the fur lining.

— Right then.

o

Fred stands teetering unsteady on the chair, wings out to balance him as he takes the clock down from the wall. He bends to hold the back of the chair as he steps carefully down from it. He can just imagine the horror on Agnes's face if she saw him doing this, like when he insisted on papering the living room himself. *Will ye get down from there, for the love of God? O, Myrrh, Mother of Tamuz, ye'll kill yersel' wan o' these days, so ye will. Ah, shusht, woman. It'll be fine.*

He sits back at his desk, a little out of breath from his adventure, wing sore and chest strained from the stretching. He's not as young as he used to be, that's true.

The second hand still ticks round—he can hear it—as he turns the clock over and finds the black plastic knob for setting it. Fingers on the low, notched disc, he turns the clock face-front and starts to twiddle. The minute hand swings by half-past and quarter to, through the hour and round. The movement of the hour hand is so slow, so slight, it's only just perceptible.

The second hand ticks of its own accord. It ticks. It ticks.

He swivels the time through all the minutes between three and four, and on.

The second hand ticks.

He stops to take his watch out of his pocket, laying the clock down on his desk. He's got the watch out and in his grasp before the second hand ticks again. The tick of the clock, the tick of the watch felt in his palm, the beat of his heart, all move at separate rhythms, different speeds. With the watch in his hand, he sets the clock to 4:29, as if ... as if he just wants to hear it from the clock, for the clock to, one last time, tell him that it's time to ring the bell.

The second hand ... ticks.

He rubs his chest, wondering if he strained a muscle trying to balance himself with his wings like that.

The second hand sits only two ticks from twelve. It sits there.

It ticks.

The watch in his hand keeps a steady rhythm, far steadier than his heart, but he ignores them both, only watching the clock.

The second hand sits one tick from twelve.

o

And Agnes stands at the kitchen window, a cloth wet with water and Dettol in her hand, poised on the counter-top as she looks out, listening for a bell that will never come. And Dan holds a glass upside down over the bristles of the brush in the sink, the bristles that should be turning, churning up water to wash it, but which are frozen in this moment, as caught in this single moment as the water, frozen and yet warm, still and yet churning, as a photograph of bubbling foam. And Malkie holds the cigarette to his lips, head tilted down to read the sports results in the paper open in front of him, smoke from his fag forming an upwards trail of curlicues, a weaving thread of involutions through the more dissipated billows of his breath and a single smoke ring that floats still in the air in front of and above his lowered horns. And Fred sits alone at his desk in his office, smiling sadly at the clock stopped at the wrong time, one hand reached up to his chest, a finger gently probing the so-slight pain there, the other hand closed around the fob watch.

But Billy walks through the factory gates, flicking the hood of his parka up over his head, sort of hooking it on his horns so the December wind won't catch it, blow it down. Huddled into himself from the cold, his wings cramped under the bulk of his coat, he hurries along past cars moving as slow as if the road were black ice, slower, slower. Eyes on the ground in front of him, his mind on other things, he hurries on towards the station and the airtram that will fly him home from Fergusley to Kentigern.

Scotland's "Auld Enemy" is England, but for better or worse, this quarrel-some pair have been partners since the Act of Union in 1707. This political marriage had a troubled beginning, of course, then the Scottish Enlightenment and the rise of the Romantic Movement in the latter years of the eighteenth century thawed previously bitter relations. Many dispa-rate characters were brought together, some of them extraordinary even by the standards of that exceptional time.

○ ○

NOT WISELY BUT TOO WELL
A. J. McIntosh

○ ○

I

I would rather be tortured than brung again to my senses by that monster of intellect and moral feeling, Dr Johnson. With a Sabbath face, he squinted down from on high and seized my big toe under the coverlet. Then he pinched it exceeding hard. "Boswell," said he, too loud for pleasantness, "I wonder that you do not tire, as the rest of us tire, of your domestic manners. But you are a filthy cur who has rolled and wallowed in his own nastiness so long he cannot sense the stink."

Johnson had, I learned later, passed the early part of that day (the 10th of September, 1773) surveying such curiosities as are afforded by the Isle of Raasay, and in confounding many of old Macleod's foolish stories anent its faerie glens and mystic antiquities. All this as that credulous rustic carried the Doctor across hags and burns and mossy protuberances. Returning home by this singular conveyance in the late afternoon, wearied but exultant, the Doctor had not even paused to wash before besting our hostess upon the matter of Ossian. Only after a 15- or 20-minute diatribe had the great man asked how I did. Lady Raasay told him there had been neither sight nor sound of poor Mr Boswell since last night's revels, that surely I must be ill or dead or beasting my pillows under some witch's curse. Johnson determined to discover which.

He came, he saw, he conquered. In the extremity of my sickness, I raised a hand and made my farewells: "My dear Doctor, a good morning to you, and an ill one." (I tried here to lift up my head an inch, but there was no moving it.) "A sad, lachrymatory day indeed, for it will be the last we share thegither. I perceive in my bodily husk only the last, sorry dregs of Life, and them ebbing fast from the shore of this world. I fear I am flitting you, my friend, alas, alas and *adieu*." In expressing these affecting sentiments, and feeling again the sensations consequent upon surfeit, a little tear started from my eye to the tune of a sigh.

"Nothing disgusts like excess," responded Johnson, "unless it be self-pity." These words he spake with such vehemence that they near split my skull. A spasm ran from the socket of my left eye to the end of the right toe still gripped between his digits.

"Oh softly, softly," I begged.

"Bugger 'Softly, softly'," he replied, adjusting his lips to my ear and bellowing within as if into some echoing cavern. "When a jobbernowl has sat drinking till 5 o' the morning, when he has so inundated with claret all notion of propriety that he thinks nothing of waking the house whistling *Lilliburlero* into the chimney, when he has so o'erbrimmed his stomach with wine and then cast up the remains of his debauch upon the stair, crashed insensible onto his bed and there soiled himself anew with all the nicety of a Tamworth hog..."

"I have heard it said that the pig or swine is, contrary to common belief, a most clean and..."

"...and there snuffled and snored and evacuated himself a 12-hour more to the disgrace of his own and his father's reputation, then, Sir, *then* I say 'SOFTLY, SOFTLY' WILL NOT SERVE!" This final section of his peroration he produced with the force of one of Mr Dennis's dramatic effects. Its effect upon *me* was at once solemnizing and concussive. I could muster nothing to excuse my wasted brains, my aching knees, teeth, and intimate privates. I mewled like a kitten.

"Boswell, you are a sot, a rogue, a grovelling sort of scarab, content only to toy with the dung of your betters, to hoard all that is horrid and roll it into little balls for future consumption." I have unremembered the rest of Johnson's summary of my character. His words were interrupted by a retch. Mine, naturally.

Recovered a little, I lay a long while silent, the smell of pukes wafting up from my shoes by the bed. Through half-closed eyelids I regarded the Doctor as he ignored me, as he concentrated instead upon my personal journal and jabbed at its pages with a prodigious fat forefinger. "Split infinitive! Error after odious error! A baboon feels more and expresses itself better. If you could once ignore a lady's particular parts and cease feeling so sorry for yourself you might advance." I thought at once of the particular parts to which Johnson referred, was stirred, and then consumed with self-loathing. This internal somersault sickened me, and I now ceased to regard my friend's comments as a noetic or noölogical tonic, as a rough but well-meant restorative, and began instead to consider them less gratefully. His rebukes, and the painless state of sobriety from which they emanated, seemed abhorrent. There came to mind earlier incidents in our tour: Johnson declining a bumper of brandy at Aberdeen, sipping spring water at Inverness, demanding tea in gloom-laden Midland accents at Fort Augustus of all places. It occurred to me at a rush that my friend was, in addition to his many fine qualities, a most pompous and self-regarding prig whom I detested from the epicentre of my kidneys.

At this moment there emerged from the river mud a swallow of a plan. It spawned, it swam, it breasted the wave and took wing, and its sole purpose was this: that somehow I would induce in that man—of all men in the world the one I most admired—a state of hideous public intoxication, here in the land of my fathers, where the memory of an eminent Englishman drunk is seldom forgiven and never forgot.

II

I own it came as quite a surprise to me that I could rise from that bed of suffering, cast off my sullied clouts, wash, powder and perfume myself like an actress, and dress in a clean suit of clothes, all within the space of three hours and a quarter. This transformation I put down not to the verbal physic of the good Doctor, but to the invigorating urge to be revenged upon him. I descended from my chamber with a tolerable impression of sprightliness, smiled brilliantly at the assembled company and Johnson, and with a graceful flourish sat down to dine.

We had boiled mutton to eat, and potatoes and cabbage, though which was which I could not tell. Johnson uttered not a word, rather directing his energies to the grey hummocks on his plate, slavering and bruzzing like a bear at shambles, gargling the grey sauce, mangling the grey gristle between his jaws. When he had done, in a mere moment, he set to belching and farting and scratching the bellies beneath his waistcoat, all of which commanded so much attention from his fellow diners that he might just as well have been holding forth on the grammar of Abyssinians or some suchlike topic. It is no wonder, given my delicate condition, that at this exhibition I felt again quite oorlich and like to spew.

Perhaps my complexion now turned ashen, or my eyes for a moment lost their customary lustre, or mayhap the lovely muse of our balls (the eldest Miss Macleod, of Raasay), alerted by some change in the gentle pressure of my hand upon her knee under the table, grew suddenly alarumed. "Surely, Mr Boswell, ye grow tae hot. I declare ye have the influenza or sommat. Dae ye no feel some wrangfu' disturbance about the heid at a'?"

"Dear Miss Macleod," I replied, "I assure you, I have never felt better."

"Damn it, Missy," interrupted Johnson, wiping the grease off his paws onto his coat sleeves, "If he has caught some cold it can only be from sleeping in puddles."

"Puddles, Sir? Puddles? Whitiver can ye mean?" Miss Macleod was intrigued. For my part, I could scarce believe this sudden turn in the conversation, and very much feared that if continued it would not display me in a good light. I meant to take charge.

"What I believe, nay am *certain*, the Doctor refers to, Madam, is my former practice of sleeping in pools of ice water, the which is not uncommon among hale young hinds about Midlothian, who swear it increases their strength and endurance in all country pursuits. I gave it up for, freezing puddles or no, I am hale and hearty always, ever upright, Madam, sappy and gallus to a fault." Miss Macleod tittered agreeably.

"When I say 'puddles'," reverberated the Doctor, "what I mean by that is ... *noisesome* puddles ... of his own making. I have seen them myself this afternoon. Isn't that so, Boswell?"

Momentarily I could think of no reply. Nothing I could say seemed equal to my predicament. The massive millstones of Johnson's wit would surely grind my reputation to dust. Was there not one atom of kindliness in him? Had he never known what it is to be young, to feel the blood bounding in one's members, to burn with a flame so ardent that only a small ocean of very strong wine can quench it? Of course he had. When he was first arrived in London and lived a libertine with the poet Savage. Now, though, now that he was old and bloated and counting his breaths, now that even the sight of a few bleached bones in a ruined kirk reduced him to melancholy, now when no sonsie besom could look with pleasure upon him nor music nor vine console, now he would play Abraham and sacrifice any sporting buck more fortunate than himself. The hypocrite! The spiteful bore! The insufferable, prating gobshite! My path was clear.

"I fear your metaphors are too erudite for a poor Scotch lawyer, dear Doctor. The only puddles I understand are the hydroptic kind, the aqueous acres which so abound in these islands." (You see what a pretty job I made of muddying the waters.) "Mr Macleod tells me that in such a liquid land and watery atmosphere it is only the native *oisquebeatha* that keeps a man from drowning in his sleep." Sandy Macleod, the M'Cruslick (or wild man) as we called him, was a dishevelled mass of hair and hodden plaid with whom I had sat at the bottle the night before. He looked bemused, for he had never said anything of the sort. Johnson looked bemused for he had forgotten the meaning of *oisquebeatha* but was too proud to admit it. "*Oisquebeatha*," I shouted to him, as if to a very deaf Methuselah, "an aboriginal potation distilled from barley."

"Indeed. Poppycock! Don't believe it," responded Johnson. At this, the M'Cruslick, in truth a sort of ill-trained wolfhound, began to growl softly in the back of his throat. He did not like to have his opinions dismissed so by a *Sassenach*, not even when they were false and not his opinions. I made him a secret signal and pressed on.

"Mr Macleod, pray tell: Is it not axiomatic in these parts that no man past his fortieth year can drink more than a dram or a scalch of the Liquor and the reason for this is that it dissolves an *old* man's intellect and renders him prone to bogles?" The M'Cruslick's matted eyebrows rose in perplexity, but he had rather be gored by a red bull than deny a single tradition he judged did honour to the remarkableness of his race. He lied without hesitation.

"Aye, och aye. Ye're no mishtook there, Meeshter Boshweel." His eyes now bulged and his head shook slowly this way and that. "Boglesh, aye, an' the brounies, oh aye, an' ghoshts an' shilkies an' the roane they shay. My ain graun'faither took a nip on hish eightieth birthday an' fram that moment he wash curshed wi' the shecond shight. Fae six lang yearsh aifter he wash purshued by the shpirit o' a deid mermaid'sh murthered bairn, sho he wash, aye. Terrible wish the mak' o' that fachar, wi' ain haund oot o' hish chesht, ain leg oot o' hish haunch, ain eye oot o' hish fache, aye an' a tuft oot o' the top o' hish heid that wid gralloch an elk, sho it wid!" Our little band sat rapt, drawing closer as the gruesome *taigh* drew forth nightmares from our minds, as his furry hands cast shadows in the candlelight.

"Tosh!" It was Johnson, waddling into my ambuscade. "That a barren islet, devoid of all fauna save a few unhappy sheep and some black-cock, could, by the simple expedient of swallowing two measures of fortified sleet, be transformed into a perfect gallery of pixies and leprechauns not only beggars belief, but then beats it over the head and violates it.

"I will happily own that any boy, man or dotard is assured of visions if he will but poison his faculties with enough pernicious and inflammatory spirits, but I aver *true* credence in these chimæras hardly fits at all with our Christian orthodoxies or our practical observations; they do not exist. In short, what you cite as evidence of things supernatural is but the foolishest sort of story-telling, a parcel of idiocies, a specious inheritance that would be risible if it did not, *ab ovo*, inspire first contempt then pity."

Johnson's trouble was that he did not know when to stop. There was a palpable hush, a dangerous frisson of which only the Doctor himself was unaware. He was hooked and I reeled him in.

"All you have said, my dear Doctor, may be true as a general rule, but Mr Macleod's proposition is more exact. He has stated quite nicely that: (1) A man of more than forty summers may cast aside the glamour or *pishogue* of the Fantastical Realm by, (2) drinking the native *oisquebeatha*, (3) here in Raasay. Now, Sir, to these precise points you have answered not at all."

"Pah!" said Johnson. "Bloody hair-splitting lawyerly claptrap." I winked at the M'Cruslick, who rose from the table, took a key from his pocket and loped to a high, dark cabinet in the room's corner. From within he removed a stone flagon and set it down upon the table. All eyes turned upon Johnson. "See how the dogs draw in," quoth he, aware now of what scheme was forming. "I have done with drinking. I have been done with it these many years. Surely

you do not think I would, for one moment, submit myself to ... ?"
No one spoke. No one moved. The Doctor looked from one to another, and last of all at me. "Very well then. I will face you down and, with each gulp of fire I survive *compos mentis*, purge this Ultima Thule of superstition. Pour away, Mr Macleod, and say goodbye to your ghoulies."

III

In the opening rounds of any bout, the prudent wrestler does not grapple in earnest but measures his opponent, ascertains his skill by way of a prelude to the contest proper. Dr Johnson knew no such circumspection, but threw back three drams of the Creature within ten minutes. He paused then for the M'Cruslick and I to catch him up, at which we all drank a toast to the ladies who dignified our proceedings from the margin by laughing and making remarks. Commencing our fifth dram, we were, I venture to say, all sensible of an enlargement to our minds, of an agreeable widening to our intellectual vistas, accompanied by sweats and shortness of breath.

The Doctor, by way of stiffening his mental sinews, began a series of emphatic monologues on matters Scottish, including the godless Hume, the dishonest M'Pherson, and a performing magpie he had seen in Piccadilly which had more sense in its head than was to be found in all the pages of Mr Smith's *Wealth of Nations* put together. We none of us interrupted once, nor contradicted him afterwards, but instead studied each convoluted sentence for the onset of inebriety or the distraction of visiting shades. Flattered by the attention, mistaking our silence for admiration, the Doctor, somewhere between his seventh and eighth drams, imagined himself now quite the most entertaining fellow of all time, and for reasons which escaped us began a braying and a mooing, a baa-ing, woofing and drintling to the consternation of all who witnessed it. This barnyard pandemonium he next ceased as abruptly as he had begun, then turned to our hostess and addressed her feelingly.

"Dear, dear Lady Raasay," said he, taking her hand in his own and petting it. "Were I a Paris, I would bestow upon you a Golden Pineapple, for sure. Thou art a radiant goddess, a star, a constellation indeed, in which hang thy bubbies like two planets—Castor and Bollux—revolving about the black fastness of that cleavage, blessèd worlds fashioned by an indulgent Deity for the enjoyment of..." To what outrageous climax the Doctor would have brung his *eulogion* we shall never know. With eyes still fixed open he slumped colossally to the floor.

Johnson did not stir for two hours, by which time the patriotic toasts had ceased and the ladies retired, and the M'Cruslick and I had laughed ourselves almost to sadness. "Dear God," groaned the Doctor. "What infernal folly have I been about?" At this, I furnished Johnson a very full account, and the M'Cruslick swore some invisible banshee must have hit him on the back of the head. "Dear God," repeated the Doctor, "no." There now glimmered in my heart a spark of pity, a familiar glow of affection for the man. Johnson seemed a sorry wreck the now, drawn upon the rocks by my spunkie deceits.

"Come, Doctor, let us take a turn about the policies. The night air will restore us to ourselves, and by some musical brook we may rinse away the stains of combat." Thus saying, like Æneas his Anchises, I carried Johnson from the field of battle.

IV

The mountain of *Dun Can* protrudes from the swamp at a distance of some three computed miles from Raasay's house, and up this noble eminence I determined we should go. It was, at the moment of its inception, a self-evidently good idea. Thereafter, it was not. So very numerous were our risings and fallings on the route, our stumblings and circumnavigations about the blasted heath, and so very onerous the weight of Johnson upon my back, that I could scarce respond to his encouraging kicks.

"You are a very half-growed, boney sort of nag, Boswell. Not at all the bouncy, fat kind we breed in England. Must be all those oats."

"Indeed, Doctor?"

"Yes, and I perceive by this uneven gait that you are spavined about your pasterns. No reply, Boswell? What a dull Dobbin you are."

"Forgive me, Doctor. Your beast is short of wind. You must dismount." My friend reluctantly got off.

"*Nota bene*, Boswell, I have drunk a skinful of your native elixir and what do I find? One hobby-horse, but not a single hobgoblin." At this sally, the Doctor let out a wheezing "heuch" which I took to be an expression of self-satisfaction. When we had both regained our equilibrium, we resumed afoot, unsure of our bearings, Johnson occasionally poking me from behind with his cane to be sure I had not fallen in some hole. I thought I would try him a little:

"'Not a single hobgoblin': most amusing, Doctor. But it is hardly to be wondered at. There are no hobs nor lobs here in the Hebrides..."

"As I said at the start."

"...but there are sundry other fiends to be found."

"Oh no, not you as well. Spare me the details."

"Perhaps we may be favoured with a sight of the *gruagach*, the hairy ones, naked and wet."

"And how would we tell them apart from all the other shaggy homuncules residing in these parts? You have merely described a Celt."

"Or the *Cailleach Bhear*, a very wicked crone with skinny arms and her face blue, who can turn herself into a boulder and moan like the North Wind."

"I have it: she was my housekeeper some years ago."

"Or the monstrous *Biasd Bheulach*, who is ravenous for human blood and prowls the loneliest quarters of the country in the form of a man or a greyhound, shrieking."

"'In the form of a man'? There is nothing so very strange about that, Boswell. Why, soon you will be calling *me* a monster if appearing 'in the form of a man' be some criterion of goblindom."

"You are very Sceptical, I see, Doctor. I cannot chill you with these terrors?"

"Why should I be scared by tales which are meant to cow children? God has blessed us with reason, and I apply my portion of that gift whenever I may."

"But what if you should see a ghost, Doctor? Would you not at least be startled?"

"No, Sir. I should frighten the ghost."

I confess to having felt somewhat crushed by the Doctor's common sense, whilst at the same time not comforted by it. In mentioning even so small a number of the nocturnal horrors which our Highland maids had recounted to me as a wean, I found that my timorous propensities had not diminished with the passing of time. In the obscurity of the Raasay night, I more than once let out a squeal as the grouse took flight at our approach. I could hear the Doctor wheezing behind me. Prod, prod went his little cane. Then there was the goat: a bedraggled, wretched, starveling thing which sprang from nowhere and made off with my hat. Prod, prod went the little cane.

Adding to our misfortunes, it now commenced to rain. Not soft, refreshing summer rain, you understand, but a cold, painful drench which penetrated from above and below with equal potency. Any thought of gaining the mountain we sought was now discarded, any hope of finding the house we had left similarly lost. It was apparent we must make camp in the middle of a lochan which had formed around us, and shelter as best we might amid the heather, bearing the deluge with a Stoic fortitude.

And so we sat and waited, watching the lochan rise, debating whether we should first drown or die of fevers. It rained and rained. We squirmed restlessly. Æons passed. "I do not like it," said Johnson.

"No," I replied. "It is very vexing, the precipitation, is it not?"

"I do not mean the rain. I mean our situation. This spot beside the lake."

"Indeed? Why not, Sir?"

"I believe I have noticed something crawling about in the water."

"Something crawling about, Doctor?"

"A vole, perhaps. I saw its hand come to the surface for a moment."

"Its hand, Sir? It cannot have been a vole if it had a hand."

"Why, then, a mole most probably. Yes, a mole. It had a long tail to it like a brush."

"No, no, Sir, not a mole, not with a..."

"Ssssh! Did you not just then remark the top of its head. It is but a rabbit after all. I saw the tuft on the top of its head."

"Tuft? *Tuft?* The M'Cruslick's grandfather! What shall we do?"

"We shall sit very still and wait for ... the rabbit ... to go away." And so we sat, drawing up our feet and knees away from the water, silent, back to back, shuddering with cold. "I can hear its claw scratching upon the bottom of the lake."

"Oh Christ! I cannot bear it," I said, breaking at last. I stood up of a sudden.

"You are not leaving me, alone?" murmured the Doctor.

"A call of Nature. For Decency's sake... I shall be but a step away."

"Do not offend it, Boswell. Of all things I should hate to meet, you know, an affronted ... rabbit."

I pished gingerly into the flood, surveying the invisible scene in hope of discerning some 'orizon or rosy-fingered dawn, but no such prospect was there. Only the dreuchit dark, and those things which I shall describe presently which no man alive will believe.

The rain plashed against my face, and I was alerted first to a vibrancy about the air, an agitation which caused all the hairs on my person, even those under my wig, wet and plastered as they were, to stiffen. This, I considered, must be some meteorologic phenomenon, some dissipation of thunderbolts in the mist, but hold! Now what was this? The ground too was in motion, not with a wanton quaking such as we have read levelled Lisbon and Santiago, but a slow and regular vibration like that of pistons. I had no notion what engineer might have builded here, and on what a scale so to disturb the *terra infirma* of Raasay, and had no chance to ponder it further before I was knocked from my feet. I raised my eyes and saw it was a luminous globe no bigger than a pomegranate but of dazzling colours which had o'erturned me as it passed, its passage marked by a parabola of sparks. This fizzing ball now stopped dead in its career—God knows how, for its motion had been incomparably quick—and, supported like a feather on the insubstantial medium, hummed overhead amid an aureole of violet shimmerings.

"Pay no heed!" commanded a voice behind me. "It is but a Will-o'-the-wisp, a bolus of bad airs without design or instinct, existing merely in the combustion of its own gas. Be sure it will soon gutter." Johnson addressed me from behind my right shoulder. "Among pouk-ledden simpletons and Scotchmen," he continued, "such freaks are held to be female sprites who dance about the moors to..." Before he could finish, the globe of a sudden dilated fully twenty times its former size, and a carpet of light rolled down, along which floated three creatures, very gigantic, wild and withered. "Merciful Redeemer!" ejaculated my friend. "Aroint thee! Be gone!" They did not move. "To which *échelon* of Hell do you belong?" added the Doctor, not, I judged, altogether helpfully. "You are vile kelpies, are you not? Or phoukas? Or the murderous cabyll-ushteys, come to abduct and drown us in the mire?" Until this moment, I had not known he was so well acquainted with our northern imps, and I was struck by the speed with which he had collected the names of three water-devils and their particular habits. To my mind, such fore-learning belied his Scepticism, undressed certain long-standing apprehensions to which he had not previously alluded.

There followed some jostling of elbows and a tearing off of buttons as we turned to run, but before we had managed a single pace, there again before us were the lurid beasts. We turned once more to run, and again, but no matter which way we faced about, there we found them still, three abreast, omnipresent, implacable. We stood fast, stupid with terror.

"In God's name, what are they, Doctor? They look not like inhabitants of the earth yet here they be. Are they of this world or the next?" I turned to my friend, and found him gaping like a squashed pudduck. I saw it fell to me to break this spell. "I wonder if I might ask a question, Sirrahs? Do you happen to know the way back to Raasay House?" At this, the ugly trio rocked to and fro, though what they meant I could not tell. "Are you familiar with the English tongue, gentlemen? Or indeed ladies. Whichever. You should, I think, be what we term *seahorses*, save that your very great size and wingless flight prohibit such zootaxological rashness."

The phantasms took turns to reply.

"Good morning to you, Samuel Johnson, doctor of letters, late of London," said the first.

"Good morning, Samuel Johnson, industrious compiler of definitions and author of *The Lives of the Most Eminent English Poets*," said the second.

"Good morning, Samuel Johnson, who shall in years to come stand as a perfect model," said the third.

Observing my friend at this moment, I noted how appalled was the expression on his phys. I asked its cause, for surely these apparitions had addressed him in very complaisant and generous terms. "Damn your meddling, man!" he replied. "You know perfectly what is the matter. You have been broadcasting my *Lives* about the town even though they are only in draft. How else could these spectres know what has appeared in no bookseller's, coffee shop or print bed?" My sincere protestations of innocence fell on deaf ears. Johnson was indeed rather offensive, his conceit of himself o'ervaulting.

"Gentlemen," I began, "I am James Boswell, *Esquire*, author and Advocate at Law, formerly of Auchinleck in the County of Ayrshire. Perhaps you have heard of me ... or perchance my faither?"

"Boswell," chorused the seahorses as one, and rather too familiarly I thought. "Lesser than Samuel Johnson but more readable. Not at first so nourishing, yet much spicier. Thou wilt gain readers though you be no writer." I did not understand these comments, or like very much how they sounded in comparison to what had been said of Johnson. The Doctor did not understand them either, but he liked the sound of them a great deal, and his opinion of the seahorses rose accordingly. With an affected little cough he declared himself charmed to have made their acquaintances, and desired to know their names and origins and whence they had acquired so many "exact" judgments.

"You must forgive us," replied the first in a melodious sing-song, "if we trespass across your manners, for we are not from these regions, are very imperfect speakers of the language, clumsy in the *comme il faut*. I fancy we fare best in Formosa, but wherever we go this business of introductions is troublesome to the extreme. Try to understand we mean no rudeness when we say our proper names lie outside your sonic range and do not bear translation.

"You have rightly noted that we are not of this earth. Boswell has been kind enough to compare us to *seahorses*. We accept the compliment. You, gentlemen, resemble creatures familiar to us at home. Delicious memories! We are, evidently, sentient and sapient beings, possessed of all the refinements and conveniences of civilization, and able—like yourselves, good Sirs—to travel prodigious distances in pursuit of instruction and diversion. We do not practise abduction or drowning.

"As your bumble-bees harvest nectar from flowers to make their honey, so do *we* gather up facts and store them in a kind of honeycomb. This honeycomb of knowledge, by the agency of a great machine, we turn into reticulated lexicons of wond'rous complexity which those whom we love may read and learn from. Our kind uses knowledge to contemplate the infinite variety of Life, the multiple plasticity of matter and non-matter, its distinctive histories, customs, contrasting truths, and tastes.

"We are always hungry for more knowledge, and to gain it we use sidereal equipages such as that you see behind us; carriages in which, by a process of shrinkage and stretching which we have never comprehended but are assured is quite safe, we voyage; journeys filled with conversation and bell-ringing, the hooting of good food and the stately *ricquochet* of thought. Thus, the further we travel, the greater grows our fund of learning, and in direct proportion increase our fascinations. You, Sirs, are two such objects of interest, though we fear we have not enough time fully to gratify our curiosity."

I believe the foregoing 332 words were the greatest number Dr Johnson had listened to without interjection for many years. He stood with chops opening and shutting, his tongue writhing like an eel in the moonlight, and then: "So, I suppose you believe in God?"

"Oh yes, tut-tut-tut-tut-tut-tut-tut," replied the seahorses, bowing and bobbing in unison. "We exist within the same *Kosmos* as you, within the same Commonwealth of the same Bountiful Creator, whom we revere and love above all things. Oh yes, tut-tut-tut-tut-tut-tut."

"But you're not Church of England, are you," stated the Doctor.

The seahorses tutted and clicked and tutted some more, before agreeing that, on balance, they were not.

"Ah well, you see, that is where you are going wrong." For Johnson, it was not enough that they should acknowledge the one, true God. He would have them Anglicans as well, and to this end adumbrated the major tenets and advantages of his faith, the splendour of its principal monuments, and the demonstrable wrong-headedness of Methody, Rome, Fanaticism, Heathenism, Atheism, Agnosticism, and Procrastination.

In a tiny *chiasm* which occurred when Johnson paused to inhale, I took aside one of our strange visitors and asked how they had come to know the Doctor's work, particularly his *Lives* which was not only out-with the public domain but had also, in great parts, still to be wrote. "We are," it replied, "a race of vagabond scholars whose harbours throng with vessels returned from the gulfs beyond. Each vessel pours out its cargo of facts and figures, *exempla*, cross-references and footnotes, and each vessel vies with its neighbour to be first to unload and take off on new adventures. This has been our way of life for years beyond count-ing. In all that time, knowledge has begotten knowledge, and knowl-edge refined and distilled has revealed inevitable consequences..."

"Like a sore heid after too much *oisquebeatha*," I ventured, seek-ing common ground.

"Quite possibly, but also pathways of truth. Some such truths are true now, some were but are not now, others still, it seems, must wait their turn upon the stage. These last, these unrealized futurities, we seek to prove. It is an holy duty which brings us closer to the Mind of

God, revealing and confirming the mysteriously thorough investment of the Supreme Presence."

"What is this poppycock?" grunted the Doctor.

"Crudely put, we infer from the past to predict the future, Sir, and with some success. We foresaw the coalescence of your planet, your species, and at last your races, occupations and manner of thought, languages, your names even, and the events of today that brought about this merry spree to gather flowers for your betrothal beside a musical brook."

Johnson and I involuntarily regarded each other, then the gurgling bog, the morbid black water lashed with rain on all sides. Without a word we agreed to overlook the errors. "But why me, of all people?" demanded Johnson. "Am I truly so remarkable?"

"Indeed. Sir, as a philosophic lexicographer you share our enthusiasm for details, yet as a lexicographic philosopher you so butcher them about as to render them meaningless. This we find droll, hugely ridiculous. To us you are the very model of a mirthmaker." This reply I fancied rather spoiled my companion's fishing trip for compliments, but there was worse to come. "Regarding Boswell," the seahorse continued, "we find that as a man of sensibility and sense he abhors the folly of his ways, his claps and crapulence, yet he will not desist; as a man of licentious habits he applies a seemly caution to his mode of thinking. This we find paradoxical, enigmatic and improving. He is much admired and cited by the educators of our young people."

I do not think Johnson or I got the answers we had expected, but I at least could reflect upon my "improving" influence, however basely earned, whilst the Doctor had to content himself with being "hugely ridiculous", something he said later "any jackpudding toper or diarist might manage". Hence our remaining time with these travellers was for the most part occupied by my friend impressing upon them his seriousness; and in consequence we learned more of Johnson's views on Messieurs Voltaire and Rousseau, and Whiggery, and the cause of Goldsmith's piles, than ever we did about our visitors' peregrinations: something I rued at the time and rue still.

"We have greatly enjoyed your conversation, Sirs, but have a deal of pressing verifications and dinner appointments elsewhere to which we must attend. You are much as we had hoped you would be, but moister. We had factored a Scotland but not its climate." So saying, these marvellous oddities bowed and bobbed, and withdrew from sight to wherever it was they sat to travel. For an instant their fiery globe pulsated, then condensed into a round unity. A crack rent the air and the cabriolet was gone. We watched it scintillate through the firmament and vanish.

The waters about our feet had retreated. The sky was blushing in the East. We bent for home, each wrapped in his own thoughts and sodden hose.

V

"Boswell, we are considered only as jackanapes in this house. Let us not represent ourselves also as candidates for the Bedlam." The good Doctor had returned to my room and once more sat at the foot of the bed. This time he kept his hands off my toe and spoke in whispers. "If the M'Cruslick or any man ask you what we saw, say only that it was remarkable, that it was beyond credence, that you will put it some day into one of your journals for the edification or bewilderment of Posterity. Are we agreed?"

"We did truly see them, Sir, did we not? Have we no duty to set these events before the Royal Society?"

"I believe we saw them. But we have a higher duty than mere anecdotage."

"How so?"

"Boswell, we have met—I will not call them fiends—but, you know, frightful fish-men from a distant strand, and found that for all their surface manners, their bon ton, they are but a species of indifferent critics. Jamie, if it knew, one half of Mankind could not bear such horror, the other such disappointment. Scribble it down if you must, but make it private I beseech you."

I have considered it every way since: my public face, my private desires, my impulse as a modern man to illumine such scroggy neuks as may be lit. And yet also there is Johnson to think of, and the simple, glaikit folk of this world, and the simple ways of Edinburgh life that would be turned head about heels at the thought of fish with feelings. (Good God, what if oysters think?) Moreover, it is the first time Johnson has besought me anything in earnest, the first he has called me "Jamie".

He is a knowing English oaf, I find at last, whom I love, honour, and abhor, and will not again betray.

It is said that only the good die young, and it's true that Scotland has lost far too many talents before their time. In a land like ours, with its hard-living culture and inclement climate, that's hardly a surprise. But what if things are not quite what they seem? Dare we suggest that only the good stay dead?

○ ○

THIRD-DEGREE BURNS
Andrew J. Wilson

○ ○

Disaffected by fame, without financial reward and overwhelmed by his complicated love life, Rabbie Burns faked his own death at 37 years of age. He hoped that the deception would wipe clean the slate of his life, and feeling in better health than he had in years, the former poet sailed for America. His experience as a farmer and an excise man, along with his literary abilities, promised to allow him to make a fortune in the New World. Perhaps, he hoped, it would also finally allow him to make peace with himself.

Burns' change of identity would never be uncovered in the newly independent United States. The infant nation had severed the apron strings which tied it to Britain with sword and musket ball, and had no interest in reminders of its spiteful parent. The dark-haired man in the sandy-coloured hunting coat, black breeks and white hose was Robert Brooks if he said he was.

His real surname was Burnes anyway—at least that was how his father had spelled it—and he had successfully played the role of the primitive poetic "natural" in the salons of Edinburgh, even though he was actually extremely well read. The convenient fabrication had been part of his life as well as his art for as long as he could remember.

Sadly, the change of name and continent were not enough to reinvent his luck, and the man who called himself Brooks found himself drifting West into the Territories, often only one step in front of his creditors. There seemed little for it, but to repeat his change of identity. He left one town in the dead of night on horseback, and when he came to the next, he announced that Robert Brooks had died of a rattlesnake bite. So the man now known as Brook Roberts moved again.

The third time was the charm for our man: Roberts would make his name as an Indian fighter and gunslinger, earning more money than he had ever done before. Finally, he was able to settle down as the sheriff of a small settlement and lived peacefully for many years.

And so my story should end, except for the dreadful twist that befell the man called Roberts in the twilight of his life. At 85 years of age, he was gunned down in a saloon by a youth whose killing spree would enter legend in the state of Kansas, a young man who was never caught and was later thought to have fled East across the Atlantic, possibly to Scotland.

I have seen a crumbling yellow poster for the man who killed Robert Burns:

WANTED!
DEAD OR ALIVE
WILLIAM TOPAZ McGONAGALL

Could it be, Dundee's own bastard poet and comical tragedian? A fragment of doggerel is scrawled on the back of the sheet:

> The marvellous, marvellous Rio Grande
> Is a great river running though the land
> That draws a line between two big countries
> And is just the place to wash your hands and knees...

The evidence is damning.

I will get back to you once I confirm my suspicion that McGonagall was also Jack the Ripper.

The old World War I song tells us that, "Old soldiers never die; they only fade away." It could be argued that those who fought in that conflict have a right to linger longer than most, but at a time when plans are afoot to disband or merge the historic Scottish regiments, perhaps we could all do with a chilling wee reminder.

❍ ❍

LEST WE FORGET
Marion Arnott

❍ ❍

> *How many miles to Babylon?*
> *Three score and ten.*
> *Can I get there by candlelight?*
> *Aye, and back again.*
> *If your feet are nimble and light,*
> *You'll get there by candlelight.*

That poem was my great-grandfather's way of saying goodnight when I was wee. Years later, when he was admitted to hospital, I murmured the words when I stopped off in his room during my ward rounds, wondering desperately how many miles away he was and whether he'd be back, and remembering too the questions I used to ask to keep him sitting on the edge of my bed.

Grampa?

Aye, hen.

How many miles is it to Babylon?

Lifetimes of miles, ower and ower.

But how many miles is that? How long would it take to walk it?

Ah don't know, hen. Ah've never been there.

Can you get back by candlelight?

Aye, hen.

How far is candlelight?

That's a daft question, wee yin.

But you get back by candlelight?

Aye. Pause. Sometimes. Pause and the long gaze that passed through me and walls, crossed seas, and ended the conversation.

❍

Sometimes, he said.

I know of at least once. Their feet, freed of the mud, were nimble and light, and their path, all the way back from there to here, was lit by the flickering gold of candle fire.

Grampa always ended the stories with the candles requistioned by his officer weeks before. They arrived on the day the war ended, crates and crates of the things. "Enough to light again the lamps all over Europe," the officer said in his dry way, "for our whole lifetime."

It was years before Grampa understood the reference, but the words "whole lifetime" held his attention because suddenly he had one: the war was over and they were moving back behind the lines, winding through the trenches on a black November night silver with frost and the tinsel mist they exhaled into the cold. They hadn't fancied lugging the crates back with them. Giddy with the silence of the guns and the need for a gesture, they snatched handfuls of candles and fixed them round the rim of their tin hats to light their way. Some of them carried them aloft like torches as well, as if they could drive back the dark with pale fire.

Once out of the trench and at the top of a rise, Grampa looked back and saw below him the long twisting column of fiery crowns floating in the still air, the faces below them gouged with shadow. The men marched in silence, but their boots rang like iron on the frozen earth. He looked up at the white moon and saw the sad dead face in it, and looked back at his pals and saw that same face over and over, shadowed and sorrowing, adrift in the night. Unbidden, his head filled with his father's favourite poem, recited thrillingly every Burns' night:

> *Coffins stood round, like open presses*
> *That shaw'd the dead in their last dresses*
> *And by some devilish cantraip slight*
> *Each in its cauld hand held a light.*

"See, hen, it seemed to me that there were mair lights than could be accounted for by the number o' sodgers, and mair boots trampin' than were feet in that file o' men. For wan wee minute, Ah had a notion that there were ithers marchin' shoulder to shoulder wi' us, ithers that were a' by wi' speakin'."

He shuddered, then smiled, half shamed. "When Ah looked again, it was only my pals trudging along, hauf deid wi' weariness and thinkin' o' home, though their hauns were cauld right enough, and they held candles."

That's how he told the tale to me. But he never told it that way to the TV people or the historians; for them, his tales of the Great War ended in a quiet walk to peace by the clean light of candles and never a fanciful notion in sight.

○

There were two admissions that day: Grampa in the dawn, and Davy Burton very late that night. I don't remember now when I first understood what was going on, but it wasn't then. That day was spent looking in on Grampa, in case he wakened and didn't know where he was. I stayed the night in his room. A steady procession of doctors came to look him over. It was a pity he was unconscious because he loved to impress the medical men: "Ah'm 106 years old, still on ma feet, a' there and roon' the corner, and a national treasure like the Wallace Monument."

"What's your secret, Billy?" they used to say for the sake of saying something about his steady heart beat and sound organs. "Mars Bars, Irn-Bru and tantric sex," he always answered, wide eyed with innocent mischief. He liked, he said, to let them know he wasn't a museum exhibit.

He was a different kind of exhibit that night. The doctors held his X-rays to the light and studied the crack in his skull, the shattered thigh bone, and the broken ribs. They didn't have to tell me the danger he was in—he was a fit man for his age, but he *was* that age. Grampa lay there like a wisp of memory. I'd swear you could see right through him to the white pillow beneath his head.

"He's your great-grandfather, isn't he?" each doctor asked. "How old?" And then, "How did this happen?"

"He was defending the War Memorial," I said with a flourish of Grampa's defiant bravado. But that wasn't the whole story. He wouldn't have wanted them to know it all—that was between him and me. "Someone pinched the bronze plaques off the plinth and toppled the lone soldier. He went out to them. They left him lying at the foot of the steps."

"All night," I wanted to scream but didn't, because middle-aged women in charge of a ward don't scream, "they left him lying out there all night!"

○

I was glad to be kept busy. I had Davy Burton to thank for that. He was brought in by ambulance, fighting, screaming, and biting like a wild animal. Two of the paramedics had to have a tetanus shot, his mother threatened with removal by the police, and Burton himself settled in a side ward, away from the other patients. I heard the commotion right along the corridor in Grampa's room.

"Ma, Ma, don't leave me here all night! Don't leave me here a' by maself!"

The soothing voices of nurses had no effect.

"Oh, don't leave me in this fuckin' place! It stinks! Stinks o' piss and crap and deid things! Ye'll no' leave me, Ma, sure ye won't? Ah'm chokin'! Ah'm chokin'! Ma! Ma!"

Ma was long gone, but the doctor gave him something and soon there was only a low, foul-mouthed muttering.

"Delirious," Nurse Smith told me over a cuppa. "Temperature's high, but not high enough to explain the raving. Infected arm."

"Another one. Is it his initials or his gang tag?"

It was the latest fad among bored youth in the town: carving their names on their arms with what must be rusty blades to judge by the number of them showing up at the hospital. You could tell the local bandits by the clanking of bottles of antibiotics in their pockets.

"His initials—right along his forearm—DB—all raised up in full technicolour. Red and green and full of putrid yellow pus. They've got him on intravenous antibiotics and..."

I didn't pay much attention really. I was more concerned about Grampa being disturbed by Burton's racket, especially by what Grampa called "language", which he hated.

○

Defending the War Memorial. No one said "Bloody old fool. Why didn't he call the police?" although they were thinking it. But Grampa was no fool and would never have confronted a gang. He was just unlucky that the theft took place on the night of the 30th of June, the night he kept vigil.

The 1st July is the anniversary of the first day of the Battle of the Somme, when men were scythed down like grass along a twenty-mile front. I know the numbers, but numbers are meaningless. More telling was the letter Grampa wrote to his mother at the end of that horrible year: *"Mother, don't tell Mrs Campbell yet, because it's not certain sure that Andra's dead, but I think I'm the only one from our street left alive."*

The TV researchers and historians always wanted to know about how he felt that day and how he felt about it now. "Glad tae be alive," he always said, as if surprised that there could be any other answer. But the questioners wanted nightmares and trauma, the never-get-over-it story so fashionable nowadays.

"Ah'm a sair disappointment tae them," he used to say with mournful pride. "Ah wisnae destroyed by the experience."

Which isn't to say he didn't remember.

○

Grampa was restless in his bed, muttering and twisting under his coverlet while Burton yelled his head off, swearing and screaming about horrible smells and the bugs jumping all over his bed. I began to think it a good sign that Grampa could hear him from inside his cocoon of unconsciousness. Perhaps he was surfacing.

Without his cheery grin, Grampa looked ancient, like a primitive tribal mask, or an ivory carving of some wise forgotten god, but the imprint of the trainer on his face burned humanly on delicate aged skin. What did they do that for? There's no answer except that it wasn't enough to knock an old man over and then run for it. It was hard to see his face grinless and dour. When I was growing up, I hardly ever saw him like that—no one did. But my grandmother told me that when she was a wee girl, she had to be quiet and not annoy her Dad that last week of June every year. "He's remembering," great-gran used to tell her. "He'll be all right soon."

And he always was. But there was a ritual to be gone through first. Each June, he would become restless and irritable, until the day came for him to load his motor bike into a luggage wagon and take the train to England and then the ferry to France. He never said what he did there exactly, not when he went by bike, and not later when he travelled by coach. When the time came that he was too old even for that, I used to escort him there by plane and then drive a hired car to the battlefields. The route was always the same: a stop at the Thiepval Memorial where the names of the lost ones are recorded in stone; a visit to an estaminet once popular with the soldiers for its omelettes and cheap wine; and then off to the Somme.

My Grampa had been many people in his life, rascally boy and soldier, father and grandfather and great-grandfather, union man and railway worker, pensioner, then national celebrity just when he thought he had nothing else left to do but die. But on that first trip, he was someone I had never seen. He was quiet, almost sullen, and stiff with tension. He stood straight as a tree at Thiepval, that big stone wedding cake, reading aloud the names of the ones he knew. Then it was away to the battlefields where he spent the night of the 30th wide awake and waiting for dawn.

"A mark o' respect," he snarled when I asked him why. He was sorry later that he'd snapped. "Ye know, hen, it's just ... a private thing."

We had a tent which had to be pitched in a particular place which he found unerringly every year, but he never used it. He sat outside on a groundsheet waiting for the sun to come up, his back rigid, his eyes fixed on the horizon, his head cocked at an angle. Under that quiet starry sky, above the whipping of the grasses in the night breeze, he heard the great barrage which was supposed to clear the German trenches—he told me once it was like standing under a railway bridge with a hundred trains rumbling overhead. I knew too that he was seeing the night sky corpse-light blue, silver with roaring brightness, screaming with scarlet and yellow flowers of flame.

It was a strange experience watching him out there, seeing the last star flicker out, the darkness thin into clear, gilded air, his set face turn bronze then pink in the dawn light. That silent time before the birdsong started was eerie. The fields emerged from under white veils of mist, and gradually unrolled before us; the sky opened up into a great arching vault of empty blue. At 7.30 precisely, every year, he rose from the groundsheet and walked forwards, rapidly but steadily. There was nothing ahead of him that I could see, only rolling fields and clumps of trees, but he walked doggedly onward, looking neither right nor left, occasionally stumbling on a tussock of grass. He was so clearly somewhere else that it made my skin crawl.

I know what he was doing of course—everyone knows the story of how the soldiers went over the top that day and walked straight into murderous machine gun fire. Grampa used to advance about 300 yards, then he'd stop and thrust his hands in his pockets and stand there staring into space, rocking slightly on his heels, communing with something. I've never told anyone this, but it seemed that the light thickened round him, that it was brighter and heavier than the air round me. Sometimes I heard a faint buzzing sound, like a chainsaw from a long way off. I don't know why that should have made me uneasy, but it did.

I always followed behind. I'd sooner have interrupted the Pope at Mass than speak to that stern face gilded by early sun, but sometimes he spoke to me. One time he pointed to a hollow in the ground—big and wide and shallow.

"That's where me and Craigie Young fell into the crater. Dae ye mind Craigie?"

Craigie had been dead since 1916, 36 years before I was born, but I minded him. He was one of my bedtime stories and I knew him as well as I knew Grampa. On summer days Grampa used to take me to the park to fish for taddies in the pond. We always stopped at the War Memorial on the way. Name after name was read out to me and a story told. I learned to read off the War Memorial, Adams to Young and all points in between, and I learned to remember their lives and deaths, although I didn't remember soon enough for Burton.

◦

Nurse Smith called me to Burton's room. She was worried about him. His heart was racing; he was raving, and alternately shivering and burning. He flicked constantly at imaginary bugs on his sheets and pillow. "Dirty things! Crawlin' a' ower me! Get them aff!"

There was nothing new about this, but the nurse was as white as the sheets he lay on.

"Look." The flesh around the letters on his arm was feathered with the red streaks of blood poisoning. "Do you see them? More letters!"

And so there were. Instead of "DB", his arm now read "D O N B".

"When did he do that?"

"He's been flat out all night, tossing and turning. He couldn't have done it." She shook her head. "And even if he could have, what with? There's nothing sharp in here."

We looked about, but the doctor came then. He was soon on the phone to the consultant. "He's been at his arm again."

Nurse Smith wilted under the angry reproach the doctor's eyes flashed at her. The doctor took more bloods, increased the dose of antibiotics, and ordered a nurse in there to stay with the patient. I returned to Grampa's room since I was officially off duty, Burton's screams that the bugs were crawling all over him ringing in my ears.

Grampa was still asleep, more lightly, I thought.

○

A psychiatrist came to see Burton in the morning because of the determined self-harming—a large "Y" had appeared on his other arm during the night. Nurse Smith was in hysterics. "He was never out of my sight!" she insisted. The psychiatrist was fine with that—hysterical stigmata, he thought. The neurologist was less impressed by Smith's denials, since she thought Burton's sensory delusions—the itching bugs, the smells which choked him, and the raving about being in a cold, cold grave, his mouth filled with earth and wriggling worms—were possibly caused by some form of brain damage or tumour. The "Y", however, she was certain was self-inflicted.

All kinds of tests were ordered.

○

Grampa was sleeping fitfully when I returned to him, muttering and sighing.

"Craigie," he said, suddenly clear.

○

Craigie Young was the one he fell into the crater with: a minister's son and very decent, read his chapter every night, never missed church parade. Even when they were out there in that crater, unable to return to their own lines because the machine gunners had them pinned down, he read his chapter, usually Ecclesiastes.

"It's a comfort, Billy, don't you think?"

"Oh, aye, it is that," my great-grandfather said, wondering how long before another shell hit them, or the gunners got them, or they died of thirst, wondering how long Craigie could last with the great hole in his thigh, and if he should attempt an amputation because

Craigie's leg was already turning black and attracting swarms of flies. Whenever Craigie lapsed into unconsciousness, Grampa sat flapping the things away. If Grampa fell asleep, he woke up to find them crawling all over his pal. He had a hatred of flies ever after. "Dirty things! Worse than the lice," he shuddered.

They were out there for two days and nights. Grampa might have made it back to their trenches, but he wouldn't go without Craigie, although Craigie insisted he try. "Go on, Billy, you can bring back help. Make a dash for it."

Grampa always told that story for the TV people—they loved it—although he never told them the whole of it. When Craigie became delirious, he clung to Grampa's arm. "Oh, don't leave me out here all alone. Don't. You'll not leave me, Billy, sure you won't?"

And he didn't. "Ah was feart Ah'd no' find him again," was all he said.

I thought Craigie's pleas were touching, but Grampa shushed me. "It was the fever talkin', no' the man."

He was loyal to the last, my Gramps.

In the end, a search party found them and got them back to safety. Craigie pressed his Bible on Grampa before they took him to the field hospital, as if he knew he wouldn't make it. "It's such a comfort, Billy."

Grampa could smell the gangrene, a gagging smell of rotten meat. He knew Craigie wouldn't make it either.

"The Good Book says a time to dance, a time to mourn, a time to live, a time to die," was all he would tell the TV people about how Craigie's death affected him. "It's such a comfort."

○

Nurse Smith fetched me to Burton's room that night. In silence she pushed his blanket down and showed me his arm. The big "Y" was now "YOU", and the other arm was "DONBRO".

"I never took my eyes off him," she insisted. "It just rose up in front of me."

I was already reaching for a pager.

"Do you smell anything?" she asked frowning.

I couldn't.

"I thought I..."

"It's listening to him is making you imagine things," I said. "Same as he has us all itching with his bugs."

She nodded, but didn't seem convinced.

○

By the time he was 90, Grampa was too old for the journey to the Somme. He was 94 before I found out what he did instead. On the night of the 30th June, he took a deckchair out to the War Memorial in the cul-de-sac opposite his house and sat behind it all night, quiet, communing, in the shadow of the trees which overhung it. I found him there when I came home early from a night shift.

"Now, hen, ye tell naebody aboot this," he insisted.

"I know, Grampa, it's a private thing."

I didn't really understand. I could see the force of the Somme visit—just. But sitting at the War Memorial—it didn't seem quite rational. He explained it to me as his way of remembering, which he only did twice a year—on the 30th June and the 11th November. The rest of the year he got on with his life. He was reaching for an explanation that made some kind of sense, but I knew it was more than that. I'd been with him at the Somme in the dawn; I'd seen his intensity, the compulsion to walk that ground again, his absence from now. In some way, the vigil was necessary to him and so I didn't intervene. I never imagined he'd be in any danger so close to home. And short of locking him up, intervention would have made no difference anyway. He was welded to those men and that time.

○

When the Great War became fashionable as a study, Grampa was much in demand. He was a good story-teller. But as the years rolled on, he became more taciturn. He didn't like the modern interviewers and their constant "How did it feel?" He preferred the serious-minded ones of the past—the like of the Dimblebys and Attenboroughs, who showed some respect. There was one time we overheard an interviewer chatting in the corridor outside the studio. "This is the old boy with the Bible that stopped the bullet, isn't it?" Chuckling laughter. "Oh, hallelujah! God be praised! Saved by…"

They were silenced when Grampa descended on them. He stared

at the young man, eyeing his expensive Boss suit, his pierced eyebrow, his gold earring and his carefully tousled, dyed-blond hair. His lip curled. Well, it would. Grampa's idea of manly elegance was a slick of Brylcreem and a bar of Lifebuoy. The young man looked away in the end and sort of drowned in disapproval.

Grampa huffed and refused to be interviewed about the Bible since they found the story so amusing. I knew what was coming next: the horrors. He fixed his gaze on that young man and it was like the Ancient Mariner stopping one of three—the interviewer was spellbound. Grampa told of the night they had to move along a trench blocked with dead bodies, treading on their mates' faces and saying sorry at every step; of the dead mangled hand that snatched and caught on his puttees so that he had to break the corpse fingers to free himself; of the head Donald Brodie struggled to clear from the bottom of a trench until he discovered it was attached to a body under the earth, and how the men in the company saluted it every time they passed it.

He kept it up till the interviewer turned green and looked away. Grampa smiled in triumph—he could be an old rascal. In the canteen afterwards, the interviewer grimaced. "Gothic old fella, isn't he?"

Grampa didn't think so much of him either. "Nothin's sacred. Nothin's serious ony mair, or respected. They'd sneer and snigger at their ain mither's funeral." His eyes rounded with indignant astonishment behind his spectacle lenses. "Was that wimmen's makeup he had roon' his eyes, hen?" A splutter of laughter. "Imagine having to crawl up the Menin Road wi' yon smirkin' wee oddity! Ach, Ah've lived too lang, so Ah huv."

○

They had to call the plumbers in. Overnight, a terrible stench had filled the hospital corridor, a sickening smell like latrines and something rotten, sweetish and decayed. It was eye-watering. Burton was going off his head with it all. So were we. The plumbers found nothing wrong anywhere. I went into Burton's room to relieve Smith for a tea break, only to find the room foul—much worse than out in the corridor. Burton ranted that he was choking on the smell. I had to agree—I could hardly breathe in there. He was being moved to another room as soon as a trolley arrived, but I had to sit with him until it did.

I wasn't thinking of anything in particular. Burton tossed and turned and his pyjama jacket fell open. That was when I began to realize what was going on. Pink patches of shiny skin had appeared on his chest, splashed diagonally across his flesh from the hip to the shoulder.

I knew what they were: old burn scars, the same as Grampa's. A suspicion grew in my mind, but I knew I couldn't be right. And even if I was, what could I have said to the doctors?

○

Donald Brodie was another of Grampa's pals. One time they went out with a party to cut barbed wire. It was a warm summer's night and they moved silently into No Man's Land, cutters in hand. Suddenly a flare went up and drenched them all in silver light. A sniper opened fire and Grampa staggered backwards, hit in the chest. The webbing across his body caught fire. He leapt like a dervish, flapping at the flames, until Donald wrestled him prone and hauled the webbing off him. Grampa screamed that he was hit, he was hit, and that he couldn't breathe. But the only damage apart from the burns was black bruising. Craigie's Bible had stopped the bullet. He swore afterwards that he'd heard Craigie speak to him: "A time to live," he said.

"But don't tell that yin to anyone, hen. They'd think Ah was saft in the heid. An' onyweys, Ah became an atheist and a socialist efter the war. It's embarrassin'."

But at the time, the Bible was the talk of the trenches. Even the officers came to see it and pat it for luck, and Donald Brodie actually had it in his hands when the shell hit and the trench caved in on him.

"We worked like blacks tae get him oot, because we all feared being buried alive, but he had suffocated. His mooth was full o' that chalky dirt the Somme has. Did ye know that, hen? The soil there is fulla chalk. It glistens in the sunlight. Whit price God then, eh? Poor Donald had the lucky Bible right in his hauns—he was readin' roon' the bullet hole. 'Vengeance is mine, saith the Lord,' it said. Whit sense tae be made o' that?"

○

There were more letters on Burton's arm. You'll have guessed by now. "DONA BRO." "CR YOUN." Their names were coming up on his arm. Their wounds were appearing on his body. Their terrors were haunting his dreams.

Before my eyes, the swollen flesh round the letters turned bronze and black, and discharged a foul frothy fluid. I thought I knew what it was because I'd read of the condition although I'd never seen it. I touched the swollen flesh lightly. It crackled like stiff paper—crepitation that's called, caused by the gas from dead tissue moving into the muscles. *Clostridium perfringens*—gas gangrene. What decent Craigie Young died of and what hardly anyone ever gets any more. I thought of a trainer coming down on Grampa's face hard enough to leave an imprint and smiled grimly.

The doctor came quickly when I called for him. He was soon on the phone to a range of consultants. "Serosanguinous discharge, sweet smellling. Bronze and brown discolouration ... amputation..."

○

It's often fatal, usually fatal in fact, because it resists antibiotics and moves so fast. I returned to Grampa's room and sat down by his bed. I remember a journalist asking him why they fought so long and hard. Was it patriotism, or religion, or duty or what? And Grampa only shrugged and said, "Maybe at the start. But efter, it wis fur ma pals. We depended on wan anither. We were loyal. We had nothing and naebody else to stand by us except wan anither."

What could I have told the doctors? That Burton was being killed off by men dead for nearly 90 years? That the old warriors were standing by their pal? And even if I had, what medicine could cure that? They'd have thought I was "saft in the heid".

Nurse Smith came through to tell me that Burton was away to the operating theatre, and that it was just as well, because the police had arrived, wanting to interview him about the attack at the War Memorial. His brother had been caught trying to sell the bronze plaques at a scrappie's.

I wasn't surprised by the news.

○

Grampa stirred awake that afternoon. There was a brightness in the blue of his eye, that last fierce flare of the candle before it gutters and dies. I wasn't surprised by that either. Burton had returned from theatre. Craigie Young's and Donald Brodie's names were complete before the amputation was over. And Grampa's name was there too, right across the pink patches on Burton's chest. "BILLY FLIGHT." Only the dead or the nearly dead could cause that.

The psychiatrist was wildly excited by the phenomenon, but cast down when the doctors said Burton wouldn't live long enough for therapy. It was hard even to find the conventional words of regret when I thought of the trainer grinding into Grampa's face.

"Ye're there, hen," Grampa said and his whisper was a dead-leaf rustle and I had to bend my head to him to hear it. "Sit me up. Ah don't want to die lyin' doon." I eased him up and handed him his specs. He blinked like an old owl. "Ah've had such dreams, hen. Good dreams. We were a' young and a' the gither again. It was just grand to see them a' one mair time."

He lay back on his pillows, savouring his dream. Then he smiled. He was looking over my shoulder at the mirror on the wall.

"Look! D'ye see them? Can ye see them there?"

A coldness chilled my mind and the hair at the back of my head stiffened. I'd have done anything not to look at that mirror—didn't I know what they looked like in death? But Grampa's smile was a 100-watt welcome, and his gaze so intense and so longing, that I felt like a coward. Hadn't I known them all my life?

I turned slowly and was half disappointed, half relieved, that the only reflections to be seen were my own and Grampa's. The light round Grampa's bed, though, was thicker and heavier somehow, white cold like candle fire, and full of a presence. There was a mild buzzing of excitement in my ears, and when I turned back to the bed, Grampa was away.

It's a comfort to know that he wasn't alone.

Has our fate already been decided? The doctrine of predestination once held considerable sway with many Scots, who believed that the future was divinely foreordained. But what if the choices we make do count for something? What if all possibilities are realized in parallel and there is an alternative to our world?

❂ ❂

THE INTRIGUE OF THE BATTERED BOX
Michael Cobley

❂ ❂

1. Harsh Reality

They finally found his body in a muddy abandoned brick tunnel a mile west of Great Waverley Terminus. Seven slender men in innocuous city wear, they surrounded the sad, rain-sodden corpse, two of them crouching to search the ragged garments and a coarse canvas bag strapped to the waist. At length the examiners got to their feet, looked to their leader and shook their heads.

"Only the box," one said. "Naught else."

The leader, a tall cloaked man with storm-grey eyes, frowned as he contemplated the oaken lockbox that he held. It was roughly a foot long on each side, had brass strapping on its corners and edges, and bore many dints and scratches on every surface. It was also empty.

"So we still have to find the Relic," he said bitterly. "We still have to stay here in this vast stone maze of a city. So be it."

He stared down at the dead man lying across the weed-choked, rusty rails, knowing that it had been love, and a fatal desire for the whore Linsel, which had brought their brother to this sorry end. That and his foolish theft of several irreplaceable instruments whose exotic and obvious value had attracted the wrong kind of attention. Luckily, all of them had been retrieved, apart from the Relic.

The leader gave the box to one of the examiners.

"Return this to the Outpost," he said. "Report all that has transpired, and inform them of the task yet to be achieved. In the meantime, we shall endeavor to retrace all of our errant brother's steps."

The messenger nodded, then bent to retrieve the canvas bag from the corpse, slipped the box inside and left, climbing back up the embankment to the rainwashed main road. Under a grey, gusty sky he took a steam omnibus along bustling Princes Street to the elaborate, soot-darkened immensity of Coronation Bridge where he alighted and hurried up onto the Imperial Mile.

But he never reached his destination. In the fifteen-storey shadow of a shipping company, a horse-drawn carriage clattered up alongside him and from its open door cruel hands lunged forth to drag him bodily inside. Moments later the carriage turned off the Mile and a lifeless body was tipped out into the gutter, its blood swirling with the rainwater. And of the bag and the box it contained there was no sign.

2. A Singular Client

Many and multifarious have been those who have sought out the services of my good friend Sheldrake Ormiston, the empire's foremost diagnostic investigator. But the client who called at the Candle Street chambers one dank Edinburgh evening in October 1881 surpassed them all with a presence and demeanour sufficiently impressive to rival that of Ormiston himself.

Announcing himself as Jason Tideswell, our visitor—a tall man in tweeds—accepted my friend's invitation to sit in the red leather armchair near the fire. Once he was settled therein, and the appropriate introductions were made, he gazed across at Sheldrake Ormiston with stern grey eyes.

"Sir," he began. "I have a private predicament to resolve, one in which I would prefer not to involve the police. Be assured that there are no gross misdemeanours in this—it is merely a matter of retrieving an item stolen from me only hours ago."

Sheldrake Ormiston glanced at me momentarily, his dark eyes aglint with amusement as he reached for the old gunpowder pouch on the mantelpiece.

"Mr Tideswell," he said as his nimble fingers filled a long-stemmed pipe with shredded leaf from the pouch. "What, pray tell, is the item in question?"

This time it was Tideswell's turn to look in my direction, but Ormiston forestalled him.

"You can be quite open before my friend here," he said. "Mr Ramsay is a former lieutenant in the 2nd Philadelphia Dragoons, and has become my invaluable companion on many an intrigue and adventure. Please—continue."

Tideswell frowned, then nodded. "Very well, Mr Ormiston. Know that the item is a brass-bound oaken box, a foot long on all sides, and of a somewhat well-used appearance. Inside is a variety of papers, documents, letters, photographs and handbills. The box was my father's and came into my possession recently after his death overseas."

"When and where was the last time you saw this box, sir?" Ormiston said as smoky threads drifted from the bowl of his pipe.

Tideswell's lips twitched with a faintly sardonic smile. "In the hands of a footpad who relieved me of it as I was crossing Coronation Bridge this morning at about ten o'clock. I gave chase but lost him in the crowds near the junction with the Imperial Mile."

"Would you recognise this malefactor if you saw him again, Mr Tideswell?"

"I believe so, sir. I looked him full in the face throughout the entire incident."

Ormiston suddenly uncoiled from his armchair. "Then I suggest that the three of us hasten forth to the City Infirmary—the afternoon edition of the *Edinburgh Times* reported the discovery of an unidentified body just off the Imperial Mile shortly after ten o'clock, and a mere two streets away from your last sighting, Mr Tideswell!"

Tideswell and I came to our feet in unison and followed him eagerly out into the hall where the redoubtable Mrs Lawrence was waiting with our coats.

3. A Degree of Certainty

Two met in the nave of Rosslyn Chapel by the golden light of oil lamps.

"So the Aquarial Brethren have called upon the Great Investigator," said the Grand Master, a portly, grey-haired man in dark green robes. "Just what is in this box, I wonder?"

The second man was taller and younger, his lean physique complemented by formal gentlemen's blacks and long cape. One hand held a hat and gloves, the other a walking stick.

"The Brethren's leader claims that it contains unimportant papers, bequeathed from his deceased father."

The Grand Master gave a contemptuous snort. "Ormiston should see through that in an instant, but he'll keep his counsel until he knows more." He gazed thoughtfully over at the intricate form of the Apprentice Pillar. "Tell me, Lachlan, do we have any notion as to who purloined it?"

"Blackwood," said the one called Lachlan. "One of our spotters happened to see the incident from across the road, and recognized the driver as one of his."

"Dr Elijah Blackwood," said the Grand Master with loathing. "The bane of Edinburgh and the Empire! Is it some Manichean curse that the mightiest capital in the world must be the source of both the best and the worst that Mankind has to offer? Hopefully, your brother will pick up his spoor in this cryptic imbroglio, and if not, we might see a way to nudge him in the right direction, eh?"

The younger man smiled. "I've never known Sheldrake to be nudged, Grand Master, but I'm sure something can be done should it be necessary. And in the meantime?"

"We keep an eye on all of Blackwood's comings and goings, but with care. Our other agents will see what progress Mr Ormiston makes—it is entirely possible that he may deduce the truth about the Aquarial Brethren and their leader!"

"Which would be a fascinating confrontation to behold," said Lachlan Ormiston.

4. Cold Storage

Our breath fumed in the marble chill of the infirmary morgue while the enigmatic Tideswell looked down at the pale body stretched out on the metal drawer. He nodded.

"This is the man," he said. "How did he die?"

"By the forceful impact of a heavy object to the back of the head." The attending surgeon was the acclaimed Dr Bellwether who on more than one occasion has provided invaluable insights to Ormiston. "Death took place perhaps half an hour later and was doubtless very unpleasant for him."

"Was there anything of note on his person, doctor?" Ormiston said.

Dr Bellwether smiled as he gazed at the three of us.

"Not a thing, my dear Ormiston," he said. "His pockets were as empty as could be, and beyond a couple of moles and a missing incisor, there are no distinguishing marks."

I watched the two face each other across the metal drawer and its passenger, suppressing the urge to smile at this friendly pitting of wiles.

"None at all, you say?" Ormiston reached down for the corpse's hand, examining it this way and that. "Hmm, not a labourer; and no ink stains, so not an office worker either. What of his attire?"

"Quite odd," Bellwether said. "Not one of his garments was a good or comfortable fit, and all were mismatched, probably second-hand—"

"And thus there is no easy way of determining their origin—"

"Nor their owner." Bellwether chuckled as he pushed the laden drawer back into its place in the wall. "It seems that this may be a fruitless avenue for your investigations, sir."

Ormiston's smile was wintry. "Perhaps, doctor, perhaps."

"Yet you have attracted the attention of an unsavoury pursuer. You recall that peculiar case involving the clockwork bears, and that family of brigands who complicated the matter?"

Ormiston nodded. "The McGurks," he said with distaste. "More than just the father should be behind bars."

The good doctor nodded. "Well, one of the sons is at your heels— I saw your approach from the upper gallery, and noticed the McGurk offspring shadowing you almost to the infirmary door."

"My thanks, doctor," Ormiston said. "We shall be especially vigilant. Ramsay—have you your service revolver?"

"Yes indeed, Ormiston!"

"Then let us venture forth. Mr Tideswell—you may elect to remain here until we have confronted this problem if you prefer."

"I have no qualms about such encounters, Mr Ormiston."

"Good! Come then!"

5. Monuments of the Imperial Mile

[Excerpt from page 9]

No. XXIV—Bishop Paterson of Mallaig

Sixty-two years after the Second Restoration, Bishop Paterson was a pivotal figure in the development of the empire's spiritual character.

In 1808 he roused the fury of the highlands and the lowlands against the Protestant pretensions of James VII, forcing the establishment of the Holy Northern Church. Later, in 1817, he organized a body of influential nobles and patricians to persuade King John III to abdicate in favour of his sister, the devout Anne, who raised the Church to the pre-eminent position it occupies today.

No. XXV—Godwin MacGregor, Duke of Kintail
The Duke of Kintail was commander of His Imperial Majesty's armies at the Battle of Philadelphia in 1829. His victory crushed the 2nd American Uprising and paved the way for lasting peace and prosperity throughout the continent. Although this statue group shows him in a warlike pose on horseback, he was known for his philanthropy and clemency, especially during his tenure as Governor General of Eastern America.

No. XXVI—Charles III
This large frieze across the front of the MacAulay Building shows the entrance of Charles Edward Stuart into London in 1745, heralding the 2nd Restoration. Amongst the many figures are the clan chieftains and their standards, Charles III's advisers, and the burghers of London welcoming him at the open city gates. Although the capital was later moved to Edinburgh, London has continued to play a vital role as the empire has grown in strength and stature.

6. Waiting in Stone

"Sheldrake Ormiston!"

The words were spoken with a level yet palpable hate in the cold, shadowy tower room. By the glow of a shuttered lamp, a pair of long, spidery hands fingered a brass-bound box, turning it this way and that before laying it to rest on a bare tabletop.

"Aye, it's empty yer honour."

"So I see, Bogston, you fool, but since it clearly once held the skull, we can now reunite them..." One of the hands produced a yellowing skull from the shadows and placed it in the open box. "And this is all! We failed to acquire those interesting instruments that Linsel saw her customer with—those mysterious men got to them before we could, but at least we were able to do for one of them ... and got this box." The cold precise voice broke into a dry laugh.

"It must be important," said the one called Bogston, "but now they've gone tae ... you know who..."

"Of course it's important, but let us not worry about Sheldrake Ormiston—I have been waiting a long time for the chance to draw him into the web of a suitable demise. Even now he will be tugging on one of its outlying tendrils, that idiot McGurk boy who I sent to follow him. That should bring him within my orbit before long, whereupon he shall be dealt with."

"Good—Ah niver liked him, or his pet sodger."

"There still remains the mystery of the box and the skull, Bogston, and those strangers." The long pale fingers removed the skull from the box, turning its brow to the lamp's yellow glow and tapped the bone. "See, there are two small holes here and this patch of bone is lighter in hue—some kind of plate was fixed here, inscribed with a name..." The skull was placed carefully on the table. "In the meantime, get out and alert your hardiest toughs and let me know where Ormiston is. If Ormiston gets too close to the McGurk boy, see he stays silent."

"Aye, Dr Blackwood—be back soonest."

As the tower room clicked shut and footsteps receded down the spiral stairs, Elijah Blackwood sighed a long sigh.

"Sheldrake Ormiston—soon you will die."

7. Twixt Cup and Lip

The moment he saw us, the McGurk lad was off into the crowd like a startled hare.

"After him!" cried Ormiston.

And it was a merry chase he led us through the tower-lined Edinburgh streets: past the great, dark facades of the empire's mightiest institutions; and down cobbled side-wynds, rank with the reek of tanneries before finally emerging on Princes Street. When it became clear that he was heading for the blackened cloisters and galleries of the immense Bruce Monument, Ormiston said to myself and Tideswell: "Keep after him, gentlemen! I shall attempt to cut off his escape route!"

Then he was gone amongst the throngs of city folk. The nearby Lochinvar Gardens were busy with people waving Union flags, and contributing to the density of the crowds, as they watched small, one-man dirigibles race slowly overhead. But Tideswell and I were relentless in our pursuit, striving to keep our quarry's head and shoulders in view even as he charged into one of the hexagonal monument's many vaulted cloisters. Yet still we kept him in sight, and were able to spy exactly which tower stairwell he entered.

After him we went, climbing the gritty, worn steps three at a time. I felt sure that we had him cornered until I spotted beyond one of the open windows a narrow iron gantry linking this tower to its neighbour, the only span out of the original six still in place. And sure enough, moments later we saw his gangling form loping across, coattails flapping.

But we were gaining on him, so onwards we pressed: venturing onto the ornate but filth-encrusted iron bridge, hurrying across with the monument's six gothic spires looming and a chill crosswind buffetting us. And we had scarcely reached the other side when a terrible shriek came from below as the figure of the McGurk boy fell in a flail of limbs from one of the tower windows. Tideswell and I stared at each other in horror, and descended the tower as swiftly as we dared, thinking to catch whoever had flung McGurk to his death. But apart from a drunk and two old women, we encountered no one until we reached the bottom and saw three policemen hurrying over, led by none other than Inspector Strang of Scotland Yard.

"Yer there, just like he promised!" he began.

"Who promised, Inspector?" I said.

"Yon Mr Sheldrake Ormiston, o' course! Said also tae tell ye both tae hurry up tae the castle, wi'oot delay!"

8. Hindsight Reflections

In his private chamber, the Grand Master sat at his desk with the works of Plato open before him, whilst pondering the enigma of the Brethren and their box. They already knew about the Aquarial Brethren: soon after their appearance several weeks ago in the ruins of the hidden Outpost, an associate of the Order had spied on them and deduced that somehow they were very familiar with the ruins' layout. It was the later discovery of the closely guarded prisoner and a room full of strange machinery that led to further deductions regarding the Brethren's origin.

But now this business involving Blackwood and Ormiston threatened to create a very public—and potentially political—crisis which could spur certain advocates of change into action. He had already despatched Lachlan with orders to curb the situation, but if he could not find a comprehensive solution, the very stability of the empire could be put at risk.

9. Sidestep Thoughts

In one of the Outpost's small chambers, with two of the Aquarial Brethren guarding the door, the inventor sat before the row of dead scrying plates and wondered where a different sidestep would have taken him.

Perhaps to a Scotland where Viking kings ruled still with bloody hands, or even where Mongol overlords held brutal sway? Or maybe one where that first legendary civilization never sank beneath the waves, leading to a world where a skull in a box would be almost meaningless?

He shook his head. It was mere poor luck that his previous sidestep had delivered him into the hands of the Aquarial Brethren just when they were at their most desperate. History had turned against them with slow, inexorable implacability, an unstoppable punishment for their forebears support of a lost cause...

And now the actions of one foolish man were drawing unwanted attention their way here, and the consequences could only be disastrous. For in this derelict version of the Outpost, the power source was a broken wreck and even though the Brethren's enginists were working on it without cease he anticipated little success. The options open to him were limited, most immediately by the two men guarding him and his apparatus.

Bored by inactivity, he turned to see if he could provoke something like discourse from his captors, and was astonished to see a slender, dark-clad figure crouched over two unconscious, prone forms.

"I take it that you are the inventor of the device," the stranger said as he straightened. In one hand he held an odd pistol with a cluster of narrow barrels, while the other gripped a grey sack weighed down by a round object.

"I am," he replied, mouth suddenly dry. "Have you come to kill me?"

"Nay, sir," the other said. "You will have only protection from myself, I swear it. Although there may still be danger if you come with me. What do you say?"

The inventor thought a moment, then shrugged, stood and followed him from the room.

10. Revenge Is Bitter

Elijah Blackwood, doctor of biology and the man dubbed the Loki of Crime, stood over the body of the dead guard and stared at the broken-open chest. The oaken box was in another chest in another room, but now the skull was gone. Outside the window, night was encroaching on sloping roofs and slender spires.

"Wis it Ormiston, yer honour? Wis it?" His trusty henchman was clenching his considerable fists with barely restrained rage. "Just say it wis, an' we'll have him an' his pet sodger!"

"Rest easy, Bogston—this is not the work of the Great Investigator. Dead bodies are too untidy for his filing-cabinet mind. No, I fear that we have been visited by the interesting strangers who brought us the artefacts to begin with." Blackwood locked gazes with the burly Bogston, who flinched under that cold regard. "We know whose company their leader is in, so let us swat two pests with one blow, shall we?"

11. Battlement Ballet

I found Ormiston up on the main rampart of Edinburgh Castle, one foot resting on a wall crenellation as he stared out at the great smoky mass of the city.

"Ah, my dear Ramsay," he said. "But where is our singular client, the mysterious Mr Tideswell?"

"I wish I knew, Ormiston," I replied. "Confound the man! We had just entered the castle gates, passing the constables who told us where to find you, when he paused to retie his bootlace in a shadowy door. A moment later I realized that he had absconded utterly and was nowhere to be seen. Thus, I dashed up here to meet you."

"I'd expected as much," Ormiston said. "Our Mr Tideswell has much to conceal, not all of which is yet clear to me. However, the convolutions of this day have revealed one thing of vital importance, namely the location of the lair of my foulest foe!"

"Good lord, Ormiston! You can't mean..."

But my words were cut short by a shot that rang out from the inner darkness of the castle. Instantly, Ormiston straightened and pointed up to where the bulk of the ancient castle abutted against the more recent towered silhouette of the Holy Cathedral of St Margaret. Figures were running along upper cloisters, past the glow of torches, while shouts came from the quadrangles below.

"Come on, Ramsay," Ormiston cried, leading the way. "Something deadly is afoot!"

12. Retribution Is Cold

Tideswell led the best and strongest of the Brethren up stairs that twisted through cold rock, then up stairs concealed in walls and floors, then up disused flues and ladders that finally led onto the high ramparts of the castle. There was anger in every eye and fist, and Tideswell was the razor-keen spearhead of their onrushing resolve. The discovery of the raid and the inventor's abduction had galvanized him into immediate action, especially since he had come into possession of the location of the man who had so disrupted their plans, the vile Blackwood. When a disguised runner had whispered the place name to him during the earlier pursuit down in the city he had almost laughed out loud, such was his amazement. But then he recalled the old adage of hiding something in full view, and had waited until he and Ramsay had entered the castle grounds before going his separate way.

It was not until he and the Aquarial Brethren reached the iron gantries linking the castle to the cathedral that the firing began. But Tideswell had planned for such a confrontation and had brought along some of their rescued artefacts—he grinned as he thought of the surprise that Blackwood's thugs were about to get.

13. Divine Decay

Cornered on the flat parapet of the cathedral roof, Elijah Blackwood peered down at the seven spires behind whose bases the Aquarial Brethren were hiding, their hideously effective weapons trained on the low wall behind which he crouched. All of his henchmen here were either dead—from lightning bolts, clouds of poisoned needles or beams of terrible heat—or horribly wounded like Bogston, who lay halfway down the cathedral roof, moaning.

He glanced over his shoulder at the main bell tower and the window sitting open just a few yards away. It was a tempting exit, but if he made a dash for it, he would immediately become an admirable target, and not long afterwards, admirably dead. He raised his combustion gun, selected his last smoke round and took aim at the base of the rightmost spire. If he could raise a good veil of smoke, it might be enough to conceal a retreat to the bell tower and the way out...

"Do not pull the trigger, doctor," said someone behind him. "Your very life depends upon it!"

Blackwood looked round and cursed—standing before the bell tower window was Ormiston and his lapdog, Ramsay, who was pointing a revolver straight at his face!

14. Terminus Opus

"There was much about Mr Tideswell's story which did not ring true," said Ormiston. "So much, in fact, that I was unsure from which angle to approach it, or how seriously. But when we laid eyes on the body at the city infirmary I knew that this was a serious matter indeed—the dead man and Tideswell had a similar cast to the skin, and also very similar fingernails, which indicates a similarity of diet and thus origins."

Light from a single lantern illuminated the cathedral roof where myself and Ormiston, and Blackwood and Tideswell, stood in different corners, three parties armed and mistrustful of each other.

"You are quite right," Tideswell said. "He was one of our compatriots, murdered by this villain, this thief." He glared darkly at Blackwood.

"For the box you came to see us about, yes?" Ormiston smiled. "The box now sitting in Dr Blackwood's lair, which I've examined closely enough to deduce that its contents were not paper, but bones of some kind, perhaps a sacred relic."

"A valuable one," muttered Blackwood.

Ormiston rounded on him. "I believe it to be a skull, doctor—do you know whose it was?"

"If I knew that," Blackwood snarled, "I could put a value on it!"

"So it is still in your possession, somewhere," Ormiston said. "Such a shame that you failed to discover the small compartment in that box." And he produced the brass plate which we had uncovered prior to emerging from the bell tower.

All eyes were on Ormiston as he held the brass plate out to catch the light from a lamp carried by one of Tideswell's men, and spoke. "It reads, 'Artorius Rex', which I take to mean King Arthur."

"The once and future king!" I exclaimed. "Some terrorist factions would pay dearly to have that in their hands."

"The value of the skull seems undeniable, my dear Ramsay, given the effort expended upon its recovery," Ormiston said. "But its identity is far from certain because this nameplate is not the original." He turned to the mysterious Tideswell. "Is it, sir?"

Tideswell smiled faintly. "Your reputation is well-deserved, Mr Ormiston. What gave it away?"

"The plate looks as weathered as the box's brass bindings, but the edges are too straight, too well-made. Which begs the question—where is the original, and what name does it bear?"

Tideswell gave a slow, unconcerned shrug. "That will have to remain a mystery in your eyes, sir."

"But not for long," came a voice out of the lower shadows as footsteps climbed the sloping roof towards us. "I believe I can clear up a few enigmas here..."

I was taken aback by the look of astonishment on Ormiston's face as he beheld the newcomer, a slender man in black coat and cape who smiled at my friend.

"Sheldrake," he said.

Ormiston laughed quietly. "So the Order has taken a hand in this, eh? Ramsay, may I introduce you to my brother, Lachlan, a knight commander in the Ordo Templar?"

15. A Leap into Unknown Providence

From a shadowy ledge halfway up the cathedral roof, the inventor listened as his erstwhile rescuer laid bare the framework of truth.

"...for you see, the nameplate was hidden within the skull itself," Lachlan Ormiston was saying. "Concealed in a slot behind the nose..." There was a pause as he removed it from the skull and handed it to his brother who said:

"It reads, 'Bonnie Prince Charlie, 1720-1788'."

There was a dumbfounded silence for a moment.

"But Charles III died in 1767," said Ramsay. "He's buried at Holyrood."

"And he was only known as Bonnie Prince Charlie during the '45 Rebellion," said Blackwood, a hungry note in his voice. "So how can this be his skull, and how could it be here ... now, Bogston!"

Suddenly shots crashed out from the other side of the roof. There were shouts and returning fire, but the inventor decided that he had overstayed his welcome and quickly retreated to the castle ramparts. He remembered the way back down into the secret passages below that led to the stone chambers of the Outpost, and knew that he had to be as stealthy as possible.

All he had to do was get to his apparatus, rewire the small internal voltaic phials, and he would be able to take another sidestep away from this world. Sadly, it would be his last since the apparatus would not be able to make the crossing without the stabilizers which the phials energized. But he reasoned that a leap into the unknown was better than a surrender to known perils.

16. Coda in Tenebris

We stood at the chamber door, contemplating the smoking wreckage within.

"So the Brethren forced him to bring them to our world," said Ormiston's brother, Lachlan. "They were really fleeing the long-term consequences of their forebears support for the Young Pretender and the '45 Rebellion, which failed in their world. Many of their secretive communities were uncovered and broken, apart from this outpost." He sighed. "But it seems that eventually they were on the point of discovery when the inventor appeared in their midst."

"Where will they go?" asked Ormiston.

"The Order has decided to help them translocate to the Scandinavian provinces," Lachlan said. "There may be other surviving outposts there." He smiled at his brother. "Sheldrake, you do understand that the details of this energetic imbroglio must remain secret."

Sheldrake Ormiston raised an amused eyebrow and was silent a moment before chuckling. "I understand fully, my dear brother. Besides, it would be difficult to prove such events with the Brethren having departed these shores."

"Going in search of the last fragments of Atlantis," I said in wonderment. "Just astonishing."

"I will be considerably more amazed," Ormiston said, "when we finally get the fiendish Blackwood in shackles and behind bars. The man is more slippery than a parliament full of eels!" He gave his brother a sharp nod. "My thanks, Lachlan, for your intriguing intervention. Please convey my regards to the Grand Master."

"I shall be pleased to do so, Sheldrake."

"Right, Ramsay, let's away—there's work to be done!"

There is a special art to writing a short story, and there is a very special one indeed involved in writing a vignette. Here Ron Butlin gives us a suite of five marvellous tales, wonderful because of both their content and their brevity. These are small stories from a small nation, but the ideas are as big as the world.

○ ○

FIVE FANTASTIC FICTIONS
Ron Butlin

○ ○

THE COLOURFUL LIFE OF CALUM McCALL

During the early years of his life, Calum McCall was surprised to find himself waking up every morning in Scotland. This was a winter country of darkened tenements, black railings, pavements and streets of harsh traffic. There was only one sun, and it wasn't even striped— which perhaps explained the look of disappointment he could see in the faces of the men and women who lived there.

Every so often he tried asking his parents: "What has happened to the multicoloured suns that used to bounce across the sky, and to the colours that trailed after like rain?"

"Aye right," said his dad.

"Elbows off the table," said his mother.

At school his teacher told him to sit up straight and pay attention—that way he would get ahead.

When he fell in love for the first time he told the girl, she was called Alice, that her kisses brought back all the colours he had known so early on, and which were now almost faded to nothing in his memory. She said he was sweet, and a few months later she got engaged to someone else.

Years later, Calum married and had children of his own. One day his baby son pointed up at the sky and gurgled with pleasure. Calum's glance followed the pointing finger, but there was nothing particularly special up there—nothing, anyway, that he could see.

That night he slept badly for the first time.

He was now in a position of responsibility and could not afford to turn up at his office dishevelled with lack of sleep, not among his ambitious colleagues. The doctor he went to gave him a packet of brightly coloured pills.

Every morning now, Calum is up bright and early, ready for the day ahead. And at night, when he closes his eyes, he knows he will soon slip from one utterly dreamless world into the next.

❋

ARNOLD SCHOENBERG'S STORY

Like everyone else at the end of the nineteenth century, Arnold Schoenberg, the great composer and musical theorist, had taken his seat on the crowded train heading towards an ever-better world. After turning the corner into the glorious future ahead, the engine started picking up speed—only to go slamming into a solid wall.

Bits went everywhere: bits of countries, bits of colonies, bits of science, art and religion. The tracks, seeming to stretch back to the beginnings of Time, were wrenched apart; buckled and bent, they clawed at the blue sky above Passchendaele.

Suddenly, the street was full of people who knew best. Their self-appointed task: to get civilization back on the rails. They all agreed that drastic problems need drastic solutions—and each had a solution more drastic than the one before.

On all sides, there began such a noise of hammering and welding, such a clamour and din of revolution, extermination, colonial expansion and unemployment; of mass production and racial purity. The Stock Exchange boomed, the trains were made to run on time.

Schoenberg, meanwhile, had decided to discard tonality. He declared that his new discovery—the twelve-note system, as he called it—would create harmonic possibilities strong enough to hold everything together. Even chaos itself.

Around him, the streets now bustled with strikers and strike breakers; cattle trucks were criss-crossing Europe, financiers went thudding onto pavements. There were parades, searchlights, flags, roaring ovens, transatlantic crossings to the sounds of restaurant orchestras, reasoned debate and orderly soup queues.

Soon Schoenberg was rushing up to complete strangers: "My twelve-note system offers real value for money to composer, player and audience alike."

Once all the lights of Europe had gone out, The Sandman tiptoed from country to country tucking the sleepers tight in their beds. That done, he began telling them their dreams. Schoenberg closed his eyes believing the time would come when mothers crooned his twelve-note lullabies to their children. This particular dream made even The Sandman smile.

o

MOSES' LITTLE BROTHER

The day after Moses and the Twelve Tribes of Israel set off into the wilderness, his little brother ran up to the head of the procession: "We'll be out of here in no time—I have a map."

Big Brother, of course, knew better. After all, God was on their side, and not just any god, of which there were plenty in those far-off generous days, but the one true God—He who could provide plagues of locusts, frogs and boils, and could part the Red Sea when required.

"No, thank you," Moses replied, "We have a cloud by day and a pillar of fire by night. We don't need maps."

"But it'll tell us—"

"When God wants to tell us anything, he'll turn into a burning bush."

That night, after Moses and the Twelve Tribes had hurried off to catch up with the pillar of fire, Little Brother shrugged and lay down in the sand. Next thing, God was shaking him:

"You're on your own!" came the Divine warning.

"Suits me." He turned over, and went back to sleep.

A few days later, Moses' little brother reached the Promised Land. Milk and honey for those with work permits—but for the likes of him, it was either the building site or delivering pizzas...

The Twelve Tribes showed up forty years later. There was a dispute. Several other gods, both local and freelance, got involved—and, three thousand years after that, everyone was still at it. A partition was followed by refugee camps, suicide-bombers, missiles. Someone produced a new map. Someone started building a wall.

God turned himself into a burning bush. No one noticed.

"Okay," He said, "No more Mr Nice Guy," and reached for his *Book of Plagues*. The updated version.

o

A VISIT TO THE ORACLE

The Delphic Oracle was having a bad day. Outside, Mediterranean sunlight was bleaching the vineyards and hillsides, and shimmering on the cobalt-blue Aegean. Inside, in the dimness, the queue of punters seeking her advice seemed never-ending: shepherds and kings, five-star generals and multinational CEOs. The holy incense was making her eyes water; her headdress of writhing snakes was a disaster; each divine utterance was becoming more enigmatic than the last. Her cave needed a makeover it would never get. She needed a break.

Next up was a politician who had turned sincerity into a brand-name stamped across his forehead. Though he had planned to present himself as a humble supplicant, PR demanded an entourage of men with mobile phones, armed guards, and soldiers who swept the cave (only electronically, the priestess was disappointed to note) for weapons. For everyone's comfort and security the skies were dark with helicopters.

"If we are not in control," this champion of world democracy was explaining, "the entire world will be out of control."

Where have I heard that before? the priestess thought to herself. Just then, one of the writhing snakes slid from her headdress, glided miraculously through the sacred fire, slithered up close and bit him. The people's representative, so engrossed in the truth of what he was saying, didn't feel a thing.

Back in his own country, he addressed his cabinet. Being brave, he said nothing about that rather nippy itch in his ankle. It was business as usual. No rest for the righteous, was his motto.

Halfway through the meeting he began talking in riddles and enigmas. No one noticed the difference. There were droughts, famines and free-market investment. Shares were bought and sold. Aid parcels and cluster bombs fell. Some cities were liberated, some became rubble. Life went on, and death.

○

A GLITCH IN THE UNIVERSE

William Littlejohn was standing at his bedroom window when he saw the falling star. He closed his eyes and made a wish.

Twenty years later, a brand-new bicycle shimmered into substantiality during a merger meeting. Mr Lofthouse, the chairman, lost his audience: all attention was on the gleaming chrome, bell, mirror and wheel-stabilizers. A bright red "whirrer" was attached to the spokes.

Lofthouse demanded to know what the game was? The ice-cold sweat of denied responsibility ran down the inside of Littlejohn's tailored shirt. Security was called, and as the bike was wheeled out of the boardroom to disappear down the corrior, its whirrer seemed to call plaintively to him. That night Littlejohn couldn't sleep.

In time, he was promoted: new office, new secretary, new view, new washroom. As he stared out over the city, he could almost believe that the sunbeams on the adjacent glass skyscrapers were dancing just for him.

Over the next year a retriever puppy and a real-life Miss February centre-fold were among a series of startling and embarrassing materializations. Clearly there was a glitch in the universe—his adolescent wishes were being granted, but too late. Every day became a torment. What wish would be granted next?

He became gaunt from sleeplessness. He married, had children, moved to a good neighbourhood. Nothing seemed to help.

One morning he found himself seated at the chairman's desk. Funny, he couldn't remember wishing to actually *become* old Lofthouse, but—ah yes!—he could recognize his former boss in the new junior partner, sharpening company pencils down at the bottom of the boardroom table.

Just then Security burst in, accompanied by police. They approached, flourished documents. Bandied about were words like "embezzlement", "insider-trading". "Jail." As he was led away, Littlejohn was certain he saw the new junior glance up—and wink at him.

Parochialism is a charge sometimes levelled at Scots culture. National pride is all very well, but a solely inward looking society is doomed to a cultural development of ever-diminishing returns. Just as well, then, that Scots do like to get out and about too. After all, no one likes a solipsist.

○ ○

RUNNING ON AT ADVENTURES
Angus McAllister

○ ○

THE TEN OBJECTIVES OF THE JOURNEY

1. To fulfil one's potential as a human being, by reaching the highest grade of which one is capable.
2. To carry out one's allotted work to the best of one's ability.
3. To achieve a harmonious work/life balance by spending non-working hours in suitable recreational activity of a cultural, social or physical nature.
4. To take care of one's health, both physical and mental.
5. To acknowledge our debt to the Creators for supplying us with food, clothing, accommodation, medical care and the rest of the world's bounty.
6. To obey the Regulations.
7. To follow the advice of one's Counsellor.
8. To treat other people with sensitivity and respect, particularly those in lower grades.
9. To procreate, in order to ensure the Journey's continuation by a succeeding generation.
10. To defer to the superior wisdom of the Creators by accepting the nature of the world without question.

The Regulatory Framework, Prologue

○

They gave him a week's leave, to make him feel better about being passed over. If he'd made it to Grade 5, he'd have got an additional week, every year, as a matter of right. And Isla might have accepted him at last, instead of turning him down yet again.

Over lunch, Gavin tried to offer consolation. "There are worse things than being a Grade 4 clerk."

"Oh yes," said Ewan. "I could be a Grade 2 cleaner or a Grade 3 porter. Or maybe Grade 1 unemployed. They get more leave than anyone else."

"Don't be daft. You'd feel better if you could stop obsessing about Isla."

But how could he? She was always there, seven hours a day, at the next desk. He sensed her presence like a constant, erotic glow, covertly observing her at every opportunity, continually seeking pretexts to engage her in conversation. His work had suffered, and that was probably why he had been denied promotion. It would never improve until she accepted him or he was moved away from her. But that would only happen if he was promoted.

"Forget about her," said Gavin. "There are other fish in the sea."

"You know," said Ewan, momentarily diverted. "These old expressions fascinate me. What's a fish? What's the sea?"

"It's just a saying. Why do you always ask so many questions? You spend too much time with Alex, that's your problem."

Their lunch shift was coming to an end; around them, people were leaving as new arrivals queued at the counter. The Canteen was a rectangular, functional room, unremarkable in a world of rectangular, functional rooms. At one end there was a series of serving hatches where each person uplifted an identical lunch. At the other end, the doorway was flanked by disposal hatches, where they deposited their trays on the way out.

"What are you going to do with your week?" Gavin asked.

"I thought I'd take a trip around the world."

"You're a hopeless case."

It was only a ten-minute walk back to work. Their office was two segments away and the journey took them down one flight of stairs, along a lengthy connecting corridor, negotiating several right and left hand turns along internal passages, up four flights, round more passages, down three flights... Ewan had worked in the same office for three years, but still often took a wrong turning.

Isla was on a later lunch shift, so he decided to spend the half hour before the return of her distracting presence to concentrate on his current project. He looked at the text on his screen and tried to think of ways to improve it. It was a complex sub-paragraph from the Regulations, with numerous cross-references to other articles, clauses, paragraphs and sub-paragraphs. Ewan's task was to see if, in conformity with the Four Regulatory Ideals of Clarity, Unambiguity, Consistency and Elegance, it should be divided into two separate sub-paragraphs.

His version, and those of the three other Grade 4 clerks working on the same project, would each be reviewed by a separate Grade 5 subeditor, and then considered, revised and, if necessary, consolidated by three committees at Grades 6, 7 and 8 respectively, before being finally appraised by the Regulatory Appraisal Committee at Grade 9 and (if not passed back down for further work) sent on for approval (or not) by the Governors.

Ewan had a vague memory that this provision had been in two separate paragraphs once before, but it was difficult to be sure. Past editions of the Regulations were no longer available.

He had changed one "under" to "in accordance with" and then back again before Isla returned and his concentration waned. At the end of his shift the redrafting was still incomplete.

He had to make a duty call to Kirk, his counsellor. Kirk was a frustrated man, who had wanted to be a governor, but had never risen above Grade 8. He compensated by continually asserting his superiority over those within his influence. He gave Ewan the usual lecture about how lazy and irresponsible the younger generation was, how Ewan was the laziest and most irresponsible of the lot, how he had predicted the outcome of Ewan's bid for promotion, and how he had been right as usual. On learning that Ewan had left his current project incomplete, he said, "Don't you understand the importance of your work? Do you think regulations grow on trees?"

"What's a tree?"

"It's just an expression. Questions, questions, questions, it's always the same with you, boy. Questions are for children. It's a sign of immaturity in someone your age. You would think you'd never heard of the Tenth Objective. I'm telling you, boy, you're playing with fire."

"What's fire?"

A further outburst followed and the call came to an end.

The call to his parents was more pleasant. Like him, they were unconventional. They had been together for twenty-five years, an almost unique situation; one of their friends described them as lovebirds, whatever that might mean.

They both appeared on the screen, sitting only a few feet from each other, as always. He told them of his failure to get promoted and about his world trip.

"Will that take you all week?" his mother asked.

"It will, if he gets lost as usual," said his father.

He had made these calls from his apartment, but decided to visit Alex in person.

Alex was the same age as Kirk and Ewan's parents, but he had never risen above Grade 1. Yet, in a single evening he could come out with more exciting ideas than Ewan had heard in a lifetime of listening to Kirk or anyone else. Alex lived in a tiny apartment appropriate to his grade, spending his perpetual leave in study and meditation. Any women in his life had long since given up on him.

Alex was enthusiastic about Ewan's trip. He suggested that Ewan visit a friend of his.

"I'll call Duncan and tell him you're coming. You'll like him. He's a kindred spirit."

Ewan was looking forward to his trip but, in fact, he could have made it without leaving his apartment. The whole world could be seen in the maps that were displayed in every public place. It could also be explored online, as a diagram, as simulated reality, or as real-time observation, picked up by the hidden eyes. He could have sat in front of his screen at home, travelling down every corridor, into every office and public place.

The world consisted of twenty-seven segments, varying in area and height. They were grouped in an irregular pattern and interconnected by a series of oblong corridors. Everything was rectangular in shape, apart from the Gymnasium, which was circular and located near the centre. The segments were not on one level plane, but sat at different heights, so that a single connecting corridor could join the ground floor of one segment to the second or third floor of another.

Ewan was hoping that in a remote corner he might find something new. Something to answer a few of his many questions about the world.

○

Some of Ewan's questions with typical responses:

EWAN: Why is the Journey called that? It suggests that the world is travelling somewhere. But that doesn't make sense.
MOTHER: Dear oh dear, where does he get all this nonsense from?
FATHER: Not from me, it must be from you.

KIRK:	The Journey should not be taken literally. It is a metaphor.
EWAN:	But what's it a metaphor for?
KIRK:	Greater minds than ours devised these things, Ewan. It is not your place to question the wisdom of the Creators.
ALEX:	It could be a metaphor for the journey through life we all make. Or possibly the Journey had a literal origin that has become forgotten over the generations. Maybe the world is a giant vessel in transit. Or the Journey may simply be a myth, invented by superstitious people to explain their existence.
EWAN:	Why do we have to work? Everything's provided for us— food, clothing, the apartments we live in. We don't make anything.
KIRK:	The answer's in the Ten Objectives. Read them again and stop asking foolish questions.
ALEX:	What else would people do with their time? They invented work to fill the emptiness in their lives. They work hard, get promoted and are given a bigger apartment.
EWAN:	If the Creators designed the world, why does its structure seem so random? The segments are fitted together in a haphazard way, almost as if there's been a gradual expansion over time, with parts added on here and there when needed. But this makes no sense: if the world is everything that exists, where would you find the space to add on an extra part?
KIRK:	Greater minds etc.
ALEX:	How do you know the world is everything that exists? Maybe the Creators are a superior, non-human, race, who keep us in captivity in order to observe our habits, or to provide them with entertainment. There may be more hidden eyes than the ones we can access online. Or the Creators may have been an earlier generation of humans, whose learning was much greater than ours, and they built the machines that feed and clothe us and keep us alive. Maybe there was a great disaster, of which our ancestors were the only survivors. The machines could have continued to function on their own, even though we have forgotten how they were made. Or perhaps there are no

	Creators. Maybe the world evolved over time by a series of accidents. That would explain its random structure.
EWAN:	But some things must have been designed. What about videophones, food and clothing dispensers, diagnostic machines? Or the human brain? How could that possibly have evolved by accident?
ALEX:	I agree, but the alternative makes no more sense. If our philosophy requires the existence of creators, then we are left with the problem of who created the Creators. It becomes an infinite regression.
EWAN:	Alex says...
KIRK:	Why do you pay any attention to that loser? Look at the size of his apartment compared with mine. That tells you all you need to know about the world.
ALEX:	What does he do by himself in that big apartment? He has as little success with women as I do.

○

Before his visit to Alex, Ewan had had no definite idea about his route. Visiting Alex's friend Duncan was as good a plan as any, since his apartment was at the opposite corner of the world. It was as long a trip as the world had to offer, particularly by the roundabout journey which its design imposed upon him. He worked out a route and set off early next morning.

He still got lost as he passed through the segments, forced continually to double back in the maze of corridors, seeming to go down as many flights of stairs as he went up. Eventually, only one segment away from the end of his journey and well after his usual lunch break, he arrived at a canteen. He stopped for a meal, then set off to find the exit for Segment M.

Duncan's segment was the smallest in the world. It was linked to only one other segment and its connecting corridor was one of the longest. It really was a far-flung outpost. As Ewan made his way along the corridor the crowds had thinned and he passed only the occasional fellow traveller.

He walked past the corridor leading to Duncan's apartment several times before he found it. It was long and narrow and eventually ended opposite a single door.

He rang the doorbell. A man's voice answered: "Ewan?"

"Yes."

"Come in."

He pushed the door open and entered the hallway of a tiny apartment. He had expected Duncan to meet him, but he didn't. It took him only a moment or two to confirm that Duncan wasn't in the apartment. He searched it again, this time more thoroughly. His next surprise came when he opened the door of the bedroom closet.

It wasn't a closet at all. The door led to a low, dimly lit passage. After only a moment's hesitation, he entered the passage and made his way along. Soon he came to a flight of stairs.

Stairs? But this segment was on a single level.

It was a spiral stairway, within a tubular stairwell. The stairs and walls were made of an unfamiliar material. It was cold, slightly damp, rough in texture, and solid, emitting practically no sound when struck. After climbing for ten minutes he had no idea how far he'd gone, but he was sure of one thing.

He was well beyond the roof of the segment. He was in a place no one else knew of, not even the arrogant and condescending Kirk who had always belittled him.

Eventually, the stairway ended opposite the entrance to a passage. He rested for a little while, then proceeded along it. The passage was different from any he had seen before. It was not rectangular in structure, but formed an irregular, roughly circular tunnel.

The light gradually got brighter. He turned a corner, entered an open area, and was dazzled.

When he managed to open his eyes, he was unable to make sense of the scene around him. Everywhere in his usual environment was bounded by walls, floors and ceilings. But not here. Gradually, the scene began to acquire meaning, as if he were cracking a code.

He was on a slope that led up to a peak far above him. At the bottom of the slope there was a flat area, grey in colour, but in places reflecting the light. The infinite space above, patched with various shades of grey, seemed to be the source of the light. The rough, asymmetrical surface on which he stood was brown in places and green in others, often sprouting sinewy structures mounted on gnarled stems. He was also conscious of movement in the space above him and realized that it was caused by things that flew about.

He had been expecting to catch up with Duncan, but there was no one else around.

It was cold, and he shivered in his thin tunic.

At first he could see nothing familiar in his new surroundings. Then he noticed that below him, beside the flat area, there was a square structure. It was like a familiar beacon in a strange and hostile place, and he made his way down towards it.

It was much further away than he had realized. He was also slowed down by the roughness of the surface beneath him. Once he was brought to a halt, terrified, when a huge animal, with an intricate array of hard-looking growths on its head, ran across his path. Later he saw a smaller animal, about the size of a cat, but with long ears and a round tail.

As he neared the structure he was walking on a softer surface, covered in an unkempt, green fur. Suddenly, water began to pour from above, soaking him. His terror grew again and he broke into a run. He reached the structure, found a door and went in.

He was in an apartment. It was gloomy, the only light coming through windows from outside. Above the ceiling he could hear the sound of the water, battering down upon the apartment's top. Near the door he found a light switch, but it wouldn't work. He was colder than ever and shivered uncontrollably in his wet tunic.

The apartment was small, but had several rooms, including a bedroom and bathroom. There was no sign of Duncan or anyone else. He found a towel in the bathroom, removed his tunic and dried himself. He was still cold. He went into the bedroom, climbed into the broad bed and wrapped himself in the thick bedclothes. The light grew even dimmer and soon it was completely dark.

He lay in the darkness for an age, in a condition of sustained panic. Eventually, worn out by emotion and the physical toll of his journey, he fell asleep.

When he awoke, the window was admitting a bright light. For a while he continued to lie wrapped in the warm bedclothes, before getting up into the cold room. His tunic was still damp, but a large, freestanding cupboard in the bedroom proved to be a wardrobe in which he found clothes. He dressed himself in a shirt, trousers, shoes and socks, all thick and clumsy, but wearable.

He still couldn't get the lights to work or get water from the taps. There was no food dispenser, no laundry hatch, no screen or electronic equipment of any kind, but most of the furnishings were recogniz-able, if basic. The only real puzzle was a number of thin, rectangular objects sitting upright, in rows, in a series of shelves that stood against the living room wall. They were of differing sizes and bore strange titles: *Little Dorrit, The Complete Works of William Shakespeare, The History of Western Philosophy, Clans and Their Tartans, The Highland-er's Cook Book, The Lady in the Lake, Stranglers in the Night, Lanark, Cumbernauld A-Z, Parkinson's Law, Catch 22, Lady Chatterley's Lover, The Holy Bible, The Mammoth Book of Vampires, Werewolves and Zom-bies*, and many others. That some of them called themselves books explained their function if not their content. Unlike normal books, which were summoned on-screen a page at a time, their pages had been separately printed on a thin material and bound together. He browsed through them for some time before an even greater curiosity took him outside.

A door on the other side of the apartment led him to the edge of the flat surface, which he could now see was a pool, much larger than the one in the Gymnasium. The light from above now appeared to come from a single source, which was too bright to look at directly. Behind him, the view was dominated by the huge structure down whose slope he had come. At the other side of the pool the terrain, though rough, was less elevated and...

There were several other apartments like the one he had spent the night in. And there were figures, moving figures.

People.

If he walked round the edge of the pool he would meet other people. Maybe Duncan would be among them. He hadn't gone far before he was stopped by a stream of water that flowed down the slope into the pool.

He realized that he was very hungry and thirsty. What happened to you if you didn't eat or drink?

He returned to the apartment and looked for food. In a cup-board, he found some, but it proved of little value. Some things were sealed inside hard, tubular containers, which he couldn't open, others—such as a packet marked Lang's Porridge Oats—required preparation from instructions that he couldn't understand. The only immediately edible things he could find were two packets con-taining some kind of biscuit: Cooper's Cream Crackers and Robb's

Highland Oatcakes. There were also several bottles, two of water, and another—labelled Laird's Sovereign Deluxe Scotch Whisky—containing a clear, golden liquid, which turned out to be an alcoholic spirit.

He ate some oatcakes and drank some water. These supplies wouldn't last long. His mobile didn't work here, so he had two options: go back the way he had come or join the people on the other side of the pool. He decided to try again to walk round the pool, but first he lifted the whisky bottle and sat down near the window to do some reading.

He skimmed through several books, including one called *Dialogues Concerning Natural Religion* by David Hume. He found its language strange and difficult to follow and was about to put it aside when a marked passage caught his attention:

> In a word, Cleanthes, a man who follows your hypothesis is able, perhaps, to assert or conjecture that the universe sometime arose from something like design; but beyond that position he cannot ascertain one single circumstance, and is left afterwards to fix every point of his theology by the utmost license of fancy and hypothesis. This world, for aught he knows, is very faulty and imperfect, compared to a superior standard, and was only the first rude essay of some infant deity who afterwards abandoned it, ashamed of his lame performance; it is the work only of some dependent, inferior deity, and is the object of derision to his superiors; it is the production of old age and dotage in some superannuated deity, and ever since his death has run on at adventures, from the first impulse and active force which it received from him.

Ewan switched to a series of books that promised to provide more enlightenment: *A Child's Illustrated Encyclopaedia*. He began to read and soon lost track of time.

Much remained beyond his comprehension, but he also learned words for many of the new things he had experienced. Other things provided references for previously meaningless words contained in traditional sayings.

Eventually he became drowsy and fell asleep. When he awoke it was growing dark outside. This time he was not afraid. It was merely nightfall, a new but explicable phenomenon. He went outside and looked at the sunset, another novel experience. At the other side of the loch—which he now knew to be the correct term—there were lights in the windows of the houses.

◦

Next morning, he identified a can-opener and breakfasted on tinned peaches and crackers. Then he began to walk round the loch, in the opposite direction from the burn. Within ten minutes he was stopped by a rock face, where a portion of the mountain protruded into the loch. He tried climbing to the top of the cliff, but was eventually stopped by a precipice. He walked back in the opposite direction, taking off his shoes to wade across the burn. Before long his route was blocked again. He tried climbing the mountain but discovered that all the paths eventually became impassable. Nor was he able to find the tunnel mouth.

His new home seemed to be cut off from the rest of the world.

But someone had lived there. There had to be a way out. As he made his way back to the house, he thought he knew what it was. Something he had seen beside the loch.

When he got back he examined the boat carefully. It was made of wood, a newly discovered material, and was larger and more clumsily built than the boats he was used to. Rowing was a sport he had often practised in the Gymnasium pool.

He pushed the boat into the water and spent some time near the shore, getting used to the new craft. From time to time he stopped to rest, and when he looked down into the water he could see dark shapes darting about. He realized they must be fish.

When he had finished, more than half the day was gone and he was exhausted from his exertions. He decided to postpone his journey another day.

He would have to move on soon. There was little usable food left, and to prepare any more he would need to make fire and boil water from the burn, difficult and dangerous undertakings he would prefer not to try.

He now knew what would happen if he ran out of food and water. He would die.

○

He set off early next morning. It was dry and the sun was out. He changed back into his tunic and also put on an overcoat he found in the wardrobe. He took his remaining provisions and the six-volume encyclopaedia that had answered so many of his questions.

He began to row towards the opposite shore. The water was calm and there was no wind. He soon realized that he had underestimated the distance, but he could see the other houses clearly in the morning light, as well as several people, and this encouraged him.

After a while he stopped for a rest. He was warm from his exertions and unbuttoned his coat.

Only now did he realize that the boat was leaking. He had been resting his feet against the other seat and hadn't noticed the puddle of water on the bottom of the boat.

He resumed his rowing. He was now more than halfway across the loch, so it was better to carry on. The sun became obscured by cloud and a wind started up. The water became choppy.

He was slowing down. The wind grew stronger, the waves higher and it began to rain. The puddle beneath him was growing. He stopped, turned round and waved to the people on the approaching shore. One of them waved back, but showed no indication of realizing that he was in trouble.

He began rowing again, but was now making hardly any headway. The wind had become a gale and the small boat was tossed about by the huge waves.

Suddenly, as quickly as the dropping of a curtain, a mist descended. Ewan stopped rowing and looked around him, trying to curb his panic. He could see nothing in front of him, behind him or on either side but the hazy outline of the boat and a pervading, opaque whiteness.

A huge wave crashed over the side of the boat and it sank.

Ewan was thrown into the water and he too began to sink. He managed to shed his overcoat and struggle to the surface. He swam in what he hoped was the right direction. He was a strong swimmer, but was tired from the rowing, and didn't know how long he could go on.

The water gradually seemed to grow warmer. The wind died down and the waves subsided. Then, as quickly as it had fallen, the mist lifted again.

It took Ewan a few moments to orient himself. He trod water and looked around. He was back among people: they were swimming around him and walking about in the middle distance. Above him, the sun was still obscured, but not by cloud. A lid had come down, shutting him off from the sky. On all sides, the horizon was once again bounded by walls.

He was back home, in the middle of the Gymnasium pool. He swam to the nearest side, his thoughts chaotic. A Grade 3 attendant helped him out. "Why are you swimming in your tunic?"

"What happened to that mist?"

"What mist?"

He walked towards the exit. Once the Gymnasium had been the biggest place in the world, but now it seemed quite small. What next? He was tired, wet and hungry. That was easy to remedy. He returned to his apartment, changed into dry clothes, then went to the Canteen for a meal.

As the turmoil in his mind began to settle, one thought obsessed him. Alex had sent him to the apartment of the elusive Duncan. Had he known what would happen? Could Alex be one of the Creators?

Next day he returned to Segment M, but couldn't find Duncan's apartment. The segment seemed different—busier and less isolated. Back in his apartment, he searched it again online, exploring every corridor via the hidden eyes.

Duncan's apartment and the corridor leading to it didn't exist.

Next day he visited Alex and told him his story. "Duncan's dead," Alex told him.

"When?"

"Two days ago. He was quite old."

Alex told Ewan that his experience seemed to confirm a new theory he had been developing. In a material world, how could Ewan have been instantly transferred from the loch to the Gymnasium? What if the world and the people in it had no reality at all? What if they were electronic simulations, assembled by the Creators in a great machine, with no more substance than the images online?

Ewan took his leave as soon as he could. What did Alex's new theory entail? That the universe in general, and he, Ewan, in particular—his body and the hunger, thirst, cold and exhaustion it had felt, the warmth and comfort it had returned to—was nothing more than an electronic phantom, with no physical existence?

The man was obviously mad. How could Ewan have suspected he was one of the Creators?

o

When he returned to work he discovered that Isla had been promoted and was now in another office. At first he was disappointed, then he felt relieved, as if an aching tooth had been pulled.

Several days had now passed since the end of his adventure. He had spent most of the time thinking about what had happened, reassessing his life, re-examining his priorities. What had he learned? In the outside world you were cold, hungry and lonely, and your life was in danger. By comparison, the old familiar world didn't seem so bad. He had much new knowledge, but no real answers: these were the sole property of the Creators, to be revealed or withheld at their whim. He could grow old and die before learning more, as Alex would before long, alone in a small apartment, with few friends. That wasn't the kind of life Ewan wanted.

Alex had called the previous evening and Ewan had told him how he felt. Alex hadn't believed him. "You're still in shock. The old, inquisitive Ewan will soon be back." But Ewan doubted it.

He enjoyed being back among his friends and applied himself to his work. If he continued to work hard he would soon be promoted. By the time he made it to Grade 6 he would be able to sit on committees and the time would drag less.

In the encyclopaedia, he had discovered what lovebirds were. It would be nice to be a lovebird, but Isla had been an unsuitable partner. There were other fish in the loch, other birds in the cage.

A week after his return Isla was replaced by a girl called Heather. It was an evocative name. She lacked Isla's cold beauty, but was vivacious and friendly. She seemed to like Ewan and enjoy his company.

He decided to ask her out.

For centuries, witchcraft has been inextricably entangled with the tapestry
of Scottish folklore. Although threaded through the warp of literature and
knotted into the weft of history, from Macbeth's blasted heath to Burns'
Alloway Kirk via the fifteenth-century pogrom ordered by James VI,
witchery is still rubbished as the stuff of tall tales and superstition. Yet,
it persists. Perhaps the reality is a mystery best left unravelled.

○ ○

A KNOT OF TOADS
Jane Yolen

○ ○

"*March 1931: Late on Saturday night,*" the old man had written, "*a
toad came into my study and looked at me with goggled eyes, reflecting my
candlelight back at me. It seemed utterly unafraid. Although nothing so far
seems linked with this appearance, I have had enough formidable visitants
to know this for a harbinger.*"

A harbinger of spring, I would have told him, but I arrived too late
to tell him anything. I'd been summoned from my Cambridge rooms
to his little whitewashed stone house with its red pantile roof over-
looking St Monans harbour. The summons had come from his housekeeper, Mrs Marr, in a frantic early morning phone call. Hers was
from the town's one hotel, to me in the porter's room which boasted
the only telephone at our college.

I was a miserable ten hours getting there. All during the long
train ride, though I tried to pray for him, I could not, having given
up that sort of thing long before leaving Scotland. Loss of faith, lack
of faith—that had been my real reason for going away from home.
Taking up a place at Gerton College had only been an excuse.

What I had wanted to do this return was to mend our fences
before it was too late to mend anything at all. Father and I had broken
so many fences—stones, dykes, stiles, and all—that the mending would
have taken more than the fortnight's holiday I had planned for later
in the summer. But I'd been summoned home early this March because, as Mrs Marr said, father had had a bad turn.

"A *verrry* bad turn," was what she'd actually said, before the
line had gone dead, her r's rattling like a kettle on the boil. In her

understated way, she might have meant anything from a twisted ankle to a major heart attack.

The wire that had followed, delivered by a man with a limp and a harelip, had been from my father's doctor, Ewan Kinnear. "Do not delay," it read. Still, there was no diagnosis.

Even so, I did not delay. We'd had no connection in ten years beside a holiday letter exchange. Me to him, not the other way round. But the old man was my only father. I was his only child.

He was dead by the time I got there, and Mrs Marr stood at the doorway of the house wringing her hands, her black hair caught up in a net. She had not aged a day since I last saw her.

"So ye've left it too late, Janet," she cried. "And wearing green I see."

I looked down at my best dress, a soft green linen now badly creased with travel.

She shook her head at me, and only then did I remember. In St Monans they always said, "After green comes grief."

"I didn't know he was that ill. I came as fast as I could."

But Mrs Marr's face showed her disdain for my excuse. Her eyes narrowed and she didn't put out her hand. She'd always been on father's side, especially in the matter of my faith. "His old heart's burst in twa." She was of the old school in speech as well as faith.

"His heart was stone, Maggie, and well you know it." A widow, she'd waited twenty-seven years, since my mother died birthing me, for the old man to notice her. She must be old herself now.

"Stane can still feel pain," she cried.

"What pain?" I asked.

"Of your leaving."

What good would it have done to point out I'd left more than ten years earlier and he'd hardly noticed. He'd had a decade more of calcification, a decade more of pouring over his bloody old books—the Latin texts of apostates and heretics. A decade more of filling notebooks with his crabbed script.

A decade more of ignoring his only child.

My God, I thought, meaning no appeal to a deity but a simple swear, *I am still furious with him. It's no wonder I've never married.* Though I'd had chances. Plenty of them. Well, two that were real enough.

I went into the house, and the smell of candle wax and fish and salt sea were as familiar to me as though I'd never left. But there was another smell, too.

Death.

And something more.

It was fear. But I was not to know that till later.

○

The study where evidently he'd died, sitting up in his chair, was a dark place, even when the curtains were drawn back, which had not been frequent in my childhood. Father liked the close, wood-panelled room, made closer by the ever-burning fire. I'd been allowed in there only when being punished, standing just inside the doorway, with my hands clasped behind me, to listen to my sins being counted. My sins were homey ones, like shouting in the hallway, walking too loudly by his door, or refusing to learn my verses from the Bible. I was far too innocent a child for more than that.

Even at five and six and seven I'd been an unbeliever. Not having a mother had made me so. How could I worship a God whom both Mrs Marr and my father assured me had so wanted mother, He'd called her away. A selfish God, that, who had listened to his own desires and not mine. Such a God was not for me. Not then. Not now.

I had a sudden urge—me, a postgraduate in a prestigious university who should have known better—to clasp my hands behind me and await my punishment.

But, I thought, *the old punisher is dead. And—if he's to be believed— gone to his own punishment.* Though I was certain that the only place he had gone was to the upstairs bedroom where he was laid out, awaiting my instructions as to his burial.

○

I went into every other room of the house but that bedroom, memory like an old fishing line dragging me on. The smells, the dark moody smells, remained the same, though Mrs Marr had a good wood fire burning in the grate, not peat, a wee change in this changeless place. But everything else was so much smaller than I remembered, my little bedroom at the back of the house the smallest of them all.

To my surprise, nothing in my bedroom had been removed. My

bed, my toys—the little wooden doll with jointed arms and legs I called Annie, my ragged copy of *Rhymes and Tunes for Little Folks*, the boxed chess set just the size for little hands, my cloth bag filled with buttons—the rag rug, the over-worked sampler on the wall. All were the same. I was surprised to even find one of my old pinafores and black stockings in the wardrobe. I charged Mrs Marr with more sentiment than sense. It was a shrine to the child that I'd been, not the young woman who had run off. It had to have been Mrs Marr's idea. Father would never have countenanced false gods.

Staring out of the low window, I looked out toward the sea. A fog sat on the horizon, white and patchy. Below it the sea was a deep, solitary blue. Spring comes early to the East Neuk but summer stays away. I guessed that pussy willows had already appeared around the edges of the lochans, snowdrops and aconite decorating the inland gardens.

Once I'd loved to stare out at that sea, escaping the dark brooding house whenever I could, even in a cutting wind, the kind that could raise bruises. Down I'd go to the beach to play amongst the yawls hauled up on the high wooden trestles, ready for tarring. Once I'd dreamed of going off to sea with the fishermen, coming home to the harbour in the late summer light, and seeing the silver scales glinting on the beach. Though of course fishing was not a woman's job. Not then, not now. A woman in a boat was unthinkable even this far into the twentieth century. St Monans is firmly eighteenth century and likely to remain so forever.

But I'd been sent off to school, away from the father who found me a loud and heretical discomfort. At first it was just a few towns away, to St Leonard's in St Andrews, but as I was a boarder—my father's one extravagance—it might as well have been across the country, or the ocean, as far as seeing my father was concerned. And there I'd fallen in love with words in books.

Words—not water, not wind.

In that way I showed myself to be my father's daughter. Only I never said so to him, nor he to me.

o

Making my way back down the stairs, I overheard several folk in the kitchen. They were speaking of those things St Monans folk always speak of, no matter their occupations: Fish and weather.

"There's been nae herring in the firth this winter," came a light man's voice. "Nane." Doctor Kinnear.

"It's a bitter wind to keep the men at hame, the fish awa'." Mrs Marr agreed.

Weather and the fishing. Always the same.

But a third voice, one I didn't immediately recognize, a rumbling growl of a voice, added, "Does she know?"

"Do I know what?" I asked, coming into the room where the big black-leaded grate threw out enough heat to warm the entire house. "How Father died?"

I stared at the last speaker, a stranger I thought, but somehow familiar. He was tall for a St Monans man, but dressed as one of the fisherfolk, in dark trousers, a heavy white sweater, thick white sea stockings. And he was sunburnt like them, too, with eyes the exact blue of the April sea, gathered round with laugh lines. A ginger moustache, thick and full, hung down the sides of his mouth like a parenthesis.

"By God, Alec Hughes," I said, startled to have remembered, surprised that I could have forgotten. He grinned.

When we'd been young—very young—Alec and I were inseparable. Never mind that boys and girls never played together in St Monans. Boys from the Bass, girls from the May, the old folk wisdom went. The Bass Rock, the Isle of May, the original separation of the sexes. Apart at birth and ever after. Yet Alec and I had done everything together: messed about with the boats, played cards, built sandcastles, fished with *pelns*— shore crabs about to cast their shells—and stolen jam pieces from his mother's kitchen to eat down by one of the gates in the drystone dykes. We'd even often hied off to the low cliff below the ruins of Andross Castle to look for *croupies*, fossils, though whether we ever found any I couldn't recall. When I'd been sent away to school, he'd stayed on in St Monans, going to Anstruther's Waid Academy in the next town but one, until he was old enough—I presumed—to join the fishing fleet, like his father before him. His father was a stern and dour soul, a Temperance man who used to preach in the open air.

Alec had been the first boy to kiss me, my back against the stone windmill down by the salt pans. And until I'd graduated from St Leonard's, the only boy to do so, though I'd made it up for that since.

"I thought, Jan," he said slowly, "that God was not in your vocabulary."

"Except as a swear," I retorted. "Good to see you, too, Alec."

Mrs Marr's eyebrows both rose considerably, like fulmars over the green-grey sea of her eyes.

Alec laughed and it was astonishing how that laugh reminded me of the boy who'd stayed behind. "Yes," he said. "Do ye ken how your father died?"

"Heart attack, so Mrs Marr told me."

I stared at the three of them. Mrs Marr was wringing her hands again, an oddly old-fashioned motion at which she seemed well practiced. Dr Kinnear polished his eyeglasses with a large white piece of cloth, his flyaway eyebrows proclaiming his advancing age. And Alec—had I remembered how blue his eyes were? Alec nibbled on the right end of his moustache.

"Did I say that?" Mrs Marr asked. "Bless me, I didna."

And indeed, she hadn't. She'd been more poetic.

"*Burst in twa*, you said." I smiled, trying to apologize for mis-speaking. Not a good trait in a scholar.

"Indeed. Indeed." Mrs Marr's wrangling hands began again. Any minute I supposed she would break out into a psalm. I remembered how her one boast was that she'd learned them all by heart as a child and never forgot a one of them.

"A shock, I would have said," Alec said by way of elaborating.

"A fright," the doctor added.

"Really? Is that the medical term?" I asked. "What in St Monans could my father possibly be frightened of?"

Astonishingly, Mrs Marr began to wail then, a high, thin keening that went on and on till Alec put his arm around her and marched her over to the stone sink where he splashed her face with cold water and she quieted at once. Then she turned to the blackened kettle squalling on the grate and started to make us all tea.

I turned to the doctor who had his glasses on now, which made him look like a somewhat surprised barn owl. "What do you really mean, Dr Kinnear."

"Have ye nae seen him yet?" he asked, his head gesturing towards the back stairs.

"I ... I couldn't," I admitted. But I said no more. How could I tell this man I hardly knew that my father and I were virtual strangers. No—it was more than that. I was afraid of my father dead as I'd never been alive. Because now he knew for certain whether he was right or I was, about God and Heaven and the rest.

"Come," said Doctor Kinnear in a voice that seemed permanently gentle. He held out a hand and led me back up the stairs and down the hall to my father's room. Then he went in with me and stood by my side as I looked down.

My father was laid out on his bed, the Scottish double my mother had died in, the one he'd slept in every night of his adult life except the day she'd given birth, the day she died.

Like the house, he was much smaller than I remembered. His wild, white hair lay untamed around his head in a kind of corolla. The skin of his face was parchment stretched over bone. That great prow of a nose was, in death, strong enough to guide a ship in. Thankfully his eyes were shut. His hands were crossed on his chest. He was dressed in an old dark suit. I remembered it well.

"He doesn't look afraid," I said. Though he didn't look peaceful either. Just dead.

"Once he'd lost the stiffness, I smoothed his face a bit," the doctor told me. "Smoothed it out. Otherwise Mrs Marr would no have settled."

"Settled?"

He nodded. "She found him at his desk, stone dead. Ran down the road screaming all the way to the pub. And lucky I was there, having a drink with friends. I came up to see yer father sitting up in his chair, with a face so full of fear, I looked around masel' to discover the cause of it."

"And did you?"

His blank expression said it all. He simply handed me a pile of five notebooks. "These were on the desk in front of him. Some of the writing is in Latin, which I have but little of. Perhaps ye can read it, being the scholar. Mrs Marr has said that they should be thrown on the fire, or at least much of them scored out. But I told her that had to be yer decision and Alec agrees."

I took the notebooks, thinking that this was what had stolen my father from me and now was all I had of him. But I said none of that aloud. After glancing over at the old man again, I asked, "May I have a moment with him?" My voice cracked on the final word.

Dr Kinnear nodded again and left the room.

I went over to the bed and looked down at the silent body. *The old dragon*, I thought, *has no teeth*. Then I heard a sound, something so tiny I scarcely registered it. Turning, I saw a toad by the bedfoot.

I bent down and picked it up. "Nothing for you here, puddock," I said, reverting to the old Scots word. Though I'd worked so hard to lose my accent and vocabulary, here in my father's house the old way of speech came flooding back. Shifting the books to one hand, I picked the toad up with the other. Then, I tiptoed out of the door as if my father would have minded the sound of my footsteps.

Once outside, I set the toad gently in the garden, or the remains of the garden, now so sadly neglected, its vines running rampant across what was once an arbour of white roses and red. I watched as it hopped under some large dock leaves and, quite effectively, disappeared.

o

Later that afternoon my father's body was taken away by three burly men for its chestening, being placed into its coffin and the lid screwed down. Then it would lie in the cold kirk till the funeral the next day.

Once he was gone from the house, I finally felt I could look in his journals. I might have sat comfortably in the study, but I'd never been welcomed there before, so didn't feel it my place now. The kitchen and sitting room were more Mrs Marr's domain than mine. And if I never had to go back into the old man's bedroom, it would be years too soon for me.

So I lay in my childhood bed, the covers up to my chin, and read by the flickering lamplight. Mrs Marr, bless her, had brought up a warming pan which she came twice to refill. And she brought up as well a pot of tea and jam pieces and several slabs of good honest cheddar.

"I didna think ye'd want a big supper."

She was right. Food was the last thing on my mind.

After she left the room, I took a silver hip flask from under my pillow where I'd hidden it, and then poured a hefty dram of whisky into the teapot. I would need more than Mrs Marr's offerings to stay warm this night. Outside the sea moaned as it pushed past the skellies, on its way to the shore. I'd all but forgotten that sound. It made me smile.

I read the last part of the last journal first, where father talked about the toad, wondering briefly if it was the very same toad I had found at his bedfoot. But it was the bit right after, where he spoke of "formidable visitants" that riveted me. What had he meant? From the tone of it, I didn't think he meant any of our St Monans neighbours.

The scholar in me asserted itself, and I turned to the first of the journals, marked 1926, some five years earlier. There was one book for each year. I started with that first notebook and read long into the night.

The journals were not easy to decipher for my father's handwriting was crabbed with age and, I expect, arthritis. The early works were splotchy and, in places, faded. Also he had inserted sketchy pictures and diagrams. Occasionally he'd written whole paragraphs in corrupted Latin, or at least in a dialect unknown to me.

What he seemed engaged upon was a study of a famous trial of local witches in 1590, supervised by King James VI himself. The VI of Scotland, for he was Mary Queen of Scots' own son, and Queen Elizabeth's heir.

The witches, some ninety in all according to my father's notes, had been accused of sailing over the Firth to North Berwick in riddles—sieves, I think he meant—to plot the death of the king by raising a storm when he sailed to Denmark. However, I stumbled so often over my Latin translations, I decided I needed a dictionary. And me a Classics scholar.

So halfway through the night, I rose and, taking the lamp, made my way through the cold dark, tiptoeing so as not to wake Mrs Marr. Nothing was unfamiliar beneath my bare feet. The kitchen stove would not have gone out completely, only filled with gathering coal and kept minimally warm. All those years of my childhood came rushing back. I could have gone into the study without the lamp, I suppose. But to find the book I needed, I'd have to have light.

And lucky indeed I took it, for in its light I saw—gathered on the floor of my father's study—a group of toads throwing strange shadows up against the bookshelves. I shuddered to think what might have happened had I stepped barefooted amongst them.

But how had they gotten in? And was the toad I'd taken into the garden amongst them? Then I wondered aloud at what such a gathering should be called. I'd heard of a murder of crows, an exaltation of larks. Perhaps toads came in a congregation? For that is what they looked like, a squat congregation, huddled together, nodding their heads, and waiting on the minister in this most unlikely of kirks.

It was too dark even with the lamp, and far too late, for me to round them up. So I sidestepped them and, after much searching, found the Latin dictionary where it sat cracked open on my father's desk. I grabbed it up, avoided the congregation of toads, and went out the door. When I looked back, I could still see the odd shadows dancing along the walls.

I almost ran back to my bed, shutting the door carefully behind me. I didn't want that dark presbytery coming in, as if they could possibly hop up the stairs like the frog in the old tale, demanding to be taken to my little bed.

But the shock of my father's death and the long day of travel, another healthy swallow of my whisky, as well as that bizarre huddle of toads, all seemed to combine to put me into a deep sleep. If I dreamed, I didn't remember any of it. I woke to one of those dawn choruses of my childhood, comprised of blackbirds, song thrushes, gulls, rooks, and jackdaws, all arguing over who should wake me first.

o

For a moment I couldn't recall where I was. Eyes closed, I listened to the birds, so different from the softer, more lyrical sounds outside my Cambridge windows. But I woke fully in the knowledge that I was back in my childhood home, that my father was dead and to be buried that afternoon if possible, as I had requested of the doctor and Mrs Marr, and I had only hours to make things tidy in my mind. Then I would be away from St Monans and its small-mindedness, back to Cambridge where I truly belonged.

I got out of bed, washed, dressed in the simple black dress I always travel with, a black bandeau on my fair hair, and went into the kitchen to make myself some tea.

Mrs Marr was there before me, sitting on a hardback chair and knitting a navy-blue guernsey sweater with its complicated patterning. She set the steel needles down and handed me a full cup, the tea nearly black even with its splash of milk. There was a heaping bowl of porridge, sprinkled generously with salt, plus bread slathered with golden syrup.

"Thank you," I said. It would have done no good to argue that I drank coffee now, nor did I like either oatmeal or treacle, and never ate till noon. Besides, I was suddenly ravenous. "What do you need me to do?" I asked between mouthfuls, stuffing them in the way I'd done as a youngster.

"'Tis all arranged," she said, taking up the needles again. No proper St Monans woman was ever idle long. "Though sooner than is proper. But all to accommodate ye, he'll be in the kirkyard this afternoon. Lucky for ye it's a Sunday, or we couldna do it. The men are home from fishing." She was clearly not pleased with me. "Ye just need to be there at the service. Not that many will come. He was no generous with his company." By which she meant he had few friends. Nor relatives except me.

"Then I'm going to walk down by the water this morning," I told her. "Unless you have something that needs doing. I want to clear my head."

"Aye, ye would."

Was that condemnation or acceptance? Who could tell? Perhaps she meant I was still the thankless child she remembered. Or that I was like my father. Or that she wanted only to see the back of me, sweeping me from her domain so she could clean and bake without my worrying presence. I thanked her again for the meal, but she wanted me gone. As I had been for the past ten years. And I was as eager to be gone, as she was to have me. The funeral was not till mid-afternoon.

"There are toads in the study," I said as I started out the door.

"Toads?" She looked startled. Or perhaps frightened.

"Puddocks. A congregation of them."

Her head cocked to one side. "Och, ye mean a knot. A knot of toads."

A knot. Of course. I should have remembered. "Shall I put them out?" At least I could do that for her.

She nodded. "Aye."

I found a paper sack and went into the study, but though I looked around for quite some time, I couldn't find the toads anywhere. If I hadn't still had the Latin dictionary in my bedroom, I would have thought my night visit amongst them and my scare from their shadows had been but a dream.

"All gone," I called to Mrs Marr before slipping out through the front door and heading toward the strand.

○

Nowhere in St Monans is far from the sea. I didn't realize how much the sound of it was in my bones until I moved to Cambridge. Or how much I'd missed that sound till I slept the night in my old room.

I found my way to the foot of the church walls where boats lay upturned, looking like beached dolphins. A few of the older men, past their fishing days, sat with their backs against the salted stone, smoking silently, and staring out to the grey slatey waters of the Forth. Nodding to them, I took off along the beach. Overhead gulls squabbled and far out, near the Bass Rock, I could see gannets diving headfirst into the water.

A large boat, some kind of yacht, had just passed the Bass and was sailing west majestically toward a mooring, probably in South Queensferry. I wondered who would be sailing these waters in such a ship.

But then I was interrupted by the wind sighing my name. Or so I thought at first. Then I looked back at the old kirk on the cliff above me. Someone was waving at me in the ancient kirkyard. It was Alec.

He signalled that he was coming down to walk with me and, as I waited, I thought about what a handsome man he'd turned into. *But a fisherman*, I reminded myself, a bit of the old snobbery biting me on the back of the neck. St Monans, like the other fishing villages of the East Neuk, was made up of three classes—fisher folk, farmers, and the shopkeepers and tradesmen. My father being a scholar was outside of them all, which meant that, as his daughter, I belonged to none of them either.

Still, in this place, where I was once so much a girl of the town— from the May—I felt my heart give a small stutter. I remembered that first kiss, so soft and sweet and innocent, the windmill hard against my back. My last serious relationship had been almost a year ago, and I was more than ready to fall in love again. Even at the foot of my father's grave. But not with a fisherman. Not in St Monans.

Alec found his way down to the sand and came toward me. "Off to find croupies?" he called.

I laughed. "The only fossil I've found recently has been my father," I said, then bit my lower lip at his scowl.

"He was nae a bad man, Jan," he said, catching up to me. "Just undone by his reading."

I turned a glared at him. "Do you think reading an ailment then?"

He put up his hands palms towards me. "Whoa, lass. I'm a big reader myself. But what the old man had been reading lately had clearly unnerved him. He couldna put it into context. Mrs Marr said as much before ye came. These last few months he'd stayed away from the pub, from the kirk, from everyone who'd known him well. No one kent what he'd been on about."

I wondered what sort of thing Alec would be reading. *The fishing report? The local paper?* Feeling out of sorts, I said sharply, "Well, I was going over his journals last night and what he's been on about are the old North Berwick witches."

Alec's lips pursed. "The ones who plotted to blow King James off the map." It was a statement, not a question.

"The very ones."

"Not a smart thing for the unprepared to tackle."

I wondered if Alec had become as hag-ridden and superstitious as any St Monans' fisherman. Ready to turn home from his boat if he met a woman on the way. Or not daring to say "salmon" or "pig" and instead speaking of "red fish" and "curly tail", or shouting out "Cauld iron!" at any mention of them. All the East Neuk tip-leavings I was glad to be shed of.

He took the measure of my disapproving face, and laughed. "Ye take me for a gowk," he said. "But there are more things in heaven and earth, Janet, than are dreamt of in yer philosophy."

I laughed as Shakespeare tumbled from his lips. Alec could always make me laugh. "Pax," I said.

He reached over, took my hand, gave it a squeeze. "Pax." Then he dropped it again as we walked along the beach, a comfortable silence between us.

The tide had just turned and was heading out. Gulls, like satisfied housewives, sat happily in the receding waves. One lone boat was on the horizon, a small fishing boat, not the yacht I had seen earlier, which must already be coming into its port. The sky was that wonderful spring blue, without a threatening cloud, not even the fluffy Babylonians, as the fishermen called them.

"Shouldn't you be out there?" I said, pointing at the boat as we passed by the smoky fish-curing sheds.

"I rarely get out there anymore," he answered, not looking at me but at the sea. "Too busy until summer. And why old man Sinclair is fishing when the last of the winter herring have been hauled in, I canna fathom."

I turned toward him. "Too busy with what?"

He laughed. "Och, Janet, yer so caught up in yer own preconceptions, ye canna see what's here before yer eyes."

I didn't answer right away, and the moment stretched between us, as the silence had before. Only this was not comfortable. At last I said, "Are you too busy to help me solve the mystery of my father's death?"

"Solve the mystery of his life first," he told me, "and the mystery of his death will inevitably be revealed." Then he touched his cap, nodded at me, and strolled away.

I was left to ponder what he said. Or what he meant. I certainly wasn't going to chase after him. I was too proud to do that. Instead, I went back to the house, changed my shoes, made myself a plate of bread and cheese. There was no wine in the house. Mrs Marr was as Temperance as Alec's old father had been. But I found some miserable sherry hidden in my father's study. It smelled like turpentine, so I made do with fresh milk, taking the plate and glass up to my bedroom, to read some more of my father's journals until it was time to bury him.

o

It is not too broad a statement to say that Father was clearly out of his mind. For one, he was obsessed with local witches. For another, he seemed to believe in them. While he spared a few paragraphs for Christian Dote, St Monans' home-grown witch of 1640s, and a bit more about the various Anstruther, St Andrews, and Crail trials—listing the hideous tortures, and executions of hundreds of poor old women in his journal entries—it was the earlier North Berwick crew who really seemed to capture his imagination. By the third year's journal, I could see that he obviously considered the North Berwick witchery evil real, whereas the others, a century later, he dismissed as deluded or senile old women, as deluded and senile as the men who hunted them.

Here is what he wrote about the Berwick corps: "*They were a scabrous bunch, these ninety greedy women and six men, wanting no more than what they considered their due: a king and his bride dead in the sea, a kingdom in ruins, themselves set up in high places.*"

"Oh, Father," I whispered, "what a noble mind is here o'erthrown." For whatever problems I'd had with him—and they were many—I had always admired his intelligence.

He described the ceremonies they indulged in, and they were awful. In the small North Berwick church, fuelled on wine and sex, the witches had begun a ritual to call up a wind that would turn over the royal ship and drown King James. First they'd christened a cat with the name of Hecate, while black candles flickered fitfully along the walls of the apse and nave. Then they tortured the poor creature by passing it back and forth across a flaming hearth. Its elf-knotted hair caught fire and burned slowly, and the little beastie screamed in agony. The smell must have been appalling, but he doesn't mention that. I once caught my hair on fire, bending over a stove on a cold night in Cambridge, and it was the smell that was the worst of it. It lingered in my room for days.

Then I thought of my own dear moggie at home, a sweet orange-coloured puss who slept each night at my bedfoot. If anyone ever treated her the way the North Berwick witches had that poor cat, I'd be more than ready to kill. And not with any wind, either.

But there was worse yet, and I shuddered as I continued reading. One of the men, so Father reported, had dug up a corpse from the church cemetery, and with a companion had cut off the dead man's hands and feet. Then the witches attached the severed parts to the cat's paws. After this they attached the corpse's sex organs to the cat's. I could only hope the poor creature was dead by this point. After this desecration, they proceeded to a pier at the port of Leith where they flung the wee beastie into the sea.

Father wrote: "*A storm was summarily raised by this foul method, along with the more traditional knotted twine. The storm blackened the skies, with wild gales churning the sea. The howl of the wind could be heard all the way*

across the Firth to Fife. But the odious crew had made a deadly miscalcula-
tion. The squall caught a ship crossing from Kinghorn to Leith and smashed
it to pieces all right, but it was not the king's ship. The magic lasted only long
enough to kill a few innocent sailors on that first ship, and then blew itself
out to sea. As for the king, he proceeded over calmer waters with his bride,
arriving safely in Denmark and thence home again to write that great trea-
tise on witchcraft, Demonology, *and preside over a number of witch trials*
thereafter."

I did not read quickly because, as I have said, parts of the journal
were in a strange Latin and for those passages I needed the help of
the dictionary. I was like a girl at school with lines to translate by
morning, frustrated, achingly close to comprehension, but somehow
missing the point. In fact, I did not understand them completely
until I read them aloud. And then suddenly, as a roiled liquid settles
at last, all became clear. The passages were some sort of incantation,
or invitation, to the witches and to the evil they so devoutly and
hideously served.

I closed the journal and shook my head. Poor Father. He wrote as
if the witchcraft were fact, not a coincidence of gales from the south-
east that threw up vast quantities of seaweed on the shore, and the
haverings of tortured old women. Put a scold's bridle on me, and I
would probably admit to intercourse with the devil. Any devil. And
describe him and his nether parts as well.

But Father's words, as wild and unbelievable as they were, held
me in a kind of thrall. And I would have remained on my bed reading further if Mrs Marr hadn't knocked on the door and summoned
me to his funeral.

She looked me over carefully, but for once I seemed to pass muster, my smart black Cambridge dress suitable for the occasion. She
handed me a black hat. "I didna think ye'd have thought to bring
one." Her lips drew down into a thin, straight line.

Standing before me, her plain black dress covered at the top by a
solemn dark shawl, and on her head an astonishing hat covered with
artificial black flowers, she was clearly waiting for me to say something.

"Thank you," I said at last. And it was true, bringing a hat along
hadn't occurred to me at all. I took off the bandeau, and set the
proffered hat on my head. It was a perfect fit, though it made me

look fifteen years older, with its masses of black feathers, or so the mirror told me.

Lips pursed, she nodded at me, then turned, saying over her shoulder, "Young Mary McDougall did for him."

It took me a moment to figure out what she meant. Then I remembered. Though she must be nearer sixty than thirty, Mary McDougall had been both midwife and dresser of the dead when I was a child. So it had been she and not Mrs Marr who must have washed my father and put him into the clothes he'd be buried in. *So Mrs Marr missed out on her last great opportunity to touch him,* I thought.

"What do I give her?" I asked to Mrs Marr's ramrod back.

Without turning around again, she said, "We'll give her all yer father's old clothes. She'll be happy enough with that."

"But surely a fee..."

She walked out of the door.

It was clear to me then that nothing had changed since I'd left. It was still the nineteenth century. Or maybe the eighteenth. I longed for the burial to be over and done with, my father's meagre possessions sorted, the house sold, and me back on a train heading south.

○

We walked to the kirk in silence, crossing over the burn which rushed along beneath the little bridge. St Monans has always been justifiably proud of its ancient kirk and even in this dreary moment I could remark its beauty. Some of its stonework runs back in an unbroken line to the thirteenth century.

And some of its customs, I told myself without real bitterness.

When we entered the kirk proper, I was surprised to see that Mrs Marr had been wrong. She'd said not many would come, but the church was overfull with visitors.

We walked down to the front. As the major mourners, we commanded the first pew, Mrs Marr, the *de facto* wife, and me, the runaway daughter. There was a murmur when we sat down together, not quite of disapproval, but certainly of interest. Gossip in a town like St Monans is everybody's business.

Behind us, Alex and Dr Kinnear were already settled in. And three men sat beside them, men whose faces I recognized, friends of my father's, but grown so old. I turned, nodded at them with, I hope, a smile that thanked them for coming. They didn't smile back.

In the other pews were fishermen and shopkeepers and the few teachers I could put a name to. But behind them was a congregation of strangers who leaned forward with an avidity that one sees only in the faces of vultures at their feed. I knew none of them and wondered if they were newcomers to the town. Or if it was just that I hadn't been home in so long, even those families who'd been here forever were strangers to me now.

Father's pine box was set before the altar and I kept my eyes averted, watching instead an ettercap, a spider, slowly spinning her way from one edge of the pulpit to the other. No one in the town would have removed her, for it was considered bad luck. It kept me from sighing, it kept me from weeping.

The minister went on for nearly half an hour, lauding my father's graces, his intelligence, his dedication. If any of us wondered about whom he was talking, we didn't answer back. But when it was over, and six large fishermen, uneasy in their Sunday clothes, stood to shoulder the coffin, I leaped up with them. Putting my hand on the pine top, I whispered, "I forgive you, Father. Do you forgive me?"

There was an audible gasp from the congregation behind me, though I'd spoken so low, I doubted any of them—not even Alec—could have heard me. I sat down again, shaken and cold.

And then the fishermen took him off to the kirkyard, to a grave so recently and quickly carved out of the cold ground, its edges were jagged. As we stood there, a huge black cloud covered the sun. The tide was dead low and the bones of the sea, those dark grey rock skellies, showed in profusion like the spines of some prehistoric dragons.

As I held on to Mrs Marr's arm, she suddenly started shaking so hard, I thought she would shake me off.

How she must have loved my father, I thought, and found myself momentarily jealous.

Then the coffin was lowered, and that stopped her shaking. As the first clods were shovelled into the gaping hole, she turned to me and said, "Well, that's it then."

○

So we walked back to the house where a half dozen people stopped in for a dram or three of whisky—brought in by Alec despite Mrs Marr's strong disapproval. "There's a deil in every mouthful of whisky," she muttered, setting out the fresh baked shortbread and sultana cakes with a pitcher of lemonade. To mollify her, I drank the lemonade, but I was the only one.

Soon I was taken aside by an old man—Jock was his name—and told that my father had been a great gentleman though late had turned peculiar. Another, bald and wrinkled, drank his whisky down in a single gulp, before declaring loudly that my father had been "one for the books". He managed to make that sound like an affliction. One woman of a certain age who addressed me as "Mistress", added, apropos of nothing, "He needs a lang-shankit spoon that sups wi' the Deil." Even Alec, sounding like the drone on a set of bagpipes, said, "Now you can get on with your own living, Jan," as if I hadn't been doing just that all along.

For a wake, it was most peculiar. No humorous anecdotes about the dearly departed, no toasts to his soul, only half-baked praise and a series of veiled warnings.

Thank goodness no one stayed long. After the last had gone, I insisted on doing the washing up, and this time Mrs Marr let me. And then she, too, left. Where she went I wasn't to know. One minute she was there, and the next away.

I wondered at that. After all, this was her home, certainly more than mine. I was sure she'd loved my father who, God knows, was not particularly loveable, but she walked out the door clutching her big handbag, without a word more to me; not a goodbye or "I'll not be long", or anything. And suddenly, there I was, all alone in the house for the first time in years. It was an uncomfortable feeling. I am not afraid of ghosts, but that house fairly burst with ill will, dark and brooding. So as soon as I'd tidied away the dishes, I went out, too, though not before slipping the final journal into the pocket of my overcoat and winding a long woollen scarf twice around my neck to ward off the chill.

○

The evening was drawing in slowly, but there was otherwise a soft feel in the air, unusual for the middle of March. The East Neuk is like that—one minute still and the next a flanny wind rising.

I headed east along the coastal path, my guide the stone head of the windmill with its narrow, ruined vanes lording it over the flat land. Perhaps sentiment was leading me there, the memory of that adolescent kiss that Alec had given me, so wonderfully innocent and full of desire at the same time. Perhaps I just wanted a short, pleasant walk to the old salt pans. I don't know why I went that way. It was almost as if I were being called there.

For a moment I turned back and looked at the town behind me which showed, from this side, how precariously the houses perch on the rocks, like gannets nesting on the Bass.

Then I turned again and took the walk slowly; it was still only ten or fifteen minutes to the windmill from the town. No boats sailed on the Firth today. I could not spot the large yacht so it must have been in its berth. And the air was so clear, I could see the Bass and the May with equal distinction. How often I'd come to this place as a child. I probably could still walk to it barefooted and without stumbling, even in the blackest night. The body has a memory of its own.

Halfway there, a solitary curlew flew up before me and as I watched it flap away, I thought how the townsfolk would have cringed at the sight, for the bird was thought to bring bad luck, carrying away the spirits of the wicked at nightfall.

"But I've not been wicked," I cried after it, and laughed. *Or at least not wicked for a year, more's the pity.*

At last I came to the windmill with its rough stones rising high above the land. Once it had been used for pumping sea water to extract the salt. Not a particularly easy operation, it took something like thirty-two tons of water to produce one ton of salt. We'd learned all about it in primary school, of course. But the days of the salt pans were a hundred years in the past, and the poor windmill had seen better times.

Even run down, though, it was still a lovely place, with its own memories. Settling back against the mill's stone wall, I nestled down and drew out the last journal from my coat pocket. Then I began to read it from the beginning as the light slowly faded around me.

Now, I am a focused reader, which is to say that once caught up in a book, I can barely swim back up to the surface of any other consciousness. The world dims around me. Time and space compress. Like a Wellsian hero, I am drawn into an elsewhere that becomes absolute and real. So as I read my father's final journal, I was in his head and his madness so completely, I heard nothing around me, not the raucous cry of gulls nor the wash of water onto the stones far below.

So it was, with a start, that I came to the final page, with its mention of the goggle-eyed toad. Looking up, I found myself in the grey gloaming surrounded by nearly a hundred such toads, all staring at me with their horrid wide eyes, a hideous echo of my father's written words.

I stood up quickly, trying desperately not to squash any of the poor puddocks. They leaned forward like children trying to catch the warmth of a fire. Then their shadows lengthened and grew.

Please understand, there was no longer any sun and very little light. There was no moon overhead for the clouds crowded one on to the other, and the sky was completely curtained. So there should not have been any shadows at all. Yet, I state again—their shadows lengthened and grew. Shadows like and unlike the ones I had seen against my father's study walls. They grew into dark-caped creatures, almost as tall as humans yet with those goggly eyes.

I still held my father's journal in my left hand, but my right covered my mouth to keep myself from screaming. My sane mind knew it to be only a trick of the light, of the dark. It was the result of bad dreams and just having put my only living relative into the ground. But the primitive brain urged me to cry out with all my ancestors, "Cauld iron!" and run away in terror.

And still the horrid creatures grew until now they towered over me, pushing me back against the windmill, their shadowy fingers grabbing at both ends of my scarf.

Who are you? What are you? I mouthed, as the breath was forced from me. Then they pulled and pulled the scarf until they'd choked me into unconsciousness.

◦

When I awoke, I was tied to a windmill vane, my hands bound high above me, the ropes too tight and well-knotted for any escape.

"Who are you?" I whispered aloud this time, my voice sounding froglike, raspy, hoarse. "What are you?" Though I feared I knew. "What do you want of me? Why are you here?"

In concert, their voices wailed back. "A wind! A wind!"

And then in horror all that Father had written—about the hands and feet and sex organs of the corpse being cut off and attached to the dead cat—bore down upon me. Were they about to dig poor father's corpse up? Was I to be the offering? Were we to be combined in some sort of desecration too disgusting to be named? I began to shudder within my bonds, both hot and cold. For a moment I couldn't breathe again, as if they were tugging on the scarf once more.

Then suddenly, finding some latent courage, I stood tall and screamed at them, "I'm not dead yet!" Not like my father whom they'd frightened into his grave.

They crowded around me, shadow folk with wide white eyes, laughing. "A wind! A wind!"

I kicked out at the closest one, caught my foot in its black cape, but connected with nothing more solid than air. Still that kick forced them back for a moment.

"Get away from me!" I screamed. But screaming only made my throat ache, for I'd been badly choked just moments earlier. I began to cough and it was as if a nail were being driven through my temples with each spasm.

The shadows crowded forward again, their fingers little breezes running over my face and hair, down my neck, touching my breasts.

I took a deep breath for another scream, another kick. But before I could deliver either, I heard a cry.

"Aroint, witches!"

Suddenly I distinguished the sound of running feet. Straining to see down the dark corridor that was the path to Pittenweem, I leaned against the cords that bound me. It was a voice I did and did not recognize.

The shadow folk turned as one and flowed along the path, hands before them as if they were blindly seeking the interrupter.

"Aroint, I say!"

Now I knew the voice. It was Mrs Marr, in full cry. But her curse seemed little help and I feared that she, too, would soon be trussed up by my side.

But then, from the east, along the path nearer town, there came another call.

"Janet! Janet!" That voice I recognized at once.

"Alec..." I said between coughs.

The shadows turned from Mrs Marr and flowed back, surrounding Alec, but he held something up in his hand. A bit of a gleam from a crossbar. His fisherman's knife.

The shadows fell away from him in confusion.

"Cauld iron!" he cried at them. "Cauld iron!"

So they turned to go back again towards Mrs Marr, but she reached into her large handbag and pulled out her knitting needles. Holding them before her in the sign of a cross, she echoed Alec's cry. "Cauld iron!" And then she added, her voice rising as she spoke, "Oh let the wickedness of the wicked come to an end; but establish the just: for the righteous God trieth the hearts and reigns."

I recognized it as part of a psalm, presumably one of the many she'd memorized as a child, but I could not have said which.

Then the two of them advanced on the witches, coming from east and west, forcing the awful crew to shrink down, as if melting, into dark puddocks once again.

Then step by careful step, Alec and Mrs Marr herded the knot of toads off the path and over the cliff's edge.

Suddenly the clouds parted and a brilliant half moon shone down on us, its glare as strong as the lighthouse on Anster's pier. I watched as the entire knot of toads slid down the embankment, some falling onto the rocks and some into the water below.

Only when the last puddock was gone, did Alec turn to me. Holding the knife in his teeth, he reached above my head to my bound hands and began to untie the first knot.

A wind started to shake the vanes and for a second I was lifted off my feet as the mill tried to grind, though it had not done so for a century.

"Stop!" Mrs Marr's voice held a note of desperation.

Alec turned. "Would ye leave her tied, woman? What if those shades come back again. I told ye what the witches had done before. It was all in his journals."

"No, Alec," I cried, hating myself for trusting the old ways, but changed beyond caring. "They're elf-knots. Don't untie them. Don't!" I shrank away from his touch.

"Aye," Mrs Marr said, coming over and laying light fingers on Alec's arm. "The lass is still of St Monan's though she talks like a Sassenach." She laughed. "It's no the drink and the carousing that brings the wind. That's just for fun. Nor the corpse and the cat. That's just for show. My man told me. It's the knots, he says."

"The knot of toads?" Alec asked hoarsely.

The wind was still blowing and it took Alec's hard arms around me to anchor me fast or I would have gone right around, spinning with the vanes.

Mrs Marr came close till they were eye to eye. "The knots in the rope, lad," she said. "One brings a wind, two bring a gale, and the third..." She shook her head. "Ye dinna want to know about the third."

"But—" Alec began.

"Och, but me know buts, my lad. Cut between," Mrs Marr said. "Just dinna untie them or King George's yacht at South Queensferry will go down in a squall, with the king and queen aboard, and we'll all be to blame."

He nodded and slashed the ropes with his knife, between the knots, freeing my hands. Then he lifted me down. I tried to take it all in: his arms, his breath on my cheek, the smell of him so close. I tried to understand what had happened here in the gloaming. I tried until I started to sob and he began stroking my hair, whispering, "There, lass, it's over. It's over."

"Not until we've had some tea and burned those journals," Mrs Marr said. "I told ye we should have done it before."

"And I told ye," he retorted, "that they are invaluable to historians."

"Burn them," I croaked, knowing at last that the invitation in Latin they contained was what had called the witches back. Knowing that my speaking the words aloud had brought them to our house again. Knowing that the witches were Father's "visitants" who had, in the end, frightened him to death. "Burn them. No historian worth his salt would touch them."

Alec laughed bitterly. "I would." He set me on my feet and walked away down the path toward town.

"Now ye've done it," Mrs Marr told me. "Ye never were a lass to watch what ye say. Ye've injured his pride and broken his heart."

"But..." We were walking back along the path, her hand on my arm, leading me on. The wind had died and the sky was alert with stars. "But he's not an historian."

"Ye foolish lass, yon lad's nae fisherman, for all he dresses like one. He's a lecturer in history at the University, in St Andrews," she said. "And the two of ye the glory of this village. Yer father and his father always talking about the pair of ye. Hoping to see ye married one day, when pride didna keep the two of ye apart. Scheming they were."

I could hardly take this in. Drawing my arm from her, I looked to see if she was making a joke. Though in all the years I'd known her, I'd never heard her laugh.

She glared ahead at the darkened path. "Yer father kept yer room the way it was when ye were a child, though I tried to make him see the foolishness of it. He said that someday yer own child would be glad of it."

"My father—"

"But then he went all queer in the head after Alec's father died. I think he believed that by uncovering all he could about the old witches, he might help Alec in his research. To bring ye together; though what he really fetched was too terrible to contemplate."

"Which do you think came first?" I asked slowly. "Father's summoning the witches, or the shadows sensing an opportunity?"

She gave a bob of her head to show she was thinking, then said at last, "Dinna mess with witches and weather, my man says..."

"Your man?" She'd said it before, but I thought she'd meant her dead husband. "Weren't you ... I mean, I thought you were in love with my father."

She stopped dead in her tracks and turned to me. The half moon lit her face. "Yer father?" She stopped, considered, then began again. "Yer father had a heart only for two women in his life, yer mother and ye, Janet, though he had a hard time showing it.

"And..." she laughed, "he was no a bonny man."

I thought of him lying in his bed, his great prow of a nose dominating his face. No, he was not a bonny man.

"Och, lass, I had promised yer mother on her deathbed to take care of him, and how could I go back on such a promise? I didna feel free to marry as long as he remained alive. Now my Pittenweem man and I have set a date, and it will be soon. We've wasted enough time already."

I had been wrong, so wrong, and in so many ways I could hardly comprehend them all. And didn't I understand about wasted time? But at least I could make one thing right again.

"I'll go after Alec, I'll..."

Mrs Marr clapped her hands. "Then run, lass, run like the wind."

And untying the knot around my own pride, I ran.

For M. R. James

We like to think we live in a rational world, one where magic is nothing more than a conjuring trick, but superstitions die hard: How many people do you know who touch wood or carry a lucky charm? Maybe there are more things in heaven and earth than are dreamt of in our philosophy. After all, although the word "occult" means hidden, it's sometimes possible to hide in plain sight.

◎　◎

SOPHIE AND THE SACRED FLUIDS
Andrew C. Ferguson

◎　◎

Wet Snot. Why oh why did I use Wet Snot to throw a glamour over Sandy Carmichael?

Of course, you have to use what's available at the time, and act on your instincts. In fairness, I could've used Blood, Sweat, Pussy Juice, even Salty Urine. The real question is, why try to put a spell on him at all, with Wet Snot or anything else? It ranks alongside all the other imponderables in my recent past; like, why did I take the job back in Edinburgh when I could've stayed in London? And what started the war between me and Christine?

Sandy was six foot three, a rugger bugger type; but in the talent-free wasteland that is our Edinburgh office, he seemed vaguely amusing, actually unmarried and virtually shaggable. When he asked me out I said yes for the same reason that I put Wet Snot under the saddo's desk in the first place.

But then I forget, I'm speaking to the Uninitiated, or the Living Dead as the four of us used to call you at Mary Seaton's School for Girls. I'd better explain.

In the Eighth Jotter of the Dead, it is written, *"All water acquires psychic force when passed through the Sacred Vessel of a woman's body. But the power depends on the ease of extraction."*

Not that our Sandy knew any of this, or of the way the dried-in nasal effluvium under his desk was playing havoc with his hormones. But after two suitably pricey dinners, and some desperately sticky fumblings back at his flat, I was beginning to think that his dark side was just a tendency towards obsession: sports trivia, the names of obscure indie bands, that sort of thing. I should've dumped him there and then.

But men have their own voodoo effect on women. It's weaker, of course, but it still makes us throw common sense out the window. I'm not sure how they get their mojo working. I've got a horrible suspicion it's something to do with masturbatory fantasies.

Whatever. I still wanted him, and that's why I found myself on the wrong side of town at 3 a.m. one night dabbing more Wet Snot onto his letterbox. Sure enough, the next day at work he was at my desk waiting for me.

"I had this weird dream last night," he said. He looked like a giant Labrador puppy in its first rush of puberty.

"I'm glad to hear it," I said. "It's the people that don't have weird dreams you have to look out for."

"Perhaps we could chat about it over a drink tonight?" he asked.

"Uh-huh." I briefly considered the feeling that he was being too needy, but dismissed it when I remembered we were not alone. "Okay, then."

After Sandy shambled off, I looked over at Christine, who was pretending not to pay attention. Her ears were revolving like one of those receivers the Yanks have to pick up any signs of alien life. I waited.

"So nice to see you getting on well with Sandy, dear," she said eventually, taking her glasses off and swivelling her chair round to face me. Her glasses dropped anchor on their chain above her still-impressive embonpoint.

"Sir Ranald has great hopes for him, you know. Very talented boy. His mother's a member of my church, of course."

Roughly translated: *My boyfriend's your boyfriend's boss, lady, and I have contacts everywhere. I can damage you any time I want.*

I smiled, waiting in the long grass till twelve, when Christine would go for lunch. Then I checked there was no one near our doorway, and laid open a paper cut I had got earlier at the photocopier.

I rose, walked casually over to Christine's workstation, and paused for a second in case she was about to reappear. I worked out an excuse—the old dropped paperclip routine—and kneeled down until I was hidden from the other worker cells by Christine's PC. Then I wrote FYB in Bad Blood on the underside of her desk.

That'll dry up her commentary on my dress sense for a while, I remember thinking. The Fuck You Bitch spell is particularly effective on snidey cows, I've found.

Christine was quieter in the afternoon, but not as quiet as I'd have liked. And there was a casual shot late on about the extra button undone on my blouse that was so unnecessary that it made me wonder if I'd said the Incantation along with the FYB spell properly. I was still thinking about this at the end of the day as I picked up my jacket and left, without so much as a backward glance at her.

Sandy and I went to Bar 38 at his suggestion. I drank orange juice, to stay sharp.

"So you were going to tell me about this weird dream," I said, interrupting his tedious recital of the no-hoper musicians he's got in his minidisc collection.

"Oh yeah. Well, it was like, we went out for a drink, just like this, yeah? And then we went back to my place and we were, you know, at it, but we couldn't wait to get in the door and we were doing it on the step. You were on top, and I was hanging onto the letterbox, and then Mrs Brotchie from next door came out with a toilet brush..."

I looked at him. "Don't even think about it. I've seen Mrs Brotchie. She isn't a three in a bed option, and doorways are bloody draughty places anyway." I paused. "But we could take the welcome mat inside if you felt the bristles were an essential part of the experience for you."

He looked back at me, slowly recognizing that I was telling him he was getting a shag, and I found myself thinking of Laura, one of our little coven of four at Mary Seaton's. Her first use of the Come Fuck Me spell was, in my view, a little badly aimed. Of course, we all had a bit of a crush on Miss Dalrymple, the gym mistress. To a greater or lesser extent, I mean.

Poor Laura. It all ended rather tragically for her during the track and field events at our fifth-year sports day. The javelin pierced her little heart even more effectively than Miss Dalrymple.

Anyhoo, there was Sandy, and there I was, and the bar in Bar 38 was an ill-fitting wall of Slater Menswear product. We left in a taxi soon after.

And if you think I'm going to go into any gory details, think again. Let's just say that Sandy was acceptable comfort food, with the portions a bit on the nouvelle cuisine side. But an hour later, my warmish glow was being spoiled by our boy, drunk on the Sacred Female Fluids and working up to the dreaded L-word.

"I mean, Soph," he said, raising himself on an elbow and pawing my shoulder, "I feel we're really good together, you know? I mean, kind of like, this is really going somewhere."

"Only if nowhere is somewhere," I said. "Sandy, there's not an easy way to say this, so learn to deal with it. Consider yourself dumped." I dressed, ignoring his pathetic pleading, and left. Oh, I know what you're thinking, but sometimes the super-turbo-bitch-from-hell treatment is kinder in the long run. Short sharp shock. Tough love. All that kind of thing.

Unfortunately, not in this case. I soon discovered that Sandy's dark side went further than knowing the dearly departed John Peel's playlist for the last twenty years.

It started with e-mails, and moved on to text messages. The texting was harder to get rid of. I could've just gone out and bought another moby, but sod it, why should I? These things cost money, and anyway, so I thought, it'll peter out eventually.

It reminded me a bit of Randy Pete, Sheena Carmyllie's first serious boyfriend at Loughborough; Cynthia McMonagle, of course, went to Oxford. Sheena and I were pretty tight, so I thought borrowing Randy Pete of an evening was—well, on a par with borrowing a pair of earrings. I mean the man was a machine.

Unfortunately, Pete didn't seem to understand the ground rules and went all obsessive on me. Sheena found out, and for a while the halls of residence were a black magic war zone: FYB escalated to DYB, body fluids of all kinds everywhere, and things got pretty heavy for a while until she and I called a truce. As I say, we were pretty close. I was genuinely upset when I heard Sheena was with Pete in the car when they fished it out of the river.

But I digress. Sandy Carmichael was the same kind of unimaginative stalker as Randy Pete, but with more means of communication available to him. I'd seen the movie before, and the ending was messy.

o

A week or so later, I was just considering what action to take when Christine stuck her nose in.

"Sandy Carmichael was looking for you," she said one morning, as I drifted in at my usual time. "It was after you left, of course."

"Of course." *That "of course" will earn you a top up FYB spell, Chrissie baby,* I thought to myself. *Or more.*

"He left a note on the computer. Looks important."

"Uh-huh." So she'd read it as well.

To be fair to Christine, the note was probably readable from her side of the room—block capitals on a yellow Post-it hanging from my screen:

NEED TO SEE YOU ITS IMPORTANT

I was tutting at the missing apostrophe when Christine said, "Not seen him round much recently, Sophie. Girls in his section say he was pretty keen on you. Can I offer some advice?"

I looked up slowly.

Christine peered over her glasses at me like some prissy school-marm instead of the sex-mad slut she truly was. "Let him down gently, dear. Men usually need these things spelled out to them gradually."

I felt a glassy smile gradually spread itself across my face. This was rich coming from the woman who was shagging the senior partner behind his wife's back, whilst treating her own husband like some kind of farm animal. A number of responses flashed through my head before an unusual tactic recommended itself: telling the truth.

"Oh dear. Too late, I'm afraid. I was a bit brutal in the way I ended it and now he just won't accept it. Making a bit of a nuisance of himself, actually."

"Oh?"

A short time later, when Christine was "popping to the loo", and no doubt spreading my story far and wide among the sisterhood, I e-mailed Sandy:

<I'll call you when Christine's left for the night.
Don't contact me before then.>

Then I popped to the loo myself, coming back via the canteen and loading up with the saltiest food I could lay my hands on. Time for some radical action.

o

Christine left at 5.25 precisely as per the last three hundred years. Quick blow job for the senior partner in his executive Audi, and she'd be home with creamy kisses for hubby by 6.00.

The first part of my evening's work should have been easy, then. Except I'd overdone the nil fluid by mouth technique and only a few drops of the precious Salty Urine squeezed themselves out into the Blessed Vessel (one of my Mum's Tupperware containers; don't ask). I decided to leave marking Christine's card until I was sure I had enough for Sandy.

There were two ways to get to his section from my office: the straight route along the corridor and down the stairs, and the other, darker path, through Legal and Accountancy and down in the lift.

I phoned Sandy, told him with a resigned sigh to come up now if he was coming, and then headed for his office by the alternative route.

A word here about the Sacred Fluids. As I said earlier, the power derives from the difficulty of extraction. Unless you've got a cold, Wet Snot is actually quite hard to get. Pussy Juice usually requires some effort unless you're a complete sex maniac; since we were all squeamish about blood, we agreed that it held power, too. Urine is easy, unless you spend all day eating salt and not drinking, as I had.

I remember us all sitting up in our dorm one night debating whether some of the Sacred Fluids had innate properties. It might've seemed surprising to you that I used Snot in a spell to attract a man; but we decided after a long and interesting discussion that all of the Fluids were above the normal labels that society gave them and could be used for any spell.

Anyway, I arrived in Sandy's office, preparing the Incantation in my head for the GTF spell when I discovered that the second part of my plan had gone pear-shaped. His geeky pal Martin was still at the next desk.

We exchanged puzzled looks. "Oh, I was looking for Sandy," I lied unconvincingly.

"But I thought I heard him say—"

"Forget it. He's misunderstood as usual. Just tell him when you see him to piss off, will you?" I told him, gathering what few shreds of credibility I had left and marching out the door.

On to Plan C. I leaped into my car and headed off for his flat, immediately getting snarled up in the West End gridlock. I reckoned I had about ten minutes on him by the time he thrashed about in confusion, got back to his office, and extracted the necessary information from Martin. We crawled through the West End, and all the way along George Street. I would've abandoned my car and run for it if I'd had sensible shoes on. I never have sensible shoes on.

I got up the stairs to his flat at last and was standing on his doorstep getting my breath back when I heard a noise behind me.

"Oh, hello. I don't think Sandy's back from work yet, my dear."

Bugger. Mrs Bloody Nosey Bitch Brotchie.

I only hesitated a second. "Oh, right. And—" I rummaged in my handbag for a few moments, careful not to dislodge the Tupperware and its contents. "—here I've come out without a scrap of paper to write him a note. I don't suppose you've—"

"Of course, my dear, of course. I'm sure I'll have something." She only half closed the door and I heard her rifling through stuff by her phone in the hall. I only just had time to take out the Vessel, pour most of the contents onto the "welcome" mat, and mutter the magic words before she reappeared. I slipped the Tupperware back into my bag with one hand as I reached out for the notepaper with the other.

"Just some of last year's Charles Rennie Mackintosh stuff, I'm afraid," she said, confusing me momentarily with someone who gave a flying fuck what it was.

"Perfect," I said, and gave her my most dazzling smile. "Sandy loves good old CRM. Can I keep the rest? That's lovely."

Mrs Brotchie's nose twitched suspiciously. "What a curious smell out here in the hallway. It's like ... tomcat. We don't have any cats in this block now, not since Miss Ravelston's Thumper died."

"Mmmm..." I nodded noncommittally, but the old bag hung around sniffing the air for a full minute before going back into her lair, still muttering about cats. She finally closed the door, but was probably still watching me through the spy-hole, so I made a show of writing Sandy an affectionate little message. It read:

SANDY
GET TO FUCK
GET TO FUCK
GET TO FUCK
SIGNED THE TORTURED GHOST OF CHARLES RENNIE
MACKINTOSH

I folded it carefully and stuck it through the letterbox of Sandy's flat. Time to go: my ten minutes' start was fast running out.

Still, I stood there for a moment. You see, writing the incantation down had given me an urge to complete it, a kind of walking-on-the-cracks-in-the-pavement, obsessive-compulsive thing. When it came to it, I couldn't fucking leave without doing it again.

I crouched down by the door and opened my handbag. I was so intent on hiding what I was doing from Mrs Brotchie's spyhole that I didn't notice Sandy Carmichael until he was about three steps away from me.

"What the—"

As I stared at him, my hands clasped around the Blessed Vessel as if it were a Cup-a-Soup, it occurred to me that his dream had been prophetic: the doormat, me, him and Mrs Brotchie. Even the toilet brush was dead on in a symbolic kind of way.

"What's that?" he said, as I edged past him onto the stairs. He lunged for the Tupperware and we grappled for a hold of it briefly before it flew out of our grasp, spraying the last precious drops of Salty Urine over the stairwell wall before clattering its merry way down the stone steps. I scrambled down after it, surprised at first that Sandy wasn't giving chase. At the foot of the stairs, I looked up.

He was sniffing at his doormat like a big Alsatian, a puzzled frown on his face. He looked down at me. "What is that?" he said again. "Is it cat's piss?"

I shook my head and smiled, grabbing up the Tupperware and heading off before Mrs Brotchie reappeared, with or without toilet brush.

○

According to Cynthia McMonagle, our scribe, writing in the Eighth Jotter of the Dead, the GTF spell is extremely fast-acting. Victims usually experience a severe sense of rejection and loss. They frequently become depressed. Some may even have feelings of revulsion and resentment against the spell worker, although these feelings are rarely acted upon.

Sandy Carmichael acted upon his.

The next morning I was keeping a low profile, trying to decide if Christine was being annoying enough to warrant another Evian-free day of salty crisps, or the pain of another paper cut. Then the phone rang. The senior partner wanted to see me in his office. Now.

My first instinct was to think Christine had been playing games, but I then had second thoughts and opened the locked drawer of my desk. There was something I needed to take with me, just in case. When I walked into the room and saw Sandy standing practically shoulder to shoulder with Sir Ranald, I saw I was right.

The old man peered over his glasses at me in a way very reminiscent of Christine. "Ah, er ... Sophie. Sandy here's been making some rather strange allegations about you. Harassment allegations. Some incident last night ... out of the workplace admittedly ... my good friend Eleanor Brotchie can corroborate you were there at least ... cat's piss? Allegedly?"

Sandy stood there ramrod straight, like a guardsman about to be court-martialled. "Really?" I said. "I presume he's talking about our encounter on his doorstep?"

"So you admit you were there?"

"Oh yes. And I did spill something on Sandy's doormat because my hands were shaking so much at the thought of meeting him. A herbal remedy recommended by my Chinese acupuncturist, designed to combat stress. I was trying to drink it to calm myself down."

The Chinese medicine bit was a moment of inspiration. Christine had told me in a pally moment that Sir Ranald bought into all that Eastern mumbo-jumbo big time.

"Stress, Sophie?"

I smiled winningly. "Workplace stress. Induced by sexual harassment by Sandy Carmichael." I produced the sheaf of papers. "Here's the transcripts of various e-mails he's sent me over the last few weeks. I went to his flat last night to try to sort things out, but I couldn't go through with it. Sandy's a litigation time bomb, Sir Ranald, waiting to go off under the firm."

The old man was leafing through the papers and coming to his own conclusions. Sandy now looked like a rabbit trapped in the headlights. I lobbed in a last depth charge.

"If you want corroboration from my side, speak to Christine Costello, my colleague. I confided in her about it recently."

Sir Ranald looked up quickly at the name, but apart from that he didn't even blink. He turned to Sandy. "Well? This puts a different complexion on things, doesn't it?"

To be fair for once to Sandy Carmichael, he accepted defeat graciously when it was rammed down his throat. He looked at me, then back at

Sir Ranald, and shrugged. "Give me a good reference and I'll have my desk cleared by noon."

My surprises weren't over for the day, though. I came back into the office to find Christine, her feet propped up on the desk, reading the Eighth Jotter of the Dead, which she had taken from my desk drawer. The one I had left unlocked after I took the smoking-gun e-mails out of it. She looked up and smiled when I came in.

"Sir Ranald called," she said. "I said you'd told me about Sandy stalking you ages ago, instead of just yesterday. Wasn't that clever of me?"

"Give me that," I said, trying to grab the jotter off her. She plucked it out of my reach, raising her other hand.

"Ah-ah-ah. This is really fascinating. Does it really work? Do you think you could initiate me, Sophie?"

I paused to consider my position when I saw she was serious. "Oh, I think so," I said.

○

Christine's not such a bad old stick. And now we've called a truce, we've got a lot in common. She blows Sir Ranald, I blow off a series of rugger buggers, and when the day gets too slow, we use some Wet Snot on anyone in the office we feel is in need of some tough love. I'm having the most fun I've had since I first flew back to the old home town on the accursed broomstick that is Easyjet.

Sandy's not been back in touch: the GTF spell seems to have done the trick. If he does bother me again, I've got a stronger spell I've not told Christine about yet involving a bit of Salty Urine and a whole lot of petrol poured through his letter box. Very effective, I've found.

In the meantime, it's good to be acting in concert again: that's how it should be done. Cynthia McMonagle's gone to ground in West Sussex these days, I hear from a mutual contact. Husband, kids, ponies, the lot. Not that I give a monkey's, since I got to keep the Jotters.

Besides, I've got my new playmate now. Christine, Queen Consort to the senior partner, who knows where all the bodies are buried in the entire corporate structure.

We've got a lot to learn from each other.

Love, it is said, is like a red, red rose. You may choose to interpret this in a number of ways: beautiful, natural, treasured, thorny. Expensive, certainly. There is a cost associated with cultivating a rose, encouraging it to prosper, but most people will agree that it is worth paying. Even if the participants are separated by ten thousand miles. Or more.

❍ ❍

VANILLA FOR THE LADY
Deborah J. Miller

❍ ❍

The pub was once trendy. Students from the University used to grace the pitted wooden trestles and sit around the oak casks, their heavy Oxfam greatcoats and unshaven chins looking casually contrived. That was last year; now they've all moved on. The pub remains, still serving less fickle denizens of the city centre, those who simply haunt its cellars because it's open until three in the morning.

The barman is tired, polishing glasses that once would have been rinsed and reused with the lipstick of the previous customer still pinkly accusing him for his lack of hygiene. At least there is a small group of people in this evening, he glances over to the chairs by the fire. One of the female occupants throws back her stiffly lacquered hair and emits a piercing shriek of a laugh.

"Christ, Taz, ye're priceless sometimes, ye ken that?"

The barman reflects that perhaps it's almost better to have no customers than *them*.

A small, muscular-looking man gets up from the table. He wears a Versace business suit and tasteful gold jewellery. His eyes, brown and hard, flicker over the assembled company.

"Who's for another round then, ladies? Not you, Sammy-Jo, you've had enough."

"Aww, Dode..." Sammy-Jo pouts at him.

"I said, you've had enough." The words contain no inflection or malice, he speaks evenly, a reasonable man. Sammy-Jo sits back in her chair, chastened as though he'd pointed a gun toward her as he spoke.

"Taz. What would you like? Same again?"

She is sitting in one of the ancient faded easy chairs, nearest the fire. Taken in isolation from her companions, she could be mistaken for anything but a whore. She wears a long black cotton skirt and a white muslin blouse, she smells of Patchouli, and her oriflamme red hair is golden at the edges where the firelight shines through. Normally her small oval face and pointed chin have a defiant air, but tonight she is nervous and allows her hair to drape down one side of her face. Her skin is beginning to redden in the heat of the fire, but she doesn't move. The faded sky of the armchair frames her like a portrait, she could be a painting of an enchantress. Then she speaks, and the spell is broken.

"Naw, no thanks, Dode. I'm fine."

He studies her face and she does not meet his searching gaze. "OK."

He turns to the barman, smug, obviously fully aware of the tension around the table. "Same again, pal, 'cept for the Bacardis. Get one for yersel'."

○

"C'mon, Sammy," she whispers urgently across the table. "Look, I'd do the same for you, you know that. It's only twenty quid. I swear, if he lays into me again, I'll kill him..."

"Taz ... Ah cannae. Honest, doll. If Ah gie ye the twenty, Ah'll be short masel'. Ah'm no wantin' a doin'."

"Peggy?"

"Sorry, Taz..."

"And here we are, Peg. Same again."

Dode's voice is airy and sociable; the merest flicker of a glance passes between him and Taz. She pushes her hair back from her face and focuses behind his shoulder. Someone has just walked in through the double doors and the fresh night air feels like ice on her cheek. For a moment, street sounds impinge on the airless security of the pub and the last buses home can be heard rolling over the Bridges. The oak door slams.

She can hear Sammy-Jo, as if from a distance, whining on in her Southern-belle monotone.

Poor cow. Who does she think she's kidding? She's never been further than Govan.

Taz watches the stranger walking toward the bar, an idea forming. He's tall, very tall, and olive-skinned. His ebony hair is swept back into a pony-tail, something she normally hates. For long seconds, she watches him, watches his movements as he takes his wallet from the deep pockets of his voluminous ankle-length coat and frowns at the money inside: a tourist. She likes his hands—she always looks at hands—his palms angular, his fingers long and tapering, spread wide across the width of leather he's holding. Feeling the short-lived but intense stare, he turns toward her and, unexpectedly bold, she holds his gaze. His eyes are navy blue.

Please don't look away. Please.

Now. Do it now.

"Peter!"

She stands up fast, too fast—the easy chair rocks backwards with the momentum. The heat from the fire and too much alcohol make her acting less than convincing. Taz desperately signals for help; and now, as she turns to look at Dode in the slow motion counted by heart beats, his expression is unconvinced for one...

Two ... three ... four... Game's up the pole.

She can feel herself screaming inside.

"Anastasia! How are you?" the stranger asks.

She smiles, confused and frightened.

What? How?

He's coming towards the group, smiling widely. He opens his arms, waiting for her long-lost hug. She stumbles past Dode, tripping over Sammy-Jo's handbag and falling forward into his waiting arms.

"Anastasia," he repeats, "it's so good to see you."

The stranger holds her against a broad, lambswool-covered chest and for a moment she just breathes deeply, feeling herself go limp. He has turned her slightly away from Dode's resentful gaze, and very deliberately and softly he whispers, "It's all right."

This is crazy. How does he know my name?

"When did you get back, Peter?"

"A couple of days ago. I leave for Hong Kong next week." He smiles. "Aren't you going to introduce me to your friends?"

"Peter... This is Sammy-Jo, Peggy, and Do—Douglas." He nods at each in turn and shakes Dode's stiffly outstretched hand.

"Look, Anastasia, what do you say we go get some supper and talk about old times? We could go back to my flat if you like."

"Great!" The less she says, the better; her voice is shaking. "I'll just go and powder my nose. 'Scuse me."

Escape. The toilet is unnaturally cold, as only pub toilets can be. The cisterns and pipes hiss and gurgle, and the glaring white tiles only compound the assault on her already overloaded senses. She turns on the tap and stares dumbly at the jet of steaming water whilst pressing her forehead against the cool mirror.

"I don't know this man," she says aloud. A small hysterical giggle escapes her and rings hollowly around the small room. She knows she is going to cry and wonders whether to just relax into the tears.

The door crashes open, bouncing on its hinges. Taz watches the reflected image of Dode swagger into her sanctuary. She is going to regret saying this, but the inevitability of the situation takes hold.

"This is the Ladies, Dode."

Her voice is trembling and she tilts her chin up with the last vestiges of her defiance to look down on her aggressor. The girls had agreed amongst themselves that "wee Dode" was a psycho. They have each been on the receiving end of his violence, compared notes in a detached and clinical fashion, as if to show that their scars are, after all, only skin deep. They make jokes about his sexual prowess that they know he would kill them for, and rumour has it, that would not be the first time one of his girls has disappeared.

o

Once, she had actually liked the man.

It was a yellow, sunlit day when they met in Princes Street Gardens. Taz had been face-painting children at the Mound, and had decided to escape for a while to buy herself an ice cream. She laughed at the ice-cream man, who, when she asked for a ninety nine, said, "For that smile, hen, y'can have a hundred..."

Still laughing, she turned, and walked straight into a silver-grey business suit, ice cream first. Her profuse apologies were met with a broad white smile. He said nothing at first, just looked straight at her. Then he reached out as though to touch her hair—she stiffened slightly at the over-familiar gesture—but when his hand came back into view, he held a white rose.

"Vanilla for the lady," he had said.

o

Dode doesn't wait for explanation, but grabs her by the throat, pushing her back against the sink, and slaps her hard. She will not cry out, not this soon, but she can hear her breath coming, sharp and ragged.

"You're a fucking whore, Taz," he leers. He has a flick knife in his pocket, she knows that. "But you're *my* whore."

Dode punctuates the sentence by jerking her head back, cracking it off the mirror. He is standing hard up against her, his proximity as menacing as his actions. He is enjoying his power. She hears herself speak and despises her weakness. "Don't mark me, Dode. Please."

"Later..." he snarls.

He pulls her forward, gripping her white blouse, and she moves limply, paralysed by fright and alcohol. For a moment, he seems calm. Then he twists her around and, grabbing her hair, rams her face into the metal box of the towel holder. The noise rings dispassionately around the tiled walls. Taz drops to the floor like a stone.

Her face is very cold, except for a warm patch around her mouth. There's a kind of rushing noise. Dimly, from far away, she can hear a voice.

"...what you and your fucking pal are up to..."

Pal?

"...you owe me lady ... bitch ... twenty quid."

Oh yes, twenty quid.

A black Gucci loafer is jabbing toward her, accompanied by a dull thudding noise. She can't feel it. She laughs, inside.

Dode had been following her for a week before their apparently chance meeting; the white rose was bought well in advance. She had been his long before she ever laid eyes on him.

The toilet door slams.

○

Awakening, to pain. There's a dull ache all over, highlighted by areas of more specific hurt. She knows that she's perversely lucky to be waking at all, and coldly wonders what sort of "apology gift" she's earned from Dode—some gold jewellery at least.

Little bastard.

She opens her eyes fast, the memories returning with the force of his kicks. A wave of nausea jolts her.

How come I'm home?

There's a naked man sitting on the end of her bed. He looks comfortable, at ease. Surely she didn't pick up a client in this state? Surely no one would want to...

"Anastasia. Are you well?" She remembers then. It's the man from the bar. Peter. No, that was only a game.

"Figure you've earned a freebie?" she rasps, suddenly acutely aware of her sore face. "Shit, some people have got no pride."

She lifts the sheet and looks down at her body. Dode has broken the rules, marked the goods. Looking back at the stranger, suddenly weary to the bone, she says, "Thanks for getting me home. Now please put some clothes on and go away."

Taz turns stiffly in the bed, groping for the sheet that has slipped over the side, regretting the exposure of her bruises, her powerlessness, to this man. Sleep tries to claim her tattered senses, but she needs warmth. And then the warmth is there. He reaches over her prostrate form, spreading the sheet and the covers, tucking them around her like a cocoon. The comfort is seductive, and her eyelids begin to close. With a massive effort she opens them again. He must be kneeling at the side of the bed, his strangely expressionless face is close to hers.

"Go to sleep," he says simply.

She smiles a sad, tight smile, reaching out to touch his face in mute thanks as sleep washes over her like the ninth wave.

✿

Awake again. Is it the evening of the next day? A sullen Scottish rain is hammering remorselessly on the sloping attic windows of her tiny apartment. The leaden grey of the sky gives the bright tones of her home a flat, lifeless look, like a seaside resort out of season. Taz doesn't mind; the sound of the rain is clean and impartial, the colours will come back. Her pain is still with her, but she feels alone and peaceful, she thinks without bitterness that she wouldn't mind dying now, feeling like this. She is gazing at the small wooden Buddha that smiles back from the windowsill, she used to rub its belly each morning thinking it would bring her luck; she wonders why she stopped, as though she is beyond luck or hope, then she remembers the man. Painfully, she pulls herself upright, wincing and scanning the room.

There he is, curled up on the big red easy chair wearing her pink silk kimono. He's a big man, broad-chested, and she can see where the stitching of her gown has stretched to breaking point across the back and shoulders. He hasn't bothered to clear the mountain of clothes that she habitually flings across the room, just moved them a bit, and they surround him with a wild splash of colour. For some reason, she decides that he looks like a large pink cuckoo, and so is smiling over at him when he wakes up.

"Anast—"

"Don't ask me how I am again," she snaps. Her smile is gone, the memories of his kindness engulfed by her cynicism. *How does he know my name?* She stares at him, a practised mask of implacability.

"Have we met? Really, I mean."

"How are you?" He says the words softly, looking mildly perturbed. She draws a long breath, unsure of the situation: he's obviously a bit odd. Her eyes flicker toward the door of the bathroom to reassure herself that she can reach its safe, lockable confines before he can.

He stands up suddenly. The pink robe falls apart and the silken belt catches, looping incongruously around his languid penis. He makes no effort to correct this indignity, but begins to pace the room with long strides, as though rehearsing a speech. Taz sits back on her pillows, frowning and waiting. He stops.

"You're not going to believe me. I know that now, I've been here for two..." He stops again and cocks his head slightly as though listening. "... years. Looking for you." There is a long pause. "I'm an alien."

She doesn't laugh. Three years spent as a prostitute have taught her never to laugh at naked men, no matter what they say. Still, the temptation is there, so she bites on the inside of her lip and says nothing.

He mistakes her silence for incomprehension: "An extra-terrestrial? A spaceman."

"OK, I hear you." He wears a look of utter desperation, a contrast to his hitherto almost blank appearance. She sighs, "Prove it, Peter. Or whatever your name is."

"Jon. My name is Jon. Well, it is the name I have chosen."

Then she does laugh. "Jon! That's a good one, Jon the John." He seems puzzled, so she shrugs and says, "Never mind..."

"I cannot prove anything to you that you do not already know yourself, Anastasia."

"Look, pal!" Her misdirected hatred erupts. "You'd better do some fucking fast talking or I'm calling the polis... What the hell is this?"

"Fast talking?" Jon is walking toward the bed, sitting down. "OK." He takes her hands and holds them within his, as though praying. She tries to pull back, shrink away.

"Please..." she whispers, "go away..." Her back is literally against the wall, pressing hard into the pillows, panic choking her words; but he is looking into her face with utter conviction.

"Be calm," Jon says, gazing into her eyes. She feels this is not hypnosis, but something shared. There is space. Blackness. Her eyes close. She is falling through the blackness. Then he is there. All around. She is trusting, and the falling stops.

○

When she wakes again, it is night. He lies beside her. She feels the emptiness of hunger, and licking her dry bloody lips, she tastes the salt of her tears.

"Jon? I'm going out to get some food. We'll talk when I get back."

He stirs slightly in his sleep and she gets up to put her clothes on. Taz is still sore and can tell that her face is badly bruised; she isn't ready to face herself in the mirror yet though. She feels strangely ambiguous about sharing her bed with an "alien". Taz doesn't really believe him yet, but he seems harmless enough. Compassion is not something she has had much experience of, so she is still wary.

She smiles slightly at the sleeping figure. Bunching her coat up against the chill, she steps out into the baleful yellow glow of the stairwell.

○

The light inside the room is off, and for a brief moment, Anastasia is in silhouette as she gazes back towards the bed. Then the door slams shut.

She has been gone for mere seconds when Jon sits up and swings his legs over the side of the bed. He has been awake for some time. He shrugs off the pink robe, frowning, then leans forwards, elbows on knees, running his long fingers through his hair.

The big recessed window has a dark-brown curtain drawn across it that is designed to shut the world out. Only a square of light from the window in the roof cuts through the darkness, the black shadows of its panes forming a cross. Jon sits immobile in the centre of that cross, listening to the rain as the minutes pass uncounted. He is soulsick—and a billion miles from the comfort of his kind.

Any watcher would swear that what happens next is a trick of the light and the rain. Anastasia, could she see, would not return.

The cross-legged figure is melting, as though from the inside, collapsing inward; all bone, tissue and blood are being burnt away by incandescent fire. The chest collapses and the face buckles hideously. The spine goes last, as the skin slides soundlessly off the bed into a lipoid mass on the floor, just outside the square of light. There is still a presence in the room, although none that could be discerned by any human sense. The darkness in the corners is moving, but that could be the shadows of clouds which are passing over the moon. Then more shadow arrives, from nowhere, and the room becomes a box of blackness. A conversation is taking place, one beyond hearing or speech.

Why do you delay?

You lied to me...

Explain.

You told me they were like vermin—nothing to trouble my conscience with—but that's not true. They feel, they have spirit... Can they really be a threat?

They have the potential to be one, and that is enough.

Some of them are dying before I even get to them—too many to be coincidence. This should have been my tenth, but she's only my seventh. Have you assigned anyone else to this city?

No. Just do it and get out of there.

This is the first female, they're different.

You don't have to talk to them.

She...

The ethics of this are not your concern. This will be your last.

○

The shadows flicker and dissipate at the hard sound of the key in the lock.

"Jon?"

He has returned to his disguise too slowly. She screams as she flicks the light on. He has only begun to fill the loose skin, and his features are not quite full, his face still crumpled and warped.

Anastasia stands transfixed for long seconds, her hand still holding the key in the door. She is preparing for another scream even as he finishes.

Jon dives across the room as she shrieks, and drawing her inside, clamps his hand firmly over her horrified mouth. Slowly, Anastasia's facial muscles relax, and she nods at him. When he lets go, she laughs brokenly. "It's OK. No one ever comes."

He frowns, not quite understanding, but realizes, that at least she is calm. She reaches out a shaking finger and prods him gingerly. "Still here then spaceman? Do you want some pizza?"

"Pizza?"

"Food."

"No. I need to talk with you."

She perches on the side of the bed and takes a dripping segment out of the box. He sits on the edge of the easy chair, still naked, unaware that he should be feeling cold. Anastasia keeps her raincoat on. He is about to begin talking when she pre-empts him; as she speaks, small clouds of her breath dissipate in the air, mingling with the steam from the pizza.

"I'm not stupid, Jon. I understand being a prostitute is not the smartest career move in the world, but that's a long story and I'll be out of this mess soon. I'm instinctive, strong, a survivor. You understand?"

He nods. Her sudden eloquence surprises him, but then he sees that her movements are slightly jerky and he realizes that there is something wrong, something other than just her nervousness. Jon is about to say something, but when he opens his mouth, she waves her hand towards him and speaks through a mouthful of dough.

"No, no, don't interrupt me. Just listen, will you? I believe what you said, now. I must admit, before you ... left your skin, I just thought you were a bit, well, strange. It shook me, I must say." She swallows and takes a slug from a bottle of white wine—once sparkling, now flat—sitting at the side of the bed. "Aren't you cold? Christ, you're sitting there with nothing on! Why don't you get in the bed?"

Jon does as he is told, watching her movements as she switches on a two-bar electric fire.

"Anastasia, you have been taking chemical stimulants?"

"You mean drugs? Yeah, speed." She smiles. "It's good when you're in pain—makes your metabolism faster. I took a lot. A hundred and fifty migs, something like that. Can you heal me? I think I have a cracked rib or something. Its just that I saw this film once—he had these things that looked like those bath oil things, you know?"

Jon shakes his head, confused.

"Just my luck, she gets Jeff Bridges—what do I get?" She is walking up and down now, rubbing her arms, trying to warm up. "Makes you talk a lot too..."

Anastasia folds up the last of the pizza slice and crams it into her mouth, impatient to finish so she can talk. Then, finally taking her raincoat off, she climbs into the bed beside him.

"Budge up," she says companionably. "This doesn't mean anything, mind, I'm just cold."

There is a long silence between them, which is surprisingly comfortable, impinged on by sounds from the street below. A taxi stops at the bottom of the stairs, its diesel purring somehow familiar and comforting. She retrieves the bottle of flat wine from the bedside cabinet and takes another slug from it.

It seems natural to sleep eventually. She moves closer and twines her legs around his, nestling her cheek against his chest. Jon lifts his arms up, away from her, unsure of what's happening.

"What are you doing?" he asks.

She doesn't open her eyes, but groping for his hands, she wraps them around her.

"Cuddle," she says.

Her breathing deepens, and he watches as she falls asleep. He finds this mute act of trust especially surprising from her, so unlike the others, so instinctive. The moonlight picks out the lines her fair lashes make against her face, and soften the hardness of the bruising. She seems fully asleep, although her hand makes a small involuntary movement against the hardness of his chest.

"I am not a 'cuddle', Anastasia," he murmurs, "I am your death."

"So, kill me."

She does not look up, and for a moment Jon wonders if she has sent the thought telepathically.

"I don't understand why you didn't do it before, when I was asleep," she continues. She sounds unsurprised, unbetrayed. "Damned bad manners if you ask me."

"I ... I don't know why either." He frowns into the darkness. I just looked at you and I wanted to know ... things." He shrugs. "I cannot explain."

"It's called curiosity," she says dryly. "So tell me, before you do it—like in the movies—why?"

"I have no choice. I am a criminal. This is my atonement. It's a bargain with our powers."

"Don't they have the jail then, where you're from?"

He makes no answer and she sighs. "Why do they want us dead?"

"They fear you not for what you are, but for what some of you might become."

"Really? Why don't they just leave us to do the job ourselves? Can't they see how bloody sad we are?"

"Not everyone feels as you do."

"How many have you killed?"

"You were to be my tenth."

Jon sees that Anastasia refuses to latch onto the straw of hope that his choice of words might imply. Does her life mean so little to her, then?

"It's hardly planetary annihilation then is it..." she points out.

"I could do it now." He wants her to react. "I could kill you this instant while you hold me. I can tell you that there is no pain."

"No pain, eh? It's tempting."

There is silence for a while.

"You do not want to die Anastasia." His voice is harsh; for some reason, her vulnerability constricts his throat. Jon is no longer sure of his reasoning, but the idea of killing one unafraid to die is somehow repugnant to him. He offers her a reason to live.

"I have killed Dode."

She sits up then.

"I am telling you the truth. He is dead. I threw him off the Bridges as a train was leaving the station. Are you sad now? Did I make a mistake? You are free."

"What did he say?"

Jon pauses, and then the corners of his lips curl with incongruous mischief: "Aaaaaaah!"

Anastasia stares at him and then she starts to laugh, a sick hurt sound, devoid of all mirth. When she stops, her eyes are brimming with tears. "He's really dead then? I wish I could feel something. I wish I wasn't so fucking numb. He made me this way..."

"But you *do* feel, Anastasia. You, and the others I have killed—I know that now..." She snorts, derisively and is about to make some derogatory remark about her fellow human beings, but he carries on, unheeding of her attitude.

"Do not confuse your reality with everyone else's. There are some visionaries here, I think." he pauses momentarily. "You are stronger than you think. You will have children... Your species will continue, even if your planet does not. That is what my people fear. They think your descendants will eclipse us."

○

Jon suddenly looks tired, and Taz imagines that all the killings he has done are showing on the lines of his face. He is still lying back on the pillows, and she reaches down and traces the tiny scar-like furrows under his left eye. Reaching up, taking hold of her wrist, he pulls her down toward him and holds her in a sad, desperate embrace.

"I am going soon," he whispers. "They will come for me and I have failed. It seems I am the victim of this assignment."

"No." She raises herself up on one elbow, her hair, swaying with the motion, brushing gently over him. "Look, you've killed Dode, haven't you? Can't you convince them that he was the real subject?"

"I have never lied before, Anastasia."

"Well, learn, for Christ's sake! This is your life we're talking about."

He laughs into the darkness. "And is my life more important than yours?"

"No," she falters, "all life is important Jon." There is a loaded silence whilst each ponders the implications of this.

"Even Dode?" he asks. It's difficult to tell whether he is teasing her, smiling whilst he speaks.

○

They make love by unspoken consent. They're not in love, each un-sure that they are capable of such an emotion, each one scarred by fate and manipulation, only seeking simple comfort. She sees herself as reborn, because of what he has told her. She is free, she will have children. Strength and courage flood through her veins carried by a rush of adrenalin. She does not see herself as a small speck in the plan of things, but looks down at her small, battered frame with fierce pride and feels ... irrepressible. She smiles as she encompasses him with her body and her will, and wonders if she looks at all predatory, like someone who could make others afraid.

○

Jon is frightened, more frightened than at the prospect of his return. He has never lost control, never let go; and that is what these beings can do, he senses it. They are capable of the most shocking vulnerability, and that is part of their strength. He wants the experience, but his body is rigid, close to panic. She kisses him. For long seconds he feels only the warm physical sensation, the sweet taste of her mouth, and then something of the kiss speaks to him, so he closes his eyes and listens to that voice.

○

And because of what he is, the worldsoul embraces them. For a while, images assail them, of other lovers, other times, the last time for many. Their sadness, transmuted, made sweet, made tangible. They flash by as Jon and Taz fall into the well, flickering glimpses of the most overpowering emotion.

It was true then, other people had this, and she did not. A tiny flame of bitterness flares within Taz and is gone as Jon pulls her closer. He is drowning, he needs her.

And then they arrive; on warm grass, looking down on a serene sea. The colours of the grass and the water are vibrant and pure. A gentle breeze blows and pulls at her hair as though she is under water. The sun is warm and languid. She looks down at Jon, his pony-tail has come undone and she realizes for the first time that his hair is as long as hers—it seems a strangely trivial thought.

"I've never been here before," she says. "It's so peaceful."

Out to sea there is something massive, far in the distance. It appears to be a waterspout or tornado of gigantic proportions. Dark clouds gather around its zenith. It reminds Taz of an umbilical cord, it twists and moves, but for some reason she is sure that it will come no closer. As she watches, fleeting movements break the surface of the funnel, limbs, bodies, occasional faces; a hand reaches out, fingers spread, groping the air, then is gone. Instinctively, she knows who they are, other travellers to the worldsoul. She reaches out her hand in mute response, then smiling, returns it to her lips and blows a gentle kiss.

Larks are calling, swooping and diving and she watches the tiny red flight with intense feeling. "It's real," she whispers. "When I was a girl, it was like this..." Her voice is carried away by the breaking of the waves, she walks toward the lark feeling its grace and fragility, its speed and spirit—but it seems to come no closer.

She gives up, bemused but smiling, and lies down again, next to Jon, who appears to be sleeping. Turning her back to him, she curls up, like an embryo. She can feel the warm ridge of his spine against her back. Listening to the wind, the birdsong and the water, she sleeps.

○

It is dawn. The water sound has changed to the familiar persistent dripping, and she knows without opening her eyes that she is in her own bed. The stale smell of her own perfume is comforting and homely. She had a good trip last night.

Taz opens her eyes. There is an naked old man squatting in the corner of the room, leaning back against the wall. His long, silver-white hair reaches down to his waist, covering most of his wasted brown flesh. The intruder has large feet and his toes are gripping the carpet ferociously, as though he feels insecure, that the floor will collapse under him. She stares at him unblinking, and he smiles back with an unconvincing grin.

She closes her eyes again and groans. "Aww shit, he must be ninety-five!"

"It's my father," a voice says—Jon.

It all comes back to her. As she turns to look at him, she suddenly feels exposed. Then touch-memories from the night before sing through her; she feels as though everywhere he has kissed her is burning. Taz blushes as only a redhead can. Jon is smiling at her, his long black hair framing his face. She can tell he is worried by the older man's presence and his smile is purely for her. "Thank you," he says. Something in his expression makes it feel like goodbye, and she is not ready.

"I've come to take him back, Anastasia."

The old man walks toward the bed, too frail to be menacing, but in her anger, she lashes out anyway. "No! Don't you call me that... Who the hell do you people think you are? Don't you ever wear any fucking clothes? Just get out of my house. Go on, get out!"

A note of pleading creeps into her last words, and she sits back in dismay, clutching the covers to her chest fighting back tears. Jon is holding her by the tops of her arms, his gentle touch cool yet burning. "Please, Anastasia," he says quietly.

Jon Senior is regarding her with interest, seemingly unused to displays of great emotion. "Can you tell us, young woman, why some of our intended targets are dying?"

She glares at him defiantly, the words "Why the fuck should I tell you anything?" already forming on her lips; but suddenly she *knows* why, and drawing a long shaking breath at the realization, she answers.

"It's to do with last night, isn't it? That thing, I mean... It wasn't just a trip."

Taz glances at Jon and he gives a tiny nod of assent. "Where we come from, our elite can access a spiritual power—the soul of our planet, if you like, by means of great wisdom and philosophy. It's not like that here..."

"No," she replies. "Our planet, takes people like me. Some of us, because of our..." She pauses, searching for words. "...sensibilities, or circumstances, are dying. Some of us can't cope, with life down here..."

Her voice cracks and the tears she has been holding back spill down her cheeks like beads of pity. She bows her head, hair spilling forwards to conceal her face.

"It's so hard sometimes, life is just so hard..."

For a moment it seems as though her grief will overwhelm her, and she rocks gently back and forth, fighting for composure, then she raises her head again, her face wet and reddened. Now her voice is quiet but calm.

"We ... well, some of us ... take drugs. Heroin." she lifts her right arm and shows the small mass of bruising near the bend of her elbow. A couple of the track marks have scabbed. "It's all right," she sniffs, and nods to reassure herself, "I'm not an addict. I know that's what they all say, but it's true. The thing is, as a prostitute, I'm a high risk." She glances at their uncomprehending faces. "It's a disease.

Many of our brightest people, our visionaries, are our weakest, loneliest people. They say that millions of people will die in the next twenty years. I've lost friends already. I could be next."

Jon's father seems shaken by the news. He walks slowly to the big red chair and sits down heavily on the mass of clothes. "Then it seems our mission is completed for us," he says dryly. He stares down almost despondently at his feet and flexes the big toes, testing the muscles and the sensation of human limbs. "Perhaps I'll leave you to your unfinished business, Jon."

A look passes between them. Taz is sure he's saying, *Kill her and we can sort this out.* Jon returns the look, but cannot hold his father's gaze. Then the old man is gone. There's no fuss, no flashing blue lights, he is simply no longer there.

Jon is out of the bed, pulling his clothes on for some reason. He has become almost used to the idea of garments now, and seems unable to take his leave of her whilst still naked.

"Your father was telling you to kill me, wasn't he?" Taz asks. Jon says nothing, doesn't look at her face. "Jon, I want to live." She gets out of the bed and comes toward him, stopping short a few feet away.

"I am in much trouble, but I could not kill you, Anastasia."

She starts to thank him, but he appears so immensely troubled that the words freeze in her throat.

"Do one thing for me, to show that I have done the right thing?" he asks. "Prove it."

She does not understand, not really, but she answers him anyway: "I will, every day."

Then he is ready to go. They have arrived at the awful moment when there is so much more to say than just goodbye, but the word has to cover everything.

"They won't really kill you, will they?"

"I don't think so. I am rehearsing my lie," he says solemnly. "Here." He hands her his long trenchcoat, "I don't think it will fit you."

"I'll wear it anyway," she says tightly. Her smile trembles on her lips. "Goodbye, Anastasia."

"Bye, Jon. Take care of yourself." She comes forward and kisses him lightly on the lips, then he is gone, like his father. The sensation of his kiss will stay with her for days.

◦

She is dressed ready to go out. She is going to Leith, to the drugs project there, and then to the Art College to beg them to take her back. The rain has stopped, and at this height, even above the traffic noise, she can hear the starlings singing. She puts some music on whilst she does her make-up, expertly disguising her black eye. The singer seems to sing through a warm smile:

I wanna fall from the stars
straight into your arms...

There is a knock on the door. She knows that knock, the sharp aggressive rhythm. She freezes, mascara brush in front of her eye.

"Taz! I know you're in there."

Dode. Jon lied to her. It all comes rushing back to her, and the bitterness and cynicism engulfs her like a sick wave. *Was it all lies then, all of it?* She stares at her face in the mirror, her lifestyle stares back at her, the tiny lines around her mouth, the hooded, haunted look of her eyes.

"You gonna let me in, or do I have to knock the fucking door down?"

She crosses the room fast, and undoes the latch, stepping back quickly.

Dode smiles brightly at her as he enters the room. "Where's he gone then? Peter. Lover boy from the pub."

"He's gone," she says, "just gone."

Dode sits down on the bed, stretching expansively, hands behind his head, taking up her space; marking his territory.

"Make yourself at home," she mutters dully.

"Oh aye, I've bought you a wee present—here." He takes a long box from his inside jacket pocket and flings it to the foot of the bed. She opens it: inside a heavy gold chain sits on a plush velvet cushion; it's a good one, Dode has friends in the trade.

"A chain, how appropriate. Is this so I won't press charges?"

Dode's smile freezes. She can tell he is astounded at her nerve, but she really is past caring.

"C'mon, Taz, you know it was strictly business. Nothing personal. I can't be seen to play favourites now, can I?"

She flings the box back on the bed beside him. "I don't work for you any more. Get out."

She is shaking, knowing this will be far from easy. To her surprise, he gets up, shrugging his suit jacket back into place, holding his hands out in a placatory gesture.

It can't be this easy, can it?

He is almost past her to the door when he wheels around, lashing out at her head with an open hand.

"You little cow," he snarls, "don't *ever* think you're too good for me!"

She is on the floor, stunned, propped up against the corner of the bed. Her head's thumping and she's confused.

"You're dead, you know," she tells him.

Dode takes this as a threat. Taz knows he's scared, scared of losing her. It's not because she means anything to him, but because she's his, part of his sick little empire. He has control. She should want him.

He hauls her up onto the bed by gathering up her blouse, then kisses her hard. She does not respond. Dode looks down at her then and grins mirthlessly. He has a piece of grey gum held between his teeth. He doesn't let her go though, but reaches into his jacket pocket to produce a knife. Meaningfully, and very slowly, sweating and sniggering, he moves the blade downwards.

From somewhere within, a tiny bubble of contempt grows, and Taz finds her anger at last.

Prove it.

"Need that to show me what a man you are, Dode?" she asks. Her voice is airy, theatrical, mocking.

"What!"

She knees him in the crotch as hard as she possibly can, and he rolls to one side, groaning, dropping the knife. She rolls off the bed—now her anger is here, she rides it like a wave. He recovers surprisingly quickly and pulls himself up by the window sill, his groping hand knocking her Buddha to the floor. Taz is shaking so hard, she can hear her breath catching in the back of her throat. There is no going back. For a moment she stares down at her leg, which he has scratched with the knife. She is distracted, her fury unfocussed.

"I'm going to *kill* you for this, you *bitch!*"

As she turns, she reads his murderous intention—he is pulling his belt from the loops of his trousers and wrapping the unbuckled end around his hand. His breathing is ragged and he sways unsteadily. A small breeze catches the curtain and the birds sing on regardless.

"C'mon, you bastard!" she pants.

He staggers one step before she rushes forward with a roar, head down, arms flung outward at the last instant; a red Fury of hate and revenge crying for justice.

Too late, Dode looks like he finally understands; that she no longer can stand the game, that he has pushed her too far. His arms flail against the window frame. The glass smashes as his back hits the pane. In the last, desperate moment, he looks her in the eye, but all he must see there is retribution.

She leans forward, eager to see his fall, so keen that she almost falls too. Dode has landed on his back. He's not moving, but no one's coming to look. A light breeze catches his hair and his sightless eyes almost look innocent. His fingers are relaxing around the leather belt. Taz finds she is holding Jon's coat, and hugs it to her, despite her earlier feelings of betrayal.

No crowd is gathering on the street below. She finds this so remarkable she frowns down at the pedestrians, one passes within feet of the body and doesn't react. Something is happening: the body is fading. Dode slowly appears to be dissolving, and as this happens, her pain, all of it, ebbs away.

Taz reaches out to steady herself and her hand touches solid glass; her windowpane, miraculously restored. She stares down mutely at her own body. She is still dressed to go out, to begin again.

I want to live, Jon.

Prove it.

Anastasia swings the trench coat around her shoulders, and as she does so, a white rose falls from within its folds. Holding the rose by the bloom, she inhales the heady fragrance.

Vanilla...

The archetype of the hard man casts a menacing shadow over the
Scottish imagination. From No Mean City *to* The Big Man *and*
beyond, hard-bitten characters have expressed themselves with their
straight razors and their fists. And the hardest of them all seem to come
from Glasgow. Maybe it's something in the water supply...

◦　◦

PISCES YA BAS
Gavin Inglis

◦　◦

Glasgow's Queen's Park has a pond. It's about a hundred feet across, and it's a real Glasgow pond—which is to say it's hardly two feet deep, you can't see the bottom for muck, and you could open a branch of Poundstretcher with the smeggy trainers, empty bottles of ginger, and old pairs of Y-fronts which choke its perimeter.

In the eighties came the first stories of a fish in the pond, from carefree lovers strolling in the park. It sounded like a real Glasgow fish—which was to say it was as long as a man's leg, its gold skin was turning a scabby grey, and it gave people the eye that said they were deid, for no rational reason.

Naturally, attempts were made to catch the fish. The next Saturday, the pond's slight wooden jetties were thronged with hobby fishermen happy to have such big game so close to home and the off-license. But after a few hours of South Side drizzle and tangling their lines on shopping trolleys, even the most hardy of them headed to the pub. There was a brief resurgence of effort after closing time, but nobody saw gold in the inky shallows of the pond. The enthusiastic ones who raked about bare-handed and then fell over discovered they had weird bitemarks along with their hangovers the next day.

The incident passed, and nobody drew a connection with the occasional missing cat or dog in the area. The problem came when the City Council decided to introduce swans to the park. One by one, the graceful birds were found hideously butchered in the pond or on the walkway nearby. The filth-caked features and torn, bleeding necks of the corpses made sensitive weans cry. So the Council sent in an ichthyological authority to assess the situation. A true professional, he located the rumoured fish. And incredibly, he was able to open communications, using techniques developed from a radioactive whale which washed up at Weymss Bay during the seventies. He donned waders and advanced into the pool, ready for the first message from the fish.

"Fuck off out ma pond," it said.

"We want to help," he said through the fish language translator. "Can we get you anything? A change of water maybe? A spawning partner?"

The fish seemed to ponder this, submerged thoughtfully, then suddenly broke the surface and leapt for the man's crotch, hooked yellow teeth glistening in its maw. The man was lucky. Its grip was imperfect, there was a jetty nearby, and the surgeons at the Southern General managed to save one testicle.

When the Queen heard about this trouble in her park, she insisted on travelling to Glasgow to deal with the fish personally. They protected Her Majesty with four Royal Marine Commandos and a giant sheet of Perspex.

"Now look," said the Queen to the fish. "This is not on. There's only one person in the country who's allowed to eat swans. That's me. We order you to desist, and to cooperate with the local authorities."

"Fuck off," said the fish.

"How dare you talk to me that way," said the Queen. "I'm the Queen."

"Fuck off, your Majesty," said the fish.

The Queen turned away with a sniff.

"Remove that odious animal," she decreed. "And make sure somebody eats him."

The Council introduced an emergency rise in the Poll Tax to deal with the fish. This was initially unpopular, but opposition faded when evidence emerged that a missing Shawlands schoolgirl had been last sighted in the vicinity of the park, and one of her shoes was found adrift at the water's edge.

A team of men was sent to sweep the pond with a long net. They got halfway across and then the fish showed up behind them. That was three men in the hospital.

Next they tried a boat and a harpoon. Glasgow University supplied a special sensor which detected movement and sound. They caught the fish singing Black Sabbath's "War Pigs", but as they aimed the harpoon, their target flipped around in the water and charged the boat. The hunters fell back, the boat capsized, and that was two more men in the hospital. One lost an eye. The other reported that the fish was chewing it as it submerged.

The Council brought in an expert from the Gourock fish farms. He recommended an expensive but lethal poison. Two hours after they dosed the pond, the fish was sighted looking happier than usual. Meanwhile the corpses of squirrels and rabbits turned up by the poolside, plus two dead crabs of a species thought to be extinct since the eighteenth century.

As a last resort, the Council drained the pool, intending to simply suffocate the fish. The pumps coughed and swallowed, drawing up the pond's filth. Inch by inch, the water level dropped, exposing beer cans and bike frames in a type of archaeology peculiar to Glasgow. The fish hunters became tense, alert for any hint of the enemy. Nothing ... nothing ... and the slimy bottom was revealed in patch after patch of poisonous sediment.

The pond was empty. There was no fish.

An explosion rocked the park as the pipe to the pump ruptured. Sewage spray blinded the nearby workers. "Get it right up ye!" yelled the fish, riding the vile jet. The men from the Council staggered, and went down one by one as the fish got to them under cover of the flying filth.

It was Brian McAllister who saved the day. His personality combined a fastidious cleanliness with a forty-a-day Benson & Hedges habit. Sensing something moving nearby, he whipped out his lighter and Blue Stratos aerosol deodorant, and rigged a makeshift flamethrower. His aim was spot on and the testy, oily fish went up like a cheap sofa.

"Ya fugginbastids!" it howled, writhing in the mud as its body crackled with a sound familiar to every chippy customer in the area. It bucked and went for Brian in its crispy rage, sinking its teeth into his welly.

"Ahh—AAARGH!" he cried and went down into the conflagration. The reek of melting plastic choked the air.

It would surely have been the end for Brian except for the quick-thinking action of Donny Dougal, the park's gardener. He steamed in with an old-fashioned rake and heaved the burning fish into the air. A flabby firework, it arced high above the heads of the surviving men, casting a magnificent incandescent trail. It carried all the way over the park railings, out onto Pollokshaws Road where it slapped hard onto the tarmac...

And was immediately run over by the Number 38 bus, a double decker.

"Urgh," gasped the fish, "youse ... yuv fuckin' killed us." It lay still, until a passing lemonade lorry ran over its face and spread it across twelve feet of road.

Some of the Council workers cheered, but others fell silent. They had admired the fish and the uncompromising way it had defended its home. Not everybody was keen on the park's royal patron. Later they had a whip-round in the pub and raised a small memorial stone to the fish, beside the pond it had so loved.

Two nights later a wee boy pissed on it.

Scotland is defined by its conflicts and contradictions, and nowhere is this better exemplified than its largest city, Glasgow. Hugh MacDiarmid, borrowing from his contemporary Gregory Smith, called this the Caledonian antisyzygy and suggested that it energized our culture. Of course, it may also be a symptom of our national illness, a very Scottish form of schizophrenia.

○ ○

THE VULTURE, 4-17 MARCH
Harvey Welles & Philip Raines

○ ○

The *magazine for Kentigern's culture dippers, diggers and dilettantes!*
Also on sale in St Mungo

COVER STORY: GLASGOW! WEEK (12-20 MARCH)

You Don't Know What You've Got Until It's Glas-gone!

At last, it's here! After twelve months of planning and an unprecedented publicity campaign, Glasgow! Week is about to start—eight days of events celebrating the shared Glasgow heritage of Kentigern and St Mungo. The Vulture caught up with Glasgow! Week's director, Debra McLaughlin, on the eve of Kentigern's most prestigious cultural festival in years.

Children who have the same parents often go their own ways and lead completely separate lives, but has there ever been a pair of siblings as wildly different as Kentigern and St Mungo? "It's true, we really are like brothers," laughs Debra McLaughlin, former head of the Glasgow Arts Foundation, now the mastermind behind Glasgow! Week. "And yes, we have gone along pretty different paths, and I guess that's no surprise—we were always going to, weren't we? But it's time to celebrate our common parentage."

And this long-awaited week will do just that. From the opening ceremony in George Square on Saturday, 12 March, to the relaunch of the restored Queen Mary on the following Sunday, Glasgow! Week will see events as diverse as new plays on the George Square riots of 1919 and the lives of the Glasgow Boys, the reopening of the Kelvingrove Art Museum, concerts by Rod Stewart and the Glasgow Bach Quartet, and a hands-on exhibition of Glasgow's industrial past, The Shipbuilding Experience, at our new Maritime Museum.

But is this all just a Kentigern publicity stunt for the tourists? McLaughlin insists not. "You'd be amazed at the support that we've had from St Mungo. Ever since the cities finally split apart four years ago, I know that relations between the two councils have not always been—well, shall we say, mutual. But the enthusiasm of the St Mungo City Council has been impressive. You couldn't ask for a better partner."

Despite McLaughlin's praise for St Mungo's authorities, many in Kentigern have criticized our neighbours for being a mite stingy. "I can't deny that Kentigern has been footing the bill for this festival. But you have to remember that St Mungo has fewer resources than us. Only last week, we were hearing about their petrol shortage—I still don't know why, I have to admit, it's not as if many of them have cars in the first place—and, of course, they don't have the same facilities we do. In Kentigern, we can hold an exhibition on Glasgow's contributions to science at our world-class Science Centre. On the same site in St Mungo, there's only the old abandoned docks. But they are helping where they can. St Mungo is supplying the extras for our full-scale recreation of a Hampden football pitch invasion. And I'm sure they're making their own arrangements."

The thought of so many St Mungites running unsupervised through Kentigern for the first time since the split has been one of the more controversial issues facing the Glasgow! Week organizers. "Security was a fundamental concern, and I can assure you that we worked on it until we got it right. There will be full stewardship at all events and specially policed routes for our visitors. They will be led to and from the crossover point at the Buchanan Galleries.

"But really, is this the right attitude for a big brother? The Hampden riot is a terrific example of this collaboration in action. The ballet is being choreographed by one of Kentigern's most talented dance directors and I'm sure St Mungo will benefit enormously from exposure to such cultural genius. After all, we were born from the same city. Old Glasgow had two different character streaks. Kentigern will always display the innovation, the vision, the drive that was behind so many of Glasgow's great achievements. But there's a need to remember its failures as well. We mustn't forget how much St Mungo has yet to show us."

○

CINEMA
Kentigern (4-10 March)
UGC Renfield Street

L'Accident Humain	13.20	16.20	19.20	
Meet the Fockers	14.10	17.05	19.55	23.35 (Fri/Sat)
Ocean's Twelve	12.30	15.50	19.20	
Sideways	12.50	16.25	20.30	
Team America: World Police	13.45	16.00	18.30	

Glasgow Film Theatre
Glasgow! Week Film Season

That Sinking Feeling/
Comfort and Joy   14.35   19.05
(Sat only, afternoon show followed
by a talk by Professor Gavin Moray
of Glasgow University on "Kentigern
and the Legacy of Bill Forsyth's
Glasgow")
My Name Is Joe/Ae Fond Kiss   13.15   18.30

St Mungo (4-10 March)
ABC Sauchiehall Street

Meet the Fockers   19.00

Odeon Renfrew Street

Meet the Fockers   12.15 (Sun only)   19.00

o

ADVERTISEMENT

o

MUSIC
Kentigern
See separate Glasgow! Week listings.

St Mungo

Irn-Bru Maiden	Doors open 8 p.m., 4 March, Hellfire Tavern
Dollar Tribute	Doors open 8 p.m., 11 March, Hellfire Tavern
Country & Western night	8 p.m., 12 March, Sighthill Community Centre
Karaoke	7.30 p.m., Tuesdays and Thursdays, DeCourcey's

Editor's note: Kentigern visitors should be advised that public transport within St Mungo has become erratic following the petrol shortages. Police are warning that anyone travelling from Kentigern should be extra vigilant at the crossover point—violent attacks on Kentigern visitors have been increasing in recent weeks.

○

ART
Ned for a Day

Enter the weird world of Baxter and Jock Schultz, the two Swiss conceptual artists who are turning the art world upside down with their recreation of everyday life in St Mungo. The Vulture ventured into deepest St Mungo to speak to the Schultz Brothers at their studio in a converted police station in Ruchill as they prepare for Glasgow! Week.

TV: "Baxter", "Jock"—is it true you've taken your names from old Glasgow football legends?

Baxter: Ja. Jim Baxter. Jock Stein. Little brother and I are big fans. That was what drew us to St Mungo first-time.

TV: You're football fans?

Jock: No, we love conflict. Glasgow is good at conflict. Celtic, Rangers, Kentigern, St Mungo. But especially St Mungo— we love all the sectarian craziness and gang-banging here.

Baxter: And the heroin.

Jock: Just like home in Zurich. Very raw. Very real.

TV: Your work has taken inspiration from St Mungo's indigenous "ned" culture. I see that you're dressed right now in the trademark Kappa tracksuit and New York Yankees baseball cap.

Baxter: Ja—we prefer the original ned. Not the later, chav variations.

Jock:	More raw.
TV:	Some of your past installations have been spectacular—covering municipal St Mungo buildings in graffiti, blocking Argyll Street with hundreds of abandoned shopping trolleys. But I gather the locals haven't taken to your "pranks".
Baxter:	No, they write FUCK OFF on the side of our building.
Jock:	Result!
TV:	You're not worried?
Baxter:	No—they react to us. The Brothers of St Mungo—that's their tag—
Jock:	Local young team, obviously.
Baxter:	—these Brothers react to us. And that's good! See—we like to soak up the local culture and squeeze it out, more concentrated, but they can't take the super-strength of our juice. We worry them! They don't like us when we sponge.
TV:	Some would say you're just slumming.
Baxter:	Yes! Exactly! We slum. We're not artists, we are critics. Art is boring. We despise the search for originality. We celebrate the hunger for the authentic.
Jock:	For the raw.
TV:	So you think that Kentigern has lost that rawness?
Baxter:	Very definitely—St Mungo was the part of Glasgow that revelled in the decay. Glasgow was always very schizo—boldly going forward to the future while wallowing in the filth of the past. Big surprise that it split into two cities? I think no. I think the city is splitting itself a long time. But this time it stuck.
Jock:	Ja. And we like to play with the shit, so we like St Mungo.
TV:	What have you got planned for Glasgow! Week then?
Baxter:	We have a performance art piece—little brother and I are going to cause as many teen pregnancies in St Mungo as possible. One week, total fucking mania.
Jock:	Watch out girls!

○

OOT AN ABOOT

Saturdays and Sundays, 1 p.m. and 4 p.m. St Mungo Adventure
tours. The popular tours of St Mungo—which include visits to a

Maryhill drug rehabilitation centre, the famous joy-rider graveyard of car wrecks along the canal and an authentic football supporters bar for the recreation of a genuine sectarian attack—have been suspended for the foreseeable future. For refunds, contact Walks on the Wild Side on Kentigern 239 0081 or through the website at www.walksonthewildside.co.kentigern.

14 March. 8 p.m. Govan Town Hall. Meeting of the Brothers of St Mungo. Planning for Glasgow! Week and petrol distribution. St Mungo residents only.

○

PROMOTION

Free tickets to the opening ceremony of Glasgow! Week in George Square (Kentigern) on Friday, 11 March for all our St Mungo readers—just show your copy of *The Vulture* at the crossover checkpoint in Buchanan Galleries from 6 p.m. Tickets include the fireworks show and a free pamphlet on sexual health. Standing room only. Over 18s only. Must have a valid commuter's permit.

○

PERSONALS

Tired of being the one who's screwed over in a relationship? Want to try something new? Your waiting is over.

The Brothers of St Mungo are organizing an evening of excitement, adventure and surprises. It's a chance to get to know your neighbour.

Meet at the crossover point at 6 p.m. on 11 March. All groups welcomed. St Mungo residents only.

Cocktails will be provided.

There is a traditional Scottish prayer that is known all over the world:

From ghoulies and ghosties
And long-leggety beasties
And things that go bump in the night,
Good Lord, deliver us!

But what do you do when prayers are not enough?

◦ ◦

THE BOGLE'S BARGAIN
Stefan Pearson

◦ ◦

The Anne Marie's inboard coughs and splutters, choking itself, the exhaust plunging into the water time and again. He's hauled in all the buoys and fenders, cursed the VHF, lamented his sodden flares and the broken bindings on his lifejacket; and he's prayed, prayed for all he's worth, opened his soul to the heavens, wind and rain. But the storm rages, unheeding.

◦

"Here, I'll get them." Dad takes the scuttle from me and heads for the door. "Don't want you blowing away now, do we?"

He's always at that: treating me like a bairn—"Daddy's special wee princess!" As soon as the slightest gale starts to blow, he'll hurry me into the croft and shut the door tight, making sure I'm wrapped up in one of his massive jumpers in front of the fire. It's like he thinks I'm made of paper and that, if I step outside, I'll get carried away across the dunes and out to sea, like a kite. Mind you, if I did go outside wearing this thing, I probably *would*.

"Here, out the way now, Sally." I roll aside. Peats tumble into the grate, tiny sparks spiralling up the flue. They smell of wee.

"Do you think Iona will be home soon?"

That frown, like a deflating football. "I shouldn't expect so, not if the weather stays the way it is. She'll have enough bother getting to the Kyle from Edinburgh, never mind the ferry here. I've no seen the Minch as wild in as long as. No doubt she'll phone."

"It's not that bad is it?"

Dad puts the scuttle back down on the hearth and paces to the window. There's a crack in the curtains as he peers out into the gloom, like he's waiting for something—that hunted look he has when there's a storm brewing.

"It's bad enough, dear, bad enough."

○

My mum died when I was five and sometimes I can't really remember what she looked like. When I see her in my head, she wears a sky-blue jacket and her long red hair is tied up in a bunch on her head. Usually I make something up, a wee scene to put her in: cooking tea, shearing or making kindling from washed-up fish boxes. There's a black-and-white photo on the mantelpiece, Mum and Dad on their wedding day. "Anne Marie and Duncan Morrison, 1968," it says, but she's like a ghost in it, whispy and pale, clinging to my dad's strong arms like a bag in a gale. He picks the picture up every day.

The thing I remember most of all about my mum is her voice: the soft, warm, sleepy voice she had when she tucked me in at night after a story. I prefer thinking of her like that. It seems more real. My big sister Iona sounds like Mum did, the same dreamy words sending me off to sleep. I miss them both.

Iona went to university in Edinburgh two years ago. She comes home during the summer holidays, when the weather's nice, but this year she said she'd be back for Christmas too, even though Dad tried to put her off, making out that the ferry wouldn't be running and that she'd be raging if she ended up having to spend the holiday stuck on the mainland. But she's coming anyway. I can't wait.

Dad taps the ageing barometer. Its needle bobs menacingly.

"Looks like it's going to get worse before it gets better. Ferry'll no be sailing in this, that's for sure." If I didn't know better, I'd swear he sounds relieved.

"I'm away up to my room," I say. To be honest, I've not been feeling that well the last few days. I keep getting these pains in my guts. Dad forced me take some milk of magnesia—yeuch!—but it didn't make any difference.

○

It's Inness's grumbling that wakes me, not the gale or the rowan bucking in the gloom beyond the curtains—Dad planted the tree a few years back, to "keep the kelpies from our door". He can be dead superstitious sometimes, it's embarrassing.

"Inness! Wheesht! There's nothing there you silly dog!" But he won't shut up, just keeps on with that throaty growl, like an outboard motor. When I slide out of bed he's at the door in a flash, barging through and down the stairs.

In the living room, Dad's poking at something in the fire, flames licking round cardboard and plastic packaging. White material, cups, straps. A bra! The one I'd ordered from the catalogue nearly a month ago.

"What are you doing!" I yell, fighting back the tears. I can't believe it! I ordered that bra ages ago, and twice the catalogue people told me it had been sent, even though it'd never turned up and I'd shouted at them down the crackling line, pleading with them to make sure.

"Sally! I was just..."

"I hate you!"

○

He's afraid. Not for himself, but for his daughters; they'll be orphaned, and the youngest only eight years old—as beautiful a creature as any in God's own creation. He's fond of telling his little girl that the Lord made her on Sunday, while he was resting: a labour of love. He doesn't pray anymore, but waits; waits and hopes that the tempest tires of its sport and lets him and what's left of his family be.

○

Dad doesn't want me to grow up. I suppose I can sort of understand why: Mum dying, then Iona going off to school and university. I'll be away to high school too next year, and Dad will be left on his own with only Inness and the storms for company. But it's no excuse. I'm not a baby anymore. Even the way he likes me to dress—like a wee doll—it didn't used to bother me before, but it's getting embarrassing. Shona and that lot take the mickey out of me and it makes me mad. They all get cool stuff from the catalogue or from the mainland. I cry too, but I wouldn't tell him.

"Sally?" I hear the door to my bedroom creaking open and turn away, pressing my face against the wall. "Sally, I'm sorry. It's just you don't really need a thing like that yet, you know? You're still young. Only eleven. A wee lassie."

"I am not! And it's a bra, not a thing. You *can* say it! Shona and Ellen both have bras. Why don't you want me to grow up? I'll be twelve soon!"

"It's not that I don't want you to grow up... I just want what's best for you. To protect you."

○

There was blood in my knickers this morning. I'm pretty nervous to be honest, even though I know it's meant to happen like this. Mrs Munro said it was all part of growing up when she took all the P7 girls aside last spring, but I wish Iona was here. It's not as if I can talk to Dad. I wipe myself and crumple some tissue into my pants. I can smell Dad cooking the breakfast downstairs.

"How are you today, my wee princess?" he asks, beaming.

"Fine," I say, squirting ketchup onto my plate.

○

One of my favourite games after a big storm is exploring the dunes. The wind tears the sand away, changes its shape and sometimes rips open the rabbit warrens that riddle the hillsides and machair like fairy mines. I dare myself to see how far in I can go before chickening out.

"Inness!" I saw a streak of black and white a while ago tearing across the top fields, but I've lost him again. Not that I really mind. He'll come back when he's ready. I hope he doesn't go too close to Peter Murdy's croft. Murdy's a miserable old sod—I once saw him throwing a clump of peat at Inness when the daft mutt was nosing about round his sheds. Got my own back, though. I left the gate open on his bottom field, and his tupping ram got out and ran riot. Served him right.

Skipping over the dune and down into a wee hollow, I edge towards the big raggedy hole. The air's still and I'm suddenly aware of the wind hissing through its shaggy mane of grass.

"Inness!" I shout again. For some reason, I'd feel better if he was with me. Maybe just because he'd go first.

There's a damp, meaty smell hanging around the hole, a hole nearly big enough for me to stoop into—the biggest rabbit warren I've ever seen, but a couple of runs could have easily collapsed into each other. I inch forward, wishing I'd brought my torch, trying to be brave, imagining I'm on a quest to slay an ogre and steal his treasure. Loose sand rains onto my shoulders and the cold hits me like an icy hammer, even through my jacket. My breath curls away in lazy clouds in front of my face. The smell gets worse too. I'm in maybe a few feet, feeling in front of me with my foot when I start having second thoughts. Jesus! How wet? *It's only a hole!* I tell myself. I go a wee bit further, glancing quickly over my shoulder every couple of seconds, trying to judge the distance I'd have to scramble to get back out into the open air.

Then there's the noise.

○

It's the scraping noise that snaps him from his melancholy, the dull scratching against the side of the hull. He drags himself from the wheel-house and sees something crawling onto the deck. Something man-shaped, but not of God's creation. The wizened thing flops onto the soaking deck in a shroud of spray, skitters across the boards and crashes into his stacked creels. His instinct is to help, but something about the stunted creature stops him in the doorway. Something unwholesome. Something ancient.

"One whore of a storm! Been trying half a bloody hour to get onto this tub. Mo Criosd!'

The thing's face is as blasphemous as its tongue: dog-like, a snout of sorts, the flesh around its hairless jaw pink and obscene. He shudders.

"What do you want?" he roars.

The creature grins. "Looks like you're in a bit of a stramash! *You'll never get back to port in this," it yells.*

"And is this why you've come, demon? To taunt me?"

It laughs, jowls quivering. "Who are you calling demon? I was here before that shower lost their wings. Besides, I'm here to offer you a deal..."

"What kind of deal?"

It turns its face as a wave crashes across the deck between them. "Is that a band of gold on your finger?" it asks, pointing.

"Yes?"

"How about your woman for your life?"

He only hesitates for a moment, stifling a smile. The thing eyes him greedily.

"Take her, and take me home, abomination!"

◉

"If I've told you once Sally, I've told you a hundred times. You know it's dangerous on the dunes after a storm—the sand shifts... Here, pass me the shampoo."

I don't know who looks more sheepish, me or Inness. The bottle makes a rude noise as Dad squeezes the last few drops into his hand and lathers them into the dog's back.

"He was down the hole ahead of you, you say?"

I nod.

"And do you know what he was chasing?"

"Don't know ... rabbits?"

"Aye," he sighs, "more than likely. Baffles me how he managed to mess himself, though. Are you sure you didn't see him rolling in anything?"

I shake my head. Inness isn't a roller. He does that tobogganing thing sometimes, when he drags his bum along the ground with his front legs, but he doesn't roll in stuff. The dog had come bolting out of the hole in front of me, howling his head off. I got such a fright I nearly messed *myself!* I'd shot out of the hole after him at a hundred miles an hour too, just as it'd started to collapse. Dad was already standing outside the door with a cowering Inness as I'd scrambled breathless back up the hill. That's the two of us in the doghouse.

Inness makes a break for it when Dad turns to plug in the hairdryer.

◉

The creature isn't stupid, that much he's learned. Angry, yes, but it has all the time in the world to take its revenge. He should have expected it, but the day he'd made his way down to the cemetery to set more flowers, he'd thrown up when he'd seen the mess it had left. The thing must have clawed her out of the ground in its anger. She was nowhere to be seen, even though he spent most of the day scouring the nearby beach and hills. Thank the Lord the girls weren't with him. There was nothing he could do but put everything back, weep and place his flowers. He changes them and scrubs the small stone every week now. It uses the grave for a toilet.

○

"The forecast says there's another storm heading our way tomorrow, Dad."

"Aye, I know dear, I know."

"Is there something wrong? Are you worried Iona won't make it in time for Christmas?"

"Aye, I suppose I am. I can't help thinking she'd have been better off staying at university over the holidays. I'm sure she could have got more hours in the shop she works in: they're always dead busy this time of year. She'll need all the pennies she can get."

"But you must be quite excited? Just the three of us for Christmas dinner. It's been ages. I wonder what she's got me?"

"I'm sure you'll find out soon enough, princess."

"She should get you a new barometer. I'm surprised that one still works, the amount you tap at it."

He smirks. "Be a good lassie. Fetch those damp towels and put them on the range... I'm sure there's a film on the telly we could watch later. There's always films on this time of year."

"Okay." I'd rather just sit and watch TV anyway, I haven't been feeling that great since my period started. I took a couple of aspirin, but my tummy's been aching all day.

○

The days seem to drag on endlessly, each one longer than the last. It's torture waiting for Christmas to creep up *normally*, but when I'm expecting Iona to turn up any day, it's even worse.

I'm up in my room, reading my magazines, when I hear the phone. By the time I'm at the top of the landing, Dad's already got the receiver in his hand.

"Hello? Iona, is that you? I can't make you out, dear... Hello?'

"Is that her, Dad?" He waves his hand at me to shush.

"Hello? Can you hear me?" Silence. He puts the receiver slowly back in its cradle.

"Was it her?" He has that hunted look again.

"I honestly couldn't tell, dear. What's the weather like?"

"Still bad and getting worse, too." The wind was making such a racket against my window I had to put a tape on. "Do you think the ferry will be sailing?"

"Hard to say. I'll away and give the mainland a call and see. If it is, John Hugh'll no doubt wait till the last minute before giving up till tomorrow. Could be he'll nose in ahead of the dark."

"Hope so."

Dad picks up the phone and dials. He pokes his head into my room a few minutes later.

"Is there a ferry?"

He sighs. "I couldn't get through at all. The phone lines must be down. I think I'll take a wander down to the point to see if I can see anything. Where are my binoculars?"

"I'll get them." I skip through to the kitchen and grab them from the back of the door. "Can I come too?" Why do I just know he won't let me?

"Best not, eh?" He loops them round his neck. "What if the phone comes back on and Iona calls the house? She'll wonder what's become of us if no one's here to answer."

"Aye, okay. Don't be long though."

"Very good." He tugs on his wellies and makes for the door. "You stay here, Inness."

○

It hadn't taken him long to understand the thing's game. It was when it began to steal his eldest's underwear from the line that he finally put two and two together. "Your woman for your life," it had said. He'd always doubted it would be content with the corpse of his long-dead wife. His daughters are obviously fair game now. He'd felt like some deranged pervert plucking the remaining clothes from the line and burying them in the sand that day. "A wind must have took them, Iona. Come in and we'll get you some new stuff from the catalogue."

○

Dad's been away ages and it's pitch black out. If John Hugh was crossing the bay tonight, he would have been here by now. I tug aside the curtains and peer into the gloom. It's still wild out to sea, and the dunes are rippling in the gale like the back of some slumbering, hairy giant.

I wish Dad'd hurry up. I walk through to the hall and stare at the phone for a second, willing it to ring. "Come on Iona!" It doesn't, of course, so I lift the receiver and place it against my ear–don't ask me why. Inness starts barking his head off and I near jump out of my skin, dropping the handset with a clatter. Jesus!

"Inness! Bad dog! Wheesht!" I snap louder than I should–it's not his fault, he's just doing his doggy duty, but he gave me such a start. Inness is worse than most dogs too, because instead of growling and then giving a wee warning bark–like proper guard dogs do on the telly–he just seems to save it all up and then erupt like a hairy volcano. He can't help himself.

○

It's up to something. He knows its habits only too well. The creature's braver when the weather's bad, especially during storms. It seems that the only time he can ever truly relax is in the height of summer, but even then he feels the fear when the wind starts to blow.

Is it paranoia, or has the thing the gall to tamper with the phone line? It's not beyond acts of petty vandalism, and he's grown used to it urinating on his peat stack and defecating in his boat.

Surely John Hugh wouldn't take the ferry out in this? The sea's increasingly broody, the rocks off the far away point casting salvos of angry spray into the dark, a dark that's spreading thickly across both sea and land. He shivers and trudges down to the jetty, binoculars thudding against his chest.

○

I'm hauling Inness away from the window when I think I see something down by the dyke at the bottom of our field. My heart trips in my chest. "Inness, wheesht!" I strain my eyes through the glass, pressing my face to it, pushing the dog aside, looking off to one side to try and make out the figure in the darkness.

It's there again–a woman waving to me from the edge of the dunes. I clap my hands and dash through for my jacket. Iona's here at last! I didn't see Dad, but no doubt he's at the jetty with John Hugh.

I'm bolting out the door as I tug the zip up on my jacket, slipping and stumbling on the wet grass, Inness racing ahead of me.

"Iona!" I shout into the storm, but the wind almost tears the words from my mouth. It's so dark I can't make her out properly, but I can see long hair rippling about her face, a big bright coat jostling around her. She waves again, but as I get closer, she turns round and leaps over the dyke into the grass and starts running across the dunes.

"Iona!" I shout, until I'm hoarse. The rotten cow! She's messing about, trying to get me to chase her. We used to spend hours racing across the dunes when we were wee—if you put your arms out by your side while you ran, you looked like a plane skimming across the sea. We'd play dogfights for hours.

"Iona, stop!" But she just keeps on going. I'm getting light-headed and there's a pain in my belly, but I ignore it and run for all I'm worth, the slick sand pulling at my feet. Iona stops every now and then until I've almost caught up, then turns away again, slipping through the grass like a ghost. My excitement's melting away now and my breath's coming in gasps, but I've nearly caught up.

o

He's panting by the time he reaches the jetty, wiping lines of water from the corners of his eyes before he can get a proper look out to sea. Is there a shape in the darkness? It's hard to be sure, but he sees something being cast about on the waves about half a mile offshore. He fumbles for his binoculars, fingers thick and numb with cold. He prays it isn't John Hugh's ferry as he twists the lenses into focus.

For once, his prayers aren't answered: he'd recognise that wee white wheelhouse and twisting mast-wire anywhere. But something's amiss. There's no light in the wheelhouse, nor on the tip of the mast. The boat is silent and black. All its fenders are out, too, and it looks to be languishing in the grip of the storm. "Christ!" He allows himself that small blasphemy and hurries down to the water's edge to launch his boat. He almost puts his hand in the sharn clinging to the rail.

o

I'm near done for by the time I catch up with her. My head's spinning and I feel like I'm going to be sick.

"Iona! Stop will you?" I plead, but I don't think she can hear me. She skips down into a gully where a strange orangey glow seeps through the grass from below. As I reach the crest, I see her dipping down into a hole, a big raggedy hole in the side of a dune. The light's coming from inside it, like the coals of a dying fire. What's going on? "Iona?" I call, but there's no answer. Has she stashed something here, something she doesn't want Dad to find? Some kind of secret present she wants to show me and me alone? I slide gently down into the hollow.

"Iona?" I call again. Is that laughter from inside? A wave of nausea pulses through my belly again and I feel sick rise to the back of my throat. There's a low tunnel ahead that curves away deep into the dunes. For some reason, I don't feel scared as I edge slowly forward into the light.

❍

It's a battle to reach the stricken vessel, but he finally manages to manoeuvre alongside and gaff the rail. Clambering aboard, he calls out, but the swelling in his throat strangles his voice. The boat's empty. My God! Had Iona been aboard? He sinks to his knees and weeps into his hands. He's lost at last, after all these years. "Blasted bogle!" he cries. "Damn you to Hell!"

❍

My head's light and my eyes are going all blurry—I feel faint. I'm sure I can here voices, up ahead ... laughter maybe, and music? Am I dreaming? Or dying? Maybe I'm lying on the dunes somewhere, unconsciousness. My feet drag me forward, but I don't know why or where I'm going.

❍

A light. On the dunes. "Damnation!" He's both sickened and elated: The creature's on the dunes, of course! Scurrying around the boat, a cursory check is all he needs to establish that the ferry's mooring rope is lying severed in the water and that John Hugh's oilskins hang undisturbed on a peg in the small wheelhouse. And where are Iona's bags?

"How could I have been so stupid?" The creature was smarter than he'd given it credit for. He'd known it would come for Sally one day, just like it had Iona, but he hadn't expected it so soon. If only he'd accepted that Sally was no longer the child he wished she'd remain, he would have been ready

for the creature. He grasps for the binoculars and peers towards the shore, desperately scanning the dunes. It's too late. Something's luring Sally towards a fey light.

"Damn you to Hell!" he curses again, leaping into his boat. "I'm coming, Sally!" he screams, "I'm coming!"

○

There's a tattered curtain hanging across the tunnel. The light and voices are coming from the other side. I must be dreaming. I hope Dad finds me soon. I try to will myself awake but can't. Then I'm pulling aside the curtain. There's a big chamber on the other side, carved into the sand of the machair. It's empty apart from the fire and the monster perched on a throne of kelp and broken fish boxes. Beside the creature, on another throne, is a skeleton with flowing red hair, leathery skin and empty, unseeing eyes. The room stinks of rotting fish and worse. I almost gag. I'm going to faint. I can feel blood soaking into my knickers.

"Sally, so glad you could finally join us," the thing on the throne says, pink wobbly snout quivering with glee. "You remember your mother?" it says as it pushes the skeleton from the chair and beckons for me to sit. I walk towards the empty throne, shaking, legs like jelly, unable to stop myself. The creature's grin splits its face like a running sore.

○

He know it's too late: he's too far off and he's sure he saw Sally stepping down into the hollow. Now the light, along with his hope, has faded. There's nothing he can do, and he knows in his soul there is only one way left to honour the bogle's bargain and save his daughters.

The rope is tight around his neck as he shifts the heavy anchor onto the rail.

○

I'm about to sit on the seaweed-covered seat when I come to my senses all of a sudden. It's like someone's slapped me hard in the face. I turn and see the smile melt from the creature's quivering lips. It makes a lunge for me, but I shove its spindly arms away and it topples backwards on its throne, screaming horribly.

Then I'm running, running for all I'm worth, out of the chamber and up the tunnel, tears streaming down my cheeks as sand rains down all around me.

○

The nurses said it was Peter Murdy that found me—in my own bed, in as deep a sleep as he'd ever seen anyone. I'd been sick too. To be honest I'm embarrassed, him seeing me in that state! I can't remember anything about the storm, but I'm in the hospital now, on the mainland, and Iona's arriving soon. The nurses gave me a proper tampon too, to stop the blood.

Christmas Eve at last! I'm surprised Dad isn't here yet, but maybe he's arriving with Iona. I asked one of the nice nurses where he was, but she just gave a forced smile and said someone would be coming to speak to me soon. She also told me they give out presents in the hospital at Christmas. Dad always gets me something good.

Matthew Fitt broke new ground by giving cyberpunk a Scottish accent in But n Ben A-Go-Go, a science-fiction novel written entirely in Scots. Irvine Welsh, no less, said: "It's making a statement that it's not necessarily a language of the past... It's quite a clever thing to do, to do a science-fiction book in a language that's supposed to be kind of extinct."

Here we're proud to present another glimpse into Fitt's future world with a self-contained extract from the forthcoming sequel to But n Ben A-Go-Go. Senator Calvin Criggie is about to be elected Lord President of the floating megacity, Muckillopolis, after years of captivity in a terrorist stronghold. What is really behind Criggie's affiliation with Congressman Athelstane, his Election Grieve? Why does the Senator's bodyguard never sleep? The answers come thick and fast in Fitt's second novel, Kaledonika.

○ ○

CRIGGIE
Matthew Fitt

○ ○

Senator Calvin Criggie opens his bawkie-bleck een an, for as lang as it taks twa ticks tae go roon, Criggie canna mind whaur he is.

The Senator's hauns jine automatically forenent his face. He canna stap his body tensin intae a foetal baw. There is suddenly swite on his tap lip. He gawks at the hauf-daurk room he finns himsel in but sees nothin throu the anonymous gloam that can reconnect him tae the world as he left it lest nicht.

He fechts tae stey calm but aweady the flegs are raivellin throu him, chappin his braith intae wheezlie pechs, garrin him howk his een wi his nieves an kick wi radge frichtened sturts at the bedclaes taigled aboot his feet. Afore he can think himsel oot, his dream-mogered imagination defaults, flingin him back temporarily tae the cauld prison cell whaur he tholed fufteen fellie year o captivity on the Asian moontain city o Nanga Parbat.

Time chitters like haar as the roch cell waws, coorse wi damp an rodent kich, close roon aboot him yince mair. He grups his wime as hunger preens stob like dirks throu his gut. An as if the menyie o Ceilidh Rescue troops hadna shoodered in the prison door a twalmonth syne on Hogmanay an shot the loun deid like a radge deleerit dug, Hahn, the Senator's cell maister, lours again as he did for fufteen year in the baillie o the room, his goat an kye bowff claggerin Criggie's throat while he baitchels tae a pouder the banes in the Senator's neb wi his iron-tappit gowk stick.

Paralysed in slow-mo drow, Criggie canna richt breathe as panic threatens tae stap his thrapple. Fae his squatterin consciousness he recaws Doctor Hazelrig's words. "Think wi yir hauns, Senator. Let the air in tae let the pain oot." Gruntlin, he steers his fingirs tae his face an manages tae claw his gab. His mou this time isna stappit wi rags. His heid isnae wabbit fae chloroform. Criggie's no back on Nanga Parbat. Hahn's no here. Hahn is deid.

Criggie snaps on a licht.

A lang elegant room wi capercaillie wawpaper jinks ontae his retinae. His siller Intimo briefcase stauns on a persian-ruggit flair. His suit jaiket an troosers hing on a peg at the door while his harrylauder oxter stick leans at a gley angle aside the bed.

His lugs register a fitstep ootside in the lobby, thon o his personal bodyguaird, Sam Boness, taragatin a shooglie board wi his Reidshank captain's tread. He spots his white pre-packit sark an senatorial Hie Hoose grauvit on the airm o a chair. Criggie's pulse resumes its regular dunt. "Jeelie-knees," he tells hissel aff wi venom. "Richt wee jeelie-knees."

Criggie has waukened in the guest wing o Windyhingin Shaw, a bonnie-plenished dryland villa on Tinto Hill abinn the wattery landward o Lanark. The hoose belangs his Election Grieve, Congressman Simon Athelstane, whase Mercedes-Romeo Landlowper flew him here across the Gless Sea late lest nicht fae the sport an recreation glebe o the City's Hietoun district.

Muckillopolis yesterday wis a bobbinquaw o haun-grippin, bairn-kissin an lest-minute canglin for votes. A denner for Loch Burgh's five thoosan firefechters follaed a tousie debate wi the weans at Ewan McGregor University in Kirk afore Criggie pit the final steek on his 2105 Presidential Election campaign wi a stoor-stompin speech tae pairty worthies at the Hietoun National Pictur Hoose, cowpin in the foremidnicht ontae his guest bed at Windyhingin Shaw wi three menyies o Reidshank snipers skailed across the law's staney ribs tae bield him in his sleep.

The alarm nock aside the nichtstand reads six-ten a.m. Criggie hirples tae the bathroom an empties a pish intae the cludge but doesnae flush. Huilin hissel oot o the silk pyjamaes lenned him by the Congressman's wife, he runs the bath tae it's fou wi a brose o almond an thrissle an then dooks his forty-five-year-auld scaur-scaddit body in tae the craigie. Echty craw-klicks awa across the Gless Sea, the electronic yetts o Port's pollin hooses hae awready opened. Later the nicht at the ballot-coont in the Jim Baxter Memorial Sports Tron, Criggie's twinty-year ettle tae become the eleeventh Lord President o Port will finally rax its knowe-heid.

He shouldna be alive. Captivity on Nanga Parbat should hae shrivelled him tae a shaup. Thae years there, thrawned in weet, nippit cells, spulyied his youthied an the yin leal love o his life, an wid hae scunnered his appetite for the stushie o politics, tae, if no for learnin on release that his captors had been in the siller-sporran o enemies at hame.

Houstoun Spink, the bygane Lord President that chored hissel three terms in Argyle Hoose, peyed in 2089 a raggitie punyie o Uighur separatists tae kidnap the twinty-nine-year-auld presidential candidate Calvin Criggie. Fleyed at the fire-flaucht popularity o the young Senator, Spink had postit his rival hyneawa tae the City's Asian Trade Staple on Bombay Island. When thon failed tae clary Criggie's wallie prospects at the polls, the auld warlock had him warsled awa in the dumb o nicht.

Spink, gollyin crocodile tears at Criggie's reportit deeth, that year bore aff the Presidential gree. Ainlie in 2103 when a glamshachie kidnapper wis deefied by Spink for blackmail siller wis the plot clyped til the Muckillopolis meeja an Criggie unthirled.

Houstoun Spink nou legislates owre a haurd bink at Inverdisney Penitentiary but Reagan Spink Jr, brou-skelped intae politics by his faither's gurr, has managed tae styter throu twa terms o office. A shooghie shadda o his faither, he is aw that stauns atween Criggie an the Lord Presidency but, wi Dada Houston's mispauchlins puddlin his son's campaign, the political spaewifes hae awready consigned the current President tae the bing o history. Gruppin his briefcase an trevel poke, he ootgangs the guest room tae the lobby, whuddin the door shut ahint him. Criggie the day has a dynasty tae cowp.

His Reidshank bodyguaird strauchles tae attention fae a weel-upholstered nicht chair an, altho Criggie touers abinn maist o his peers, Captain Sam Boness meisures a heid an spauld-bane taller than him. His premature-lyart hair frames a youthfu face chowed at the edges by a lifetime's cark an care for bodies ither than himsel.

"Mornin, Senator."

"Ay, Boness. How's wir weather?"

The caber-boukit guaird gaithers up his guns. "No joco, sir."

A keek throu the lobby windae advises him o the day's coorseness. Awready, a string o kate-o-shanters has daurkened the Gless Sea atween Tinto an the City while, in the east, the turbulent lift is busy smiddyin thegither bigger, mair girnie altocumuli.

"The Congressman awa yit?"

"Haein breakfast, sir."

Criggie hauns his bodyguaird the briefcase, poke an jaiket. "Let's get tae it then, Sam."

They track their wey doon throu corridors lined wi McVeighs an Vettrianos tae the villa's laich kitchen, a space barely heid-hicht riggit wi bleck steel an reconditioned widd. The flair-tae-ceilin ermoured gless windaes airt sooth owre cushat-gray watter an the din mowdy tummocks o the Sooth Upland Hills.

"Senator. It's yirsel. Park the auld bahookitie. Birgitte's juist waashin the sleep fae her oxters, if ye ken whit ah'm sayin." Simon Athelstane slaisters milk intae a joog an flits glegly owre fae the solid birk breakfast bar. The Congressman, wi a tae still in his thirties, hurls raither than walks as if he has sma time tae skail atween destinations. Birgitte is Athelstane's gudewife. Criggie's thochts jink instantly tae Birgitte's lang sunbed-broon legs glisterin as they did for maist o lest nicht in white cut-aff bermudas at the lanimer o his vision as he an Athelstane slainte mhath'd brandies on the villa's shadda-deck.

"Muckle day the day, Senator." The Congressman thrusts his richt loof at him. Three-oorly workoots an a cockapentie personal tailor keeps his figure trig, his appearance swack. The man reeks o new siller an altho three gurlie parliaments has learned him a meisure o sophistication an moyen, tae Criggie's mind an tae ithers', Athelstane has aye aboot his gait the guff o a used-body-pairts salesman. Walin him aheid o a dozen brawer politicians tae be his Election Grieve wis nae a decision cawed by the Congressman's barra-boy chairm. Criggie prefers no tae wunner hou mony in his pairty an the meeja micht hae guessed the richt reason for the choice, even if Athelstane hasna jaloused it for hissel.

"Nane bigger, Simon." He returns the birkie haunshake an pous oot a lang-backit chair.

Athelstane clatters an ashet, spinn an coggie doon in front o Criggie an scowks at Boness, staunin wi his airms plettit aside the siller-steel jawbox. "You no hae plenty maitters tae attend tae, Captain?"

The bodyguaird ill-ees Athelstane. He has his sodgers oot on the law tae de-redd an the hoose needs tae be swaibled again for bugs an eemock-cams but Boness is supposed tae tak orders ainlie fae Criggie. The Senator howanever has his gruntle in a spreid o the day's papers. Boness smiles. Considerin hou easy it wid be tae sned Athelstane's thrapple-pipe, the bodyguaird retreats fae the kitchen.

"Richt, know whit ah'm sayin?" The Congressman stobs open the weescreen o a personal-redder an leets aff tae Criggie the day's programme. "Doc Hazelrig will see ye at eleeven for yir physio. Then a Senate Launlowper will tak ye tae the City for twa o'clock. Wir first TV tryst is at Channel 8. Then we've Shammybraw, Port The Day, Campsie Cooper Wants Tae Ken an the Josie Bryce Shaw aw the wey up tae seeven. We're pairty-hoppin until the votin staps at midnicht an then—ah hope ye winna mind—ah've pinselled ye in for a wee snotter o sleep at wir private suite—the Presidential, allow me, eh?—at the Pyot Knowe Hotel on Hietoun whaur we'll hing on for the result. That's due in juist efter three a.m. the morn's morn."

"Nae time for a quick roond o gowf, then?" Criggie raxes for a daud breid an smeerichs it wi hinnie.

"Ah'm afraid no, Senator." Athelstane pooches the redder. "When ye're no speakin til the meeja, ye'll hae tae be oot hauncreeshin until the pollin hooses shut. We've got three hunner thoosan pilgrimers stowin oot the hotels in Ocean Haven aheid o Max Jaffray's arrival on Wednesday. An fufty thoosan Azeri fitba supporters stottin aboot still tryin tae find their hotels efter lest nicht's gemm."

"Oh ay, whit wis the score?"

"Scotland Wan, Azerbaijan Nil. A fou hoose at Hampden an fowre million watchin at hame."

Criggie tummles ane o the papers owre tae its hin-page. "Fine that. Naethin like a Scotland win tae pit the folk in a guid tid, especially on election day. We'll hae tae invite Chae Whitlaw owre tae Argyle Hoose tae git his photie took."

"We'll hing on tae see if they qualify first." Athelstane scarts a note in his diary. "The return leg's mid-week at Alta Tehran. If the General can pauchle us a draw, then we'll think aboot photies."

"The General? Is that whit we're cryin him? Well, ah'll certainly need tae gie Field Marshall Whitlaw a phone afore he leaves."

"An can ah spier aboot yir speech?"

Criggie claps his heid. "In here, ma freend. Dinna you fash. Ah've had fufteen year tae work on it an ah ken it like ah ken masel."

"Ah'm shair it's braw." Athelstane nods an pits his pen an redder awa intil a briefcase. "Calvin, ye mibbe ken whaur ah'm comin fae wi this but ah've a couple o blackdugs nippin ma back."

Criggie kens exactly which airt the Congressman's comin fae. Athelstane, the electronics exec that bocht, bullied an whistle-binkied his wey tae a Laich Hoose portfolio, has been guddlin for weeks tae finn oot if he'll be offered a post in the new Lord President's Cabinet.

"Can we no dae this efter, Simon?"

"Weel, see, ah'm fleein tae North Law Burgh in aboot ten minutes. An awfie lot o dinnae-kenners owre there. Need tae mak sure oor chapfolk are wearin oot the richt doors. An ah'd raither no talk aboot this in front o the wife, if ye ken whit ah'm..."—Athelstane grups his briefcase ticht til him—"but see the morra when ye wale yir cabinet. Will ye be mentionin ma name?"

The Senator, if he could, widna hae Simon Athelstane in his road. Aneth the ootward nouveau-lairdie exterior, the man is aw wee-time geck an grab. Criggie tries but canna ayewis keep his puggie cool. "Sure, ah'll be mentionin it. Nou is that awthin or have ye ony ither bleck dugs nippin at yir taes?"

Criggie watches the anger staun up an jig in Athelstane's een. "Ah thocht the university wis interestin yesterday, if ken whit ah'm gettin at?"

"No really," he replies, harlt for a moment he micht hae chauved the Congressman tae sair.

"Well, ye'd hae tae be a richt cauld tattie tae no notice the stramash o bonnie lassies up there. When ye're President, ye'll need a wife. Canna hae the Lord President high-kiltit an the claik o the toun. Ken whit ah'm steerin at. Ye'll juist hae tae nip yirsel a bonnie wee postgrad."

"Dinna be daft, Athelstane. Ah've got a face like an auld baffie."

"Are you kiddin? They'll lap ye up. Get them gaun aboot yir trevels, fleg the g-strings aff them wi yir wee stories aboot Nanga Parbat."

Bealin, Criggie scuds the cafetiere back ontae its coaster. He'd been, twa year, tap-bannock wi a staff o three thoosan at the Himalaya mission on Bombay Island when they took him. Heid in a poke, airms in airns, fourteen an a hauf year wi Hahn an his gowk stick, jabbin, clourin, kittlin. The trauma a year efter is still fresh scartit on the circuits o his harns. Ony mention o Nanga Parbat, even in glaikit banter, channers him tae the pock. The body-pairts salesrep should ken better.

He taks his coffee tae the kitchen windae an glowers doon ontae the jabblin expanse o the Gless Sea.

Deef an blinn in his middenie Kasmiri tolbooth, the Senator didna witness the eldritch alterations nature wrocht on the planet an the gleebries o ocean controlled by Muckillopolis. The continent-happin floods, that had drooned the earth tae its tapmaist kips, peaked at the century's hin end, subsequently dwynin, devallin ten meter a year owre the next decade. A gowp at a time, the Atlantic an Pacific returned bittocks o whit they had smoored durin God's Flood in the form o lang, thin dry-land whangs that appeared, like the runkled gairters on a pillie-wanton's leg, roon escarpments, alpine-plateaux an on the laicher braes o the Hieland an Lowland hills, cowpin real estate prices tae the bottom o the meal bowie.

Afore, ainlie Port's high-heids an siller-daddies could afford a hoose on the bens whaur men like Athelstane plenished their palaces wi Tuscan foontains, brushbox timmer flairs an gowd-gildit cludgies. But since the watters' retreat, clamjamfries o middle-cless beengers an ledder-spielers hae been fechtin like caterans tae clatch up dream bothies on every spare rig an neb o grund gaun. On the rocky hochbands o Tinto Law, Criggie merks that the auld-empire villas like Windyhingin Shaw are weel on the road tae lossin the gree tae the condos an broon-tiled howfettes that run doon in heeligoleerie order tae the watter's edge.

"Dat's wis oot a Bollinger, Simon. Du should buy some mair. Hit fairly luiks ta me lik we micht be needin hit." Birgitte Athelstane, a watergaw kimono loose owre her lythe hurdies, sclaffs intae the kitchen in licht espadrilles.

"Ay." The Congressman meets her wi a grin that isna returned. "An whit else for ma darlin?"

Birgitte poors a gless o orange an taks a lazy gowp at it. "Naethin else."

"Ah wis juist sayin tae the Senator here that we should see aboot gittin him a bidey-in. Whit dae ye think?"

Birgitte snakes an airm roon her gudeman's waist. Even in hodden hoose sandals, she is taller an brawer than him. Criggie finds her sair tae look at, this twa an thirty year auld beauty wi a lassie's body an howtowdie's smile.

"Göd idee," she snirls. "Lat's reffel him up richt noo wi Frieda Ramsay. Pass du me da phone."

"Frieda Ramsay? Her? Naw, ken whit ah'm sayin. Weeter than the gravedigger's neb, that yin." Athelstane gruggles up his face, then dichtin a dry brou, grins owre at the Senator. "Got ye oot o that, Criggie. You owe me guid style."

Criggie nods his heid. "Oh, ah owe you awricht."

His host glisks theatrically at the gowd watch on his sheckle. "OK. That's me got tae buzzle. Ah'd love tae gab here aw day but ah seriously have tae nash. Somebody's got tae mak sure we win this election, if ye ken whit ah'm on aboot."

While he pinkie-dials a code intae his phone an the rotors o his Mercedes-Romeo Landlowper croichle intae motion on the heli-plet ootside, Criggie's an Birgitte's een scance at each ither a second.

"Channel 8. Hauf-twa. Dinna be late."

"Mind da champagne." Birgitte's voice tails aff intae the eemock o a whisper while aye at the windae Criggie sweels the coffee roon the bottom o a gless mug. Nane speaks. They listen as the copter's blades tuilyie the air an heeze the Congressman intae the weatherie Tinto sky.

"Tinks du dat he kens?" Birgitte flits tae the kitchen's french windae an stares throu the buhlitt-resistant pane.

"Mibbe." Criggie glaiks at Birgitte's back. The mornin sun taigles aboot her silhouette wrappin her in a rosie o licht.

"He tinks du'll gie him a post i dy cabinet. Hit's aa he spaeks aboot."

"Ah'll likely work him in somewhere." Criggie moves tae staun forenent her.

"Calvin. We hae tae white dis. Hit's jöst gyaain ta hurt wis. I mean, du wis boarn ta steer dis toun." Birgitte spins roon, the strang line o her face blearie wi concern. "Hit's dy life. Hit's whit du kens."

Criggie raxes Mrs Athelstane tae him an, doucely fauldin back her kimono, kissocks her bare shooder. "Ah ken nothin. Juist that ah miss you."

"Du sudna be here, Senator. Du sudna even be here."

Birgitte turns awa till she is atween him an the windae but wi his braid bouk, Criggie caws her gently forrit an hauds her. His tongue trevels doon the lang curve o her neck an she closes her een, airchin hersel against the gless o the buhlitt-proof windae. The goun slidders tae the flair. Her breists press at the cauld pane. Criggie haps her completely in his airms an a sab cuts in ablow each short braith she taks. His mooth spiers for hers as he pugs her roon an they kiss.

"Du's no listenin ta me," she says, pushin awa fae his passionate slaichs. "Du'll loss aathin dis wye."

"Wheesht, lassie," Criggie whuspers an, wi a harlie fingir, staps a tear on her cheek an cairries her ben tae hers an her gudeman's bedroom.

*They say that to sup with the Devil, you need a long spoon. Well,
now's the time to open the cutlery drawer, grab a piece of the best
silver and stand well back. Just make sure you know who you're
dealing with.*

o o o o o o o o o o o o o o o o o o o o o o o o o

SNOWBALL'S CHANCE
Charles Stross

o o o o o o o o o o o o o o o o o o o o o o o o o

The louring sky, half past pregnant with a caul of snow, pressed down
on Davy's head like a hangover. He glanced up once, shivered, then
pushed through the doorway into the Deid Nurse and the smog of
fag fumes within.

His sometime conspirator Tam the Tailer was already at the bar.
"Awright, Davy?"

Davy drew a deep breath, his glasses steaming up the instant he
stepped through the heavy blackout curtain, so that the disreputable
pub was shrouded in a halo of icy iridescence that concealed its flaws.
"Mine's a Deuchars." His nostrils flared as he took in the seedy mixture of aromas that festered in the Deid Nurse's atmosphere—so thick
you could cut it with an axe, Morag had said once with a sniff of her
lop-sided snot-siphon, back in the day when she'd had aught to say to
Davy. "Fuckin' Baltic oot there the night, an' nae kiddin'." He slid
his glasses off and wiped them, then looked around tiredly. "An'
deid tae the world in here."

Tam glanced around as if to be sure the pub population hadn't
magically doubled between mouthfuls of seventy bob. "Ah widnae
say that." He gestured with his nose—pockmarked by frostbite—at the
snug in the corner. Once the storefront for the Old Town's more
affluent ladies of the night, it was now unaccountably popular with
students of the gaming fraternity, possibly because they had been
driven out of all the trendier bars in the neighbourhood for yacking
till all hours and not drinking enough (much like the whores before
them). Right now a bunch of threadbare LARPers were in residence,
arguing over some recondite point of lore. "They're havin' enough
fun for a barrel o' monkeys by the sound o' it."

"An' who can blame them?" Davy hoisted his glass: "Ah just wish they'd keep their shite aff the box." The pub, in an effort to compensate for its lack of a food licence, had installed a huge and dodgy voxel engine that teetered precariously over the bar: it was full of muddy field, six LARPers leaping.

"Dinnae piss them aff, Davy—they've a' got swords."

"Ah wis jist kiddin'. Ah didnae catch ma Lottery the night, that's a' Ah'm sayin'."

"If ye win, it'll be a first." Tam stared at his glass. "An' whit wid ye dae then, if yer numbers came up?"

"Whit, the big yin?" Davy put his glass down, then unzipped his parka's fast-access pouch and pulled out a fag packet and lighter. Condensation immediately beaded the plastic wrapper as he flipped it open. "Ah'd pay aff the hoose, for starters. An' the child support. An' then—" He paused, eyes wandering to the dog-eared NO SMOKING sign behind the bar. "Ah, shit." He flicked his Zippo, stroking the end of a cigarette with the flame from the burning coal oil. "If Ah wis young again, Ah'd move, ye ken? But Ah'm no, Ah've got roots here." The sign went on to warn of lung cancer (curable) and two-thousand-euro fines (laughable, even if enforced). Davy inhaled, grateful for the warmth flooding his lungs. "An' there's Morag an' the bairns."

"Heh." Tam left it at a grunt, for which Davy was grateful. It wasn't that he thought Morag would ever come back to him, but he was sick to the back teeth of people who thought they were his friends telling him that she wouldn't, not unless he did this or did that.

"Ah could pay for the bairns tae go east. They're young enough." He glanced at the doorway. "It's no right, throwin' snowba's in May."

"That's global warmin'." Tam shrugged with elaborate irony, then changed the subject. "Where d'ye think they'd go? The Ukraine? New 'Beria?"

"Somewhaur there's grass and nae glaciers." Pause. "An' real beaches wi' sand an' a'." He frowned and hastily added: "Dinnae get me wrong, Ah ken how likely that is." The collapse of the West Antarctic ice shelf two decades ago had inundated every established coastline; it had also stuck the last nail in the coffin of the Gulf stream, plunging the British Isles into a sub-Arctic deep freeze. Then the Americans had made it worse—at least for Scotland—by putting a giant parasol into orbit to stop the rest of the planet roasting like a chicken on a spit. Davy had learned all about global warming in Geography classes at school—back when it hadn't happened—in the rare intervals when he wasn't dozing in the back row or staring at Yasmin MacConnell's hair. It wasn't until he was already paying a mortgage and the second kid was on his way that what it meant really sank in. Cold. Eternal cold, deep in your bones. "Ah'd like tae see a real beach again, some day before Ah die."

"Ye could save for a train ticket."

"Away wi' ye! Where'd Ah go tae?" Davy snorted, darkly amused. Flying was for the hyper-rich these days, and anyway, the nearest beaches with sand and sun were in the Caliphate, a long day's TGV ride south through the Channel Tunnel and across the Gibraltar Bridge, in what had once been the Northern Sahara Desert. As a tourist destination, the Caliphate had certain drawbacks, a lack of topless sunbathing beauties being only the first on the list. "It's a' just as bad whauriver ye go. At least here ye can still get pork scratchings."

"Aye, weel." Tam raised his glass, just as a stranger appeared in the doorway. "An' then there's some that dinnae feel the cauld." Davy glanced round to follow the direction of his gaze. The stranger was oddly attired in a lightweight suit and tie, as if he'd stepped out of the middle of the previous century, although his neat goatee beard and the two small brass horns implanted on his forehead were a more contemporary touch. He noticed Davy staring and nodded, politely enough, then broke eye contact and ambled over to the bar. Davy turned back to Tam, who responded to his wink. "Take care the noo, Davy. Ye've got ma number." With that, he stood up, put his glass down, and shambled unsteadily towards the toilets.

This put Davy on his lonesome next to the stranger, who leaned on the bar and glanced at him sideways with an expression of amusement. Davy's forehead wrinkled as he stared in the direction of Katie the barwoman, who was just now coming back up the cellar steps with an empty coal powder cartridge in one hand. "My round?" asked the stranger, raising an eyebrow.

"Aye. Mine's a Deuchars if yer buyin'..." Davy, while not always quick on the uptake, was never slow on the barrel: if this underdressed southerner could afford a heated taxi, he could certainly afford to buy Davy some beer. Katie nodded and rinsed her hands under the sink—however well sealed they left the factory, coal cartridges always leaked like printer toner had once done—and picked up two glasses.

"New roond aboot here?" Davy asked after a moment.

The stranger smiled: "Just passing through—I visit Edinburgh every few years."

"Aye." Davy could relate to that.

"And yourself?"

"Ah'm frae Pilton." Which was true enough; that was where he'd bought the house with Morag all those years ago, back when folks actually wanted to buy houses in Edinburgh. Back before the pack ice closed the Firth for six months in every year, back before the rising sea level drowned Leith and Ingliston, and turned Arthur's Seat into a frigid coastal headland looming grey and stark above the perma-frost. "Whereaboots d'ye come frae?"

The stranger's smile widened as Katie parked a half-litre on the bar top before him and bent down to pull the next: "I think you know where I'm from, my friend."

Davy snorted. "Aye, so ye're a man of wealth an' taste, is that right?"

"Just so." A moment later, Katie planted the second glass in front of Davy, gave him a brittle smile, and retreated to the opposite end of the bar without pausing to extract credit from the stranger, who nod-ded and raised his jar: "To your good fortune."

"Heh." Davy chugged back a third of his glass. It was unusually bitter, with a slight sulphurous edge to it: "That's a new barrel."

"Only the best for my friends."

Davy sneaked an irritated glance at the stranger. "Right. Ah ken ye want tae talk, ye dinnae need tae take the pish."

"I'm sorry." The stranger held his gaze, looking slightly perplexed. "It's just that I've spent too long in America recently. Most of them believe in me. A bit of good old-fashioned scepticism is refreshing once in a while."

Davy snorted. "Dae Ah look like a god-botherer tae ye? Yer amang civilized folk here, nae free-kirk numpties'd show their noses in a pub."

"So I see." The stranger relaxed slightly. "Seen Morag and the boys lately, have you?"

Now a strange thing happened, because as the cold fury took him, and a monstrous roaring filled his ears, and he reached for the stranger's throat, he seemed to hear Morag's voice shouting, *Davy, don't!* And to his surprise, a moment of timely sanity came crashing down on him, a sense that Devil or no, if he laid hands on this fucker he really would be damned, somehow. It might just have been the hypothalamic implant that the sheriff had added to the list of his parole requirements working its arcane magic on his brain chemistry, but it certainly felt like a drenching, cold-sweat sense of immanence, and not in a good way. So as the raging impulse to glass the cunt died away, Davy found himself contemplating his own raised fists in perplexity, the crude blue tattoos of LOVE and HATE standing out on his knuckles like doorposts framing the prison gateway of his life.

"Who telt ye aboot them?" he demanded hoarsely.

"Cigarette?" The stranger, who had sat perfectly still while Davy wound up to punch his ticket, raised the chiselled eyebrow again.

"Ya bas." But Davy's hand went to his pocket automatically, and he found himself passing a filter-tip to the stranger rather than ramming a red-hot ember in his eye.

"Thank you." The stranger took the unlit cigarette, put it straight between his lips, and inhaled deeply. "Nobody needed to tell me about them," he continued, slowly dribbling smoke from both nostrils.

Davy slumped defensively on his bar stool. "When ye wis askin' aboot Morag and the bairns, Ah figured ye wis fuckin' wi' ma heid." But knowing that there was a perfectly reasonable supernatural explanation somehow made it all right. *Ye cannae blame Auld Nick for pushin' yer buttons.* Davy reached out for his glass again: "'Scuse me. Ah didnae think ye existed."

"Feel free to take your time." The stranger smiled faintly. "I find atheists refreshing, but it does take a little longer than usual to get down to business."

"Aye, weel, concedin' for the moment that ye *are* the Deil, Ah dinnae ken whit ye want wi' the likes o' me." Davy cradled his beer protectively. "Ah'm naebody." He shivered in the sudden draught as one of the students—leaving—pushed through the curtain, admitting a flurry of late-May snowflakes.

"So? You may be nobody, but your lucky number just came up."
The stranger smiled nastily. "Did you never think you'd win the
Lottery?"

"Aye, weel, if hauf the stories they tell about ye are true, Ah'd
rather it wis the ticket, ye ken? Or are ye gonnae say ye've been stitched
up by the kirk?"

"Something like that." The Devil nodded sagely. "Look, you're
not stupid, so I'm not going to bullshit you. What it is, is I'm not the
only one of me working this circuit. I've got a quota to meet, but
there aren't enough politicians and captains of industry to go around,
and anyway, they're boring. All they ever want is money, power, or
good, hot, kinky sex without any comebacks from their constituents.
Poor folks are so much more creative in their desperation, don't you
think? And so much more likely to believe in the Rules, too."

"The Rules?" Davy found himself staring at his companion in perplexity. "Nae the Law, right?"

"Do as thou wilt shall be all of the Law," quoth the Devil, then he
paused as if he'd tasted something unpleasant.

"Ye wis sayin'?"

"Love is the Law, Love under Will," the Devil added dyspeptically.

"That's a'?" Davy stared at him.

"My employer requires me to quote chapter and verse when chal-
lenged." As he said "employer", the expression on the Devil's face
made Davy shudder. "And She monitors these conversations for com-
pliance."

"But whit aboot the rest o' it, aye? If ye're the Deil, whit aboot the
Ten Commandments?"

"Oh, those are just Rules," said the Devil, smiling. "I'm really
proud of them."

"Ye made them a' up?" Davy said accusingly. "Just tae fuck wi'
us?"

"Well, yes, of course I did! And all the other Rules. They work
really well, don't you think?"

Davy made a fist and stared at the back of it. LOVE. "Ye cunt. Ah
still dinnae believe in ye."

The Devil shrugged. "Nobody's asking you to believe in me. You
don't, and I'm still here, aren't I? If it makes things easier, think of
me as the garbage collection subroutine of the strong anthropic

principle. And they"—he stabbed a finger in the direction of the overhead LEDs—"work by magic, for all you know."

Davy picked up his glass and drained it philosophically. The hell of it was, the Devil was right: now he thought about it, he had no idea how the lights worked, except that electricity had something to do with it. "Ah'll have anither. Ye're buyin'."

"No I'm not." The Devil snapped his fingers and two full glasses appeared on the bar, steaming slightly. Davy picked up the nearest one. It was hot to the touch, even though the beer inside it was at cellar temperature, and it smelled slightly sulphurous. "Anyway, I owe you."

"Whit for?" Davy sniffed the beer suspiciously: "This smells pish." He pushed it away. "Whit is it ye owe me for?"

"For taking that mortgage and the job on the street-cleaning team and for pissing it all down the drain and fucking off a thousand citizens in little ways. For giving me Jaimie and wee Davy, and for wrecking your life and cutting Morag off from her parents and rais-ing a pair of neds instead of two fine upstanding citizens. You're not a scholar and you're not a gentleman, but you're a truly professional hater. And as for what you did to Morag..."

Davy made another fist: HATE. "Say wan mair word aboot Morag..." he warned.

The Devil chuckled quietly. "No, you managed to do all that by yourself." He shrugged. "I'd have offered help if you needed it, but you seemed to be doing okay without me. Like I said, you're a profes-sional." He cleared his throat. "Which brings me to the little matter of why I'm talking to you tonight."

"Ah'm no for sale." Davy crossed his arms defensively. "Who d'ye think Ah am?"

The Devil shook his head, still smiling. "I'm not here to make you an offer for your soul, that's not how things work. Anyway, you gave it to me of your own free will years ago." Davy looked into his eyes. The smile didn't reach them. "Trouble is, there are consequences when that happens. My employer's an optimist: She's not an Augustinian entity, you'll be pleased to learn, She doesn't believe in original sin. So things between you and the Ultimate are ... let's say they're out of balance. It's like a credit card bill. The longer you ignore it, the worse it gets. You cut me a karmic loan from the First Bank of Davy MacDonald, and the Law requires me to repay it with interest."

"Huh?" Davy stared at the Devil. "Ye whit?"

The Devil wasn't smiling now. "You're one of the Elect, Davy. One of the Unconditionally Elect. So's fucking everybody these days, but your name came up in the quality assurance lottery. I'm not allowed to mess with you. If you die and I'm in your debt, seven shades of shit hit the fan. So I owe you a fucking wish."

The Devil tapped his fingers impatiently on the bar top. He was no longer smiling. "You get one wish. I am required to read you the small print:

The party of the first part in cognizance of the gift benefice or loan bestowed by the party of the second part is hereby required to tender the fulfillment of 1 (one) verbally or somatically expressed indication of desire by the party of the second part in pursuance of the discharge of the said gift benefice or loan, said fulfillment hereinafter to be termed "the wish". The party of the first part undertakes to bring the totality of existence into accordance with the terms of the wish exclusive of paradox deicide temporal inversion or other wilful suspension contrary to the laws of nature. The party of the second part recognizes understands and accepts that this wish represents full and final discharge of debt incurred by the gift benefice or loan to the party of the first part. Notwithstanding additional grants of rights incurred under the terms of this contract the rights responsibilities duties of the party of the first part to the party of the second part are subject to the Consumer Credit Regulations of 2026...

Davy shook his head. "Ah dinnae get it. Are ye tellin' me ye're givin' me a wish? In return for, for ... bein' radge a' ma life?"

The Devil nodded. "Yes."

Davy winced. "Ah think Ah need another Deuchars - fuck! Haud on, that isnae ma wish!" He stared at the Devil anxiously. "Ye're serious, aren't ye?"

The Devil sniffed. "I can't discharge the obligation with a beer. My Employer isn't stupid, whatever Her other faults: She'd say I was short-changing you, and She'd be right. It's got to be a big wish, Davy."

Davy's expression brightened. The Devil waved a hand at Katie: "Another Deuchars for my friend here. And a drop of the Craitur." Things were looking up, Davy decided.

"Can ye make Morag nae have ... Ah mean, can ye make things ... awright again, nae went bad?" He dry-swallowed, mind skittering like a frightened spider away from what he was asking for. Not to have ... whatever. Whatever he'd done. Already.

The Devil contemplated Davy for a long handful of seconds. "No," he said patiently. "That would create a paradox, you see, because if things hadn't gone bad for you, I wouldn't be here giving you this wish, would I? Your life gone wrong is the fuel for this miracle."

"Oh." Davy waited in silence while Katie pulled the pint, then retreated back to the far end of the bar. *Whaur's Tam?* he wondered vaguely. *Fuckin' deil, wi' his smairt suit an' high heid yin manners...* He shivered, unaccountably cold. "Am Ah goin' tae hell?" he asked roughly. "Is that whaur Ah'm goin'?"

"Sorry, but no. We were brought in to run this universe, but we didn't design it. When you're dead, that's it. No hellfire, no damnation: the worst thing that can happen to you is you're reincarnated, given a second chance to get things right. It's normally my job to give people like you that chance."

"An' if Ah'm no reincarnated?" Davy asked hopefully.

"You get to wake up in the mind of God. Of course, you stop being you when you do that." The Devil frowned thoughtfully. "Come to think of it, you'll probably give Her a migraine."

"Right, right." Davy nodded. The Devil was giving *him* a headache. He had a dawning suspicion that this one wasn't a prod or a pape: he probably supported Livingstone. "Ah'm no that bad then, is that whit ye're sayin'?"

"Don't get above yourself."

The Devil's frown deepened, oblivious to the stroke of killing rage that flashed behind Davy's eyes at the words. *Dinnae get above yersel'? Who the fuck d'ye think ye are, the sheriff?* That was almost exactly what the sheriff had said, leaning over to pronounce sentence. *Ye ken Ah'm naebody, dinnae deny it!* Davy's fists tightened, itching to hit somebody. The story of his life: being ripped off then talked down to by self-satisfied cunts. *Ah'll make ye regret it!*

The Devil continued after a moment: "You've got to really fuck up in a theological manner before She won't take you, these days. Spreading hatred in the name of God, that kind of thing will do for you. Trademark abuse, She calls it. You're plenty bad, but you're not that bad. Don't kid yourself, you only warrant the special visit because you're a quality sample. The rest are ... unobserved."

"So Ah'm no evil, Ah'm just plain bad." Davy grinned virulently as a thought struck him. *Let's dae somethin' aboot that! Karmic imbalance? Ah'll show ye a karmic imbalance!* "Can ye dae somethin' aboot the weather? Ah hate the cauld." He tried to put a whine in his voice. The change in the weather had crippled house prices, shafted him and Morag. It would serve the Devil right if he fell for it.

"I can't change the weather." The Devil shook his head, looking slightly worried. "Like I said—"

"Can ye fuck wi' yon sun shield the fuckin' Yanks stuck in the sky?" Davy leaned forward, glaring at him: "'Cause if no, whit kindae deil are ye?"

"You want me to what?"

Davy took a deep breath. He remembered what it had looked like on TV, twenty years ago: the great silver reflectors unfolding in solar orbit, the jubilant politicians, the graphs showing a 20% fall in sunlight reaching the Earth ... the savage April blizzards that didn't stop for a month, the endless twilight and the sun dim enough to look at. And now the Devil wanted to give him a wish, in payment for fucking things up for a few thousand bastards who had it coming? Davy felt his lips drawing back from his teeth, a feral smile forcing itself to the surface. "Ah want ye to fuck up the sunshade, awright? Get ontae it. Ah want tae be wairm..."

The Devil shook his head. "That's a new one on me," he admitted. "But—" He frowned. "You're sure? No second thoughts? You want to waive your mandatory fourteen-day right of cancellation?"

"Aye. Dae it the noo." Davy nodded vigorously.

"It's done." The Devil smiled faintly.

"Whit?" Davy stared.

"There's not much to it. A rock about the size of this pub, traveling on a cometary orbit—it'll take an hour or so to fold, but I already took care of that." The Devil's smile widened. "You used your wish."

"Ah dinnae believe ye," said Davy, hopping down from his bar stool. Out of the corner of one eye, he saw Tam dodging through the blackout curtain and the doorway, tipping him the wink. This had gone on long enough. "Ye'll have tae prove it. Show me."

"What?" The Devil looked puzzled. "But I told you, it'll take about an hour."

"So ye say. An' whit then?"

"Well, the parasol collapses, so the amount of sunlight goes up. It gets brighter. The snow melts."

"Is that right?" Davy grinned. "So how many wishes dae Ah get this time?"

"How many—" The Devil froze. "What makes you think you get any more?" He snarled, his face contorting.

"Like ye said, Ah gave ye a loan, didn't Ah?" Davy's grin widened. He gestured toward the door. "After ye?"

"You—" The Devil paused. "You don't mean..." He swallowed, then continued, quietly. "That wasn't deliberate, was it?"

"Oh. Aye." Davy could see it in his mind's eye: the wilting crops and blazing forests, droughts and heatstroke and mass extinction, the despairing millions across America and Africa, exotic places he'd never seen, never been allowed to go—roasting like pieces of a turkey on a spit, roasting in revenge for twenty years frozen in outer darkness. Hell on Earth. "Four billion fuckers, isnae that enough for another?"

"Son of a bitch!" The Devil reached into his jacket pocket and pulled out an antique calculator, began punching buttons. "Forty-eight—no, forty-nine. Shit, this has never happened before! You bastard, don't you have a conscience?"

Davy thought for a second. "Naw."

"Fuck!"

It was now or never. "Ah'll take a note."

"A credit—shit, okay then. Here." The Devil handed over his mobile. It was small and very black and shiny, and it buzzed like a swarm of flies. "Listen, I've got to go right now, I need to escalate this to senior management. Call head office tomorrow, if I'm not there, one of my staff will talk you through the state of your claim."

"Haw! Ah'll be sure tae dae that."

The Devil stalked towards the curtain and stepped through into the darkness beyond, and was gone. Davy pulled out his moby and speed-dialed a number. "He's a' yours noo," he muttered into the handset, then hung up and turned back to his beer. A couple of minutes later, someone came in and sat down next to him. Davy raised a hand and waved vaguely at Katie: "A Deuchars for Tam here."

Katie nodded nonchalantly—she seemed to have cheered up since the Devil had stepped out—and picked up a glass.

Tam dropped a couple of small brass horns on the bar top next to Davy. Davy stared at them for a moment then glanced up admiringly. "Neat," he admitted. "Get anythin' else aff him?"

"Nah, the cunt wis crap. He didnae even have a moby. Just these." Tam looked disgusted for a moment. "Ah pulled ma chib an' waved it aroon' an' he totally legged it. Think anybody'll come lookin' for us?"

"Nae chance." Davy raised his glass, then tapped the pocket with the Devil's mobile phone in it smugly. "Nae a snowbaw's chance in hell..."

We Scots like to believe we know a good tune when we hear it. Scottish bands continually reshape the music scene, our folk songs fed the roots of American country and western, and it's even been argued that black gospel music derives from the psalm-singing of the Hebridean churches. Cultural elitists, then? If only everyone shared our tastes...

❂ ❂

TOTAL MENTAL QUALITY, BY THE WAY
William Meikle

❂ ❂

I'd never heard him so excited. Not even when he got his first CD player.

"Ye've got tae come an' hear this," he said on the phone. "Total dead mental, so it is."

I was used to John's enthusiasm, but I couldn't prevent a small sigh escaping. He caught it, even over the crackling line.

"No, Ah mean it, man. It's pure brilliant."

On the way over I wondered what it was now. Last time it had been the new speakers—the ones which let you hear the band breathing. Before that it had been laser discs, before that quadraphonic and so on, as far back as eight-track cassettes.

John was a hi-fi bore. I put up with him because he was generally a good guy and we enjoyed much of the same music. But get him on to the subject of equipment and he was off and running—tweeters, woofers, RMS, crackle and hum ... he could bore you for hours about any one of them. Recent advances in technology had sent him into heaven, and he spent most of his waking life studying the magazines and buying the latest add-ons. You probably know someone just like him.

There used to be a lot of them around.

When he opened the door, he had the happy look of a puppy that had just wet all over the new carpet.

"Come away in, ma man," he said. "Ye're no' gonnae believe this shit."

John led me into the living room. I could see that he'd cleared out even more furniture. Now all he had was the system, his albums and a sofa, placed in exactly the optimum position in the room.

"This is it!" he said. "This is effin' it."

He was dancing around on his toes, full of nervous energy. I didn't want to get too close to him—he might have been giving off sparks. I finally managed to get him calmed down enough to tell me what was going on.

"It hasnae even made the mags yet," he said. "Ah got it fae a contact out in Livingston, in Sony's labs. Ah'm unner strict orders no' tae let it oot o' ma sight. It's, like, gonnae be the biggest thing since the telly wis inventit."

John plunged on, almost talking to himself.

"TQ—that's whit they're gonnae ca' it—Total Quality—the ultimate in biotechnology. Dae ye see this wee beauty here?"

He held up a box, about the size of a packet of cigarettes, but black and shiny with strange nodules protruding from its surface. It was sleek and strangely organic, like something Giger might have designed. It made me want to stroke it, and get as far away as possible, both at the same time.

"Those fiendish Orientals have done it again, have they?" I asked, more to slow him down than out of any genuine desire to be illuminated.

"They hiv that," he said, shaking his head in admiration. "It's a new form of computing, all based on a single chip. It's built around a genetically engineered cell, a bit like an amoeba really, but what they've done is pump it full of intelligent proteins and attach it up to the latest in microcircuitry."

"What's it for?"

"Well," he said. "Originally it was for the home entertainment industry. They wanted something that could track and monitor how you played games ... you know, all the little twitches and movements of the controller that are different for every individual? They wanted to use the learning power of the new chip to tailor each game to each person, so that the computer can learn what you're good at ... and more importantly, what you're bad at. They've even been experimenting with voice recognition and vocal control to get rid of manual controllers completely."

"That must take a lot of computing power."

"You'd better believe it," he said. "This wee beauty can go ten times faster than anything else on the market. It's right up there with the Cray that gets used for weather forecasting."

John hadn't noticed it, but he'd lost his accent as soon as he started talking technology, and lapsed in to his "Sunday" voice. He stopped talking when he saw that I had switched off.

"Okay," he said, taking pity on me. "Here's the gen. Once they started building it in the lab they realized they had a side-effect. It worked even better than they imagined at collecting information and recording it." His accent began to broaden as his enthusiasm bubbled over. "It'll record onythin' that ye play to it, and they havnae reached its limit. It's a bottomless pit, like."

I'll admit it, I was amazed. "You mean you could put the complete works of Dylan into that little box? Clear off a whole shelf of albums and replace it with a fag packet?"

John laughed. "Ye can dae that already wi' an iPod," he said. "Naw. This is a wee bit special ... there's mair tae it," he moved over to the stereo and plugged his new toy in. "Just ye wait. It's gonnae blaw yer heid aff."

The box intrigued me, I must admit. I'm not too hot on technology, but even I know that Sony don't let stuff like that out of their research labs—especially not to an ageing, long-haired hippie enthusiast who just happens to want to hear how it sounds.

I suspected a put-on. "Hey, John, what else does it do?"

He turned, a questioning look on his face. "Whit dae ye mean?"

"Well, does it make coffee? Or does it light your fags for you?"

He was annoyed with me—I could see it. It was a rare sight. John rarely lost his cool, but he was close to it now.

"Ye think Ah'm hivin' ye on? Let me tell you, boy, this is effin' huge. The hail world needs tae ken aboot it."

I finally saw the look of guilt on his face.

"Oh, John. You didn't?"

"That Ah did," he said, finally smiling. "And no' fae Sony either. This wee beastie came fae the Uni ... fae the biotech research lab. Ah heard aboot it on the grapevine, like. Ah wis oot the back hivin' a fag and wan o' the techie guys telt me a' aboot the side-effects they'd found. The gadgie telt me it sounded better than his Hi—Fi ... and he's got a Bose 1740! Ah kent there and then that Ah hid tae hiv a look at it. Ah slipped in tae the lab later. There wis naebody lookin', so Ah thocht Ah'd jist take it for the night, just tae try it oot."

I saw now why he had invited me—he needed someone to tell him it was all right. He'd stolen a piece of technology, worth God knows how much, and was using it to record his album collection, and he wanted my approval. Sometimes I wondered if he would ever grow up.

"Ye hiv tae hear it," he said, fiddling with something at the back of his box of tricks. I knew that it didn't matter to him what the connections were—he was able to knock up anything electrical in no time. He was talking, still trying to convince me that what he'd done wasn't really bad. He was back in geek-speak, and his accent disappeared again.

"They've been having some trouble with the buses and RAM connectivity in the lab. And they've not quite found the correct resistor to maintain a steady current through the bionic parts of the cell. But the recording and playback has been perfected, and you know what I'm like with the electrics. I've knocked up an interface for it. Just wait till you hear it."

He did something at the front of the box and the music began.

Have you ever wanted to hear John Lennon sing "Bat Out of Hell"? Or Madonna murdering "When I'm Sixty-Four"?

"Whit is this shit?" John whispered.

"Sounds like those intelligent proteins learn just a wee bit too quickly," I said.

We both sat there, stunned, as the amalgam continued. Celine Dion and Janis Joplin duets, Jimi Hendrix and Slash throwing riffs at each other. Weird is not the word for it.

After we'd had a beer, John did some experimenting. What he had stolen turned out to be the world's best mixing machine. It could pick up the nuances from one musician and transport his playing style into any other song. After a while we had Hendrix playing on "Stairway to Heaven", and Eminem dueting with Otis Redding and Sam Cooke.

"Yer bloody right," John said. "It's effin' brilliant man. It's yer ultimate karaoke box!"

I could foresee some problems, which I pointed out to him. It wasn't ours, we didn't know how it worked, we had no idea how to program it, and it seemed to play what it wanted, not what you wanted it to. We were arguing about it while Elvis sang with Robert Plant on "Bohemian Rhapsody". Then Hendrix came back ... only it wasn't quite him.

"Hey Joe" started.

"Haw Jimmy, where ye gaun wi' yon shooter?"

It had picked up John's accent perfectly.

"Did you record yourself?" I asked.

He stared back, wide-eyed, and shook his head.

"Then I think we're in trouble."

I turned towards the machine, but my coordination was off. I knocked over my beer can. It fell on its side and eighty shilling bubbled over the box.

It soaked in, and the box seemed to swell and grow, so slightly that I wasn't quite sure what I was seeing.

Britney Spears came on singing "Little Old Wine Drinker Me", then thick black smoke started to curl from the rear of the box.

We both lunged for the power cable. I reached it first, but I was too late to stop the box from overheating. It exploded, blowing a small cloud of oily smoke into the middle of the room. That wasn't all. Our clothes were covered in tiny yellow dots, like pollen grains. Looking around I could see that the whole room was spotted with them, including the sleek black casing of John's stereo.

I managed to pull one off my T-shirt and rub it between my fingers. It burst with a tiny popping sound, leaving an greasy smear across my palm.

"What the hell is this?" I asked, showing John the smear.

He looked over at me, eyes wide with a mixture of fear and wonder.

"Spores," he said in a hushed voice.

We spent the next hour cleaning up, breaking the remains of the box into as many pieces as possible and cleaning the oily muck from the surfaces in the living-room. The yellow dots were the most persistent, but we managed to get rid of most of them after I discovered that they could be taken off our clothing with a piece of Sellotape. We spent a good half hour trying to track them all down, then burnt the Sellotape. Afterwards, we went for a walk, distributing the remains of the black box in various locations as we made our way round the pubs. When we split up later that evening, both more than a little the worse for drink, John made me swear an oath of secrecy, just like when we were kids.

Over the next week we scanned the newspapers and TV reports for any mention of the black box, but all was quiet. John was getting paranoid, seeing secret service agents around every corner, and it was becoming harder and harder to coax him out of his flat. He kept complaining about problems with his stereo system, but that was an old story. He always had problems with his system.

Maybe I should have listened more when he was talking about the problems—but then again, I don't think it would have made any difference. There was only one thing that stood out as being unusual that week, and I didn't make the connection at the time, but I can now see how it all fits in.

It was Wednesday night. John called me and his tone was strange. I'd heard him excited before, of course, but this time there was something else there, something that sounded like fear ... or madness.

"Pit yer telly on tae BBC 1," he said. "Tell me whit ye see."

I did as I was told.

"The Prime Minister is giving a party political broadcast," I told him. "He's sitting at a desk looking serious."

And then John asked a strange question. "Whit's he wearing on his heid?"

I was stumped. "Just his hair," I said. "What's the problem?"

"Ye dinnae see the 'See You Jimmy' hat?"

I laughed, at just about the same time he started to sob.

"Are you all right John?" I asked.

He took a while to answer.

"Just a wee bit worse the wear for drink," he said. "Dinnae mind me." He hung up.

I didn't think any more about it until later that week.

I was watching the news on the TV. The Prime Minister was on again, being interviewed over foreign policy.

"So Prime Minister," the interviewer said, "what are you going to do about the situation in the Middle East?"

The PM jutted out his chin.

"Let me tell ye, boy," he said, "Ah'm fair scunnered wi' the hail business. As Ah wis telling the Chooky Embra ower a swally, it's lang past time we gave them a doin', so it is."

I watched, open mouthed, as he put his arm around the interviewer.

"See you, ya bampot; ye're ma best pal, by the way."

I realized how far things had gone when I was walking over to John's place. Several people walked past looking at their iPods; they were obviously not playing what was expected. I stopped one of them—a guy I knew vaguely through an old friend—and he let me listen to what was supposedly Franz Ferdinand, but had turned into Harry Lauder. And instead of "Roamin' in the Gloamin'", he was "Wankin' Doon the Bankin'".

I passed the TV rental shop and Billy Connolly was being interviewed by Ewan McGregor, followed by Sean Connery reading the weather, while on another TV set in the window, massed ranks of pipers and drummers marched through all the capital cities of the world playing "Scotland the Brave". And everywhere, if you looked closely enough, there were thousands of the tiny, yellow, pollen-like grains.

It took five minutes shouting and three minutes' worth of threats of physical violence before I could get John to open the door. He was drunk and had been crying, and I could see why as soon as I entered the living room. His stereo system—all those sleek black boxes on which he'd spent the best part of ten thousand pounds—had been reduced to a pile of broken rubble, its electrical intestines strewn across the floor.

I was almost speechless.

"Who? What?" I managed to say, then, seeing the look in his eyes, "Why?"

John motioned at the centre of the room. He'd moved the television back in and he was watching a game show. Rabbie Burns was the question master, and the panel contained Scotty from *Star Trek*, Lulu, Sir Walter Scott and Mel Gibson in full *Braveheart* make-up. Suddenly it changed to a football match. I didn't have my glasses on, but I knew something wasn't right. As I moved closer, I could see what it was. The players were all mutton pies on legs, kitted out in full football strip.

Behind me, John roared with laughter and cried heavy, sparkling tears.

"Ye see whit we've done? We've made telly watchable. We let the wee buggers oot and they've gotten everywhere."

He seemed to be genuinely amused.

"Is it no' just pure brilliant?"

After thinking about it for a bit, I had to agree with him. The programmes were a definite improvement on what passed as entertainment on British television.

"But what if the authorities find out?" I wanted to know.

He passed me a beer and we settled down in front of the TV.

"Ye'll be a hero. Apairt fae wan wee thing."

He was being serious for a moment and I saw his look stray to the remains of his stereo. The tears were back in his eyes.

"Just dinnae try listening tae the radio. The wee bastards are mad for Jimmy Shand."

One of Scotland's proudest boasts is the number of inventors it has produced; James Watt, Alexander Graham Bell and John Logie Baird, for example, all made revolutionary discoveries that brought people closer together, each in their different way. But while we have seen more than our fair share of innovators, not all of their remarkable creations have managed to change the world; well, not this world at least...

○ ○

THE BENNIE AND THE BONOBO
Neil Williamson

○ ○

George Bennie watched the future glide to a halt on the track above his head. He smiled. Waiting at the foot of the gantry stairs as the invited dignitaries and potential investors disembarked from his gleaming railplane, he grinned. And he beamed at the excited chatter that he could hear over the purr of the fore and aft prop screws easing down to a lazy birl.

He was going to be vindicated. Applauded. Rich.

It was 1930 and, with the wounds of the Great War beginning to heal at last, the country was ready to move on. And what better way to do that than replace the ponderous, dirty railways with this sleek, elevated wonder? People had a right to travel in speed and comfort.

The queue of passengers reached him. Hands pumped his, faces glowed, lips spilled excitable platitudes.

Such a smooth ride.

Bennie felt the charge off them, the genuine thrill.

The stained glass windows are darling.

And every single one of these people had influence, would carry away the message that the Bennie Railplane was the mode of tomorrow, and anyone not on board with a sizeable investment would be left behind in the past.

Imagine, Glasgow to Edinburgh in twenty minutes.

And all this from a public demonstration in a sidings in Milngavie. There was so much more he could do to refine the design. The engines for instance, now just a pair of standard, noisy diesels...

"It'll never happen."

The voice—soft, female, American—snapped him out of his thoughts. The rest of the passengers, having made their congratulations were now trudging back towards the offices, leaving a lone figure: really no taller than a child, shawled and bonneted so that her face could not be seen, and hands in a muff, which Bennie thought odd for July. Mentally he scanned the passenger list—of course, it was the widow from New York, the late addition: Mrs ... Mrs ... *Blanchflower*, that was it.

It seemed she alone had not been impressed by the railplane's demonstration. Well, that was hardly surprising for an American. They were never impressed by anything they hadn't made themselves.

Bennie adopted his most reassuring tone. "I guarantee you, Madam, the concept is sound, and the vehicle perfectly safe."

"Oh, I know it is," replied the voice from the bonnet. "But even still, your dream will be strangled. You will die a broken and destitute man."

With that outburst, the tiny woman hirpled away, as if plagued by bad joints, in the direction of an open workshop door. Bridling, but beginning to suspect this antagonsim as that of a competitor's investor come to inspect the opposition and finding it frustratingly superior, Bennie followed. It took a moment to spot her in the dimness, but there she was, in the lee of a stripped-down engine block.

"I should warn you," he began, "that my designs are fully patented—"

She removed a hand from her muff, holding it up to stop him. He stared at the hand. It was long-fingered and covered in thick black hair.

The hand loosened the ties of the bonnet, slipped it back. If she had not silenced him, the face which was revealed would have left him speechless anyway. Huge chocolate eyes under bony brows, a toothy mouth, wide nostrils, and more of that strange hair.

In his astonishment Bennie couldn't help himself. "You're a mon—"

The visitor bared impressive teeth with a soft growl.

Bennie realized his taxonomical mistake. "Sorry, a chim—"

"If I had been a '*chim*', I'd have bitten your testicles off at '*mon*'." She sighed. "The word you are looking for, George, is *bonobo*. Other side of the Congo River from the *chims*. Look, we don't have time for lengthy explanations, but I can see you will need an explanation of *me* before we can progress to the matter at hand." The ape stroked the hair under her chin, as if choosing her next words with care. "In the future," she said, "humans will find ways to make modifications to the body that would make your hair stand on end. Literally, if that's what you desire."

Bennie's hand went reflexively to smooth his receding Brylcreemed hair.

"Where I come from, they can—and you'd better believe they do—boost and alter any physical human attribute you can name."

The obvious question dutifully formed on his lips. "Then you're not *really* a mon...?"

She was ready for it. "A *bonobo*," she repeated. "Yes, I am. *Of course*, they had to experiment on someone else before they were allowed to go to town on human bodies, didn't they? I may be fourth-generation enhanced, but I'm still one hundred per cent bonobo, thank you."

Bennie, not yet close to appreciating any of the bewildering volley of concepts that had been hurled at him in the last few minutes, did manage to catch the inference in this. Four generations of radical genetic experimentation must have produced a lot of dead-ends before they got it right. "I'm sorry," he said.

"Don't be," she said matter-of-factly. "I'm more intelligent than the average human. And I've got my own apartment in the East Village, not to mention a research grant. I've even got the vote, although given that it's still only white human males that ever make it to the election platform it's frankly no use to me at all. They'd be better off with chimps."

"Did you say, the *future?*"

The bonobo scratched her nose. "Catch on fast, don't you? How else would I know that your beautiful railplane is doomed to failure?"

"Please don't keep saying that." Bennie felt unwell. His head was light and his stomach was hollow, and he felt as if, just as he had been gathering momentum down the gleaming railway track of his life, someone had switched the points and diverted him into a most peculiar siding. In such circumstances there was only one thing for an engineer to do: throw the vehicle into reverse, and back up carefully to rejoin the main line.

"Well, Mrs Blanchflower," he said. Ignoring the disturbing question of who *Mr Blanchflower* might be, he smiled more brightly than he felt able and took one step, two, back towards the door. "Many thanks for coming to my little demonstration. I'm sorry you've come so far only to be disappointed. However, you will understand that I have a number of other guests, who I seem to be neglecting—"

"Nineteen fifty-seven."

"I'm sorry?" The ape had the rather irritating habit of blowing up the tracks in front of his train of thought.

"I didn't mean to put it so bluntly," she said softly, "but that's the year you will die. Having spent all of your money on travelling the world looking for investors in the railplane, you eventually give up and take over the running of a small shop to make ends meet. The year before you die, this demonstration track, along with the carriage that sits on it right now, which will have been rusting flake by brittle flake among the gorse bushes and weeds for more than twenty-five years, will finally be dismantled. That's when the dream that has been worn down to a hard nugget inside your heart will finally wear so thin that it'll break and vanish. You won't live another year after that."

Part of Bennie's brain had been aware all along that he really shouldn't be standing talking to an ape in a dress, especially one with such an eloquent—even lyrical—turn of phrase, but that part was overruled by the part that took umbrage at the decidedly insulting tone to her speech. "I'm sorry, madam," he said stiffly. "The evidence is to the contrary. I have a number of *very firm* expressions of interest already, and..." His composure broke. "*By Christ*, did you see the looks on their faces? Did you hear what they were saying? They're up at my office right now, stuffing themselves with French canapés and waiting to throw money at me."

The bonobo simply shook her head, a sort of mournful look in her soft, brown eyes.

"Well, give me a reason then," Bennie blustered. "What's to stop them?"

"There's a war coming."

"Ha!" Now he knew what this was: a prank! His visitor was nothing more than an actress in an ape costume—a very convincing one, granted—her acting, however, was far more persuasive than her grasp of world affairs. "A war indeed. Who put you up to this? It's barely a decade since we won the war to end all wars. There will be naught but peace and prosperity for the rest of our lifetimes."

"So you say," she replied, unfazed, "but nevertheless, there is one coming, and before the decade is out. And what's more it'll be worse than the last one."

"Nonsense." In the face of her calm conviction, this didn't even sound convincing to his own ears.

"And it's not just the war. The railway owners will call in favours with persons of influence. With all this apparent peace and prosperity you're talking about, business is looking good for them. The last thing they need is a cheaper, faster, altogether better alternative to the train."

"When the railplane network is in place there will still be a role for the traditional railways," Bennie protested, but he'd used that argument so often that, true as it was—the railplane would only ever be suitable for express passenger conveyance—it sounded glib even to him.

"George," the bonobo blinked, and wiped at her eye in such a natural and non-human fashion that Bennie's brief fantasy about the actress in the ape suit was blown apart like a dandelion head in the wind. "Do you really think they'll be content with *goods haulage?*"

The logical part of Bennie's brain gained the upper hand then: and it found her argument, if not persuasive, then at least coherent. Even likely.

Bennie pulled up a three-legged stool and sat on it, clasping his hands in front of his eyes. Was it really possible that all his bright plans would come to nothing? He felt warm fingers, soft as leather gloves pat his head. A gentle squeeze of solidarity.

"Very well," he said at length. "Assume that I take you at your word—that you are an intelligent ape that has come from the future to ruin my entire life just at its happiest moment to date. But I have to ask you: Why? What have I done that you should hate me so much?"

"That's complicated, George."

A muffling of her voice made him open his eyes and look. She was nowhere to be seen.

"I certainly hated you at one point," she continued. The voice was coming from behind a row of lathes and pedestal drills. "Or at least hated you in *principle*. In much the same way as pretty soon you'll grow to hate the railway owners." There was a grunt of effort and the sound of something heavy being dragged on the floor. "But now I know how things are, I empathize." As Bennie approached the bank of machines, the ape's head suddenly popped up.

She smiled in a not particularly wholesome fashion. "We're the same, you see? So, I've not come to ruin your life, but to offer you ... something which should help." Mrs Blanchflower ducked down again, and apparently did something that began a noise like rice grains being dropped onto a skillet.

Bennie didn't see. How he could be considered in any way the same as this perplexing creature, he had no idea. Then, as he got a clear sight of what was behind the lathes, a glimmer of understanding was finally lit.

Mrs Blanchflower had dragged a rusting bogey assembly into an empty area of the floor. She looked up from a device cradled in her hairy hand. "You don't need this, do you?" She indicated the scrap.

Bennie shook his head.

"Good, iron is about as good as we could hope for here for a substrate."

Something was happening to the old bogey. The metal was flowing, beading like condensation and dripping to the floor in a rattling rain of spherules that bounced and rolled in all directions. Mrs Blanchflower tapped at her device and the skittering balls underwent a miraculous change in direction, reversing and converging on a structure that, as he watched, rapidly rose from the floor.

Bennie watched with admiration as balls flowed together into strands that entwined, becoming cables that rose up like charmed snakes and met at the top to form a shape recognizable as a doorway. "What's this then?" he asked.

"This?" the ape said, stepping over what was left of the pile of scrap to inspect the completed arch. "This will take you to any point on the planet, and as I discovered by accident during the development phase, any point in history."

Bennie peered at the iron archway. This was what she had meant when she said they were the same. The ape was an engineer. "You designed this ... process?"

She bobbed her head. "Indeed. You just tell it where you want to be, and there you are. It's the transport of the future." She paused, looked at him in a curious fashion with her unreadable, inhuman eyes. "Or at least *a* future."

"What do you mean by that?"

"It's best if I show you."

"It's *best* if you tell me," Bennie replied. As far as he could see, the archway was only that. Standing a little off true, and with something of a kink near the apex, it resembled a piece of modern sculpture more than any mode of transport he had seen. Yet, close to it, there was a charge in the air, a potential, that made him cautious.

Mrs Blanchflower sighed, looked at the floor. "I have a confession to make," she said.

"Yes?"

"The reason I came here was to stop you. Stop the railplane before it ever got developed. Originally, I mean."

Bennie shook his head. "I thought you said the whole project was doomed to failure?" he said, bitterly.

"For the most part, yes it is." She shuffled, less confident now than she had been earlier. "George, I didn't know until I came back, but my future is one of the very, very few where you did succeed."

"Your future? You mean there's more than one?"

She shrugged, an odd gesture he thought for an ape. "Potentially infinite futures. But it turns out most events coalesce towards one probable outcome. I've been to 1957—dozens of times, by dozens of routes—and the outcome's always the same. You should have been designing a new kind of engine then that was going to give the bennie a real edge over the train, but all I found was a rusting heap on the sidings and a disillusioned inventor."

Bennie stuck his hands in his pockets, walked away from the bonobo. This was madness. Twenty minutes ago he had been watching the evidence of his assured fame with his own eyes. It was a *certainty.* It was in the sunbeams bouncing off the polished steel carriage and it was in the faces of the passengers. How could it not be, after all this time, all this hard work? And yet, he had already had prickly dealings with the railways. *He felt his certainty crack.* And if the world did indeed go to war again so soon... *He felt it crumble.* There'd be no investment, not even from the Americans. *He swore he* heard *it crash.*

Mrs Blanchflower must have heard it too. "You see," she said softly, "we're the same."

Bennie rounded on her then, finding that anger had replaced the denial. "Exactly *how*, madam, can we be considered *the same...*" he began.

It was that sad look in her eyes again that killed the anger as quickly as it had arisen. "Because in *my* future, George, the one that's virtually impossible to locate unless you already came from there and know how to get back—the one where, despite everything, you did succeed—it's the centuries-long, world-wide dominance of the Bennie Transport Corporation that stifles new ideas, new inventions—like this one, yes—if there's even a possibility that they might challenge a fraction of its monopoly."

Mrs Blanchflower stepped in front of the archway and held out her hand. "Would you like to see?"

❂

The future was exactly as Bennie had dreamed it. Glasgow had grown larger, taller, brighter, and its four great railway stations had become the looms for gigantic silver ribbons of clustered bennie lines that spun out of the city to the north, the east, the south and the west; to the rest of Scotland, and the United Kingdom, and via miraculous bridges to Europe, and beyond.

Their journey across the Atlantic would take no more than an hour and a half. Bennie had wanted to stay in Glasgow, but Mrs Blanchflower pointed out, somewhat peevishly but correctly enough, that there was nothing left there of the city he knew in his time.

Since they had arrived in the future, the bonobo had become withdrawn. She clearly had plans she wanted to be getting on with. It was as well, then, to accompany her to New York. If he wanted to come back later it was only a short hop after all.

The view from the upper level of the triple-decker behemoth as it zephyred along the gentle sine of its track was stunning. The great grey North Atlantic reared and swirled as a storm raged below them. Rain rattled against the observation windows, but the megabennie—as he was told it was called, and he was pleased to recognize many similarities to his original design despite the various improvements that had been made—continued on, smooth and true.

Marvellous.

Mrs Blanchflower coughed to attract his attention. That was when he realized that the rattling he had heard was not the rain. She had pulled up a section of deep-pile carpet and was busy turning a square of metal decking into another of her archways.

"I thought I was going to see New York," Bennie said, disappointed that she was sending him home already. Home, it was suggested, to humiliation and failure. She'd shown him 1957. It had been horrible.

"This isn't for you," she said, and nodded to the chair next to his. Where she had been sitting, there was a plastic card. "The keys to my apartment and my bank account," she said. "It's not much, I'm afraid, but then you know how it is being a struggling genius and all."

So he was staying here? But that meant...

"What are you going to do?" Bennie asked.

That sad look came over her face again. "This is *your* future, George," she said. "I'm off in search of *mine*."

She was wrong on that account, or at least unspecific. This wasn't *his* future, or that of thousands of other versions of himself, but it was the future of some randomly favoured George Bennie who had somehow fluked his dream into actuality. Since this remarkable trip had begun, he had clung to the slenderest hope that he would return to his 1930 and, armed with the certainty that his vision could be fulfilled, would make it so. The very fact that Mrs Blanchflower was leaving him here with no opportunity of return, and that *here*, and in particular the vehicle he rode on, still existed, proved that it wasn't he after all who had succeeded.

Bennie appreciated the fact that she didn't make any more fuss than that. One minute the talking ape was standing beside her invention, the next ... the archway encompassed her in a complex and quite frightening folding motion, and both she and it were gone.

Bennie stared at the hole in the floor, and the two stumps of slag that marked where the arch had stood. *Where's the elegance in that?* he thought. *It'll never catch on.*

Then he settled back in his seat and enjoyed the rest of his trip to the capital of a New World where they clearly knew a good prospect when they saw it.

The question of identity is one much considered by Scots, both at home and around the globe; a national obsession easily assuaged with flags, football songs and lorne sausage. For most, this is a harmless exercise, a simple matter of regional pride, but for those from other backgrounds the question "Who am I?" can be much more difficult to answer. And finding an answer requires something a little stronger than our other national drink.

○ ○

THE HARD STUFF
John Grant

○ ○

We saw things in Falluja that no one should be expected to see and want to carry on living. People fused together by the flames, pregnant women with their guts splayed out and the unborn child among them, infants with their limbs blown away. All the time our superior officers kept telling us it was the insurgents who'd done this with their car bombs and their mortars, and all the time we knew they didn't even believe this themselves. We'd rained high explosives and incendiaries and hell upon these people. Some of them had probably been ready to kill us; the vast majority of them were just ordinary men and women and kids who'd been caught underneath the technology we'd let fall on them; none of them deserved what we'd done to them. What made it worse was that all of us knew by then there was no real reason for us to have done any of it. We'd been lied into this place by people who used human beings' lives as rungs on a ladder of personal greed.

We moved forward through the smoke and the stink of burning masonry and people's flesh. Some of us threw up, some of us did terrible things to the occasional survivors we encountered, all of us had no expectations that we'd ever be the same again.

I don't remember anything about the moment when the ghosts of the dead took their revenge on me. Their tool might have been a home-made incendiary that somehow hadn't detonated earlier, during the bombardment. It could have been one of our own bombs. All I knew was that one moment I was probing through the smoking hinterlands of Hell, my rifle at the ready, and the next I was ... somewhere else, a place where there was nothing to be seen or sensed except the agony that devoured me. Every cell of my body had been replaced by a flame. The whitest heat of the fire was in my arms; from there it spread to fill everything.

Then there was a time when the world was a polychromatic fan of constantly shifting images, none of which made any sense at all even though they seemed like memories I might once have had. But this time of release couldn't last for long—never long enough—before the fire returned to claim me. There was a thunder in my ears that was either the roaring flames or my own bellows of pain and terror. Occasionally I had fleeting glimpses of faces that were trying to look kindly, but succeeded instead only in looking routinely resigned.

Someone told me I was lucky still to be alive, to have all my senses and my "good looks" intact, but it was only later that I was able to stitch those words together, like someone painstakingly repairing a ripped piece of lace. At the time they were just stray torn threads that didn't seem to have any relation to each other, dancing along in a gale of raw heat. Then I was told, repeatedly, that I was going home. That didn't make sense to me either. Didn't these people realize I *had* no home? That all I had was that I *was*? I had no past, unless my past was an infinity of the fire that was the present. I wasn't a human being any longer, had never been. I was just a construct woven from filaments of everlasting pain.

But one more thing I didn't have was any words with which to say any of this. So I just carried on through the tunnel of eternity until at last I noticed things were different.

○

"Your trouble, Quinn," said Tania, "is that you're forever filling your head with all the things you can't do any longer. It makes you think there's nothing you *can* do."

We were sitting on the porch watching a late-Fall sun head toward the horizon. The sky was painting the tree-splashed hills the colours of toasted bread. It was the end of another day marked by little except the fact that I'd lived through it.

I made no reply to her. Most of the time I didn't.

"You should wipe those thoughts out of your head, Quinn," she continued, nodding as if I'd said something. She was standing with her hands on the porch rail, looking out defiantly toward the sunset. There was enough of a breeze to press her dress against her legs. "If you don't, you're letting them be the bars to the prison cell you've locked yourself into."

She turned to face me, and I tried to meet her gaze. I couldn't, so instead I looked down at my own arms, what was left of them.

The months had etiolated them. They looked like empty denim shirt-sleeves hanging on a line, one of them tucked up by the wind more than the other. The people with the resigned faces had saved my left arm down as far as the wrist, my right not so far as that, only to a few inches below the elbow. Freakishly, the explosion hadn't harmed the rest of me at all beyond a few superficial shrapnel wounds that had soon healed, leaving scars that looked like nothing more serious than long, pale crinkly hairs plastered by sweat to my skin. My "good looks", as the medics had called them, were still the way they'd always been, except for the waking nightmares that seethed behind my face.

I didn't have much use for mirrors, but sometimes Tania made me look into them as she shaved me, or trimmed my hair, or brushed my teeth.

As the sun came into laborious contact with the cut-out hilltops I spoke at last.

"Time for a drink," I said as I always did this time of evening. "An aperitif. Fuck the meds."

Tania slapped her hands against her cotton covered thighs and let out a gasp of exasperation.

"Have you been listening to a single word I've been saying?"

"Yes. You've been telling me I should look on the bright side, think positive, all that."

She sighed.

It was a constant bone of contention between us, like my refusal to wear the clumsy prosthetic hands I'd been given, which lay in their box upstairs. If I wanted a more sophisticated pair we were going to have to find the money for them—a lot of money for them—from somewhere. All the government would spring for were lumps of pink plastic that looked ridiculous because of their colour and chafed my stumps to agony within minutes. That was what the country could afford, they said. There were, after all, tax breaks to pay for.

"But I'm a stupid self-pitying bastard," I said, "so I just carry on wallowing in my misery and bitterness, or dreaming up crazy schemes about what I'd like to do to the fat-cat fuckers who made me like this." I raised my shorter arm, the one that seemed always to be wanting to hide itself within the sleeve of my teeshirt. "The trouble is, I can't nuke Crawford, Texas, and fry Il Buce and the Stepford Wife alive because how the fuck without any fingers could I set the"— I formed the word fastidiously—"*device*? I can't strangle Rumsfeld in his own intestines, which is what I'd dearly love to do, because he hasn't left me with any hands to strangle him with. As for those fuckers Darth Cheney and Kindasleazy... So all I have left is talking about how I'd like to do every one of those things and more, and getting my jollies by dreaming about those bastards' screams and them begging for a mercy I won't give as they choke on their own severed genitals, because every time I ask you for your help making my dreams real you just look disgusted or your face twists up in pain or you pretend you've not heard me, which is probably the worst and cruellest thing you could do to me. And somehow in the middle of all that I can't find room to cram in a Dale Carnegie course on encouraging my positive thoughts."

It wasn't one of my longer speeches. I was just getting started. I could go on for hours, when the spirit took me, detailing the medieval tortures I wanted to inflict on the shits who'd stolen my hands and put me here.

"I'll get you that beer," said Tania, heading for the screen door. "And something a bit stronger for myself," she appended under her breath, thinking I couldn't hear her.

She came back out a few minutes later and plonked the beer down on my chair arm. In her other hand she had something cheerily red and toxic-looking with a parasol sticking out the top. My beer was in a plastic beaker with a screw-on top and a straw. The condensation wouldn't form properly on the plastic sides, which looked blotchy and diseased rather than enticingly misted. Nonetheless, I bowed my head and sucked and the liquid was tart and cold, like the ice no one had been able to put on me when the fire possessed me.

Tania flopped into the other chair on the porch, and let her free hand dangle as she took a sip—a gulp—of her drink. Two chairs were all we needed out here these days because we didn't have visitors very often any more, and most of them didn't want to stay long. I thought it was because they were sickened or embarrassed by my deformity. Tania thought the same, only it was different deformities we were thinking of.

Dad didn't come here at all, now. A soldier without hands isn't a soldier any more. He'd made himself forget about me.

"I'm taking you away on a trip," she announced abruptly in an alcohol-coloured voice.

"Yeah. Right. Another psych checkup by those terribly nice people at Newark General?"

"Nope." She put her glass carefully down on the armrest of her chair and stared at it. "I'm taking you to see my folks."

That caught my attention. Her folks hadn't come across from Scotland for the wedding, although they'd sent a bunch of tartaned ethnic objects for us to fill the attic with. We'd kept planning to go over to what Tania called, with a curious twist of her lip, "the old country", but somehow as the years passed we'd never gotten around to it. And then, of course, there'd come my Iraq posting, the murderer of all plans, real or otherwise.

I looked at her, questioning.

"I think I need their help," she said. She was still staring at her half-emptied glass of red stickiness. For once she seemed doubtful of her words.

"Their help with _you_, Quinn," she added, as if the glass didn't know already that this was what she meant. "I've booked us tickets for Friday. Return tickets from Newark to Glasgow. We're going for a week, just over."

"You didn't think this was something we should discuss?" I said, purely for the sake of saying it. She was the one who took my decisions for me. I was happy enough about it, because it was one less thing for me to make a mess of. But that didn't mean I couldn't voice a few words of false independence from time to time.

"I knew you'd just argue about it for days, so I thought I'd pre-empt you."

She winced. "Pre-empt" wasn't the most popular of words around our house. She gave a flutter of her hand as apology, then took another swig of her drink to distract my attention.

"I think it's a good idea," I said, surprising her. "I just wish you'd asked me first."

She grinned at me, for the first time in days. For the first time in weeks or years, I managed a grin back.

"Just remember who's the boss, woman."

"Yes, boss."

My good mood was covered over by the usual black tar before she'd finished the second word. I stood nine inches taller than her, but she'd be the one carrying the baggage or struggling with the trolley. I wondered how many times during the trip I'd reach instinctively with my left arm toward my inside right jacket pocket for the tickets or the passports or the money before realizing that, of course, these days they resided in Tania's pocket, not mine. I wondered how many times I'd force that embarrassed little "silly me, it doesn't really matter, honestly" laugh for the benefit of the people around me.

I didn't say anything more that evening until after she'd led me inside and fed me fried chicken and microwaved sweet potatoes followed by praline caramel ice cream, and then taken me into the bathroom and unzipped my trousers and pulled them down around my knees so I could have a shit.

When I finally spoke it was just to say thank you after she'd wiped my ass for me.

The one time I wished my pride would take a holiday so I could use my cheap, wrongly coloured, hated prosthetics.

○

My dad made it to be a five-star general, unlike his farm-labourer father before him. Dad wanted lots of sons who'd all make it to be five-star generals, so the family tree would glow in the night like some spiral galaxy and impress the hell out of the Hubble Telescope.

It didn't turn out that way, because my mother never properly recovered after giving birth to me. I have vague recollections of the smell of soap and soft skin and summery cloth; there are other memories, too, of the smells being not so good, but by then my father had decreed it was probably best if "his little man" were kept out of the sickroom. Clear as a colour photograph in my head is what I saw when, at the age of three and a half, I was held aloft for one final look at my mother, framed by the oblong of her coffin. I gazed down at the face of a stranger who bore a casual resemblance to someone I'd once known.

Dad never married again. He had a succession of lady friends, one or two of whom he succeeded in coaxing out of their military uniforms when he thought I was asleep. But their visits were few and far between. Mainly it was just him and me.

And his ambitions for me. If he couldn't have a passel of sons, then the one son his weak vessel had borne to him should fulfil a passel's worth of his dreams. I was a soldier from even before my mother died. I could get my bedclothes as tight as a drumskin by the time I was five.

Tania shouldn't have found me, but she did. Why her eyes ever alit on the stuffy youth with the micrometer-precise haircut, whose personality was hardly more than the uniform he wore, is something I've never been able to fathom. But she bubbled up to me at my cousin's wedding and introduced herself, asking me if I agreed with her a cow had probably sneezed into the vol-au-vents. Young women were a slight mystery to me at the time, although I'd read all the usual magazines, gazing with a sort of astonished fascination at the glistening revelations; and so I didn't know quite what to do with myself during that first conversation. But she was persistent, and without my ever understanding quite how it had happened I had a date with her the following week.

The years didn't change Tania. The faint accent she had, which wasn't so much an accent as a startling lack of one, never went. She had a face you'd dismiss as nothing special, really rather plain, except that at the same time you'd find yourself thinking it was maybe the most beautiful face you'd ever seen. Around that oval hung straightish blonde or muddy-mousy hair that was either lank or aethereally fine, like the flimsy webs that billow across the blackness between the stars. Her eyes were green, or perhaps brown, or perhaps even darker than that. Her skin was pallid; her skin was deliciously porcelain-pale. I wasn't so dazed during our first meeting that I didn't notice, with the highly trained reflexes of military men everywhere, that she significantly lacked the generous frontal rations enjoyed by the women in the magazines. Curiously, this made her seem far more feminine than they were.

(No, there was one thing about her that changed. She gave up smoking after she'd been properly introduced to Dad. He had moral compunctions about women smoking.)

What else did she look like?

She looked like Tania. That's all the description necessary. Certainly it's the only real description I can come up with.

Born in Scotland, midway between Glasgow and Edinburgh and a bit to the north of both, she'd been raised in a village that sounded more like a few houses, a shop, a pub and a post office than anything you'd recognize as a settlement. About the family business she was always charmingly imprecise: I got the impression her father wasn't really a farmer and not really a trader, but somewhere midway between both and a bit to the north, just like where they lived.

Somehow she'd ended up training as a dancer in London, and had come to New York as an understudy in a touring production of something by Chopin, or maybe it was Delibes. But then she'd sprained her knee. (Did I not mention the slight limp with which she walked ever after? It was something I had a hard job remembering, even as I watched her.) And after that there could be no more question of her pursuing a career as a dancer, except perhaps along Eighth Avenue, a performance art she wasn't prepared to countenance. So she turned instead to production. She already had a work visa, and she was able to wangle that into an assistant position somewhere far enough off Broadway it was probably in the middle of the Hudson.

That was not too long before she found me.

Dad and the army laid on a hell of a military wedding, I'll give them that, even though he hid his disapproval of this "Bohemian" so deeply and effectively that it was the first thing strangers became aware of when they met him. She turned to costume design so we could be together as I finished college and then wherever around the country the army's whim took me.

My posting to Iraq represented the first time we'd spent more than a day apart since our wedding.

Dad's eyes were watery with pride as he wished me *bon voyage*. He put on all his old medals, the better to show off the puffing of his chest.

"Go serve your country and kill those heathen motherfuckers, son."

I'm surprised the stare Tania gave him didn't boil the flesh from his bones.

o

"I don't care what you say, sir. I think that's liquor."

Tania and I looked at each other in frustration. Behind her face, the depth of the moulded plastic window frame gave me the illusion I was looking out not upon sunset-painted clouds but upon the ocean floor, where weirdly coloured coral formations sprouted.

The chief stewardess, who looked like an advertisement for the Aryan race after a teenager had doctored it with Photoshop, had spied the plastic bottle full of glucose solution sitting on the fold-down tray in front of me and gotten it into her head that I was sipping scotch or brandy through the bottle's built-in straw. On these planes, she'd informed us coldly, it was a Federal Offence to drink any alcohol except that sold to us at great cost by the cabin crew.

"I strongly advise you, sir, not to drink any more out of that bottle," she concluded, fixing us in turn with a stare borrowed from an old Gestapo movie. "Know what I mean?"

She flounced off down the aisle, doubtless to phone her mother for a good weep.

Tania began to giggle. So, after a few moments, did I. My laughter felt very distant from me, but the emotion was perfectly genuine. Adversity was bringing Tania and me closer together than we'd been in months.

We'd navigated Newark International with the usual dehumanizing and, in my case, emasculating hindrances. The clerk at check-in had seemed sickened by my vulgarity in putting my elbows on the counter in front of him. The security people had taken one look at my dark face and my truncated arms and decided I was obviously a mad Arab suicide bomber—who else would go around with his hands missing, after all? We'd dissuaded them from the full body-cavity search, but they'd done just about everything else they could think of. We'd discovered the eateries and drinkeries behind the security gates all worked under the assumption that their customers could carry their own plates and glasses; burdened by our duty-free bags and our carry-on luggage, Tania had done her best to cope for two, but even so there was a corner of the hall that was going to be forever beer-stained. After she'd fed the both of us, there were still two hours to go before departure; I got through the first hour OK but eventually confessed I needed a leak, so there was a whole round of further complication when we found the disabled bathroom was closed for repairs...

I was dreading our arrival in the airport at Glasgow, where presumably we'd have to go through the entire rigmarole all over again.

"Put it this way," said Tania, reading my thoughts, "it couldn't possibly be any worse."

"You bet?" I said, though in fact I agreed with her.

"Have a nice glug of glucose, Quinn. It'll make you feel better. If that nasty lady comes back I'll deal with her."

I chuckled again. Tania was grinning. Before Iraq, her grin had always made me chuckle. It was one of our countless ways of making love.

Time passed.

We watched a movie in which Cameron Diaz waggled her rear end at the camera. No change there. I slept for a while. A different stewardess, younger, woke me up to ask if I wanted a breakfast that I took one look at and didn't, although I accepted the coffee and the plastic demi-tasse of orange juice.

"I'm lucky," I said to Tania as she peered out the window into the beginnings of sunrise to see if Scotland were visible yet.

She turned from the window, surprised. "It's been a long time since I've heard you say that, Quinn."

I knew she was expecting me to tell her I was lucky because I had her, so instead I said: "There are countless other poor assholes who've come back who would envy me for having got off so lightly."

Her face fell, but she rallied. "Taken you a while to realize that, hasn't it?"

"And at least we've got enough money to cope," I went on. Dad might have decided I was a lost son, but either he'd forgotten to cancel his monthly allowance to us or it was his way of cancelling out his guilt for the abandonment.

"That certainly makes it easier," she said, nodding, her eyes narrowing.

I felt the corners of my mouth twitch, even though I was trying to stop them doing so.

She saw.

"You're a bastard, Quinn Hogarth," she said, the disguised offendedness draining out of her eyes, leaving behind sparkle. "But I knew that when I married you."

She took one of my ears in each hand and dragged my head towards her for a kiss.

"Say it," she whispered in my ear.

"Those are the least important things of all," I murmured back to her. "You're my luckiness, Tania, and always will be."

"You don't know the half of it," she said.

○

The airport in Glasgow was a bit of a disappointment—which was to its credit. Our adrenaline levels had geared themselves up for another dose of Newark International, only worse because of being in a foreign country. But there was neither subservience nor bored resentment and suspicion on display. The place was about a tenth the size of its Newark counterpart, which might explain some of this—not all. The attitude of the various uniformed officials seemed to be that we were all equal colleagues in achieving a common aim, which was to get arrivals through the bureaucracy as quickly and comfortably as possible.

Tania joined me in the All Other Passports line at immigration. When the guy at the counter saw her UK passport he frowned and was halfway through pointing her toward the queue for EU nationals when he realized why she was here.

"The business in Iraq?" he said, nodding toward my stumps. His accent was quite thick, and totally different from Tania's non-accent, but I had no difficulty understanding him.

"Yes." I tried to soften my curtness with one of those instant smiles in which I specialized.

"I'm sorry you had the evil luck to be sent there," he said offhandedly, shrugging as he stamped my passport.

I caught my breath. It was exactly the right thing he'd said. No overweening sympathy. No gung-ho denunciations of towel-heads. Just a sort of acceptance and sharing of my misfortune.

He looked me in the eye. "I hope you're bringing the lady back home to stay. It's an ill thing when all the best and prettiest ones get taken away from us."

I laughed. "Just a holiday, I'm afraid."

He shrugged. "Ah, weel."

"Is everyone in Scotland like this?" I asked Tania later, jerking my head toward the terminal building we'd just come out of.

"No," she said with a smile, looking around her for the taxi rank. We'd decided beforehand that it'd be silly to try negotiating the buses into the city centre, me with my handlessness and Tania with all the luggage. "But a lot of them are. It's a more laid-back country than you're used to, Quinn. And freer."

As the taxi driver loaded our cases and bags into the trunk of his big black vehicle, he told us he'd take us to Glasgow Central, where our hotel was, for twenty pounds.

"Twenty pounds?" I hissed to Tania as we settled ourselves into the back seat and she reached across me for the tongue of my seat belt. "That's well over fifty bucks! It's only about ten miles, isn't it? He's ripping us off."

"Some things are more expensive here," she replied, jiggling the belt's tongue into its socket. "A lot of things. Just get used to it."

"But..."

"Think of it as your payment for medical insurance."

That ended the discussion.

Everything in Scotland seemed to be smaller, more enclosed-feeling than at home, I mused during the drive into the city. The dinky little airport. The three-lane highway whose lanes seemed narrower than I'd have expected. Most of the cars were actually *cars*: there were hardly any SUVs on the road. The transport trucks and buses seemed half the size of real ones. The overall effect was to make me feel I'd strayed into a model of the world, somewhere slightly enchanted. I recognized the sensation. It was the same as I'd felt when visiting miniature villages as a child.

Tania and a uniformed valet whipped us from the taxi into our hotel—which was not so much next to as half-inside Glasgow Central Station—through registration and up to our room. As she stowed away our clothes in drawers and a wardrobe I gazed out the window onto a vista of the railway station, sensing again that odd magic, this time because the double-glazing muffled into silence all but the very loudest of noises. I could hear the announcements over the loudspeakers, but only very faintly and fuzzily, as if they were a long way away and I was wearing faulty earplugs. There was far more grime than would have been tolerated in a station back home. From where I stood, high above, the passengers scurrying around in obedience to their own motivations were as incomprehensible as roaches on an unswept kitchen floor.

"Are you tired?" said Tania from behind me.

I turned and saw she was sitting on the bed, hands between her knees, all our kit and caboodle safely tidied away into appropriate places where I'd be unable to find any of it unassisted. On the bedside table, beside the telephone, lay a stick pen; there was one beside every phone at home, too. It was there for me to pick up in my teeth and dial with in the event of emergency. Next to the pen she'd put one of the bottles of bourbon we'd got at the duty free in Newark, as well as a carton of cigarettes I hadn't realized she'd bought. She'd opened the carton. A pack of Basics lay on the coverlet beside her.

"Smoking?" I said. "I thought you gave that up."

The edge of her mouth quirked. "Your father's three thousand miles away."

"Even so."

"Even so, I've not got anything to light the damn things with. And I'm too shagged out to go downstairs and get a box of matches from the lobby."

I nodded toward the table underneath the window. Alongside the slightly creased advertisement-stuffed tourist guide to Glasgow, the hotel stationery and the anachronistic blotter, were a book of matches and an ashtray.

"Compliments of the house," I said, trying to keep any judgemental note out of my voice.

"Just be a dear and bring..." She stopped. Resignation crossed her face as she heaved herself to her feet. "Sorry, I forgot."

She tossed the book of matches onto the bed and went into the bathroom, where I could hear the clattering of glass. A moment later she emerged with a tooth mug.

"Cigs. Booze. Sleep," she said, gesturing at the bourbon. "The recipe for a happy wife right now."

We kicked off our shoes and lay side by side on the bed, drinking the raw whiskey. Tania had rinsed out my plastic cup, getting rid of the remains of the glucose drink and replacing it with neat bourbon—to the brim; she wasn't a woman who believed in doing chores twice when once would do. I don't know why we hadn't bought scotch in Newark. Maybe it would have seemed blasphemous, or something, to bring a bottle of scotch to Scotland. I made a resolution to get some in the morning, or, if we woke early enough this evening, tonight. But just at this moment, lying together in what was for me a brand-new country and for Tania a long-abandoned homeland, the bourbon seemed perfectly in keeping. It was a symbol. We were using up, so that we would eventually piss away, the last vestiges of all the emotional and intellectual encumbrances we'd brought with us. I even smoked a couple of her cigarettes—the first time I'd smoked since the stolen guilts of adolescence—although they made my head spin and she laughed at my coughing.

Later, a little clumsily, we got off the bed and I watched her as she bent to pull back the sheets. She undressed me for sleep, and then undressed herself. I don't know if it was the booze or the tiredness or the fact that we were shedding our old selves just as we'd shed the noises of America, but for the first time in four months we made love.

We did this a little clumsily too, but that didn't matter.

○

Two days later, we were driving away from Glasgow, heading roughly north-eastward. Tania seemed far more at ease behind the wheel of the rental car than she ever did driving the Nissan at home. Maybe it was that the driver's seat was on the opposite side; maybe it was just because the car was that little bit smaller in every respect. I don't know. Whatever the case, I myself had found the differences initially disconcerting, then within a few minutes strangely liberating. They were part and parcel of the past forty-eight hours or so. We'd spent most of one day just wandering around, picking up a few things (including a bottle of Laphroaig) in the Glasgow shops; we'd spent most of the second day in the Burrell Collection, where I gazed at the foreignness of the Scottish exhibits while Tania gazed at the foreignness of everything else. In between, we'd eaten two excellent Indian meals and a bad hamburger meal. We'd also made love half a dozen times more, another rediscovery of the ancient arts.

"Where are we going?" I asked for the thousandth time.

"You'll find out when we get there," she said, laughing at the repetition of the exchange.

I glanced sideways at her, watching suburbs speed backwards past her face. There was a shiny vivacity in her eyes, focused on the road ahead, that I'd not seen in far too long.

"Second glen on the right, then straight on 'til morning, sort of thing?" I said.

She began to speak, then paused, then spoke. "That's probably a more accurate description than most," she said primly.

I brushed my hair back from my forehead with my smaller lump of pink plastic. There was still novelty in the gesture. Since Iraq I'd let my hair grow, and it was now longer than I'd ever had it. The other, larger, prosthetic was still in their shared case, somewhere in the trunk behind us.

Unknown to me, Tania had packed the plastic hands for the trip to Scotland, "just in case". When I'd discovered this, instead of flying into a temper I'd asked her to strap on the left one for me—just the one, as a form of compromise with my arrogance. The thing itched like hell sometimes if I kept it on too long, but the agonies of my previous experience were just a memory. We'd discovered in one of the Indian restaurants that, if Tania wedged a spoon firmly between the useless thumb and the equally inflexible fingers, I could feed myself—messily and sloppily at first, as the biriani-streaked front of one of my shirts testified, but I'd improved rapidly with practice. Spaghetti was a distant dream, but perhaps the day would come.

The waiters in the restaurant had watched the performance with a friendly amusement, once or twice pointlessly offering help. This was the curious thing I'd discovered in Glasgow: the complete acceptance by everyone of my disability as just a part of who I was, nothing special. There was the occasional startled glance when people first encountered me, but otherwise it was as if handless men were on every street corner. At home in Jersey, on the rare occasions when I allowed Tania to take me out, I received looks that could be pitying, or sickly fascinated, or even derisory. Once in a supermarket, as I'd dawdled aimlessly behind Tania and her shopping cart, a trio of prepubescent boys had seen fit to follow me, taunting. Their parents, nearby, hadn't intervened until Tania, when she'd finally cottoned on to what was happening, had laid into the kids with a few—quite a lot of—acid words. One of the mothers, springing to the defence of her little angel, had angrily retorted: "Well, what can you *expect?*"

There was none of that in Glasgow. Nor, either, was there any perceivable reaction to our being a "racially mixed couple". I suppose the fact that we were both Americans outweighed any differences there might be between us.

In Scotland it doesn't take you long to drive anywhere. The kind of journey I was accustomed to at home would have had us driving into the sea before it was halfway through. Even so, it seemed to take a good while to leave the urban smear behind. At last, though, the road narrowed from four lanes to three, the central reservation being discarded. Then we were down to two lanes, and ultimately to what seemed to my American eye to be more like one and a half. The countryside we went through was at first rather drab, in terms of both its landforms and its vegetation; the greens were duller and more muted than at home, as if they'd forgotten to wash their faces this morning.

And then things finally began to change. The road became twistier, its progress punctuated by lots of small rises and falls—some of them not so small. The car laboured in a few places as we struggled to reach a crest. The hills were taller and rockier, crowding around us; when we saw them ahead of us in the distance, they had that mysterious purple colour I'd read about but only rarely seen at home. We had the way more or less to ourselves; on the rare occasions we came across a tractor or another car, Tania slowed down as the two vehicles manoeuvred carefully past each other. Each time, she and the other driver would say a few words of greeting, usually about the weather, in one case about a lost sheep. As far as I could gather—the accents were becoming less intelligible to me here, directly counter to Tania's predictions—it was an extremely interesting sheep.

"Tell me something more about your folks," I said when we'd left him and his battered paint-free zone of a truck. She'd never mentioned anything except the basics: Dad, Mom—"Mum", I mean—sisters Alysson and Joanna, brother Alan. Unlike me, who had two fat albums filled with badly focused snapshots and stiff formal portraits of my family, she possessed no photographs of her kin. There were phone calls every week or two—in the old days I'd been required to say a few phatic words to one in-law or another, but not since Iraq—and letters from her mother at least as often, although I'd never noticed Tania writing back. My wife's memories seemed to begin when she'd moved to London. It wasn't as if she were particularly secretive—far from it, in fact. I once joked that I knew more about what her boyfriends before me had been like in bed than I did about her family. She'd given me a cold look and asked me to pass the potatoes.

"I'm going to be meeting them soon enough," I added. "You might as well warn me what to expect."

She thought this over for a few moments, frowning to herself, tilting her head to one side while still watchfully regarding the next curve in the road, letting her foot ease off the pedal a tad as if that would help her deliberations.

"They're the kind of people that you just need to take them the way they are, Quinn. You've got a vile habit of trying to mould people into what you want them to be—you got it from your dad, although heaven be thankful you're not as bad as he is. My folks, they're ... they're not *mouldable*, if that's a proper word. If you try to think of them as anything other than themselves, they won't change. But maybe you will."

It wasn't much of a description, and she refused to add to it. I had images of a commune of merry left-over hippies passing the joints around and forgetting to wash.

Well, I could cut it—of that I was sure. Despite what Tania had said, I was as adaptable as anyone. There'd been plenty of dope in Iraq—it was the only way most of us knew how to get through what was happening—so the prospect of the drugs didn't bother me. Might take a toke or two myself, if...

We came to a place where the road faded out, just beyond a small, dilapidated farmhouse that seemed to be entirely populated by mangy-looking dogs, who watched with suspicious boredom as we drove by. The metal and the low roadside walls stopped abruptly, but two confident-looking ruts carried on across the fields. Tania didn't slow the car or otherwise seem to notice the change in surface.

"It's pretty remote where they live, is it?" I said.

She giggled, and now she did slow the car a little. "I can't see too many townships around here, can you, Quinn?" She nodded ahead of us, where there was little to be seen except sheep-spattered browny-green slopes and, beyond, two greater hills seeming to intersect in a pronounced V-shaped notch. "That's where we're heading. To the—what was it you called it? Ah, yes. To the second glen on the right, straight on 'til morning."

"Not literally, I hope?"

"Hmm?"

"'Til morning, I mean. That's about fifteen, sixteen hours away."

She threw back her head and laughed. If it hadn't been for the ruts we might have driven off the track.

"No," she said. "Mornings are the last thing you'll need to worry about."

It was a puzzling remark, but then a lot had been puzzling me since—oh, since about the time we'd said our goodbyes to the man who'd lost his sheep. Tania was changing, changing even as I sat beside her in the car. We'd pulled into a layby at one point so we could both have a pee (an operation whose mechanics were made possible for me, just, by the lump of plastic at the end of my arm). She went first, and as she emerged from the scraggly bush there'd been no earthly reason to hide behind, I observed the way her stride had changed. It was as if she'd lost about half her weight and was in danger of floating off the ground if she didn't remember to tether herself there. And there was a glow about her that wasn't entirely explicable by the prospect of her seeing her family for the first time in years. I had the odd illusion that the land across which we moved was *feeding* her, somehow—and doing so with a full willingness. This was *her* country. She reigned here with the contented respect of her great, silent subject. There was a communion between her and the very soil unlike anything I could imagine myself experiencing back home in my own native land.

As she'd climbed back into the car and I rocked myself to and fro in my seat, preparing to swing myself out for my own pee, I'd noticed how many birds seemed to be singing around us. God knew where they'd been perching—the trees in this region weren't anything to write home about, being largely of the variety that are obviously not dead yet, but thinking about it. As we bumped along the rutted track, now, I wondered if, were I to roll my window down, I'd hear the songs of just as many birds, even though we were in the middle of nowhere.

"How long to go?" I asked after a few more minutes' silence.

"We'll be there very soon, Quinn," she reassured me, adopting the voice of mothers everywhere when the brats in the back are being a pain in the ass.

"Yes, Mommy," I responded, joining in the game, "but *how* soon?"

"You haud yer wheesht, Jimmie, or yer dad'll stop the car and gie ye a good skelping."

"Huh?"

For the next half hour or so, as the ground beneath us got less and less kempt and the sun, poised midway down the afternoon sky, pondered whether or not to call it a day, she regaled me with Scoticisms. Before giving me the translation in each case, she insisted I make a few guesses myself. The laughter between us got louder and more uncontrollable as my guesses grew progressively more obscene.

"No, Quinn"—this in schoolmistressly tone— "'fit rod?' does *not* mean a healthy..."

She suddenly paused. We'd gone round so many twists and turns since leaving Glasgow that I'd lost my orientation, but we were clearly now heading more or less due west. Directly in front of us, the sun was settling into the notch I'd seen earlier between the two hills.

When Tania spoke next, her voice was different—quieter, lower, slower, barely more than a breath.

"Oh, Quinn, we're almost there." This seemed to be as much to herself as to me. "The sun's opening the gates for us."

I squinted at her, wondering what in the hell she was talking about. She didn't notice my attention.

And, as I watched, she quite deliberately lifted her hands off the steering wheel, leaving the car to guide itself.

In any other circumstances I'd have panicked entirely. No way was I able to grab the wheel, not with a single chunk of badly sculpted, lifeless plastic in place of hands. As it was, there washed across me like calming warm air the conviction that her action was a perfectly natural one, that everything around us was as it should be, as if ourselves and the car scuttling along the now nearly invisible track were tucked inside a cocoon where things were...

Where things were *done differently.*

That was how it was as we drove through the gateway filled by that blood-red sunshine.

o

The blinding glare of the sunlight shattered, revealing itself to me as clouds of rusty-winged insects that fluttered away, their group interest caught by something else as I waved my arm, shooing them.

How could I have imagined they were sunlight? The sun was at its noon height in an unblemished silver sky. Tania and I were walking hand-in-hand through ankle-deep grass and little black-button-eyed wildflowers across a gently curving foothill. The flowers were mainly pink and white, though there were blues and yellows scattered here and there, as well as some distinctly more exotic colours, ones I couldn't quite find a name for. The grass was the unnatural green of Astroturf, but its fresh smell told me it was real, not plastic. There was a curious blur across the ground; it took me a few moments to realize that the tip of each blade of grass was stained a faint, airy violet, the colour that ultraviolet might have if you could see it, the colour of the faint breeze that both warmed and cooled my face.

And all around us there was birdsong, although I could see no birds.

My mind hopped back a pace or two.

Real, not plastic, I had been thinking.

I could feel Tania's fingers curled around mine.

I glanced down at the hand that was holding hers, then at the other.

"I'm..." I began.

"Hush," she said quietly. "There's no need to be saying anything, Quinn."

Again her voice had changed. The precision of her non-accent had become more than it had ever been, so that I had the impression I was listening not to a voice but to pure language. At the same time there was something archaic in it, too.

I dragged my eyes away from the hand of mine that was in hers and followed the line of her bare arm up to her face. Gone were the blue jeans and the sensible striped blouse she'd put on this morning. She was wearing a dress the same colour as the tips of the grass-blades, and as insubstantial-seeming. The neck of it was high, prim, so that the bareness of her arms was a near-uncanny incongruity. The hem of the dress, I saw out of the corner of my vision, brushed the grass we walked upon, and trailed out behind her like half-seen downy feathers.

She trod the ground as lightly as the feathers rustled, as if her body had given up all of its matter to the sky.

Tania turned her head slowly toward me, meeting my gaze.

These were the eyes of my wife I was looking into, of my Tania, and yet they were no eyes I'd ever seen before. I was gazing into shady green corridors that retreated infinitely far back, into places and times where I was not entirely certain I wanted to go. Her lips were thinner, her mouth a little wider, and was there a trace of an unaccustomed cruelty in the laughter lines at the corners? The porcelain whiteness of her skin had become almost opalescent. Her hair was the pale, pale shade of highly polished pure gold, where the yellowness is more of an idea than a hue. In it she wore a coronet plaited of the variously coloured flowers that sprinkled the field we walked through. Her forehead was unmarked. The eyebrows beneath it, darker than her head hair, were fine lines that seemed to have been painted on rather than grown; one was raised a little above the other, giving her an expression I might have interpreted as cold cynicism had it been on any other face.

"Who are you?" I said so softly I'm not sure I spoke the words aloud. "Where are we?"

She laughed.

"Less of your questions, questions, questions all the time, darling Quinn." She lifted my hand as if it were a plaything and skipped forward a step or two, pulling me into the dance with her. "You know you have always wanted to see my folks. Well, now you shall. They have been waiting so long and eagerly to meet my lover from the west, and to share with him the love they have for me. They have a ripe welcome waiting for you, my Quinn. But do not pester them with your questions, the way I allow you to pester me. They might not be so gracious if their tempers frayed."

Again she glanced at me. Her eyes were wide, mocking.

I suppose I should have begun to get frightened around now. Who was this stranger I'd thought I knew through and through? Where was she leading me? Who were these enigmatic people who might harm me if their "tempers frayed"? Had I entered some hallucinatory madness? Was the madness even my own?

But, gazing into those antiquity-coloured, teasing eyes of Tania, I trusted her entirely—trusted her far more even than I ever had. Wherever I was, I was here because of her love for me. This world was an extension of her. I could no more come to any real harm here than she would strike me a fatal blow with her own hand.

"Watch where you're going, Quinn," she said lightly. "If you trip and fall I'm not sure if I could hold you."

Obediently I turned my head forward. The curved rim of the hillside was approaching us faster, it seemed, than the steps we took could account for.

"Where are we...?" I started to say, then remembered her stricture.

"Stop asking," she said anyway. "There is nothing you know how to ask about. Just *be*, Quinn."

And then we were over the breast of the slope and looking down from its small height onto a little valley. A stream curled along the bottom. By the stream's side there gathered like idly curious spectators a collection of small stone houses with grassed roofs—they looked like pictures I'd seen of Highland crofts. A white horse grazed unfenced. Two dogs cavorted together, warring over something I couldn't see from here that floated in the air above them. A ram looked up towards us as if it had been observing our arrival, its twin horns like hard nails. Smoke coiled from the chimney of the largest of the houses, which was still small.

"The second glen on the right," I said quietly.

Just a few yards ahead of us, a notice had been stuck into the ground—a flat sheet of wood nailed to a stake. The untidily painted letters read:

ABANDON YOURSELF

All Ye Who Enter Here

There was no sign of any other human being but us.

"Everyone's inside," explained Tania before I could break her rules again. "They're preparing for us."

"No need for them to dress up specially," I said, making a joke of the remark's inadequacy.

"Oh, but they will, they will," she assured me. "Come on, Quinn. Time to meet the folks."

◦

Much later, although it was still noon, there were nine of us crammed into the only room of what I was told should properly be called the Bothy. In Tania's absence, her sister Joanna and her brother had both wed; they had brought their spouses. Meanwhile Alysson, the unmarried sister, was showing a generous bulge; she proudly informed us the baby was due in under four months. We'd had plenty of beer to drink as we ate what seemed to be an entire sheep, with potatoes and a coarse kind of beet called a turnip. The air was thick: everyone but me was smoking the cigarettes Tania had brought with her from the States. The noise level was getting high. Faces were getting red. Eyes were getting bloodshot and watery.

I'd expected Tania's family to be as aethereal as she herself had become while we were approaching this place, but instead they were of big-boned, broad-shouldered country stock, as assuredly physical as an ox. And Tania herself was no longer the unworldly creature she'd seemed to be on the hillside. As we'd descended into the valley she'd shed her strangeness like steam; by the time we reached the Bothy she was the same Tania who'd long ago seduced me, then married me. But perhaps not the same Tania who'd left America with me, for this one bore smiles that seemed to come all the way up from the soul.

The only thing left of the hillside Tania was her dress, which was made of a fabric that fascinated me. As I sat on the floor at her feet, leaning against her knees—there weren't enough chairs to go around, and we'd eaten off big wooden plates on the floor—I repeatedly, however hard I tried to stop myself, took a fold of the garment's hem between my fingers and rubbed it back and forth. It felt as if it were made of woven water. I couldn't decide if it was the peculiarity of the fabric's texture that drew me again and again, or just the fact that I had fingers against whose skin I could feel it. Her calves beneath the cloth were slender and smooth and cooler than they should have been in the heat of the room. Whenever I thought no one was looking I'd covertly caress them, making her stir in her seat.

Outside, it was still broad daylight. Inside, it was night, and we depended on the guttering flames of half a dozen oil lamps placed strategically around the room. We could see the sunshine through the Bothy's half-open door and its three or four small grimy windows, but it seemed to be unable to penetrate more than a few inches into where we were, as if the air itself snuffed out the brightness.

Tania's family all called her by one of those affectionately derogatory nicknames families often use among each other. In her case it was Loachy. I knew there must be a tale behind the name, but somehow I never thought to ask her for it. Soon enough, I found myself using the name myself, sometimes. A love-name.

For the third time that evening I needed to go take a leak. I was apparently the only one of the company who had any such requirement, but earlier Tania's father, James, had pointed out a tiny stone shack, like an upright sarcophagus, inside which I'd sure enough found an earth privy. The pit was perfectly clean, when I glanced down into it. My guess was it had been specially dug for me just a few hours ago.

Explaining quietly to Tania, who was busily occupied in laughing at one of brother Alan's more ribald jokes—my scatologies earlier in the car had been as nothing compared to the stuff this family regarded as commonplace—I hauled myself to my feet, marvelling yet again at the way my hands obeyed the commands I gave them. Taking exaggerated care not to trip over the bakelite telephone which sat anachronistically in the middle of the floor, or the flex that snaked off from it into an unexplored corner, I made my way haphazardly out into the daylight. I'm sure they all of them knew of my going—knew precisely which muscles I'd moved and the number of breaths I'd taken—but not one of them gave the slightest sign of registering any change. Indeed, there was something quite unnatural about the way the hubbub of excited chatter and laughter stayed totally unaltered, I thought woozily as I shut the door behind me and made my way to the privy. It sounded somehow ... orchestrated, somehow prerecorded, like the laughter track on a bad television sitcom. What were they really thinking, these people? What were they communicating to each other under the cloak of smutty jokes and oddly unpin-downable reminiscences?

What did they truly look like?

Tania had told me they'd been preparing themselves for my arrival, and I'd assumed they were putting on finery, adding final touches to make-up or hair. But that most certainly hadn't been the case. The men were in farm-soiled loose trousers, James's held up despite the overhang of his belly by a piece of hairy string knotted around his waist; their shirts were coarsely woven cotton. The women were in smock-like dresses with torn hems and cooking stains. If any of them had brushed their hair—or their teeth—in a week there was no evidence of it. All the men needed a shave, and, although I'd never dream of saying a word about this to Tania, so did her mother.

If they'd not been dressing up for me, was it conceivable they'd been dressing *down*? Could it be that Tania's family, in their natural state, resembled the loved, the lovely, yet the in some measure terrifying creature who'd accompanied me across the grassy hillside to reach here? Had they donned solidly corporeal bodies, convincingly detailed right down to Alysson's pregnant swelling, in order to make me feel less of a stranger?

Or might they have had some other motive for adopting their guises? Was their intent, less benevolently, to deceive?

I shivered as I creaked the privy's wooden door open. For a while up there on the hillside I'd been certain that the place to which Tania was leading me was Fairyland, and I still wasn't sure this conclusion had been too far askew. The face I'd gazed into on the slopes, the face with the eyes of a lost and ancient time, could have been the quintessence of La Belle Dame Sans Merci. At military school we'd studied Shakespeare's A Midsummer Night's Dream as one of our few concessions to culture, and I'd learned enough to know that fairies weren't the cute little bundles of mischief the Victorians had turned them into. They had cruel ways with mortals who strayed into their realm.

Again, I should have been frightened, but I wasn't. Wasn't Tania here? In both of her guises, I knew, she loved me. She'd not let grief befall me.

When I returned to the Bothy and pushed on the door, the sound of raucous laughter was cut off abruptly. The daylight followed me as I slowly entered the room, which was now as silent and empty as if it had been deserted for decades by all except spiders. The dust on the floor showed no foot-trails except my own. The air smelled musty and disused; all trace of cigarette smoke had vanished. What had been gravy-streaked platters just a couple of minutes ago were now loose boards warping up from the floor's level. The picked bones of the sheep's carcase had become a grey skeleton so desiccated it looked as if it would collapse into dust if I trod too heavily.

Where the quaint heavy old telephone had sat, the chrome of its dial mottled by the corrosion of at least one generation's fingertips, there was a glass bottle, with the hipflask shape and about the size of a pint of liquor. The bottle's shoulders were the only thing in this room that still gleamed. I moved to pick it up, pausing reflexively for a moment as I bent toward it and then remembering that here, in this land of Tania's, I had the fingers with which to grip it.

It felt chilled in my hand.

I took the bottle out into the full sunlight and held it up. The contents were that pale straw colour that denotes either one of the finest single malts or a healthy urine specimen. I had a suspicion they weren't the latter.

The bottle didn't have the usual liquor screw-top but a cork not unlike a champagne cork, fastened in place with a splotch of hard red wax. There was some kind of hieroglyph on the seal, a logo, but the wax had squished around it so I couldn't make out any of the details. For a label, the front of the bottle bore what seemed like just a scrap of paper torn off a larger sheet and hurriedly stuck on. Handwritten on it was one of those long, complicated Gaelic words that make you think the monkey's been at the typewriter again. I hadn't the remotest idea what it meant. Probably DRINK ME.

I broke the seal and squeaked the cork out, sniffed. Decidedly not a urine sample.

"Quinn!"

I looked around, then up. At the top of the slope down which we'd come, Tania was standing, waving at me. The breeze was pressing her dress flat against one side of her body; on the other side the dress's long feathery tail was blown out like a flag, becoming progressively less discernible the further it was from her until finally, I could see, it was the gauziest of clouds in the silver sky.

She saw that she'd caught my attention, and beckoned.

Quickly, touched by an irrational guilt, I wormed the cork back in and started to put the bottle down by the Bothy door, but she gesticulated wildly with her arms that I should bring it with me.

Relieved that my beloved was still here, in whatever form she might now be bearing, I almost ran up the gentle grade, arriving beside her hardly out of breath. One glance as I approached her was enough to tell me that the slightly tipsy giggler of the Bothy was gone, replaced by the severe monarch whose eyes held too many years.

I almost tripped over the little wooden sign in the grass. Someone—Tania?—had turned it around, so that now it faced the valley, and myself. I hesitated briefly, expecting the wording to have been altered, but it still read

ABANDON YOURSELF
All Ye Who Enter Here

For a moment it struck me that the message had it wrong this time—I was, after all, not entering but leaving—and then I shook my head. The sign was perfectly correct. I was entering a world that was far smaller than the one I'd been visiting. Yet, for all that, the instruction made little more sense than it had the last time. How could I abandon myself? Why would I want to? Had I abandoned myself in the valley and not realized I'd done so? Was it *myself* that I had to abandon, or my *self*—my selfhood?

I opened my mouth to ask Tania, but then I remembered the stern way she'd told me I should stifle my questions, just *be*.

But human beings aren't really human beings unless they're inquiring about everything around them. Without realizing it was a question, I said: "Where are James and Ellen, Alysson, the others?"

I expected a snapped response, but instead Tania smiled.

She reached out and with a long fingernail, almost a talon, tapped the side of the bottle I held.

"They're in here," she said. "Where they've always been."

What she'd said didn't seem to have any meaning, but I didn't dare push my luck and probe further.

"Now, Quinn, it's time for us to go back to a place where this day can end."

She turned away from the valley. Somehow her dress shifted on her body so that it was still the same as before, one side close against her and the other petering off infinitely into the sky.

I took the hand she held out to me, and kept pace with her as she half-walked, half-skipped away across the field full of violet-tinged grass and multicoloured flowers. Yet again we were surrounded by birdsong and by the little rusty insects we'd first encountered when we'd driven into the sun. Was it these insects, not unseen birds, that were the ones chirping and trilling? Or were they not insects at all but the actual bird calls themselves, visible and tangible in this land of Tania's?

We tore across the grass, far more quickly than our legs could actually be taking us. I felt as if I were the camera strapped to the front of the express train in one of those old sped-up movies they used to show to impress small children, me among them. Faster and faster we went, until the low hills in the distance became little more than purple blurs, even though the grass blades and the starry flowers on the ground beneath us were perfectly clear.

Tania turned to me, then glanced back over her shoulder. Without thinking, I followed her gaze.

Behind us the sky was growing dark. The great train of her dress seemed to belong to both of us, not her alone, as it spread itself across the swathe of night.

Earlier it had been the clouds. Now it was the moon and stars.

And:

"Damn that fucking idiot in the Volvo," said Tania, jamming her foot down on the brake.

○

All the way back through the outskirts of Glasgow, she prattled away about how good it had been to see her family after such a long time, how she was worried her dad was looking so much older these days, how Alysson had settled down a bit now she had a wean on the way...

I just let the words pass by me at a distance, much like the tenements and shop windows on the far side of the car window. Wherever Tania had spent the afternoon, it didn't seem to be where I had been. We'd driven out to some place in the back of beyond by the side of an anonymous loch, and we'd met the new in-laws and had a meal and watched Dad show off his new electrically powered lawnmower, and Alan had nicked his finger while carving the lamb—probably because he'd had a drop too much of the sherry while we'd been waiting for the recalcitrant potatoes to cook. A perfectly normal afternoon meeting in-laws, in other words. This surely must have been what really happened.

So then how the hell had I managed to hallucinate that we'd gone somewhere else entirely?

I didn't have much experience of hallucinations—although I'd smoked the occasional joint in Iraq and before, I'd steered well clear of anything harder, including the hallucinogens that were endemic in the camps—but it seemed to me that my experience had been far too vivid, far too complete, to have been simply a fever dream. I could still taste the frothy beer we'd drunk, still touch with my tongue the greasy scum the mutton had left on the back of my teeth. Yet ... yet wouldn't those sensations be just the same if instead we'd had the cozy family visit Tania was describing? In themselves they proved nothing at all. Besides, the things I'd thought I'd seen—the shiny silver sky, the dress that became the clouds or the stars, the grass blades tipped with a colour the human eye couldn't encompass—surely none of these could have any existence outside of dreams, or fevers, or both?

By the time we'd handed over the car to the hotel valet for parking and made our way into the supremely gilt and polished lobby, I'd more or less succeeded in persuading myself that everything I'd undergone during the afternoon had been a product of abnormal psychology. Perhaps I'd picked up a dose of food poisoning at one of the restaurants we'd been in. It was evident from Tania's still flowing chatter that I'd acted completely normally during the visit to her family, that no one had noticed me behaving in any way unusually—or, if they had, they hadn't commented on the fact to Tania. Perhaps they'd simply put down any apparent eccentricities of mine to the fact that I was a Yank—hell, a country that could have Il Buce as its leader must be straining at the seams with people who were a bit touched in the head.

As we waited for the elevator—the lift—I felt the weight of a bottle in my coat pocket.

"...and what was nicest of all, I think," Tania was saying, her fingers laced beneath her chin, her face glowing with happiness, "was that when Mum and I were alone in the kitchen coping with the dishes, she said how much she and Dad liked you, really *liked* you. They both fell in love with you, Quinn. They both think of you now as being truly their son. Mum was so funny. She told me, all very sober and pompous, you understand"—Tania dropped her voice into an appropriate caricature—"that, a fine man like you, I was to be sure not to be such a silly wee flibbertigibbet that I went and lost you. I just about *died*. I mean, she hasn't spoken to me like that since..."

"Loachy," I said quietly as the elevator pinged to announce its arrival. We were the only ones waiting for it. "Tania, Loachy, however you want me to call you, none of this is anything like what happened to *me*."

The almost manic vivacity stripped itself away from her instantly. In its place there came across her face an expression I couldn't at first identify.

Then I recognized it: *contentment*. What had confused me was its complete lack of correspondence to her words and her body language. Clutching my left arm and its lifeless hand, she pulled me into the elevator car and stabbed at the button for our floor, all the while continuing to yammer about the perfectly ordinary family reunion we'd enjoyed. She was sending me two messages at once, the more important one being the one that wasn't conveyed in her words: that I'd in some way lived up to her aspirations for me by remembering the truth of the afternoon, not the official account. I was the investigative journalist who'd come good, who to everyone's surprise had succeeded in weaseling his way behind the curtain of propagandist lies and got the scoop—only for some reason my editor wasn't allowed to congratulate me publicly on the feat.

The same forked understanding hung around us like a haze all the way along the plushly carpeted, tastefully decorated, forbiddingly empty corridor from the elevator to our room. Once we were inside, I expected her to open up to me honestly, but still she persisted in the pretence, moving briskly about, hanging up her coat, spending a couple of minutes in the bathroom peeing and sprucing up her face, talking incessantly about nothing that mattered. After I'd used the bathroom myself—"Look, Ma! No hands! Well, not really..."—I came out to find her sitting on the bed holding the pint bottle, turning it over in her hands, looking at it the way you look at a book you've already read. She must have fished it out of my pocket while I'd been doing my best not to spray the apricot floor-tiles.

"I can't read that," I said, sitting down beside her, reaching out to touch the crudely lettered label with fingers that couldn't feel it. "What does it say?"

"It's in the old tongue."

"Yes, darling, I'd guessed it was Gaelic from the way it looks like someone's sloshed their alphabet soup over the edge of the bowl."

Tania shook her head, not smiling, still looking at the bottle, not at me. "An older tongue than Gaelic, Quinn," she said so softly I could hardly hear her.

I narrowed my eyes, trying to think what languages might have been spoken in Scotland before Gaelic came along.

"Pictish?" I hazarded.

Now she turned her head toward me. She smiled, but it was the saddest smile I'd ever seen on her face.

"You're getting warmer, husband mine, but you've centuries more to go."

I gave up. "What does it say?"

She looked at the label as if reading it again. "Near as it matters, it says, 'The Hard Stuff'."

I tapped the bottle again. "Pretty potent, huh? A hundred-and-fifty-proof sort of thing?"

"Potent, yes," she said, inclining her head. The warm glow of the bedside light paradoxically returned to her face some of that cold austerity I'd seen earlier in the day. "You'll be finding out soon enough."

"A single malt, is it?"

She thought about this, still holding her head to one side.

"More like a blend."

I was disappointed. To be honest, although I could tell the difference between Laphroaig, which I liked in small quantities, and Glenfiddich, which I thought was more like paint stripper than liquor, most scotches tasted about the same to me. But I'd been told countless authoritative times, not least by Tania herself, that the malts were the aristocrats, the blends merely stopgap measures or "cooking whisky". I'd expected a bottle with this provenance to contain something more exotic than I could have found in the room's minibar.

Tania could tell what I was thinking by the way I shifted my seating on the bed.

"It depends on what you put into the blend," she said, "how fine it turns out to be. I told you what was in this one, Quinn."

"Your folks?" I'd assumed her comment back at the valley's rim had been whimsical.

She nodded. "This isn't just a whisky we're giving you. As it says on the label, it's the hard stuff."

"It *smells* like scotch."

"Well, it would, wouldn't it?"

"Shall I get the...? Oh." Sometimes even I forgot about my disability.

"Yes," she said, to my surprise. "You do the fetching. Just the one glass, though. You can manage that, can't you?" She cast her eye at my plastic hand, lying on my knee. "This is a drink you'll be having on your own, lover man. It's not one I can share with you."

Perplexed, I went and got one of the glasses from the bathroom. If I put my hand vertically above it and then jammed the rim between the thumb and the side of the index finger, I could carry it. The stratagem wasn't going to work for drinking out of it, though.

I put the glass down on the bedside table, shaking it free with a little difficulty. "Fill 'er up."

"Not yet, Quinn. You're not ready yet."

"Who says? It's been a long day, and an extremely confusing one— for me, at least—and I cannot remember a time when I've needed a belt more than now."

"Stay standing," she said, looking up at me as I moved to sit down beside her again. "It'll be easier for us that way."

I didn't know what she was talking about, but of course I did what she told me.

Tania stood up and, facing me, pushed my jacket back off my shoulders, then worked the sleeves off my arms. The garment dropped to the floor. Then she got to work on the buttons of my shirt, which in due course followed the jacket. All the while, her fingers moved with an almost trancelike slowness, performing each action with the minimum of effort and yet with the grace and flow of some stately parade.

The net effect was to make me more rampant than I could remember being since my teens.

With the same exquisite slowness, Tania unbuckled the belt of my pants and worked the zipper down.

"A fine upstanding military gentleman, I see," she remarked with an affectionate little grin. It was the same cliché with which she'd teased me when first we'd undressed each other, years ago. Her hair brushed the side of my erection as she pushed my pants and shorts to the floor, but she didn't react in any way to the contact. Instead, kneeling there, she pulled the laces of my shoes untied.

"Sit down on the bed now, Quinn," she said.

I sat, and raised my legs to let her tug off shoes, socks, the rest of my clothing.

When she had me completely naked, still kneeling in front of me, she looked me in the eyes with that same sad smile I'd seen before. It was the kind of smile lovers or kin bear when one of them is about to depart on a long journey.

She stood up and leaned across me, pulling the pillows out from under the coverlet and puffing them up against the headboard. I put my arm as much around her hips as I could, feeling the denimed curve of her rear against the soft skin above the tangled mess of scar tissue where my wrist had once been, and tried to pull her down to me.

"No," she said, quietly but firmly, like a nurse rejecting the advances of a bedridden lecher. "Not now, Quinn. Not now."

Once she had the pillows arranged to her satisfaction, she took a pace back from the bedside.

"Prop yourself up against them, darling. Make yourself as comfortable as you can. You've got the night ahead of you."

The words were like a splash of cold sea spray on my face.

"What do you mean? Won't you be here? Where are you going?"

"It's where *you're* going that matters, Quinn."

"I'm not going anywhere. I'm naked as the day I was born, woman. I'd get arrested. Particularly with..."

Tania glanced at my tumescence with a sort of weary but loving spousal tolerance: men will be men, they think with their balls, what can you expect?

"It's been pleasing to see my old friend back in the landscape again," she said with a dry little chuckle. "Seems a shame to waste it, but..."

She let the word hang.

"Later?" I said.

"Aye, later, maybe. Have you not got yourself settled yet? You've got some serious drinking to do."

Not until I was arranged to her satisfaction on the bed, with my back against the pillows on the headboard, would she speak again. By this time my penis had quietened. I'd begun to realize that this whole ... whole *ceremony* had far too much of the nature of a farewell about it.

"Where are you going?" I said again to her, this time putting it into my voice that I was wanting an answer.

"Oh, just somewhere around."

"Where?"

"You don't need me any longer, Quinn."

I struggled to sit more upright. "What are you trying to tell me, Tania? Are you leaving me? Is that what you and your mother were *really* talking about in the kitchen? Or wherever. I know I've been a bastard to live with ever since Iraq, but ... but this afternoon taught me something—this whole trip to Scotland has taught me something. I can feel the old me, the old Quinn, coming back, and he's here to stay. Now's not the time to give up on me, darling—I promise you... Or is there someone else I don't know about?" It wasn't credible, but it was the best straw a perplexed and bleeding man with a plastic hand could find.

The cruel monarch was suddenly back in the room, her eyes a green blaze of fury. When she spoke, her words were clipped into arrows of ice that pinned me to the pillows.

"That is a question you should never have thought to ask, Quinn Hogarth. You have demeaned me, and I do not take kindly to that."

And then she relaxed her shoulders again. "No, darling. There's no one. I love you as much as I ever have—more, if anything. Believe me, this is all because of the love I have for you. If I loved you any the less, I'd ... well, I'd not have wasted the ... the opportunity you presented me." She bit her lip, eyes dancing. "To put it in the politest possible terms."

Despite myself, I smiled too—more in relief that I'd escaped the full force of her regal ire than anything else.

"And now," she said.

Tania didn't complete the sentence, but, her movements crisp, reached for the bottle by the bedside and twisted its cork out. She sniffed the open top, appreciating the fumes, then poured the pale amber liquid into the hotel's tooth-glass.

When she'd done and the tumbler was full to the brim, there was still about an inch left in the bottle. She looked at the remaining liquid accusingly, then very deliberately tipped it, too, into the glass.

It all went in, but the glass didn't overflow.

"Wait a moment," she said, and went to burrow through one of the drawers, pulling out the screw-topped plastic drinking cup I'd barely used since our arrival in Glasgow. For a moment I thought she was going to decant the liquor into it, but instead she just pulled out the straw.

"You'll need this, at least at first," she said, popping it into the glass. Still the meniscus held and there was no overflow.

"Kiss me," I said. "You owe me a kiss. Please."

"Before I go," she replied. "I'm not gone yet."

I knew I should be doing something more by way of protesting—I should be leaping from the bed and having a showdown with her, or going on my bended knee to plead with her—but it was as if there was something hypnotic in the air, so that all I could do was follow the flow of events with a sort of unhappy complaisance. She was the one who was in entire control of what would happen. For me to try to redirect things would be not just a challenge to her authority but a disruption of the natural order. I had the sense that all this had been written down before somewhere, and that I—and, for that matter, Tania—had no choice but to follow that unread script. A tiny part of me rebelled against this uncomfortable tranquility, but I ignored it as I would have ignored a butterfly on the field of battle: something irrelevant whose prettiness I might have the time to appreciate later.

So I watched her lethargically as she neatly folded my clothes and piled them on the ottoman that sat in front of the window table. She unravelled my socks and tucked them neatly into the openings of my shoes, then placed the shoes side by side under the ottoman. Lastly she came across to the bed once more and, assuming no disagreement from me, unstrapped the sad pink prosthetic from my arm. She placed the parody of flesh on top of the heap of my clothing.

Then she stood facing me, her hands cupped together like a virgin's in front of her crotch.

"Don't ever, ever forget how much I love you, Quinn. And ... and remember what I said. I'll be around."

She took two quick, determined steps to the bedside, as if concerned her resolve might desert her, and looked down on me where I sat.

"I believe you requested a kiss, sir," she said with mock coyness.

Her lips were fire on mine.

I don't mean what the words would mean in a purple novel. I felt as if I were being kissed by and kissing flame. The pain was nearly as intense as I'd suffered when I'd first come stumbling back out of unconsciousness after the device had exploded in front of me in Falluja, but where that had been hostile agony this was exquisitely pleasurable. Her tongue-tip flickered against mine and I almost screamed, but still I forced myself against her.

Then she was on the far side of the room, standing by the door, her hand on its handle, half-shadowed because the weak glow of the bedside lamp barely reached that far.

"Drink, Quinn," she said, gesturing with her head to tell me what I should do.

I leaned to my side, fumbling the bent plastic straw around with the stump of my arm until it pointed toward my lips.

I took it into my mouth, my eyes still on Tania's silently standing figure.

"I've enjoyed beyond words having you as my husband, Quinn," she whispered. "My sweet lover. But you no longer need me."

Before she'd finished speaking she'd turned the handle of the door and was gone into the anonymity of the hotel corridor.

I let out a long breath, and drank.

○

I was a mist, a haar, that clung close to the land, creeping into every last one of its crevices, becoming almost absorbed by it yet retaining my own self, my own separateness. I became the inverse of trees, taking their shapes into myself, their convexities being reproduced with perfect fidelity as concavities within me. Flying birds and running animals—human animals among them—were streams of their passage through me. Stones and mountains formed new parts of me, too, as did valleys and the shore.

None of them paid the least bit of attention to my presence. I had been here not forever but for far longer than any of them had. I was simply a part of reality to them, like the air they breathed. As with the air, I was invisible. As with the air, they could not be if I were gone.

Formless, I had all forms. Formless, I was able to make of myself any form I chose, following whatever was the whim of my moment.

In this particular moment of mine I watched myself deciding that a piece of me should be thickened, twisting streamers of intangibility coming together in a swirl and coalescing around each other in countless layers to create physical essence where before there had been none. The creation emerging from the mist, taking shade out of the greyness only I could see, had two legs, two arms, a head, a momentary identity, a name.

That name was Quinn, and the creation talked—I could see it doing so, even though I couldn't be troubled to listen. I did, however, trouble to give it the power to see through my eyes, hear with my ears.

There were others like me. I knew this in the same way the small creatures knew of me. It had always been so. Like me, they toyed with their world, creating and destroying, most of eternity just playing. At our edges we blended with each other, enriching each other, delighting in each other. But not all of us did this, not always. Some chose the route of dying.

Through my eyes the Quinn-creation could see one of these entering its death throes. It was taking physicality around itself, binding itself in an armour of steel to defend itself from all that was not itself, even though it had no attackers. I watched, passive, as it did this. I knew what would happen to it next—we all did. Self-caged, unable to bear the surrounding weight of its idiot armour, it would shrink, growing ever more bitter and miserable as it did so, like an old man seeking impotently to destroy all around him rather than confront the failure he has made of his life. The entity had become engrossed by its own madness, the madness that fed it and fed upon it. There was nothing any of us could do to save it.

The Quinn-creation, however, wished to try.

Had wished to try.

Seeing it through my eyes, he saw the infeasibility of the task. Feeling its dying through my emotions, he was able to strip himself of his pity. The entity had not been struck by death, but had instead chosen of its own free will to die, and the manner of its dying. Through stupidity it had embraced insanity. Existence does not tolerate stupidity long.

We watched the stupid, shrinking, dying entity, did the Quinn-creation and I. Perhaps there was a chance for it, perhaps it could save itself. It was difficult to care, although I sensed the Quinn-creation retained some vestige of caring.

Certainly the Quinn-creation, the name-taker, as it melted back into me—abandoning its self as it discovered that its selfhood was all that had held it back from being truly free, truly individual, truly something other than just another faceless unit in a millions-strong temporary flock, truly everlasting—possessed enough compassion for the one that was approaching its death to be a name-giver as well as a name-taker. The Quinn-creation gave the self-condemned, self-armoured, self-narrowing entity a name.

The Quinn-creation, its shared thoughts fraying with regret, called the dying entity Fortusa.

○

I awoke with what I believed at first was the hangover to end all hangovers. My plastic beaker, empty, had found its way into my naked armpit. I squinted painfully against the grey light streaking in from the station; neither of us had thought to draw the curtains last night. Barely audible, like thunder beyond the mountains, a voice announced that a train for a destination was now boarding at a platform. The tiny noise made the spiritual silence, the utter Tania-less loneliness of the room—of the cold hill side—all the more profound.

I swung my legs over the side of the bed, got to my feet, swayed. No wonder the liquor was called The Hard Stuff: it had a kick like nothing I'd ever drunk before...

Yet my vision was clear. My mouth was no fouler-tasting than on any other morning. My stomach wasn't unsettled.

The pain in my head didn't come from the liquor—or, at least, it did, but not from the alcohol. The pain was from the still-healing surgery the dream had performed in my mind.

Dream?

That had been no dream. It had been a glimpse, for the first time in my life, of reality. Reality makes us, moulds us, nurtures us or rejects us, but it is also made *by* us, by all of us, even though we are unconscious creators.

The incisions in my mind would heal soon. Already the stitches could be pulled out.

Half an hour later I was at the hotel's reception desk. The clerk glanced at my hands, my plastic hands, as I leaned on the counter in front of her. The left one was now accustomed to me; the right was still an intruder, but I wore it this morning anyway. It held my room card-key.

"My wife—she seems to have gone missing."

The receptionist raised an eyebrow, smiling. "Perhaps she'll still be at breakfast, sir, or in the..."

I shook my head impatiently.

"She's gone. I know that. Did she check out, or did she just ... go?"

Frowning now, the receptionist checked my card-key, then turned to her keyboard, tapping a few times as she called a new display up on the screen.

"We have you registered as a single occupancy, sir. Perhaps, ah..."

"It's all right. Forget it."

I walked away.

Part of me knew the futility of what I was doing, but there was still enough of a part of me stuck in the old ruts that I felt compelled to go through the formalities.

I made towards a pay phone, then realized I'd never be able to get the coins into the slot. Back upstairs in my room, I picked up the ballpoint pen in my mouth, ready to tackle the phone with it, then let it fall again. If I really tried, I had enough control over my artificial hands to...

That was when I realized I'd dressed myself. Not just dressed myself but strapped on the hated plastic prosthetics. Which had I done first? How the hell had I strapped on the prosthetics before I'd strapped on the prosthetics?

Distracted by the realization, I froze for a full minute, perhaps longer. Then I sat down on the bed and shuffled my way out of my shoes. Standing up again, I went to the closet and tussled with the door until I had it open. From the row of my shoes there I selected a pair of slip-ons, and slid my feet into them.

Back on the bed, I clumsily pressed the 0 for an outside line, waited for the dialling tone, then with care hit the 9 and the 1 and the 1 again.

I put the phone back on the receiver before the ringing had time to start.

What the hell had I been doing? It wasn't 911 for the cops in this country: it was 999. Tania had told me that on the plane, and repeated it once we'd arrived in Glasgow until she was sure I had the information firmly imprinted on my brain. In my distraction I'd succumbed to an old habit.

But wasn't everything I'd been doing for the past few minutes just exactly that—succumbing to old habits? I knew that Tania had gone, and I had a slowly clearing understanding of why she had. I wasn't going to be able to find her unless she wanted to be found, which she didn't. What was the point of all this rigmarole I was putting myself through? Why was I still reciting the lines of the play when the curtain had long ago come down on the final act?

Sitting on the bed, I let my shoulders sag. Packing the suitcases would be a bit of a nightmare, but I guessed I could always heftily tip one of the hotel's maids to undertake the chore for me. Half the stuff

I could leave behind anyway, although I found I was irrationally reluctant just to dump Tania's shoes and clothing and general clutter—if they were still there—into the room's wastebins. Even if I took everything home with me—yes, that was what I would do—the journey would be manageable. The hotel's valets or the taxi driver would get the baggage into the taxi, and at the airport I could use one of their trolleys or find a handler to cope. At the other end, in Newark, things might get a bit more difficult, but not if I explained my plight at the Glasgow check-in desk and asked them to signal the details through to their counterparts in the States. And from Newark International I could get a taxi all the way home, screw the cost. My wallet was fat with notes in both currencies, and my credit cards were—thanks to Dad's allowance—in reasonably healthy shape. The trip was going to be a challenge, all right, but it was all perfectly feasible...

My thoughts ran down like a clockwork toy.

Old habits again. My first impulse had been to try to trace Tania somehow. Once I'd accepted that this was a fruitless endeavour, my next urge had been the primitive one of scuttling for home as fast as I could go. But home is more than a place, more than a geographical location, more than a set of names and empty symbols. There was a place where I'd lived my whole life, but it had been usurped by name-shifters—by people who seized the names of things, changed their meaning, and pretended they still meant the same. Freedom, on their lips, had become synonymous with slaughter and repression, democracy with the law of the concentration camp. The house in which I'd dwelt, whose every corner I'd thought myself intimately familiar with, had been invaded by thieves, and now I was on the outside gazing in through the window, watching them smash up my property. Whump—there went the microwave. Zip—and a razor sliced through one of the pictures on the wall. Crash—there went the valueless but infinitely valued glass vase Aunt Millie had given me before she died. And all the while the fire the usurpers had lit was blazing merrily in the middle of the living-room carpet, fueled by the chairs and the coffee table...

The place I thought of as home wasn't home any longer—not *my* home.

I lay down on top of the bed, its coverlet still in disarray from where I'd slept on it last night. The pillows were slightly damp from when I'd been sweating into them, but they were comfortable enough.

I put my plastic pseudo-hands behind my head and stared up at the ceiling. There was no need to go scurrying back to the States just yet. The cash and credit cards I'd been planning to use to finance my dash for the solace of familiarity might just as well fund a few extra nights here in this station-side hotel—that's what they'd been intended for in the first place. We'd sampled only a couple of the Indian restaurants, and there must be hundreds more in Glasgow for me to pick among. Was it not the case that Dalí's painting of the crucifixion hung in one of the art museums here?

If I ran away, my flight would be a mourning. To mourn Tania would be fully to lose her, forever. If I stayed here a while longer she'd always be...

...around.

I wondered where that train had been departing for.

○

Every day as I arrive at my office, having climbed the last flight of stairs, I pause in front of the glass case that stands just inside the main door. I touch the top of the case, and perhaps it's true that I feel what I think I can feel: the cool smoothness of the glass against my artificial fingertips.

No. Of course that can't be right. The prosthetics I wear these days are much better than those dreadful pink plastic ones I once so loathed, but even they can't perform miracles.

The office is in one of these big old residential houses in Grampian Way, in one of the posher parts of Glasgow. Before that it was, briefly, the room over a garage. I've moved up in the world, and nowadays no one seems to notice I'm not Scottish. For four years I've been spearheading a charity devoted to organizing the endeavours of lawyers internationally to get the inmates out of the concentration camp at Guantánamo Bay. We win a few, we lose a whole lot more ... but at least we do win those few.

I pay myself enough of a salary that every Saturday there's enough left over for lunch at an Indian restaurant. Oh, and for me no longer to need the allowance cheques that Dad's anyway stopped sending.

Inside the glass case is a life-souvenir that is one of the reasons I'm here: the pair of shoes that long ago I pushed off my feet in a hotel bedroom, and have never worn since.

Their laces tied with perfect bows.

As I pause by the case this morning, I hear, rippling down the corridor, a sound that is one of the other major reasons why my home is in Glasgow, why I'm doing what I'm doing. A cascade of dearly loved laughter. As is almost always the case, she left our somewhat seedy flat before I did this morning, to get to work as early as she could. She's on the phone to a potential donor, perhaps, chatting him up for a few hundred or a few thousand euros extra, or perhaps it's a moral rather than a financial squeeze she's putting on someone: from time to time we gain the ear of a significant legal or political figure here in my chosen homeland, and then there can be a spurt in our achievements.

I thought I'd lost Tania forever, back on that first morning after she'd told me I no longer needed her and I'd accepted her gift of The Hard Stuff. She said she'd always be near wherever I was, but I didn't believe her—I assumed she was talking purely figuratively. What neither of us recognized then was that the day might come when she'd realize that, though I might no longer need her, she might find herself needing me.

She found me again—easy enough to do, because I was hardly likely to hide from her. And, of course, I was waiting for her return.

Her name is Alysson now, and she has wavy copper hair rather than fine, straight and pale. She's a couple of inches shorter and a few years younger than she was before, and her accent is broader, but I knew her for Tania the moment I set eyes on her, that day in The Record Exchange on Jamaica Street when we were both trying to browse through the Savourna Stevenson CDs at the same time. Should I have had any uncertainty, I needed only to look into her eyes, which are brown sometimes and green sometimes, but always with the sense of an infinite past behind them. We have a baby on the way—my younger sibling, Alysson often teases me, gazing fondly at her sometimes puerile lover. I eagerly anticipate the day when she'll announce that it's maybe time for her to take me to meet her folks.

I pat the top of the case one last time, smiling at the sound of her laughter, before I head down the passage to whatever Fairyland the new day brings.

One question that Scots always ask is, "Wha's like us?" Now Jack
Deighton gives us an answer.
Perhaps his strange characters are the inhabitants of a distant world who
share our dour outlook on life. Or perhaps they are our inheritors, the
last intelligent creatures left on what has become of the Caledonian land
mass in Earth's far future.
Will the last person to leave Scotland please turn out the lights?

◦　◦　◦　◦　◦　◦　◦　◦　◦　◦　◦　◦　◦　◦　◦　◦　◦　◦　◦

DUSK
Jack Deighton

◦　◦　◦　◦　◦　◦　◦　◦　◦　◦　◦　◦　◦　◦　◦　◦　◦　◦　◦

It was broad-limbed Artelmin who first voiced the doubt. Artelmin the proud.

"We cannot survive here," he said, warping his feasils to shape the words, channelling the wind through with deft strokes of his nether blinds. "The sun no longer provides for us all. We block each other's basking in our struggles for the failing light."

"But what else can we do?" Shiazu asked, her feasils a-twitter. "Where else can we go?"

"We must follow the sun," he said, simply.

A chill settled on me as he uttered the words, a premonition of loss. None of my forebears as lorekeeper had ever contemplated such a thing. My outermost feasils almost trembled at the thought of it. Yet mindful of my responsibilities, I restricted them to a single twitch.

"To where?" I asked. The rustle and swish of a concerted folding of the group's blinds formed a backdrop to the question. My unease was evidently widely shared. "The sun has not gone," I added. "It rises and falls as it always did."

"But ever nearer the horizon," Artelmin argued, "and for a shorter time each day. If we follow it west we may catch it in its fall, have the benefit of a full day's light again. Be restored to our former estate."

He swept his blinds roundly in a gesture that encompassed us all: sturdy Fenroth; poor lopsided Bertellon, whose oft-retold encounter with a fangwin had stripped his feasils all down one flank; the wily

Shiazu, adept in the luring arts; Hooglis, with his blinds formed into that strange brush on top; stolid Krugg; the younglimbs, feasils held to rigid attention, not daring to interrupt in such an argument. And Valatha, my dear Valatha, rootlimbs curled just so in that way I found irresistible, whose blinds were sublime, whose shimmering feasils spread in a perfect arc.

"We are not as we were," continued Artelmin. "We spend our days bickering, jostling amongst ourselves for a few meagre rays of light. There is no future for us here. We must follow the sun."

"But this is our home," I reasoned. "Lorekeeping holds no hint of any other browsing ground. This is where we belong."

"Yes, yes!" a chorus of rustled whispers assented. The agitated flickerings of feasils attested to the unease amongst the group. Artelmin's was an awe-full proposal. Most of us were eager to grasp at any reassurance.

"There were good times here once," I argued. "There will be again. The day's length has always changed with the season. This is only a more pronounced variation. Things will surely soon return to their proper state."

"That was before the new sun," Artelmin said. "Before the change."

Instantly I sensed the mood alter. Feasils drooped in apprehension as individuals sought to shut out the unwelcome implication. Blinds sagged on all sides as the air of dejection rippled through the ensuing silence.

As Valatha too succumbed, even I was touched by the contagion, withdrawing deep within myself, blinds drawn down tight in an instinctive reaction to threat.

◊

The new sun, for so long an expanding glow in the night sky, is all but gone now. I can barely detect a residual trace whenever the clouds of night part and the empty skies draw away my precious warmth. It had promised much as it drew near, of perpetual days and boundless drafts of energy for our feasils to absorb at will.

All sad illusion. Soon, as mysteriously as it had arisen, it began to fade, having reached barely a quarter of our true sun's intensity.

But by then it had set those strange wandering suns of the night whirling into crazier dances against the sky, and somehow altered the normal seasonal balance between night and day into something new. Something strange and terrible.

I suppose I should be grateful for small mercies. The true sun still rises each day and rolls along the horizon, warming my fibres for a few precious hours before it slowly sinks again and I must retract my rootlimbs, draw down my blinds and fold my feasils about me against the cold. I am still able to convert enough life-giving energy to delve into the earth, to scrabble amongst the crevices in the underlying rock, seeking out nutrients and the surface meltwater which forms after each noon. My feasils may be pale imitations now of their former gaudy glories, may look faded and draggled, as if pest-ridden; my rootlimbs may no longer be so sensitive to the conditions beneath my four basal stalks, but they still function. I strain enough sustenance to last me through the static hours, the long hours of darkness when all my senses seem to fade to black and white. I am still alive, if only just.

And it could be worse. At least the fangwen no longer roam the plains. With my grouping dispersed, drawn one by one somewhere over the horizon by the uncertain prospect of greater sunlight and richer pickings further west, I would be an easy target for any of the once troublesome beasts which remained. But I have sensed none of those sharp-toothed, mournful-voiced creatures for many seasons now. Too many seasons to keep count.

Likewise, I have no knowledge of those of my grouping who have gone west. Nor of the other groups which, on glorious sunlit afternoons, used to dot the plains with shimmering pools of colour as blinds were outstretched, feasils spread wide as an allure to poach potential partners from other groups, or sometimes (oh, happy decadent days) purely for the pleasure of it.

The plains are empty now, the pallid, dispersed light which does fall on them reflecting only from bare rock or sparse scrubgrass. For all I know, I may be the last of my kin.

I receive but poor reward for my daily basking. I struggle to feel replete, even under the afternoon sun. It is strange how, at such a low angle in the sky, the sun looms so large: yet its warmth seems as nothing compared to the splendours I recall from my youth. Then, each day seemed a carefree stroll from one browsing patch to the next—with hardly ever a need to spread my blinds to their fullest extent to catch its bounty.

So much has disappeared since the change, not much of it for the good.

○

Artelmin was first to leave. A particularly fierce storm had just subsided and the dulled disc of the late afternoon sun was creeping through the departing clouds when he declared his intent.

"I have endured enough," he said. "There is nothing for us here but endless storms and a cold chill in our fibres. I will leave now before it is too late—alone if necessary—and follow the sun. Should any of you wish to accompany me, I will be grateful for the company."

There was a moment of silence as the group absorbed the finality of his announcement, some sage folding of blinds in acceptance of his decision, a few whisperings of anguish.

"What say you, Borellan?" he asked me. "Will you accompany me?" For that brief moment, I thought his manner might have held an air of uncertainty, even pleading.

"You know I cannot," I told him. "A lorekeeper stays always with his kin." Then he was Artelmin once more, rustling his blinds decisively, angling his feasils to express understanding and regret.

"Then I will take my leave," he said. "Those who decide not to follow my path I hope to meet once more in the Great Browsing Grounds Below."

At this, Shiazu began to rustle and twitter, shimmering her feasils in a simultaneous expression of distress and coquetry before falling on him in a flurry. Perhaps embarrassed by her unseemly display, Artelmin quickly disengaged himself from contact.

Hooglis and I dipped blinds with him, our tips touching his in a formal farewell. Valatha embraced him in a suitably decorous fashion.

Artelmin saluted us all in turn, even down to the smallest younglimb—a thin and reedy specimen, deprived of sufficient energy and consequently lacking in growth for her age, but nonetheless delighted by the compliment. The contrast between the two—one still strong and full of vigour despite a few ragged edges, the other pale and etiolated, barely able to function—was, I am sure, a contributory factor to the subsequent exodus, preying on the minds of those who witnessed it, speaking more eloquently for Artelmin's case than any words of his could.

Artelmin paused only a moment to see if anyone would join him before lumbering away with a jerky gait, front rootlimbs anchoring in the cracks in the rocks, the tops of his blinds swaying heavily as he brought his rear stalks forward, rootlimbs trailing, to set base for the next step.

He seemed to make slow progress at first, pausing at times to replenish his energies, his spread blinds curiously dark against the lowering red sun. But all too soon he was but a dot in the wide expanse of the western plains.

○

The weather has settled into a new pattern. The wild storms, ferocious, unpredictable—whipped up out of nothing, or so it seemed—no longer rage as they did. They have been replaced instead by a long, bitter wind spiralling continuously out of the north and east, too often laden with flakes or balls of ice. A wind which never ceases, day nor night, which ruffles my feasils in their daily attempts to trap the solar warmth, mocks their efforts to maintain my body temperature during the long dark nights, which has no trace of heat, which fills my weary fibres with a cold, dull ache. Which dumps its frozen loads on my feasils, ripping and tearing at the strands; batters my rootlimbs so that I have to retract them, reducing the precious time I have for browsing.

Where is the rich, warm, cleansing rain that used to fall so joyously in its season, ridding our feasils of the accumulations of dust that dulled their shine, filling the cracks and hollows of the land to overflowing, leaching out essential food elements from the soil and rock?

○

The next day Shiazu prowled the browsing grounds, pestering first Hooglis, then Fenroth, proceeding at length to the younglimbs, hoping to flatter them with her attentions.

Me she did not approach, correctly assessing that my bond with Valatha was too strong. In the end, she turned to Bertellon, shimmering her blinds at him shamelessly, bewitching him with attentions he had long since forgotten. By late evening, their interlocked shadows beckoned to us from their position partway to the horizon.

A few more left over the following days, during the lulls the storms allowed us. That trickle was soon to broaden to a flood. On one dark day of glowering clouds and howling gales, fully half of the remaining group set off in pursuit of better pastures—even Krugg, the least likely of deserters—driven before the wind like so many discarded feasils.

○

I grow steadily more tired. Sometimes it seems as if time stands still when I hang my blinds in the sunlight, the constant wind ruffling my limp feasils as I attempt to take in the elusive warmth. No longer can I simultaneously move nimbly among the rocks as I do so, there is too little energy to be had. I spend my days greedily absorbing as much as possible and it is still a pitifully small amount. All too quickly the arc of the sun's circle dips below the horizon and I must make my mad dash to meet my body's demands, stocking up suste-nance, drinking in enough moisture to last through the long, icy night and scarcely warmer morning ahead.

If it were not for the regular nightly accumulation of clouds, I doubt I could survive. Despite their cargoes of snow and ice, they provide a blanket of sorts against the cold, cold sky. In their absence only the prickle of feeling from the many tiny suns of the night—too weak ever to fuel my needs—counteracts the loss of heat from my exposed feasils. After such nights, it is late indeed the next day be-fore I recover sufficiently to spread my blinds. Two in succession may be the end of me.

○

The saddest departure was Valatha's. It still pains me to recall our final embrace when, entwined rootlimbs anchored deep into the rock, our blinds came together, and hidden within the folds, I extended my plins into her carpla and shuffled off the gifts-of-life, savouring her sweetness for the last time. Though we both knew there was little chance of issue from such a union, her season not being due, it some-how felt the only way to honour the end of our long relationship.

"Why must you leave?" I implored her, feeling the weight of her impending departure throughout my limbs.

"I have stayed too long for all the good it has done," she replied. "The days grow ever colder, the sun ever lower in the sky."

"I am afraid, Borellan," she continued. "Afraid that if I do not leave now, I never shall. Afraid that if I remain here, my fibres will return too soon to the earth from which they sprang."

My blinds sagged with the thought, for I could not agree. "Let others do what they will," I said. "I did not quicken under a wandering sun of the night. Nor, I trusted, did you. Think well, Valatha. This is where we first took root, grew up as younglimbs together, shared our first embrace."

Her feasils shimmered in distress, but their cruel angle was a message in itself. They were turned away from me. In all the years I had known her, I had never seen them held so.

"I have thought, Borellan," she said. "Look around you. Artelmin had it right; there is nothing left for us here. Can you not see that? Why do you cling so stubbornly to what is clearly lost? Beyond the western plains there is at least hope. Here there is none beyond the prospect of an early death. I feel it in every fibre. Even through the bitter chill, its rank odour fills my pores whenever I take breath."

I had no reply. What reply was there? I too had felt the sense of rot and decay, suffered the cold embrace of the encircling gloom, desired a more kindly light to pluck me from its clutches.

But my life had been spent on this one small browsing ground. I knew of little else. I could not share her belief, her hope. All that I could think of was to endure. Even though all the light I had ever known was dying, I had no faith that salvation could be found somewhere over the horizon.

"Go, then, if you must," I told her, and sensed her flinch. In remorse—I could not bear her to think ill of me—I added, "And take my blessing with you," to help ease the pain of parting.

The angle of her blinds altered in response. I shuffled hesitantly towards her. We matched tips awkwardly, moving slowly to a fuller union. Our intertwined limbs in the end became racked with convulsions of sorrow rather than pleasure. Finally she extricated herself gently from the embrace and turned to follow in the rootsteps of Artelmin, Shiazu and Bertellon; Fenroth, Hooglis, Krugg and all the rest. She did not look back.

I stood, my sad blinds outstretched to catch the dying light, and watched her shadow, in a miserably elongated distortion of her perfect shape, extend eastwards back to me, across the plains.

I have felt the urge for her many times since then, my plins aching with the weight of unshed gifts-of-life, but there has been no Valatha to receive my bounty. I doubt, too, that she would still embrace me with that old fervour. My plins are dry and shrivelled now, my dishevelled feasils a poor invitation to a union.

○

It seems it is I, who held to the ancestral browsing paths, who have been the most deluded. It was not enough to torture my soul that the others should leave, especially my poor sweet Valatha, but now my steadfastness in remaining has been mocked, and most cruelly. I never thought to see life bring forth such bitter fruit.

Today the full arc of the sun did not rise above the horizon. The perpetual wind threw a blanket of cloud over the sky for much of what little daylight I was granted, and chilled my fibres anew with its frozen cargo, but a tiny wedge of the disc remained always beyond my senses. A thin wedge, true, but tomorrow it will be thicker. Today, from the sun's pathetic rise to its final set, like too many days past, has been but a long, slow dusk compared to the full glorious summers of my youth.

Were those golden years the greatest delusion? It is hard to remember them now, with the daily struggle to survive uppermost in my thoughts. Sometimes it seems that they are only a dream, of a different life in some strange place of the imagination, yet at others they are bright and clear in my mind's perception, a softly glowing vision of better days in times past.

But I must shake myself free of all such thoughts. I have more pressing matters to consider.

The western plain lies before me in all its emptiness. I must draw down my blinds against the fall of night and prepare as best I can for the long journey (to what nameless destination?) that tomorrow I must start across it.

I suppose I must travel in hope. Who knows? I may once more meet with Valatha.

○

I have come upon an eerie place, one made worse by the murkiness of the light. Weird shadows seem to lurk in the gloom cast by the cloud cover. My senses are plagued by transitory miasmas conjured from the swirling mists.

I cannot be sure whether my lumbering progress towards the sun is succeeding or not. Whenever the clouds part, the furthest extent of its disc remains always tantalizingly beyond the horizon. But at its fullest, it seems no smaller, as far as I can tell, than when I set out.

Each "morning" I wait with impatience for its heat to warm my fibres, hoping to lumber as many extra steps forward as possible before the meltwaters form in the late afternoon and I stop to browse. Without the daily thaw, I would find it harder to break into the frozen land, lose more precious time.

To my surprise, the soil here is good. There is little beyond scrubgrass to compete with me for nature's bounty. Once the ice has melted, my rootlimbs can roam freely in the quiet earth.

But each short day's journey is ever more wearisome, my active moments are taken up with absorbing the sun's rays, or pressing ever forward, or finding food. I have little energy left over for reflection, nor for remembrance, the sacred duty of the lorekeeper.

o

I have lost count of the days. The western plains are long behind me, the scene around me now is one of desolation.

The soil is poorer here, a bare covering on the underlying rock. Any sustenance it provides is hard won. Were it not for an intermittent few misshapen hummocks which provide a richer fare, I might not have survived this far. There is something increasingly familiar about those shapes. But their lines are distorted, worn away by erosion and decay. I have no time to ponder the mystery; I must move ever onward if I am to catch up with the sun.

o

I have made no progress for several days. Despair has held me locked and unable to function. My only motions have been the reflex raising of my blinds to catch the brief day's light and the involuntary shudderings of my outraged body.

Ah, that curled rootlimb! To my horror and disgust it made me realize that I have been feeding on the decaying bodies of my dead kin.

Which of those shapes was Artelmin, I wonder, which Hooglis? Have I been feasting on the remains of Shiazu or poor Bertellon? That stout one there, is it Krugg? The taller one beyond, Fenroth?

It is a good thing to enrich the soil, to return dust to dust, and eventually to feed the goodness that was in your fibres on to your descendants, to give young limbs you have never seen a solid start to life. But there is a time to such sombre feastings, a due season. Not now, so soon after the deaths, and without the proper ceremonies. I was too close to those who have fallen to face the thought of what I have done—albeit unknowingly—with any equanimity.

The rootlimb was unmistakable. It could only be Valatha's. Dear Valatha, whose feasils shone the brightest of us all.

Why have I alone been spared, when the brightest and best of us are gone?

o

I stagger on. Daily, I follow the sun, wending my way ever westward in forlorn anticipation of finding the sunlit pastures we all set out to reach spreading at last before me. But that land of promise lies as far away as ever. My quest, it seems, will never end.

The true sun still hugs the horizon, making a mockery of my efforts to catch up with its decline and fall. At night, whenever the clouds part, I scan the skies in constant hope of finding another new sun swelling there, that might restore order to the swirling chaos left by its predecessor. But it is a useless longing. Visitations like those are beyond rarity. Nothing will bring back the halcyon days of memory.

What dreadful sin did we commit that we should have been subject to this fate? In our delusion we accepted the coming of the new sun with joy. None of us saw in it the seeds of our destruction.

Those dreadful mounds are long behind me; the memory of Valatha's rootlimb a reproof and inspiration both. To keep travelling, in constant battle against the interminable chill wind behind and the ever-retreating sun ahead, is the sole tribute I can make to the vain efforts to survive of Valatha, Artelmin and the rest.

The winds still wail incessantly, like a continuous chorus of demented fangwen. Occasionally one howl will stand out from the rest, more mournful, more full of regret, as if a fangwin is truly near and on a hunt. But surely none of those once most feared of beasts can have survived where we did not. And yet, I almost hope for it. How fitting it would be if I should, at the last, provide sustenance for at least one of my poor fellow creatures.

The days of my life wear down in the same exhausted, dulled routine.

With every dawn the creak as my blinds fan slowly outwards, feasils spreading wide to catch the feeble light. The all too few hours hanging in the sun—an agonising effort barely worth the reward. The scrabble amongst the rocks and soil in search of food and water. The short day's journey into night, scrambling slowly towards the setting sun.

And, at the close of each slow dusk, a drawing down of blinds.

NOTES ON THE CONTRIBUTORS

MARION ARNOTT's short stories have appeared in a wide range of independent publications, including *Peninsular, Solander, QWF, Hayakawa Mystery Magazine* (Japan), *Chapman Magazine, Scottish Child, Books Ireland, West Coast Magazine, Northwords* and *Crimewave*.

She has a couple of awards to her credit including the QWF Philip Good Memorial Prize for Fiction for "Fortune's Favourite" and the CWA Short Dagger (2001) for "Prussian Snowdrops". Her story "Marbles" was shortlisted for the Short Dagger in 2002 and was also nominated for a Derringer Award.

She also has a story in the Paisley Writers Group anthology, *A Strange Place*. Marion's story "Dollface", from her collection *Sleepwalkers*, was shortlisted for the 2003 CWA Short Fiction Dagger.

o

RON BUTLIN was born in Edinburgh. Having worked variously as a footman, a male model, and a barnacle-scraper on Thames barges, he has become one of the acclaimed Scottish writers of his generation. His works include the novels *Night Visits* and *The Sound of My Voice*, which has won several international prizes. As well as many short stories, he has published four books of poetry. His most recent collection is the highly surreal *Vivaldi and the Number 3*. This summer sees the publication of *Without a Backward Glance: New and Selected Poems*.

o

MIKE COBLEY read his first SF story at the age of nine, and had his first story published in 1986, after which he enjoyed a meteoric rise to fame over the course of, er, the next 20 years. Or so. During which time he has seen a good number of short stories published in a variety of magazines and anthologies (since collected in *The Iron Mosaic*, published by Immanion Press), not to mention the dark, epic *Shadowkings* trilogy, which reached its culmination this year with the final volume, *Shadowmasque*.

Mike has an abiding fascination with Scotland's place in the UK and Europe, and aims to write more stories set in the alternative past/future shown in "The Intrigue Of the Battered Box".

o

JACK DEIGHTON was born and brought up in Dumbarton and attended Glasgow University. Apart from two years spent working as a research chemist near London, he has always lived in Scotland. He now teaches in Dunfermline, while living in Kirkcaldy with his wife and two sons.

His short stories have appeared in *Interzone, New Worlds* and *Spectrum SF*. His first novel, *A Son of the Rock*, was published in 1997.

HAL DUNCAN was brought up in small-town Ayrshire and now lives in the West End of Glasgow. He works part-time as a computer programmer to subsidize his writing habit. His first novel, *Vellum*, is available in the UK in hardback and trade paperback from MacMillan.

○

ANDREW C. FERGUSON was born in 1962 and lives in Glenrothes, Fife, with his wife and daughter. He has had around thirty stories and poems published in various UK and US markets, including *Interzone*, *West Coast Magazine* and *The Hope That Kills Us*, an anthology of Scottish football stories.

In addition, he has co-authored a body of non-fiction work with Bruce Hunter on the Knights Templar, Freemasonry and the Holy Grail. Their book, *Legacy of the Sacred Chalice*, was published in the US by Macoy in 2003.

Current projects include: a nineteenth-century horror novel; a biography of Doctor Knox, Burke and Hare's main client; and a work on one of the wilder shores of the law of Scotland.

○

MATTHEW FITT was born in Dundee in 1968. A graduate of Edinburgh University, he has lived in New York and the Czech Republic. The second holder of the Brownsbank Fellowship, he has been a full-time writer for five years. His choice of Scots for SF prose is a challenge to those who like to think the language is backward, sentimental and near extinction, and a shot in the arm for those who believe that Scots has much to tell us about ourselves in this century and the next.

○

JOHN GRANT (real name Paul Barnett) is the author of about 60 books, of which about one-third are novels. His *The Encyclopedia of Walt Disney's Animated Characters*, currently in its third edition, is regarded as the standard work in its field. As co-editor with John Clute of *The Encyclopedia of Fantasy*, he received the Hugo, the World Fantasy Award, the Locus Award, the J. Lloyd Eaton Award, and the Mythopoeic Society Scholarship Award. As managing editor of the Clute/Nicholls *Encyclopedia of Science Fiction*, he shared a rare British Science Fiction Association Special Award. He received a second Hugo in 2004 for *The Chesley Awards: A Retrospective* (done with Elizabeth Humphrey and Pamela D. Scoville). Recently published major books, all as John Grant, include *Masters of Animation*, the "book-length fictions" *Dragonhenge* and *The Stardragons* (both illustrated by Bob Eggleton, the former shortlisted for a 2003 Hugo Award), the novels *The Far-Enough Window* and *The Dragons of Manhattan*, and the art/reference book *Renderosity: Digital Art for the 21st Century* (done with Audre Vysniauskas). His story collection *Take No Prisoners* was published in 2004.

His website is at www.hometown.aol.com/thogatthog.

GAVIN INGLIS was born in Paisley, saw St Mirren win the Anglo-Scottish Cup, and later moved to Edinburgh. He gave up eating animals in 1993, but still likes to wear parts of them.

His writing veers between mainstream Scotlit, uneasy relationship humour and dark little tales aimed at grumpy goth teenagers. It has appeared in publications as diverse as *Scottish Book Collector*, *Crap Ghosts*, *The Journal of the Society of Archivists* and *Grunt and Groan: the New Anthology of Sex and Work*. His novel *Mirror Widow* won the Instant Books competition at the 2002 Edinburgh International Book Festival.

o

ANGUS McALLISTER initially qualified as a solicitor, though now earns a living as a lecturer in law at the University of Paisley. In 1978 he was a runner-up in the BBC's Read All About It short story competition (science fiction section) and in 1980 a runner-up in a competition run by the British edition of *Omni*. The first story, "What Dreams May Come", was sold by the BBC to a woman's magazine and appeared in a German SF anthology as well as being reprinted in *Starfield* (1989), an anthology of Scottish SF edited by Duncan Lunan. His novels include *A Variety of Sensations*, *The Krugg Syndrome*, *The Canongate Strangler* and *The Cyber Puppets*.

o

ALAN McINTOSH was born in 1960 and educated at York and Stirling Universities. For the last 20 years he has pursued a successful and financially rewarding career in publishing, but not caught it. He now lives in Edinburgh, where he shirks from home as an editor of dictionaries and journals. As well as writing fiction, poetry and biography, he researches and talks (to anyone who will listen) on Victorian funerary culture.

o

KEN MacLEOD was born in Stornoway, Isle of Lewis, in 1954, but spent his teenage years in Greenock. He studied at Glasgow University and did postgraduate research in London. He worked as a lab technician, factory worker, motor depot cleaner and clerk before discovering that the money was better in computer programming. After ten years in IT he became a full-time writer and is the author of nine novels, the latest of which is *Learning the World*. He lives in West Lothian with his wife and children, and still feels a slight presbyterian guilt at making money from telling deliberate lies.

o

WILLIAM MEIKLE is forty-something and Scottish. Originally from Kilbirnie in Ayrshire, he now lives in Kinross in a permanent state of culture shock. William's four novels to date have all been published in the independent press in the USA, the most recent being the *Watchers* trilogy, where Bonnie Prince Charlie, and his whole Highland army, get to be vampires. William has three more novels scheduled for 2005–2006.

"Total Mental Quality, By the Way" is dedicated to the 1981 drinking crew in the Rubyiat in Byres Road. You know who you are.

○

Like most overnight sensations, DEBORAH J. MILLER has been writing fiction for almost twenty years. She was born in Edinburgh, and currently lives in beautiful East Lothian. Deborah is an Author Ambassador for Book Aid International.

Her first Fantasy trilogy, *The Last Clansman*, was set in both "real" Scotland, and a mythic, alternate country based on Celtic and Scots folklore. *The Times* hailed the series as "evocative and powerful".

Deborah's new series is titled *Swarmthief's Dance*, and the first instalment is due for publication by Tor UK this autumn. The story is set during the build-up to the ending of the world of Myr and features her most fascinating character yet: Vivreki Monvedrian.

○

EDWIN MORGAN is Scotland's greatest living poet. He was born in Glasgow in 1920. The great range of his poetry in style, form and subject matter reflects his lifelong interest in areas as diverse as languages, technology, art and film. He has travelled widely and translated poetry from many languages. His science-fiction poems broke new ground for both poetry and the genre.

He was made Glasgow's first Poet Laureate in autumn 1999, and was awarded the Queen's Gold Medal for Poetry in 2000. In June 2001, Edwin received the prestigious Weidenfeld Prize for Translation, the winning book being *Phaedra*. He was given the title of "Scots Makar", the first Poet Laureate of Scotland, by the Scottish Parliament in 2004.

Edwin has published numerous volumes of poetry, as well as collections of essays, most of which are available from Carcanet Press and Mariscat Press. His official website is www.edwinmorgan.com.

○

STEFAN PEARSON hails from the far North West Highlands, and his experiences there colour much of his writing. He has written a novel, *Worse Things*, which is set in a remote Highland fishing community and deals with themes of isolation, loss and redemption — it doesn't sound funny, but it is.

Stefan has read his stories at Edinburgh's premier horror film festival, Dead by Dawn, and Bloc Press recently published a chapbook of his short stories entitled *The Chronicles of Vinegar Tom*.

He is currently working on two more novels, one of which is a children's story about flatulent fairies, roadworks, hippies up trees and chronic asthma. The other is a Highland novel again, but this time features robbed mobile banks, defaced statues, Gruinard (the anthrax island), gannet hunters, slaughtered pilot whales and Faeroese gangsters.

○

Raised in Washington DC, **PHIL RAINES'** first contact with Scotland was his grandfather's gift of a Celtic football supporters kit and a copy of the utterly incomprehensible *Oor Wullie*. His second was sharing a train north from London with returning Scots after a rare Scottish victory over England when he was shown a Gladstone bag holding a chunk of Wembley's turf. Scotland has been full of surprises ever since. Now living in Glasgow, he is a member of the Glasgow Science Fiction Writers Circle.

○

DAVID PRINGLE, born in 1950, in the late-Victorian writer and editor Andrew Lang's birthplace—Viewfield, Selkirk—was editor and publisher of the science-fiction magazine *Interzone* from 1982 to 2004. He has written or edited a number of books, ranging from the critical study *Science Fiction: The 100 Best Novels* (1984) to the anthology *The Ant-Men of Tibet and Other Stories* (2001). He is currently living once more in Scotland, after more than 40 years away, in a stone cottage just a few minutes' walk from his birthplace, and also just five minutes away from the wooded site of King David's original motte-and-bailey castle, the long-lost Selkirk Castle, built circa 1110 and in effect a royal hunting lodge which commanded the riverine routes into the great Ettrick Forest...

○

HANNU RAJANIEMI was born in Finland, but has lived in Edinburgh for four years, working on his Ph.D. in string theory. He is also a member of Writers' Bloc, an Edinburgh-based spoken-word performance group.

Hannu's work has previously appeared in the webzine *Futurismic* (http://futurismic.com) and a chapbook containing short stories involving Finnish mythology is forthcoming from Bloc Press.

○

Born in Yorkshire, **CHARLES STROSS** moved to Edinburgh ten years ago, where he currently lives and works as a full-time writer. His latest novel, *Accelerando*, is published in the UK by Orbit and in the USA by Ace.

○

HARVEY WELLES doesn't live in Scotland, but in Milwaukee. He tried Irn-Bru once, but didn't like it.

○

NEIL WILLIAMSON was born in the heart of Lanarkshire, surrounded by Scotland's fading heavy industries. Studies for an engineering degree imbued him with a love of Scotland's technological history—both its triumphs and its failures.

Neil's short fiction, which has been published in magazines and anthologies on both sides of the Atlantic, will be collected in book form by Elastic Press in 2006.

○

ANDREW J. WILSON was born in Aberdeen and now stays in Edinburgh, but he lived near Glasgow for a while as well. His short stories have been published in anthologies and magazines in Britain and the USA, and he has read his work on BBC Radio Scotland.

He has written two plays, *The Terminal Zone* and *The Black Ambulance Gang*, which were performed at the Edinburgh Festival Fringe, the latter on a moving bus. He also reviews science fiction and fantasy for *The Scotsman*.

○

JANE YOLEN, called by *Newsweek* "the Hans Christian Andersen of America", and by the *New York Times* "the Aesop of the twentieth century", lives half the year in Massachusetts, USA, and half the year in St Andrews, Scotland. At present count, she has published over 270 books. She has also produced three children (all of whom have published books) and six grandchildren. (We are still waiting to hear from them. Half of them still have to learn how to read and write first.)

ACKNOWLEDGEMENTS

Thanks to everyone who helped in the making of this book, in particular: Lorna McLaren, Emma Taylor, Jim Campbell, the *Herald*, who originally commissioned Ron Butlin's "Five Fantastic Fictions", Iain M. Banks, Alasdair Gray, Muriel Gray, Colin Fox MSP, The Scottish Arts Council, Glasgow City Council, The Glasgow SF Writers' Circle and The East Coast Writers' Group.